THE WINI
OF THE WASTE.

Antony Swithin was born in England but now lives in Canada. While still a child, the mysterious Atlantic island of Rockall came to haunt his imagination; and it has done so ever since. Over the years, his concepts of the island have evolved into a whole imaginative tapestry, rich in detail — of its geography, its fauna and flora, and the history of its peoples, so that the island emerges in his writing as a land as real as any to be found on our maps.

The Winds of the Wastelands is the third volume in a series of novels about Rockall. The first and second were *Princes of Sandastre* and *The Lords of the Stoney Mountains*. The fourth will be *The Nine Gods of Safaddné*.

THE WINDS
OF THE WASTELANDS

The Perilous Quest for Lyonesse

BOOK THREE

Antony Swithin

Fontana
An Imprint of HarperCollins*Publishers*

Fontana
An Imprint of HarperCollins*Publishers*
77–85 Fulham Palace Road,
Hammersmith, London W6 8JB

A Fontana Original 1992

9 8 7 6 5 4 3 2 1

A catalogue record for this book
is available from the British Library

ISBN 0 00 617940 1

Set in Linotron Ehrhardt

Printed in Great Britain by
Hartnolls, Bodmin, Cornwall

TO LINDA
not only for her hard work on,
but also for her appreciation of,
these stories of Rockall

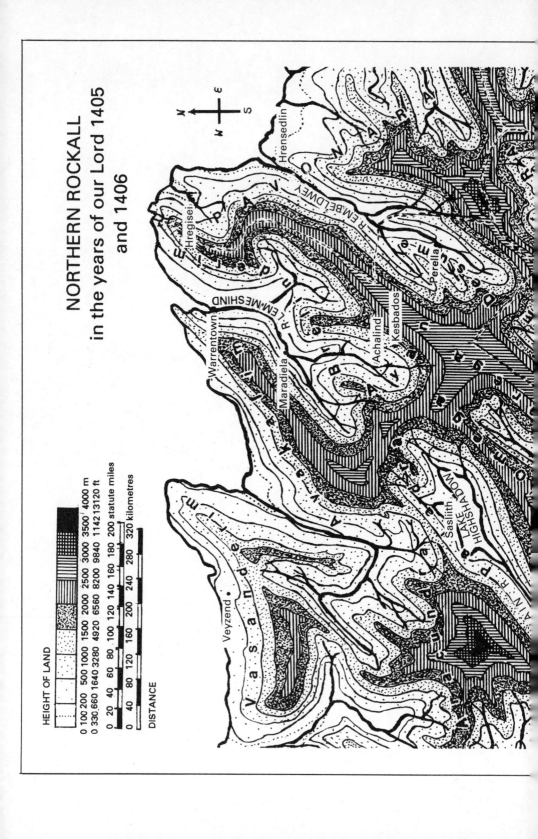

NORTHERN ROCKALL
in the years of our Lord 1405
and 1406

HEIGHT OF LAND

0 100 200 500 1000 1500 2000 2500 3000 3500 4000 m
0 330 660 1640 3280 4920 6560 8200 9840 11421 13120 ft

DISTANCE

0 20 40 60 80 100 120 140 160 180 200 statute miles
0 40 80 120 160 200 240 280 320 kilometres

Veyzend

Warrentown

Maradiela

Hregisei

Hrensedlin

R. LEM-MESHIND

Achalind

Kesbados

Perella

Saslith

LAKE HIGHSHADD

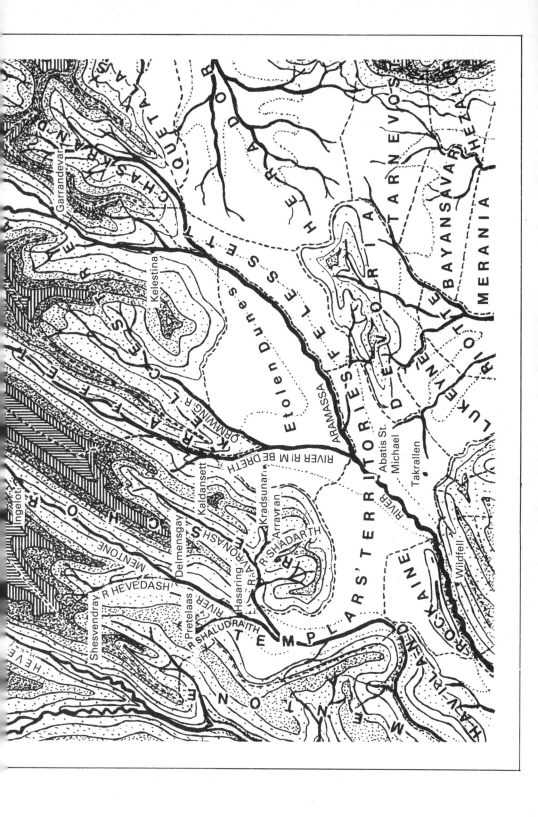

CONTENTS

One   A SWIRL IN THE WATER   1

Two   THE BOAT PEOPLE OF THE ARAMASSA   7

Three   SIR ROBERT RANDWULF'S STORY   17

Four   STORM ON THE RIVER   29

Five   THE MEN OF THE LORDLESS LANDS   39

Six   PRISONERS IN KRADSUNAR   47

Seven   ESSA   57

Eight   PURSUIT   69

Nine   AN UNEXPECTED ENCOUNTER   77

Ten   THE TIME OF DARKNESS   85

Eleven   IN THE CASTLE OF INGELOT   97

Twelve   TORIL EVATENG ENDS HIS TALE   111

Thirteen   A PEACEMAKING AND A LEAVETAKING   123

Fourteen   THE GOLDEN BIRD   131

Fifteen   INTO THE WIND-FOREST   141

Sixteen   THE CREATURES IN THE GLADE   149

Seventeen   THE WAIL OF THE WIND   157

Eighteen   BACK TO THE WIND-FOREST   167

Nineteen   A BRIDGE AND A TUMBLE   177

Twenty   THE GOD IN THE PASSAGE   189

Twenty-one   THE COMBAT IN THE CORRIDOR   201

Twenty-two   SNOW IN THE HIGHSHADOW MOUNTAINS   211

Twenty-three   THE CITY BY THE SHORE   225

Twenty-four   THE EYE OF THE GOD   233

Twenty-five   SNOW AND SPECULATION   245

Twenty-six   A FALCON IN THE SKY   255

Twenty-seven   A CLIMB FROM DANGER   265
Twenty-eight   A CHANGE OF DIRECTION   273

GLOSSARY OF ROCKALESE WORDS   283

ILLUSTRATIONS

I.   Map of Northern Rockall   vi & vii
II.   Comparison of the Sandastrian and Reschorese
Alphabets   289

Chapter One

A SWIRL IN THE WATER

In the days before my father's friend Henry Hotspur had quarrelled with the king, I had been taken to London and had sat on the Thames banks, watching royal Henry's great barge being rowed by and seeing the barges of his wealthier nobles following. I remember the bright sails and gilded outworks, the rich costumes, and the music of psaltery, rebec and sackbut. I recall also the regular and leisurely fashion in which the oars dipped into the river, as if effortlessly; and how, as they were all feathered together, droplets of water glittered jewel-like in the sunlight before falling back into the shining stream. It had been a splendidly colourful scene and I had envied even the busy watermen. How glorious, to be rowed up some great river in the sunshine!

Yet, now that I was being rowed on a bright day of late spring up a still greater river, I felt no faintest sense of satisfaction. Instead, I was acutely bored. On a great, multi-oared barge like the king's, there is colour; there is space to amble up and down; there are refreshments and there is music. The Aramassa is Rockall's greatest river, but it is broad, shallow and very muddy, with many shoals just below or just above the water surface. All its hues are subdued, dun and green and grey; even the fishes we glimpsed seemed to echo those same drab shades. The craft in which we were plying that river had not a great bank of oars, but only two pairs. Though my companion in the Lazadels' boat was Prince Avran of Sandastre, neither his workaday costume nor even his weapons smacked of royalty, pomp or riches. Sir Robert Randwulf, our companion in the Garavets' boat, was almost hidden by piles of the merchandise that the cousins hoped to trade upriver. Certainly none of us had room in which to move about.

1

Before we boarded them, the two craft had seemed spacious enough. They were called *yildrihen* and were flat-bottomed and fairly broad, somewhere between a scow and a coble in size. When we said farewell to our friends of the wizard's company under the shade of the doramek trees and embarked on our voyage to Reschora, both boats had been empty and we had ample space.

Since then, we had passed a night in a boatmen's village on a mid-river island. Its huts had walls and roofs made of reeds woven between the branches and stems of still-living withies; they were hard to see even from a few yards' distance, let alone from the river, and could be abandoned with little loss at times of flood. Our night had been enjoyable enough; we had been treated to fish grilled on hot stones and to a curiously salt-tasting wine, then had slept in one of the cluster of huts. However, when we woke next morning, it was to find the two boats so packed with trade goods — dead and sun-dried fish; oblongs of mud containing still-living fish that, we learned, would stay asleep and fresh till the mud was washed off and they were cooked; fish-nets and hooks; and delicately woven baskets in nests of diminishing size — that there was scarcely room for us even to stretch.

Sir Robert had complained vigorously, only to be told that he had a choice; either we might travel with the boatmen to Reschora under the conditions they set, or we might be returned to the doramek grove and the wizard's gold given back to us.

This further aroused Sir Robert's wrath, but to no effect. Etvan Garavet, who served as spokesman for the four boatmen, merely smiled complacently. Surely they were being fair, he protested; after all, if they took us back and refunded the gold, would they not have wasted much time for no profit?

The boatmen knew well, I am sure, that we would not dare to return. Not only would we have had to endure the wrath of the Lord of Pochardsvale, but also the embarrassment of admitting our failure to our former companions. Rather than that, we had capitulated.

Thus we were voyaging on upstream with as little space afforded to us, and little more consideration given to us, than if we also had been merchandise. Indeed, I am sure that is how the boatmen regarded us — as goods to be ferried, differing only from their other merchandise in that our transport had been paid for in advance.

My legs were feeling cramped; I shifted them and gazed out across the river. So broad a stream is the Aramassa that the very banks seemed far away. The sun was high and the Ferekar Naur to the south of us, those Stoney Mountains where we had met with such varied adventures, were dim in the haze. By now, perhaps the conference at Rewlenscrag would be over and the jousting begun. I remembered Lauretta Saville who had loved me, wondering uneasily where she was and how she was feeling since fleeing from Becketsward. Then I thought of Ilven, princess of Sandastre and my bethrothed, so far away in Sandarro. Five months had passed since our parting; many more must go by before we might hope to meet again.

Five months since leaving Sandarro and less than a year since I, Simon Branthwaite, had left my Hallamshire home to search for my father and brother in Rockall. All I had known, on leaving, was that they had followed other English adventurers and fugitives to a new land that, in echo of romantic tradition, had been given the old name Lyonesse. Yet neither my friend Avran, third son of the eslef (ruling prince) of Sandastre and brother of my beloved Ilven, nor any of the savants of his father's realm had ever heard of Lyonesse. They had guessed it might be in the great central forests of Rockall, where many English fugitives had found new homes. However, Lyonesse was not there, nor was it among the patchwork of holds in the Ferekar Naur. So now we were travelling to Reschora as prelude to traversing the great northern mountains. If Lyonesse were anywhere in Rockall, it must lie beyond those mountains.

When I had left my home of Holdworth, I had thought I might find my father and brother, if not within the week or so that a voyage to France might have taken, at least within a few months. I had not reckoned with the size of this island of Rockall, nor (despite the stories I had heard back in Hallamshire) had I expected its ways to be so different from those of England. I had been ignorant and optimistic indeed!

Well, now I was much better equipped to travel about Rockall. I had learned not only to speak and write its principal southern language, Sandastrian, but also its more difficult northern tongue, Reschorese. I had learned not only to ride, and control by my thoughts, the four-horned sevdru of the southern mountains and the three-horned rafenu of the central forests, but also gained an affection for those animals stronger than I had felt for any horse. In my practices with Sandastre's leading swordmaster, I had enhanced immeasurably my skill with that weapon, even though it would never approach Avran's or his. My facility in using the bow had not only secured for me more respect than it would ever have earned in England, but also had served Avran and me well on several occasions; and my more secret skill, with the throwing-knife, had likewise proved of value.

Avran, who had a capacity for relaxation I could not equal, seemed to be fast asleep, while Sir Robert, in the other boat, looked remarkably contented and at ease. For my part, small though I was, I could not attain comfort in these accursed yildrihen. I shifted again and strove to stretch my cramped limbs, wishing the boatmen would allow me a spell at the oars; at least it would make a change! But they would not; Avran had asked already and been rebuffed.

I gazed over to my left, to the northward. Those lower hills that marched with the river were the Ferekar Rokanair, the Rockaine Hills, a feoff held by knights from Gascony. That brought to mind the French knight we had encountered in Dellorain, Sir Guy de Something-or-Other; I wondered whether his broken leg had yet healed. So much had occurred in the few months of our journey; there was so much to call to mind, to ponder upon. Rascal, that strange little arboreal animal who had claimed and returned my affections; what had happened to him? Had he been returned safely to Sandarro and, if so, had he settled down with Ilven? Thus again, my thoughts returned to her whom I loved. I relapsed into wistful rememberings and forgot my discomforts for a while.

My revery was rudely interrupted. Suddenly I heard shouts of dismay from the first boat and was jolted by the abrupt halting of our own craft. This wakened Avran. Sir Robert, in the other yildrih, had stiffened and was gazing ahead in the direction of Etvan Garavet's frantic gesturings.

Yes, there was a swirl in the water. Something seemed to be rising from the shallow bottom of the river, some great shape as broad and brown as a sandbank — but a sandbank does not move!

The Garavets' boat was swinging about, the brothers paddling with desperate speed, while Sir Robert, who had drawn his sword, clung on to the gunwale. Our boat was also swinging, as the Lazadel cousins drove their oars deep into the water to port. Avran was bending sideways, trying to pull his bowstave free from the bundles that had been placed on top of it overnight.

I strove to do likewise, only to be thrown forward violently. The yildrih, turned with too much haste and too little thought, had struck a shoal.

Instantly the Lazadels, by adroit manipulation of the oars, halted the turning of the boat and strove to thrust us away from the sandbank. However, the damage had been done. While the Garavets' boat was already racing away downstream, we were left full in the path of the creature, whatever it was, that was coming at us!

Like Avran, I had failed to free my bowstave; it was too firmly entrapped by the tight-packed fish bundles. What fools we had been, when we embarked that morning, not to insist that our bows be freed from these encumbrances! Yet somehow one does not think, as a landsman, of needing such a weapon in mid-river. Cursing my own stupidity, I pulled myself back onto the thwart and gazed apprehensively upstream.

I could see the creature clearly now — all too clearly. It was almost as big as our boat, but broader and more squat. Two enormous limbs at the front were thrusting aside the waters to form great bow-waves; there was a high-arched carapace, dully brown in colour and knobbed like a Scottish soldier's targe; and, more distantly, I could note the swirls caused by the two hind paddles that were powerfully propelling the beast towards us. Its head was massive, blunt at the front like the stump of a felled oak, with two huge nostrils whose fleshy rims twitched unpleasantly at each drawn breath. Yet its eyes were what alarmed me most. I saw them as its head undulated; set slantwise on the upper side of its head, they were palely yellow, with pupils that were greenish slits — baleful and yet dead-looking, like the eyes of a resurrected corpse in a nightmare.

Our craft was swinging over to port now, as the cousins strove to get clear of the sandbar. Already we were almost broadside to the current, but we could not complete the turn before the creature was upon us.

I had not realized the fact till then, but I had not perceived its mouth. Now, as it opened its jaws, I saw why. The upper jaw was bigger than the lower, overhanging it, with a huge hook at the front

5

like an immensely enlarged eagle's beak; and, like an eagle, the creature had no teeth, just sharp chopping rims of yellowish bone that would close together like clippers. Larger and larger its open jaws were looming; I could see right down into its throat, the pale pink, palpitating flesh, the greyish tongue with tip flicking as if anxious to taste its prey . . .

Terim Lazadel, in the bows, was still labouring with his oars to make our yildrih complete its second turn; but Ulim Lazadel had drawn in his oars. He had seized a fishing-spear and, as I glanced toward him, he cast it at the beast.

He threw badly; the spear missed narrowly and passed in front of the creature's head. Instantly the great jaws closed on the spear, bit it neatly into three pieces and spat them forth, then opened again for its next bite — a bite at me, for the continuing swing of the yildrih had placed me directly in its path!

The waves generated by the rapid approach of that massive creature were causing the boat to buck. Ulim threw a second spear, but it bounced harmlessly off the thick carapace. Avran had his sword at the ready, but he could not hope to reach the beast with his blade in time.

I had been watching the creature's approach with a sort of helpless horror; but suddenly I regained the power of movement and reached desperately to my belt for one of my knives. Too tiny a weapon to stop the beast's approach, but all I had . . . The open jaws were reaching for me when, with the force of desperation, I hurled the tiny blade down into the pink funnel of the creature's throat.

The beast gave a sort of coughing retch and, just before it was upon us, the great jaws closed. Even so, its head hit the boat with the force of an enormous hammer-blow. The yildrih was tilting under the impact and rising up under me; I was being thrown backwards; the boat had turned onto its side now, was hurtling towards me, falling upon me!

I plunged head-first into water that seemed to be boiling in the forward rush of the great beast. Gasping for breath, I thrust out with arms and legs in a desperate, convulsive attempt to swim clear.

Too late; the overturned hull of the boat was above me, bearing down on me! As I strove frantically to dive out from under it, something struck my head and all went black.

6

Chapter Two

The Boat People of the Aramassa

When I came to my senses, I was lying on a sandy beach. My clothes had been stripped from my body and I had been wrapped in a warm, dry blanket, with another rolled up under my head to serve as pillow. Sir Robert was kneeling beside me, his hand upon my brow. As I opened my eyes, he withdrew it and called: 'Avran, Simon's recovering his senses!'

I closed my eyes and, when I opened them again, saw that Avran had joined Sir Robert. He was wearing only a piece of cloth wrapped kilt-like about his waist. His shoulders had suffered a grievous scrape, but otherwise he seemed well. His expression, at first strained and anxious, relaxed as he looked at me. He gave a deep, sighing breath and then smiled.

'Well, I feared I'd lost you that time, my friend,' he said. 'Truly, when Ulim Lazadel brought you ashore, I thought that he was carrying a corpse!'

My forehead felt tender; I reached up and touched it, promptly wincing and wishing I hadn't. 'No, I seem to be alive,' I responded huskily and then coughed, for my throat felt almost as sore as my scalp. 'The boat hit me; it fell on me.'

Sir Robert smiled. 'I don't think it was the boat, by the shape of your bruise. I believe it was your own bowstave! When the Lazadels recovered the yildrih and brought it ashore — yes, it's on the beach over there' — he gestured behind him — 'they found your bowstave protruding from it at an angle; it had wedged between two of the thwarts. As that accursed creature toppled the boat over onto you, you received quite a clout! The stave must have hit you as hard as a kick from a rafenu.'

I groaned. 'What a thing to happen — to be knocked out by one's own bowstave!' I stretched, then shivered convulsively.

'Just a moment; I'll fetch you a drink.' Avran leapt to his feet.

In a few seconds, he returned with a flask and set it to my lips. This was a better-tasting wine than that we had consumed last night, and very strong. After a few gulps, I began to feel better. While I drank, Sir Robert was speaking again.

'The boatmen are quite delighted with you, you'll find, Simon. No, you didn't slay the creature, though I don't doubt that you gave it severe indigestion! The point is that you caused it to close its jaws, and thus you saved the Lazadels' boat. Those jaws would have taken a great piece out of the yildrih's side — no, I don't believe the beast was reaching for you, though I cannot blame you for thinking it was! — and the boat would have sunk into the sand. I dare say the creature would have eaten Avran and you afterwards, of course, but that doesn't worry the boatmen so much. As it is, your action saved their yildrih and they've been able to salvage their merchandise, so they're well pleased. Indeed, they fished you out of the river even before diving for their possessions; which, I gather, is a great compliment!'

I laughed at this, even though rather shakily, and then asked: 'What happened to the others — to you, Avran?'

'Oh, I swam ashore. It wasn't too comfortable, though, for the hull of the boat hit my shoulder and I had difficulty in using my right arm. Believe me, I was glad to get to the bank!'

'I'm sure you were,' I commented with a renewed shiver.

My friend smiled affectionately at me, then went on: 'As for the others — well, as soon as the beast went off downriver — and with your knife in its throat, it didn't linger! — the two Garavets went after the boat. They swim like fishes; they never even bothered to come ashore. While the Lazadels fished you out of the water and helped Sir Robert to pump you out, the Garavets heaved the boat up onto the beach. Then they and the Lazadels started diving for the merchandise. If you look around, you'll see everything strewn about us and drying out in the sunshine — your clothes and mine included.'

I was feeling better with every minute that passed. 'That's good . . . Whatever *was* that creature?'

8

It was Sir Robert who responded. 'A glagrang, they call it. Did you ever see a tortoise? No? Yet there are quite a few in Rockall — my people keep them as pets — and I saw many more out in the Saracen lands. They're lizard-like creatures that have a box-shaped shell; they eat plants, snails and insects. Well, there are some water-living types also. One can find them in all the rivers that flow into the Great Marshes, I'm told, lying on the bottom until some prey swims over, then rising to attack it. Mostly they're small and harmless enough, though they might bite off the odd finger. However, they live a long time — you can count the growth-rings on their shells to know their age — and some become quite huge. That one would, I'm sure, be a few centuries old. The older they get, the more evil they become; or so the boatmen say. Ugly beasts, too; very ugly.'

'Are we likely to encounter any more, then, Sir Robert?' I enquired apprehensively.

He smiled. 'I don't think so. Such giants are quite rare, I gather; and that particular beast was the only one living so far upstream, if Etvan Garavet is to be believed. Your little knife has sent him away downstream and we don't think he'll be back.'

'Good,' I said with deep feeling.

He laughed outright at this, then said: 'It will be an hour or more before your garments are dry enough to wear, Simon. Why not sleep for a while? I'm sure you'll benefit from a further rest. And, er, we're just fellow travellers now, you know. No need for formality. Might you not just call me "Robin", as Vedlen Obiran does?'

'Thank you; yes, indeed I will,' I responded, quite touched by this unexpected gesture of friendliness. Then I closed my eyes again and was soon tranquilly asleep.

As matters turned out, it was late afternoon before we re-embarked. While I was sleeping, some farmers from a Wildfell stead, who had spotted the boats drawn up on shore, came down and bought largely from the boatmen, paying in good Heradorian silver. During this trading, there was no reason for me to be roused. I was able to slumber for fully four hours and woke feeling greatly refreshed. There was still a dull ache in my right temple and I found it a mistake to shake my head, but otherwise I felt well enough.

The trading had two other beneficial effects. First of all, it gave us a little more room in the boats and secondly, it cheered the

9

boatmen immensely. Not only was I thanked most ceremoniously by the Lazadels for saving their yildrih, but also we were thereafter all three treated not just as burdens to be conveyed, but as friends.

As we set off upstream, the four boatmen began singing lustily, a song of the pleasures of being a boatman and the freedom of life on the great river. They were delighted when Avran, picking up the tune, started to play along with them on his pommer and when Sir Robert and I joined in their choruses:

> Oh river, thou who art our home,
> Thou on whose waters we ride,
> Wandering from green marsh to grey mountain
> Day upon day, night upon night.
>
>> Deep flood waters,
>> Summer sandbars,
>> With thy seasons
>> We are one.
>
> Oh river, our father and mother
> Providing our food and our drink
> Giving us pleasures and sorrows
> Thou who art our life.
>
>> Spate-brown channels,
>> Sun-probed shallows,
>> With thy seasons
>> We are one.
>
> Oh river, our past and our future,
> Who bore our forefathers' yildrihen
> Whose reeds hide our children from danger
> Carrying time to the sea in thine arms.
>
>> Hastening currents,
>> Slack backwaters,
>> With thy motions
>> We are one.

As the daylight waned, Sir Robert called across from the other boat and pointed to the southward. The Ferekar Naur were already black against the sky but, high on a shoulder of those hills, a slim tower was bathed by the sun's waning rays in a bright, roseate light.

'Wildfell,' he called. 'Sir Amyas Aydenburgh's stronghold.'

Soon the shadows were falling across the river itself. As the last light faded from the Rockaine Hills to the northward, the yildrihen swung across to that side of the river and were guided into what looked like an entirely weed-choked backwater. But no, there was a narrow, clear channel up which we steered. About twenty rods in from the main river, we drew up alongside what had looked like a mass of low bushes among the reeds. Perceiving that these were in reality the huts of a second settlement of the boat people, I was relieved but not surprised. I was beginning to learn some of the ways of this water world.

The people of that village received our boatmen gladly, us others with initial suspicion. However, this turned into open-hearted welcome when they learned of our encounter with the glagrang and were told that it had fled away downstream. The creature, it seemed, had been much feared and had taken several lives.

Suddenly we found ourselves at the centre of a party. Fires were lit, a great deal of wine and beer was drunk, and there was much music. Men played on drumheads stretched over holes delven into the mud or blew on reed pan-pipes: women strummed harps with frames of withy and strings made from dried waterplant stems; Avran tootled on his pommer; and I did my best to play a citole-like stringed instrument that someone had set in my lap. Children danced gaily about us in the narrow lanes between the little huts, until one by one they crept away to sleep.

It was a merry evening, but in the morning we rose late and with aching heads. Avran's shoulder, which looked in worse shape after that night, was treated with ointment and bound up in strips of plaited reed by a kindly boatwoman. After that, affectionate farewells were said to us and we set off again upstream.

Terim Lazadel, who had been yesterday so silent and had seemed so surly, was today in cheerful and talkative mood. We learned from him that the boatmen were a sort of freemasonry of the river, living by their fishing and trading and owing no allegiance to any lord of the lands about. Indeed, since the river served as a frontier between realms for much of its length, it would have been hard to decide to whom their allegiance should be owed! Their boats travelled regularly up the Aramassa to Vachnagar in far Chaskrand or up its tributary the Garrowand to Kelestina, chief town of Kelcestre. Occasionally they would even travel as far upstream on the Garrowand as Garrandevor, the many-towered lakeside capital of mountain-girt Adira. However, the higher reaches of both rivers were swift-flowing and hazardous, only to be ventured upon when there was promise of good trading returns. Downstream among the Great Marshes, where the Aramassa became ever lazier as it approached the western sea, the boatmen ventured equally rarely; those marshes were a dangerous place and, though the boat people of that region were friendly enough, their way of life was too alien for comfort.

Of the realms that marched with the rivers they travelled, the Lazadels seemed to know little and to care less. Even the riverside cities were regarded merely as places where goods were unloaded or loaded, bought, sold or bartered. The boatmen loathed having to stay overnight in any town and, indeed, insisted always on sleeping in their yildrihen. Only when on the water, or with friends in some little village hidden among the reeds, were they truly happy. The Aramassa was the parchment on which the colour of their life was painted; for them, away from that river, everything faded into dinginess.

Around noon, we came upon a place where a little wooden jetty had been built out over the riverside mud into deeper water, to form an easy landing-place for boats. Some way back from the water, out of the reach of the spring floods, there was a group of wooden houses within a high palisade and deep ditch bristling with stakes. This place was called Abatis St Michael by the Templars who now ruled the lands athwart the river thereabouts, but the boatmen gave it their own, older name of Adyaneng.

Here the yildrihen were drawn up, while the boatmen went ashore to trade. Sir Robert was content to drowse at ease in the Garavets' boat. However, Avran and I, our bodies still aching from yesterday's bruisings and stiff from a morning in the confinement of the boats, were glad to be able to walk around for a while. A small crowd had assembled to view the boatmen's goods; we talked with those of the women who spoke Reschorese, but found that most spoke only languages unfamiliar to us both. I presumed these must be tongues of those distant lands from which the Templars had come; Greek, maybe, or Cypriot, or the language of the Holy Land itself? Sir Robert might have told us, but he was sleeping; and I have never since heard those languages spoken.

There was little among the boatmen's stock that attracted purchase but, when we re-embarked, the Lazadels seemed not at all disconsolate. At a place so often visited by boatmen, good sales would have astonished them.

The sun was high now and the day becoming very hot. The river, which had been broad enough already, seemed to be becoming yet broader and the Garavets' boat, which was again ahead of ours — Etvan Garavet seemed to like always to be in the lead — was steering ever further across toward the northern bank. Indeed, though the haze over the water made distances hard to judge, we seemed surprisingly far already from the southern bank.

I had been leaning backward drowsily against the heap of fish-parcels, but now I sat up and paid more attention. Looking overboard, I noted that the very colour of the water seemed to be changing. To our right and behind us, the Aramassa appeared as brown and muddy as ever. To our left and before us, however, the water looked lighter, more transparent somehow; less silt-laden, cleaner.

I was about to comment on this to Avran when, glancing ahead, I saw a broad promontory of land extending towards us. Then I understood — or thought I did.

'We're passing an island, Avran,' I observed to my even drowsier friend. 'I wonder why it has caused the colour of the water to change?'

'Eh, you landsmen, you landsmen!' Etvan Lazadel was chuckling. 'Why, you've no eye for a river! Nay, that's no island; it's the separation of two streams! We could follow the Aramassa eastward and northward, sure enough, but that would not get you to Reschora, where you're bound. Nor will this river, for that matter; but it'll take you closer. The waters ahead are those of the Rimbedreth. It's a grand enough stream, but not so mighty as the Aramassa.'

'So we'll be following the Rimbedreth henceforward?'

'Following? — that's a funny way of putting it. We'll be rowing up it, lad, if that's what you mean! If all goes well, you'll be at Kaldansett in three more days.'

'Kaldansett? Is that in Reschora?'

'No indeed. It is the southernmost town of the Kingdom of Raffette. To reach Reschora, you'll be needing to cross over the mountains — or, at least, that seems to be your friend Sir Robert's plan. I've never been to Reschora; this river doesn't run there. Folk say that, should a man voyage all the way downstream to where the Aramassa meets the great waters, he can travel up another great stream, the Mentone, all the way to Reschora. That might be so; but me and mine, we stick to our own rivers. The Aramassa, the Garrowand and the Rimbedreth are good enough for us — and we're not that keen to be voyaging the Rimbedreth, I can tell you!'

As he was speaking, we had been moving steadily across into the waters of that river; clearer, cleaner waters, as it seemed to me. His comment puzzled me, so I asked: 'Why, what's the matter with the Rimbedreth?'

'Nothing at all, as a river. It's the lands about it that cause the trouble. What do you see over there?' Terim gestured towards the northeast.

I gazed intently into the haze. 'Why, I seem to see hills,' I said surprisedly. 'Are we so near to the mountains already?'

'Nay, lad.' He was chuckling again. 'Not mountains, those, but hills right enough — hills of sand! They're the Etolen Dunes — a dry place and a dangerous. And the few folk that live among the Dunes, they're dangerous also. In the Etolen Dunes and in the Lordless Lands west of the river, you can find the ragtag and bobtail of all the villainy in Rockall!'

'I thought the Templars held these lands?'

'They hold the better lands, south of Reschora and north of Rockaine; and, of course, they hold lands east of the Aramassa. But, in the Dunes, there's almost no water; there's little provender for beasts and there's no ground where crops will grow. And the Lordless Lands, they're quite as dry, if not so sandy. They stay lordless because no lord desires to rule lands so barren.'

Avran had subsided quietly back into a doze, but I was finding all this alarming. Our experiences in the Ferekar Naur had left me with a deep apprehension of any region where robbers roamed unchecked. 'How shall we manage to pass safely through those lands, then?'

He laughed once more. 'Why, by sticking to the river, of course!

Out on the water, we're safe enough. And, for the nights, we boatmen know a few spots where we can be secure from danger. You've no cause to fret; leave it to us!'

I hoped he was right. Yet his words had planted the seed of a fresh anxiety in my mind; or was it a premonition of trouble to come?

Chapter Three

SIR ROBERT RANDWULF'S STORY

The boats had travelled almost a league upstream before Avran roused himself from his doze. With eyes still sleep-hazed, he gazed idly about him; but then surprise caused him to jerk into complete wakefulness. 'What has happened, Simon? Where are we? This doesn't look like the Aramassa!'

It is always a delight to be able to impart, as if from a personal store of knowledge, information recently gained. 'That's because it *isn't* the Aramassa,' I responded crisply, before Terim Lazadel could deprive me of that pleasure. 'We left the Aramassa some time ago. We're on the Rimbedreth now and travelling directly northward.'

'Oh indeed? What strange country!'

The comment was justified, for this river and its valley were like no terrain either of us had ever seen. The Rimbedreth was a big enough river, even if not such a giant as the Aramassa; but it was somewhat faster-flowing and its waters were very pellucid. The bottom was sandy rather than muddy, with patches of curious, bluish-grey weeds sending up wavy tendrils almost to the water surface.

Among these weeds there swam a multitude of small fishes, some as brown as the bottom, some as transparent as clear glass, all of them visible only when in motion and impossible to perceive when still. Some had broad heads with snub noses, much like the bullheads of our English brooks; others had feelers about their mouths, like the whiskers of a farm kitten. Every so often a creature like a crayfish, its carapace as palely blue as the water-plants, would shoot out from one weed cluster to the next. The little fishes seemed to regard such events with sublime indifference. When any bigger fish swam by, however, there would be a brief flicker and then stillness, as each small fish sought concealment on the bottom.

17

Yet, fascinating though it was to gaze overboard and watch the fishes, the landscape about us was so dramatic as to demand attention. Instead of gliding through a broad valley, we were travelling now between cliffs. They were not exceptionally tall cliffs, being indeed no more than three or four poles high. However, if one looked to right and then to left, the cliffs proved to be startlingly different in character — and the terrain beyond even more so.

On the left-hand, western side, the rocks were mostly dark in colour, blacks, greys and purplish browns, their thin layers thrown into the strangest of convolutions. Above the cliff was a broad terrace of dark rock, mostly bare. Though angular, spiky-leaved plants had found shelter in places, their leaves were a dull grey and did nothing to enliven the landscape. On three occasions, a sudden movement caused me to notice a lizard. Though they were quite big and as scaly-backed as a heraldic dragon, these creatures were not easy to see, for they were as dark in hue as the rocks about them. The only bright colours were produced by little patches of sand, seemingly blown across the river by easterly gales. Altogether it was a bleak and unencouraging prospect, as cheerless a terrain as any I had seen. I could well understand why those lands were lordless and populated only by fugitive criminals. What man would choose to live in such a place?

Quite different was the right-hand, eastern bank. There, all was bright colour. The low cliffs were made up of a sandstone which, in the intense light of that late April afternoon, seemed as scarlet as the petals of a pimpernel. Patches of pale green flecked them, where plants had found lodgement for their roots, and the cliffs were topped by an irregular line of green, with even a few thorny bushes. There seemed to be no soil; I presumed that the river vapours sufficed to keep the plants alive. However, this line of green was a tenuous frontier between life and death. Pushing across it in many places, and serrying behind it everywhere for future wind-driven assaults, were the dunes.

Avran and I had ridden among sandhills when in flight from the Montariotans, but those hills had been benign enough, with an abundant vegetation in the hollows and sparse grass even on the slopes. These dunes were quite different. They were sharper-crested and steeper-sloped, too dry and too often shifted by the winds, I

18

guessed, to allow any plant to grow. And their colour — why, they were as bright as the palette of a herald! Their crests were saffron, the very hue of the cloak Avran had worn in Bristol, but on their slopes the colour changed to crimson and, in shaded places, to maroon or to a rich brown.

Where the green barrier had been breached and the dunes had advanced to the river's edge, high walls of sand overtowered the cliffs. From their faces and especially from their bases, sand trickled down steadily, the trickle growing or waning at each gust of the fitful breeze. As we passed such dunes, we could hear the trickling, a dry rustle as uneasy as the ticking of a death-watch beetle in a wall.

Terim told me that, when a high wind was blowing from the east, the boatmen kept over to the west side of the Rimbedreth, in fear that a dune might shift forward and collapse into the river. Even so, there remained the danger that a boat might fill with wind-blown sand and sink.

It was sand from the dunes, I presumed, that formed the river bed; and indeed, beneath each towering sand cliff there was a low bank of sand, curving out into the river and fading away downstream. Yet the sand beneath the water seemed quite pale in hue, white or even silvery. This puzzled me and, while Avran had been drowsing, I had made up my mind to ask Terim Lazadel about it.

However, my friend's torrent of comments and questions swept the matter from my mind. What was the name of those dunes? What was the country to our west? How far would we be travelling and where would we disembark?

My thirst to impart information was soon sated and I redirected the flow towards Terim, who had been listening amusedly as he and his brother rowed onward so steadily, so tirelessly. Predictably, Terim had little to say about Reschora. He had heard tales of its wizards, of course, and the brothers had even ferried some of them, though without ever experiencing anything very miraculous. Their land, however, the Lazadels had never visited; it lay too far from the river to interest them.

Of Raffette, in contrast, Terim had much to say, for the Lazadels had travelled several times to Kaldansett and even beyond. We learned that the monarch of Raffette was young and easy-going, popular enough but so simple and so trusting as to cause anxiety

19

among a people ever conscious of rapacious Kelcestre on their eastern border. Terim told us much else about Kaldansett and about Raffette. However, since I was destined never to visit either that land or Kelcestre, the matter of his talk has slipped like a fish out between the meshes of my memory.

To row up the Rimbedreth is, even for the skilful and muscular Aramassa boatmen, a harder task than rowing on their own slow-moving river; but Ulim and Terim would not trust us with their oars, even though our relations were now so much friendlier.

Long before the setting sun left its glittering trail on the Rimbedreth's waters, the Garavets' boat led us to a flat platform of rock, jutting out into the river beneath an overhang of the western cliff. There we landed and had a cold supper, for the boatmen thought a fire too much of a risk. I think they took turns to keep watch, but I am not sure. Weary as I was from the after-effects of my near-drowning, I was asleep even before the sun set and did not wake until daylight returned.

The next morning's journeying saw a change in our disposition. Instead of having Avran as my companion, I had Sir Robert Randwulf — or rather Robin Randwulf, for so he had bidden me call him. This change was made at Avran's suggestion, for my friend felt that Robin had been required to spend too much time alone with the boatmen. Moreover, Avran was anxious to learn the tunes of some of the boatmen's songs from Etvan Garavet; indeed, my friend spent much of the morning playing on his pommer while Etvan and Dazlan sang. The Lazadels, Robin and I also sang along for a while; but I was not sorry when the Lazadels fell silent, for there was much that I wanted to ask Robin.

At first I cross-questioned him about Reschora. He had been several times to that Kingdom and was able to answer me very fully. Since much that he told me will transpire as this narrative proceeds, I need not detail his words here.

However, I had another matter in mind. From the time when Felun Daretseng had so firmly avoided my questioning, I had been wondering about the dark tragedy that had caused Vedlen Obiran, the benign wizard who had aided us so generously, to forsake his homeland. I was sure that Robin, for so long the wizard's friend, must know the details, but I was less certain that he would be

20

willing to satisfy my curiosity. Consequently I approached the topic as cautiously and obliquely as a hunter stalking a stag.

'How long have I known Vedlen? Why, we met soon after I left my home in Jarmswayle and took to wandering. Where is Jarmswayle? Well, 'tis the chief town of Odunseth, my own land, far away to the east of here, where the Green River enters its estuary. It is not a large realm. Two small rivers, the Beleth and the Chillrun, define its boundaries to east and west, with the Green River itself to the north and the great Moor of Rann to the south. A fair land it is, lush and lovely; the corn grows tall there and the hasedain wax fat. Many years have gone by since I saw my country; nor shall I ever go there again.

'Why did I leave? Well, you know, my father was its ruler and 'twas my great-grandfather that had built the high keep of Jarmswayle, after the fortunes of war drove him from England. Yes, I was the son of the Earl; but I was my father's fifth son, the child of his second wife. There were four stout elder brothers to govern Odunseth under my father, all sons of his first Countess. With so many other sons, he did not truly need me; and my half-brothers, they were not so very fond of me, though they did not treat me unkindly. What is more, I had a great desire to see the world beyond the confines of my own little land. So, in the summer following my sixteenth birthday, I put a pack on the back of my favourite rafenu, set a sword to my belt and slipped away.

'I went first to Warringtown. That city had seemed to me the very hub of the world, with its ships voyaging to Bordeaux and Calais, London and Lubeck — all the ports of all the great nations. However, I could gain no employment from Warringtown's fat merchants, who would not open their money-bags for any young stranger; and I had no gold to pay my own passage over the seas. So I turned back inland, crossing Quenslang and following the north bank of the Green River to Quincemail. There the King of Herador held his court in those days; it is now at Thraincross.

'By misfortune, I fell sick — or perhaps, after all, it was to prove good fortune. Mayhap it was some disease picked up from the foreign seamen in Warringtown; mayhap it was a consequence of starvation, for I had eaten little in a long time. Well, when I reached the gates of Quincemail, so sick was I that the guards would not let me enter.

Clearly they thought I carried some dread plague and feared what might happen if they let me within their city. I cannot truly blame them, but I was ill and desperate, and they drove me away from the gates . . .

'As I was stumbling away, with my rafenu following — I was too weak, by then, even to remount him — a young man chanced to be riding along the road toward Quincemail. You may guess the rest. Of course it was Vedlen Obiran, come from Reschora in quest of necromantic employment; in those days, his inclination was more toward sorcery than medicine. Yes indeed, he stopped and tended me. Then, since I might not enter the city, he persuaded a villein to give me a cottage bed and stayed with me till I was well. Nor would he accept my offer of payment by service, for I had no gold. He told me that I had become his friend, and that no friend need offer recompense for such small favours. Yet his favours to me were not small. I am glad to know that, over the years, I have been able to repay a little of my debt to him.

'What happened to me after that? Well, I joined a mercenary band for a while. We fought in a whole tangle of little wars that ravaged the disputed lands south of Herador. Then I sickened of such service and, having saved enough gold for my passage, I travelled to London. Did I enjoy the voyage? No, not at all; I have never found pleasure, and often endured great discomfort and danger, on the sea.'

I agreed fervently, remembering my own voyage to Rockall: but I did not speak of it, for I did not wish to snap the thread of Robin's discourse.

'I did not stay long in London,' he continued, 'for it was not a happy city in those days. Instead I went on to Brabant. For a while I found employment among the many little dukedoms and prince-doms of the Holy Roman Empire. When I tired of their petty quarrels I went to Rome and saw the Pope himself — or one of them! Onward then I made my way, to the very Holy Land itself. What is it like? Oh, hot; almost as dry as the Etolen Dunes and even more dangerous, nowadays, for a Christian. Yet I survived, albeit perilously, and I travelled westwards again to Navarre, Aragon and Castile, where good Christians are still battling the infidels. You have heard some-thing of that story already; I need not repeat it. In the end, I wearied

22

of all those strange lands and came back to Rockall, resolved never again to cross the seas.'

'That is my own resolution, after much lesser dangers,' I said firmly. Then, noticing an amusement in his eyes and remembering the last few months, I qualified this: 'Dangers at sea, that is. Yet did you not return to Odunseth?'

He grimaced. 'Aye, I did; but too late. I had been away for fourteen years — too long, alas! In the very autumn after I had left home, my father died, quietly in his bed. Nor did my eldest brother long survive him, for he was killed that very winter in an affray with the mountain folk of Hevelestre. My second brother, Ethelbert, drove them back onto the moorlands and, indeed, ruled peacefully for six years; but then he broke his back in a fall while out hunting and died soon after.

'Well, that left two other brothers; but Cuthbert died when a boat overturned in a tide-race and a winter sickness carried off Hubert before ever he gained the earldom. Both Ethelbert and Cuthbert had married, but Ethelbert's countess proved barren and Cuthbert's only child, a daughter, was but an infant when he died. Meantime the court chamberlain, a man I had neither liked nor trusted, had persuaded my mother to wed him. Since I was gone, that made him the foremost claimant; but the councillors, I gather, were not pleased by the prospect of having Clerebald as earl. Then my mother died — rather too conveniently, I have always felt, though I have no proper grounds for any suspicion of misdoing — and Clerebald sought to strengthen his claim by a new marriage. Cuthbert's widow resisted his coercions and fled away, to Mionia I think; so he wedded Ethelbert's widow instead and took Odunseth under his rule.'

'Yet surely, when you returned, you could reclaim the earldom from him?'

Robin laughed ruefully. 'As I said, I'd been gone too long. After fourteen hard years of travel and war, I looked little indeed like the young man who'd fled away. Earl Clerebald received me graciously enough — or so it must have seemed, to his courtiers — but, when I tried to advance my claims, he merely smiled. 'You allege you are Sir Robert Randwulf, the youngest son of my revered late master, Earl Leofwin,' he said smirkingly. 'Then I trust you have documents to prove it? If so, gladly will I cede my place to you. No documents?

23

Well then, does anyone here recognize this man? If so, let them speak up.' No-one answered, of course, though I am sure that some present did recognize me. So I was conducted firmly from the court, escorted to the borders of Odunseth and told never to return, on pain of execution.'

He paused, then went on reflectively: 'Indeed, I am of opinion that Clerebald sought to dispose of me anyway, for I was waylaid by six cutthroats when only a few miles beyond the border of Odunseth. Happily for me, they were not good fighters; less happily, they were swift riders. I could not catch any of the three who survived, to ask who had set them to ambush me, so I cannot be quite sure it was Clerebald. Nevertheless, I do not doubt it.'

I was shocked at the story. 'Yet did you not return anyway? Surely you went back and roused the people against the usurper?' Knowing Robin to be a formidable warrior, I could not believe he had accepted that dismissal passively.

He gave me a twisted smile and shook his head. 'No, I did not go back. Had I started a revolt against Earl Clerebald, many would have supported me, for he is neither a popular nor a just ruler. However, there would certainly have been fighting and I was not willing to gain the earldom at a cost in blood to my own people. I had learned that they had forgotten me — and why indeed *should* they remember the fifth son of an earl who had died so many years agone? It seemed simplest that I should remain forgotten. So I have never gone again to Odunseth, nor shall I.'

Robin fell silent. Finding nothing more to say myself, I gazed outboard into the river waters for a while, watching the fishes as they darted about the sandy bottom. The river was narrower here, I noticed, and the cliffs steeper; the Lazadel brothers' strokes were shorter, so the current must be a little stronger. Perhaps that was why they had fallen silent? The wind seemed to have dropped altogether; or maybe the cliffs were shielding us from it?

I turned again to Robin. 'How did you come to meet Vedlen Obiran again, after so many years?'

Distracted from his dark thoughts, Robin brightened. 'Why, I set out to find him! Having lost my home, it was natural for me to seek out the one friend I had in all these lands. The task of seeking was not hard, for Vedlen's renown had grown during the years I had been gone — renown as physician and chirurgeon, renown also as one who could foretell the future, whenever willing. We met at Francassel in Tarnevost and for a year I travelled with him through the forestlands. Eventually he decided to go back again to Reschora and I took service under the King of Herador. After the tragedy that befell the Obirans, I joined Vedlen again for a while, staying with him for two more years and striving to cheer him. Then, when he needed me no more, I took service in Merania.'

I felt like a hunter who, after a long stalk, has come at last within bowshot of his stag. 'Tragedy? What was that?' I asked innocently.

Robin sighed and shook his head in sad remembrance. 'Vedlen does not like it to be spoken about, for he does not wish anyone to pity him. Yet, now that his tent is far behind, I can see little harm in telling you.'

He hesitated, as if uncertain where to begin. Then he spoke again, gazing not at me but outboard, as if seeing visions of the past.

'She was a girl of Kelcestre, a lovely creature. Her father had been a possible claimant to the throne, so the King of Kelcestre had him murdered. Then the daughter fell sick; heart-sick, I would suppose. The King did not wish her to die, it would not look good so soon after her father's death, so Vedlen Obiran was engaged to tend her, to make her well again. And so he did; but they fell in love and fled away together, back to Reschora.'

He paused, staring once more into the distance. Then, with evident reluctance, he continued.

'At first all went well for them. They found a fine home, a fortified farm in an isolated valley beyond the Windrill Wall — the high ridge that divides the Rivers Rimbedreth and Alinglim, north of the Trident Mountains. It should have been a safe enough place; and so indeed it seemed, for a long while — quite seven years. They lived together in joy and their son was born and growing.

'But then Vedlen Obiran was called away. The daughter of his good friend, the Earl of Marcanlon, was desperately ill and the Earl would place reliance upon no other physician. So away Vedlen hastened, on that errand of mercy. While he was gone with his men — and he did save the girl's life, rarely indeed does he fail — his home was attacked and burned by some murderous marauders. Vedlen returned to find only its blackened ruins and the charred remains of his people lying among those ruins. Though some neighbours had seen the flames of the burning, they had not striven to pursue the marauders. You will understand why Vedlen reacted as he did at Owlsgard; and maybe, as I did, you will marvel at his fortitude on that occasion.'

'But who were the marauders? What happened to Vedlen's wife and son — were they both slain?'

'As to the identity of the marauders, we never learned for sure. I shall always believe that they were agents of the King of Kelcestre, who is a deeply evil man and a vengeful; but it has never been proved. As to Vedlen's wife and child, I think their bones must lie among the ruins of their home. Yet my friend will not accept that. He is convinced his wife and son were merely abducted, that they yet live somewhere, can he but find them. Hence all his restless wandering. However, it is quite ten years now since their farm was put to the flames and nary a trace of his wife and child has he discovered. Even his staunch hope must be fading by now.

'Why does Vedlen not use his powers, to foretell whether that quest will succeed? You may well ask. From two causes, I think. First, because he believes he should never use those powers for selfish ends. He did so, I understand, during earlier years — it is always a temptation for wizards — but never any more. I think he believes that great tragedy was, in some measure, a judgement on him from God for misusing his skills. Of his second reason, I am much less sure; but I suspect he may be afraid, strong though he is, to discover the future. That discovery might end his hope forever.'

Again Robin fell silent. Seeing etched upon his lean features the sadness that these memories had brought, I felt ashamed of my curiosity and asked no more questions.

Gazing about me, I saw that the river valley had become yet narrower, though the cliffs seemed lower hereabouts. To our right, the dune walls had entirely gnawed away the green line of vegetation and were towering high over the river. I noticed also that in the other boat, though Avran was still blowing quietly on his pommer, the singing had ceased.

Our own two boatmen were evidently uneasy; yet, with the sun still high in the sky behind us and with no wind, I could not understand why. Terim was rowing at the stern, behind Robin, so it was to Ulim Lazadel that I spoke.

'Something seems to be troubling you, friend. What is the matter?'

Ulim glanced at me briefly; all the scorn of an expert for a simpleton was in that glance.

'Can you not tell that the river is rising? Why, the water is halfway up the cliff, much higher than it should be in this place and at this season! Though there's been no rain here, there must have been storms in the mountains. This is a bad stretch to be caught in. If the water rises no higher, all will be well enough. If it keeps rising much longer and flows much swifter, then we'll be in dire peril!'

Chapter Four

STORM ON THE RIVER

Now that Ulim's words had alerted me to the situation, I realized how unobservant I had been. Gazing overboard, I saw that the river bottom was indeed much further beneath us. If any fishes were swimming there, they were now too deep down to be seen. The weed tendrils were no longer reaching upwards, for the force of the rising water was thrusting them all downriver. Moreover, the very water was cloudier; the sand of the bottom must itself be moving.

As for the cliffs, they did indeed appear lower here, though I was depressed to notice that they seemed steeper; the contorted rocks of the western cliffs were actually overhanging the river in places. Moreover, as Ulim had said, the cliffs were not truly any lower; it was just that the rising river was lifting us so much higher, though not nearly high enough to give us hope of an easy landing. There remained forty feet or more of rock above us to our left and much more than that, of rock and dune, to our right — an unappealing prospect, indeed.

Robin had been roused from his revery by Ulim's words. 'What should we do, then, Master Lazadel? Might we not turn back and allow the current to carry us to some landing-place?'

Ulim's voice, as he replied, had all the strained patience of a mother speaking to a tiresomely importunate child. 'Now, Sir Robert, reason it out, won't ye? We've been rowing all morning, four hours and more. In all that time, we've passed no good landing-place. Turning back would mean a long run back downstream and much effort lost. And you know, even the rock where we spent last night must be under water by now, with the river rising as it is. To turn back would be just daft!'

'Can we hope to reach Kaldansett ere nightfall, then, if we go on?'

'Nay, not Kaldansett.' The boatman's contempt for that question was evident. 'Even had the river been normal, we'd not have reached Kaldansett before eventide tomorrow. Yet there *is* a good landing-spot on the east bank, that we might reach in another hour or so if all goes well. If we can get that far, I don't think we'll chance travelling any further till the river falls.'

Terim Lazadel, who seemed either more tired or more dispirited than his normally quiet brother, grunted an amen to this. Then, after Ulim had brusquely repulsed my hesitant offer to assist in the rowing, both brothers fell grimly silent. I noticed that the sound of Avran's tootling on his pommer had ceased; he also must now be aware of the danger.

For my own part, striving to appear relaxed, I engaged Robin in renewed conversation. He responded politely enough. I recall that we talked about his life at the courts of Herador and Merania, but beyond that point memory does not carry me.

While I was listening and asking questions with part of my mind, at a deeper level I was counting the minutes. My eyes strayed ever and again to the river. Even to my uneducated perceptions, it was evident that matters were getting, not better, but worse. The water was still rising and the boatmen were finding it increasingly difficult to battle against its quickening current.

Abruptly Ulim capitulated, in one regard at least. 'Happen you'd better do some rowing after all, Sir Robert,' he said. 'I don't doubt that you'll be more expert than Simon, even though you're not so young. There's a spare oar, slung underneath the right thwart beside you. Ah, you've found it; good! Just unfasten the cords tying it in place; a couple of tugs should suffice. Well enough; now shove it in the water to port, opposite to Terim's oar. Right; now let's see how we manage!'

I saw, by Robin's expression when first he dipped his oar into the water, that the current was much stronger than he had anticipated. Soon, however, he began rowing with a skill I could never have matched. With this assistance, our yildrih began to move forward much faster, gaining so rapidly upon the Garavets' boat that we were abreast of it within minutes. They gave us a startled glance and exchanged rapid comments, but we passed them with ease.

Looking back, I saw that Avran was being equipped with an oar. However, though he strove manfully, he was much less expert than Robin and their boat remained well behind ours. Possibly Etvan Garavet, with his liking for being in the lead, was annoyed at this. More probably, in such conditions he did not care.

For a while, the extra impetus given by these third oars seemed to be solving our problems. Certainly we were progressing faster, even though the river still appeared to be rising. My heart lightened.

However, soon there came a breath of wind, a stirring of the air about us. At first I welcomed this, for I thought it would cool the oarsmen pleasantly and make their task less onerous. Then I noticed that the wind was coming from the northeast and saw clouds massing in that quarter; and suddenly I felt afraid.

Ulim looked upward at the sky, then glanced backward at me. He said not a word but, by the furrowing of his brows and the pursing of his lips, I knew his thought as clearly as if he had spoken: 'That looks like trouble!' He had been using his oar alternately at left and right but now, with powerful strokes at left, he guided the yildrih over until we were beneath the very overhang of the dark western cliff.

The water was becoming ever more turbulent, so that the sound of the sand grains dribbling down from the dunes was quite drowned out. However, I could see that, as the wind freshened, more and more sand was coming down, in steady runnels or sudden rushes. The great wall of red and yellow seemed now as menacing as the brightly tinted shields and helms of an approaching hostile army.

On we went, each minute and even each second a crucial advance. The other boat was still several poles behind us. I could no longer see Avran, but I knew his lips must be drawn back and his brow furrowed in concentration as he strove with the stream. In our own boat, Ulim had assumed complete authority; clearly, although the less talkative of the Lazadel cousins, he was the stronger.

Suddenly, over to our right and a little way ahead, the face of a towering dune seamed and crumpled. There was a dull roar as the mass of sand cascaded into the water. The resultant waves scarcely affected us, though they caused the Garavets' boat to bob. However, we were caught in the edge of the cloud of sand that was blown cross-river. I shut my eyes and lowered my head; the three oarsmen merely blinked and continued grimly rowing.

Ulim had said it would take us an hour to reach the landing place. How many minutes had gone by? I was not sure; thirty at least, I trusted, but was I counting correctly? I called out to Ulim: 'How long to go?'

His response was entirely disheartening. 'Not so far to the place I mentioned, but I doubt that we'll dare to land there. It's over to starboard — and just see the state of those dunes!'

As he spoke, another dune crest collapsed forward into the water, some distance ahead of us this time, causing our boat to pitch and a second hail of sand-grains to sting our faces. The dangers of that eastern bank were indeed all too apparent.

'What's to be done, then?' I asked desperately.

He glanced back at me again. I was surprised at his expression, for it was not at all one of fear; instead, it showed a wry amusement. 'Aye, that's a fair question. What think you, brother Terim? Have you any ideas?'

Again a dune front collapsed and again we endured a hail of sand-grains. I noted with concern that sand was beginning to accumulate within the yildrih; a bright, menacing line of it was growing beneath the thwarts, and there were pockets of it in crevices among the piled-up trade goods. Terim had not responded and I wondered if he had even heard his brother's words.

Ulim, while maintaining his stroke, managed somehow to pull a cloak about his shoulders — a greenish cloak, the colour of the withies that grow beside the Aramassa. Lifting his oar from the water momentarily — the action caused the boat to check — he fastened the cloak's loops with quick fingers and shrugged the hood forward, so that it would protect his face from the sand rain. Then his oar was back in the water and we were gaining way once more.

Hitherto so useless, I was able at least to help Terim and Robin into their cloaks. Robin thanked me with a nod, but Terim said never a word; he seemed to be pondering deeply. I put on my own cloak; when the successive collapse of two more dune-faces sent further clouds of sand rolling across the river, I was grateful for the protection its hood afforded.

Suddenly there came a voice from the stern. 'Ulim, do you mind that gully on the port bank, where the cliff collapsed last year? The gully shaped like an hour-glass, with the mound beneath? Happen we've a chance of landing there, if the river hasn't washed the rock pile away by now.'

'Aye, 'tis a good thought, Terim lad.' Ulim sounded perfectly calm. 'How far ahead would that be, do you suppose?'

'About half a league, I'd reckon. Not so far, but quite far enough, with the water as it is and the wind rising.'

Indeed, it proved an arduous passage. The wind was building itself into a gale and was full of sand, perhaps from the collapse of further dune-faces upriver, more likely because sand was being carried from shifting dunes to the eastward. There was rain in the wind also, fine drops only but driven so hard as to sting like thorn-pricks. It was ever more difficult to see upriver, through the sand-haze and the rain. To make matters worse, the river was becoming ever more turbulent, so that the oarsmen were having to row from a continuously pitching boat. For my part, I was beginning to feel quite seasick — or rather, river-sick.

The Garavets' boat had fallen so far behind that it was quite out of my view. I trusted that all was well with Avran; at least he had a task to perform, while I was merely an encumbrance. Suddenly feeling cold, I shivered and huddled deeper into my cloak.

Ulim glanced back at me and gave me another of his wry smiles; I am sure he perceived, from the pallor of my countenance, what was amiss with me. He and Terim were still contriving to use their oars effectively, despite the conditions. After rowing for, why, quite five hours, I felt that they ought to be exhausted, though I was grateful they were not; they must have muscles as tough as bog-oak!

Robin was faring less well. Several times, as the boat pitched, his oar missed the water entirely and he endured a shoulder-wrenching jolt. In contrast to the brothers, he was already beginning to look tired.

Where was that gully and rock pile? Clinging to the thwart of the yildrih, I strove to gaze through the haze of rain and blowing sand; but the dark, overhanging rocks showed no interruption.

There was an especially mighty surge as a huge dune-face collapsed; Ulim crouched forward as the blast of sand hit us and I followed suit. The yildrih pitched to port and came close to overturning; but it did not.

The bottom of the yildrih was filling with sand, especially on the port side; the weight of it must be affecting the boat's balance. Well, that was one job I *could* perform! Gazing about me, I noticed a baler affixed under the thwart. I tugged it free from its cord and began to shovel sand overboard, striving at the same time to avoid altering the yildrih's trim. This was not an easy task, with the boat bucking and more sand blowing inboard at every moment. Whether my efforts significantly lightened the labour of the oarsmen, I do not know, but the job kept me occupied and distracted my thoughts from my stomach.

After a while — ten minutes? twenty minutes? I could not estimate the time or our progress clearly — I noticed that, while the rain was coming ever harder, there was less and less sand in it. Already I had shovelled overboard all the sand I could reach. No doubt the boat would be filling with rainwater next, I reflected gloomily; but, for a while, I could suspend my efforts. I straightened my back thankfully.

Almost as I did so, Terim called from behind me: 'Look ahead, brother! I believe I see the gully!'

Eagerly I gazed ahead. Yes, there *did* seem to be a break in the overhang of the cliff; but was there still a mound of debris beneath to make us a landing-place, or had the Rimbedreth indeed gnawed it away? I could not tell.

Ulim seemed doubtful also. 'Aye, that's the place; but shall we be able to get ashore there? Well, we can but try.'

As he was using his oar to steer us yet closer to the western cliff, another sand-dune collapsed forward into the river, just upstream from us. This generated a further great surge of water. Within seconds we were being borne sideways, at an alarming speed, right under the rock overhang and in toward the cliff.

For a horrid while, I was quite certain that we would be wrecked. I loosed my hold from the thwart and flung myself down, clutching frantically at the ropes that held the cargo in place.

Fortunately, both Ulim and Robin responded swiftly to the danger. Each raised his oar and, crouching over it, held it tightly. In consequence it was the oars, not the boat, that hit the rock face. There was a sickening jolt, then both men gave a mighty thrust. I heard

34

Robin's oar crack and split; but the immediate danger was past and the backwash was carrying us out again toward midstream.

As I straightened, I saw that the break in the cliff-line was just ahead of us. A gully it was, but a very steep one, little more than a vertical groove in the cliff. Beneath it a narrow pile of rocks, the reduced residue of the cliff collapse, protruded only just a few feet above the water and extended scarcely a yard outward into the river. Well, it was a refuge of a sort.

With Robin unable now to assist, those last few yards were a hard struggle for the brothers. I could hear Terim's gasping breaths as he plied his oar. Then, abruptly, we entered quiet water in the lee of the rock ridge and the bow of the yildrih grounded against those rocks.

In a single flow of motion, Ulim dropped his oar, unrolled with quick fingers a coil of woven-reed rope fastened to a bar at the bow, and leapt ashore. At this the yildrih bucked, then swung sideways. While Robin fended her off from the cliff with the broken butt-end of his oar, Ulim tied the rope about one of the rocks. Then he straightened and laughed at us. There was no hysteria in that laugh, just a deep amusement.

''Tis the Rimbedreth for excitement,' he said. 'Myself, though, I prefer the Aramassa. Come ashore, now, Simon; and you too, Sir Robert.'

I was eager to leave the yildrih but clumsy in doing so. Indeed, had it not been for Ulim's steadying hand, I might well have fallen sideways into the river as the boat pitched. Sir Robert stepped ashore more gracefully. He seemed inclined to apologize for breaking the oar, but Ulim silenced him gruffly.

'Nay, Sir Robert, we can make another easy enough. We're beholden to you for your assistance; it saved us much sweat.'

Terim seemed in no haste to follow us ashore. Perhaps this was not surprising, for the rock pile gave little shelter. It was no more than a narrow, very irregular shelf at the cliff foot, not so long as a refectory table and little broader. Moreover, it afforded no shelter from the driving rain. Directly above was the steep landslip-track and, on either side, overhanging cliffs.

'We cannot remain here,' Ulim observed calmly. 'One of us must climb the gully and let down a rope, if we're to keep ourselves and our merchandise from the river. Simon, you're the smallest and nimblest; d'you fancy a climb?'

I did not, for the gully was almost as steep as a house side and the dark rocks were wet and slippery. However, having done so little in the boat, I could scarcely decline the task.

'Most certainly I do,' I answered untruthfully. 'Moreover, there's a rope in my pack, if you'll toss it to me, Terim.'

After catching the pack I took off my cloak, folded it, and then strapped it about my shoulders beneath the pack; better to be wet, I felt, than to be encumbered. Then, taking a deep breath, I turned to the cliff and began my ascent.

Forty feet is no great distance to climb. However, when every deep crevice is full of wet sand, clinging to one's boots but providing no secure hold, and when every shallower crack is greasy with rainwater, it can seem a long, long way. Yet somehow I scrabbled and scrambled upward, at last heaving myself thankfully onto the broad, flat rock shelf that topped the cliff.

There was another slope, shorter and less steep, behind this shelf. A straggly growth of narrow-leaved shrubs grew in its lee, blown sand being heaped about their trunks. One of the shrubs was close enough to serve as anchor for my rope. Having taken off my pack I put on my cloak again, though I was so wet by then that it served little purpose. Then I fetched out that rope, partially uncoiled it and secured it to the gnarled trunk of the shrub before turning back toward the river.

The rope was a dozen ells in length and, though thin, extremely strong. Crouching at the cliff top, I threw the remaining coil outward and downward. Ulim caught this deftly and fastened the rope's lower end under a rock.

Promptly Robin climbed up to join me, carrying his own pack and using my bowstave as staff. Thus assisted, he found the ascent easy enough.

Almost at that moment there came a delighted shout from Terim. Looking downriver through the rain, we saw the second boat wallowing laboriously towards us. At the sight of our yildrih, the foremost oarsman — I could not recognize him, cloaked as he was, but presumed it was Etvan Garavet — swung the boat's bow towards the bank. After a further interval of effortful rowing, the Garavets' yildrih nosed in between ours and the cliff.

That oarsman tossed his rope to Ulim and leapt quickly onto the rocks; yes, it was Etvan. Avran stumbled ashore next. He seemed utterly exhausted, for he collapsed in a crouch, burying his head between his arms. Dazlan Garavet tossed Avran's pack, and passed his bowstave, to Etvan. As he came ashore himself, he shook the rain from his cloak in the fashion of a dog emerging from a pond.

Meantime, Terim had got ready a satchel of foodstuffs. Soon all four boatmen were nimbly ascending the cliff, scarcely troubling to use the rope. My weary friend Avran needed it, however, hauling himself laboriously up to join us.

Terim lit a little fire, using flint, steel and dried leaves dug from under the sand, then feeding the flames with dead branches broken from the shrubs. We huddled round it gratefully, cooking and eating a welcome meal in the poor shelter of the scrub. So good did it seem to rest and eat that we were quite uncaring even when the smoke, tossed about so unpredictably by the gusty wind, blew into our eyes.

Avran's hands were raw-red from the unaccustomed labour of rowing. He was very much tireder than Robin, presumably because his lack of skill had caused him to expend more energy than was really necessary. Consequently he lay back and said little.

In contrast Robin, who had recovered faster, was quite bright and talkative. The boatmen, though they had laboured so long, were in equally good spirits. However, Terim seemed restless. Twice he walked over to the cliff-top to be sure all was well with the boats; the water, he told us, was still rising, though the rain had slackened. After only a half-hour, he went back down the cliff, for he was unhappy away from his yildrih.

Ulim, Etvan and Dazlan sat much longer by the little fire before rousing themselves. Eventually Etvan said: 'Well, the river will not drop till past nightfall; we'd best be getting our merchandise ashore. The yildrihen'll float lighter then and, if the Rimbedreth keeps on rising, 'twill not harm them.'

'Aye, you're right,' responded Ulim. All three boatmen rose and we rose with them, to walk over to the cliff-edge again.

'It would surely be easiest if you three went down to unload,' suggested Robin. 'You'll do it more quickly than would we. I'll haul the bales up on the rope. Then, Simon, perhaps you and Avran might carry them over and stack them under the trees?'

So the boatmen went nimbly down the gully again, this time using the rope to steady themselves, while we three travellers watched them and waited for the first load.

We were being doubly unwise, had we but known it. To advertise one's presence by lighting a fire in lordless lands, and to maintain no watch, is to take unjustifiable risks. However, I'm sure we were all afflicted by the carelessness that so often follows survival of one danger and makes one so vulnerable to another.

That must serve as poor excuse for the fact that the armed men came unnoticed upon us. We were looking down towards the river, into the howling gale, when we became suddenly aware that we were surrounded; or was it the warning cry of Ulim Lazadel, gazing upward, that alerted us too late? Before even Robin could draw his sword, we were seized.

As for the Lazadels and the Garavets, they leapt into their yildrihen and, cutting the ropes with swift knife-strokes, slipped away downstream into the turmoil of the waters. Whether they survived that long and perilous passage down to the Aramassa we were never to learn, for we never saw or heard of them again.

For our part, with wrists bound firmly behind us, we were marched away from the cliff-top into captivity.

Chapter Five

THE MEN OF THE LORDLESS LANDS

Three months earlier, when Avran and I had ridden into trouble amid the ruins of the Elvenostan city, our captors had proved to be a horde of ruffians; but at least those men had all worn uniform and had shown some sense of discipline. No such qualities, of appearance or of order, were to be noted among the band that had seized us this time.

There were around thirty of them, thirty of the raggedest and dirtiest rogues it had ever been my misfortune to set eyes upon. A few wore ancient coats of mail, rent in places and streaked brown with rust; some others wore gambesons of leather, roughened and with edges frayed by over-long use; several wore surcoats over their tunics, in a variety of faded colours and with devices almost indistinguishable; and the rest wore just jupons or tunics of cloth or wool, torn or roughly patched. All carried weapons, most often a battered-looking sword, though some had spears or axes and two bore only long-bladed knives.

As for a sense of order, they showed no such thing. They had seized, disarmed and bound us efficiently enough but, almost before we had been herded away from the clifftop into the poor shelter of the spinney, they were quarrelling.

'Ye're a fool, Ulseg,' growled one of them. He was a hulk of a man with thick black hair and beard, as surly as a bear at a baiting and speaking in some dialect of Reschorese which I could comprehend only with difficulty. 'Ye launched the attack too soon! Why did ye not delay till them boatmen had brought their merchandise out of the yildrihen? We'd 've had much handsomer pickings.'

'Ach, ye think ye're so clever, Vatsarg!' spat back the man thus addressed. He was a shorter but very burly man, clad in a mail-coat made for a much bigger soldier, for it hung about his knees. There was a sword at his belt and a short axe in his hand. 'So clever ye are that I'll split your skull for ye, some day soon. How could we have got down the cliff fast enough? They'd 've been away down river long before, as ye know well.'

'Aye, maybe; but their goods would've been ashore for us to seize, had ye not been so accursed hasty, and we much richer. I repeat it; ye're a fool!'

'Richer? What d'ye think those goods would be worth, anyway?' asked the other disgustedly. 'Fishing nets, woven baskets and parcels of dried fish, that's all they'd be. We've captured the men with the wealth! These three 'll be carrying gold, be sure of that.'

'Let's search 'em, then, and share it!' A third man was eagerly speaking now. He was a lean creature with dirty, straw-coloured hair and palely blank eyes, clad in garments that seemed to have been fabricated by stitching together the contents of a rag-sack.

'We'll have none of that!' asserted Ulseg, who seemed to be their leader. 'We'll search 'em back at Kradsunar, and not before! Those are Lord Darnay's orders, as you know well! He'll divide up the gold and we'll be given our proper share, all of us.'

'And what about their weapons, and their clothes? This is good cloth.' The pale-eyed man had his hands on Avran's cloak until Avran twitched it disgustedly away.

'All will be shared, like usual.'

'Aye — like usual!' Vatsarg was contemptuous. 'We all know what that means. Lord Darnay takes what he wants and you take what you want. Then, if anything be left, the rest of us might just be permitted to share it.'

'Are you seeking to be leader, then, Vatsarg?' The burly man was speaking more quietly now, but with vicious ferocity. 'Well, I think the time for our reckoning has come!'

With a sudden swing of his right arm, he threw the short axe, blade foremost, at the bigger man. Vatsarg had not been ready for this; moreover, he wore no mail. The axe took him in the lower chest. He crumpled forward with a shuddering groan, the blood spurting between his fingers as he clawed frantically at the axe-haft.

There was a gasp of shocked horror from the other villains, but there was no real protest; evidently such incidents were not unusual

40

in their lives. As for Ulseg, he paid no further attention to his dying adversary.

'Beremond, you'll stay here and watch the river, with six men. Clean up that axe and keep it for me, mind! The rest of you, move! And mind you hold your mouths shut; ye've seen what happens to men that exercise their jaws unduly. Move, I said!'

And move they did, though in no sort of order. The seven who were to stay behind shifted reluctantly over to one side. The rest of us set forth in an irregular straggle, with Avran, Sir Robert and me each escorted by two armed ruffians. Past the clustering shrubs we went and up the short slope beyond. As we crested it, I glanced back and saw our little fire still burning. Well, the rain would soon put it out — or perhaps the seven left behind would choose to refuel it, to cheer their dismal watch.

For the moment, they had other concerns. They were surging round their fallen comrade — not to succour him or comfort his dying, I was sure, but rather because they were eager to despoil him of whatever they might. I shivered at the thought, and at the memory of the horror just witnessed. Then, trying to put it from my mind, I looked ahead.

The country we were now entering was little more inspiring than that on which we had turned our backs. It was not without splashes of colour, for there were patches of red sand, wind-transported, in the hollows. However, all other hues seemed mere shades of grey or black; black slates and grey soils, thickets of greeny-grey thorn-bushes here and there and a general scattering of bulbous, spiny plants of a sort I had never seen hitherto, as dull in colour as the thornbushes. It was as if the whole landscape had been covered by ashes, half-burned coke and brick-dust from some gigantic brick-kiln; a dismal place, indeed. As we were marched along, I wondered whether it was always thus or whether the rain might bring forth a new growth of grasses or flowers to brighten the dreariness.

For the rain was coming down harder now. The unruly wind tossed it wilfully at us, sometimes from left or right, sometimes into our faces, though most often it came from behind. Now that we were away from the river, I realized that the day was quite warm. Our march — none of the band seemed to have rafneyen, or even hase-dain, to ride — was in consequence an unpleasant and sweaty one.

41

The straggle became ever looser. Ulseg strode along foremost. Immediately behind him were a couple of particular cronies, each with a second sword-belt — Sir Robert's and Avran's — girt over his own, so that a sword swung at each hip. Three other ruffians followed, bearing our three packs; one had on my belt, with its sword and knives, while the other two carried the bowstaves and quivers. Evidently Ulseg was keeping the loot close to his hand; he knew his associates too well to trust them.

Indeed, despite the shock of Vatsarg's murder, the men further back were soon at their grumbling again, mostly in Reschorese, though I thought I heard some English words also.

Robin, over to my left and a little way ahead, was striding along briskly; his two guards were finding it hard to match his pace. Avran, in contrast, had fallen back and was shambling along exhaustedly between two impatient ruffians, who cursed him at intervals and groused the rest of the time about the evil weather and the hardness of their lot.

My own two guards presented a considerable mutual contrast. One was quite silent; he was tall and wall-eyed, wrapped in a long cloak that had faded almost white, with a spear slung across his shoulders. The other was shorter and particularly ragged; he was perpetually muttering to himself and fingering his axe, as if anxious to use it on me — or someone . . . Neither seemed especially watchful, but I was at the centre of the straggle and had little chance of escape.

Since I had laboured so little in the boat, I was in good shape for this march — better than Avran or even than Robin, for all his hardihood. Yet, when one is a prisoner, with no sense of the distance to be covered and no prospect of joy at the destination, any march swiftly becomes wearisome.

As the Rimbedreth was left further behind, the sand patches became ever fewer till they vanished altogether. With this colour gone, the landscape seemed even more dreary.

The Lordless Lands — yet these villains had spoken of a lord. What was the name I'd heard? Oh yes, Lord Darnay. Well, if these ruffians were typical of his vassals, he was little to be envied! What would he do with us — or, more to the point, what would he do *to* us? We were much too far from home to be subjects for ransom and, I feared, by now altogether out of the beneficent reach of the wizard.

Our prospects seemed poor indeed — and yet I retained some optimism. They had taken my sword and my belt with its knives, but they had not searched me. Consequently they had not found the knives hidden in the shoulders of my jupon and in the shanks of my two boots. Though it seemed probable that, following arrival at their camp (if camp it was), we would ultimately be deprived of our good clothes, that might not happen immediately. All hope was not yet lost.

We marched through the waning of the day into darkness. By then Ulseg and his companions had allowed us to catch them up, no doubt so as to ensure that their prisoners remained secure and unmolested. Indeed, the ranks of our captors had become much tighter, either through a common distrust of each other or through apprehension of danger in the darkness. In part because of this new proximity to the formidable Ulseg, in part through sheer weariness, the grumblers had fallen silent; even my guard had ceased his mutterings and axe-fingerings.

My taller, wall-eyed guard stumbled at one point and fell heavily. However, the other ignored him and urged me on, leaving him to scramble unaided to his feet and catch us up. No-one commented on the happening, not even he.

As the daylight faded, the rain slackened and eventually ceased. The earlier warmth was waning; I found myself shivering anew. Heavy cloud still arched over us but far southward, to our left, a band of brightness showed that the sun was setting — as narrow a line as the crack under the door which allows light into some dark cupboard. Surely our march must end soon?

Gratified murmurs from the ruffians about us provided the first intimation that, at last, we were approaching our destination. Then I perceived blacker masses against the dark sky, knew them to be the outlines of buildings, and realized Kradsunar must be, not a camp, but a city.

The march quickened in the excitement of arrival and, though we prisoners did not share that emotion, we were borne along willy-nilly. There was a sharp question from guards, a brusque response, and then we were entering under the arch of a gatehouse.

43

This was lit only by a single, guttering torch. Even so, I could perceive that it had been in semi-ruinous condition until hastily repaired with unshaped stones by unskilled hands. Beyond was a narrow way between high buildings: it was too dark to see them clearly, but they were unlit and had an odour of dusty aridity that convinced me they were neglected and uninhabited.

Whether by Ulseg's design or through the careless ineptitude of his ruffianly band, only he and his two cronies were now ahead of our guards and us. The men bearing our packs had dropped back and the rest of the raggle-taggle were even further behind. Robin and his guards were walking along just in front of my own escort and me; Avran, so entirely weary that he was staggering and only kept moving by the support of his grumbling guards, was immediately to my rear. There was even less light amid these ruins and the alley bent crookedly.

We had several minutes of shuffling along in deep gloom before I noticed a pool of light ahead of us. We made an abrupt turn to the left and entered blinkingly upon a market-place, lit brightly by bonfires and torches and thronged with people.

It was immediately evident that a carousal was in progress and, indeed, had been happening for some while. Hunks of meat were charring neglected on spits over fires; broken loaves of bread and masses of sliced meat were scattered upon roughly made tables; empty barrels, intended to serve as seats, stood upright by the tables or had been tumbled over; and everywhere, among puddles left by a rainstorm that must have been much briefer here, there lay earthenware goblets and beakers with beer spilling from them, some intact and some smashed, and the other unattractive debris of a riotous feast.

Among all this disorder there stepped, staggered, swayed, sat or slumped as unattractive-looking a rabble as ever I have set eyes on. All of them were ragged, many of them misshapen and most of them wild or evil-looking — the very scourings of this island of Rockall. Some were perched on the barrel-tops, either singing and flourishing their beakers of ale or sprawled forward over the tables; a few lay intertwined in love or combat on the ground between the puddles or had fallen inert into them; and many were dancing in a drunken fashion, with arms interlinked in a ring or in single solemn rotation.

Music of a discordant kind was being furnished by two men with bagpipes, the first examples of that instrument I had seen since leaving England; but even that strident sound was almost lost in the general hubbub of songs, shouts and curses that filled the air.

On the side of the square furthest from us was an elevated dais made from blocks of cut stone piled roughly together. Upon this was set a rather better-constructed table, behind which there were seated — or, in two instances, upon which there had collapsed — men in much richer attire. Midmost was a huge, squat creature with a tangled mass of greying hair and a bunchy beard. He had a great silver tankard clutched in one massive paw and was surveying the scene with the satisfaction of Satan contemplating the antics of his devilkins. Could that be Lord Darnay? If so, he was a fitting ruler for this tumultuous, disorderly mob.

Ulseg had halted upon entering the square. 'Ah, of course, 'tis the celebration of the anniversary of our seizing of this town! I had forgotten. We must hasten to pay our respects to our lord.'

Did I detect some irony in his tone? I was not sure; but certainly his words provoked a fresh outbreak of complaint among the ruffians pushing out into the square behind us. Why had they been excluded from this debauchery? Why could not others have been sent to watch the river? Why had not Ulseg brought them back earlier?

Ignoring all this, Ulseg and his two cohorts began pushing their way through the drunken throng towards the dais and we, perforce, must follow them.

As we approached Lord Darnay's table, a girl who had been serving him with beer from a tall jug scurried towards us, presumably in haste to refill the jug from a broached barrel nearby. Gazing at us too interestedly, she failed to watch her footing, slipped in a patch of spilled ale, and cannoned into the man at Ulseg's right.

Instantly and viciously he struck her with his fist, so that she tumbled onto the ground, the earthenware jug shattering into pieces. Nor was he satisfied at this. He turned upon her with a curse and drew back his booted foot, intending to give the poor creature a mighty kick.

However, Robin was too swift for him. Murmuring reprovingly, 'Come, sir, that is scarcely gentlemanly!' he hooked his own right foot about the upraised boot. With a quick twist, he so upset the girl's assailant that the villian staggered sideways and tumbled, splash! face foremost into a deep rainwater puddle.

As he fell, the girl scrambled to her feet, lithe and swift as a lizard, and fled away into the crowd.

Robin's guards seized him and shook him angrily. However, a great, rumbling laugh came from the huge man on the dais, to be echoed swiftly by the men about him and by Ulseg and his other crony. Within moments, the whole square was in an uproar of amusement.

When Robin's victim, striving to rise, tripped on one of the two swords that hung from his waist and fell again into the puddle, the laughter redoubled.

Upon his second rising, he shook a dripping fist at Robin and would clearly have assaulted my friend, had not two other ruffians prevented it. This vain defiance aroused further amusement, Lord Darnay throwing back his great head and positively roaring with laughter. Only when the hilarity had died down did he beckon over Ulseg and ask about us.

'Huh! Passengers from a yildrih? They won't amount to much. Any wealthy lord would be riding in his own barge or travelling with an escort by land. Don't bother me now; I'll see to 'em in the morning. Put 'em in the guardhouse for the night, Ulseg, and come back to join our celebration. Ay, take their packs along with 'em. We'll sort everything out in the morning. Hurry, now; you're wasting good drinking time!'

He took a quaff from his great tankard, hastily refilled by another scurrying girl, and waved us from his presence. We were hustled out from the brightness of the square into the gloom of another backstreet of that ruinous, riotous city, the tumult of the carousing fading away behind us.

Chapter Six

PRISONERS IN KRADSUNAR

'Well, we have survived the river only to encounter troubles quite as severe — we have weathered Charybdis, only to be savaged by Scylla.'

Robin was speaking and, though I did not understand his allusion at the time, I shared fully his feeling of anticlimax and frustration.

The room in which we had been incarcerated was fairly large, but almost bare and extremely dirty. It was dimly lit by a single candle-wick, floating in tallow in a shallow bowl. Presumably this illumination had been intended to enable our guards to inspect us at intervals. Predictably, however, on such a night of celebration and with such men, they could not be troubled to do so. In any case, they would have argued, why need they bother to inspect prisoners who were without weapons and tied up firmly with strong ropes? Even if we freed ourselves, was there not a roomful of armed men — themselves — outside? How could we hope to pass them and escape?

That, indeed, was the principal problem. We were in the inner of the two lower chambers of what I presumed must be the keep that had once guarded this town, there being in the outer chamber a stone staircase to upper rooms. When Ulseg and his ruffians had brought us to this place, they had been not only bickering as usual, but also impatient to return to the square and the festivities. Of the original party of twenty or so, six had slipped away already between city gate and guardhouse, while the man whom Robin had tripped was gone in quest of dry clothing. Those of Ulseg's band that remained were all most unwilling to stay on guard. It had needed not only the full exertion of an authority strengthened by his slaying of Vatsarg earlier that day, but also the promise that food and drink would be brought to them in ample quantity, before Ulseg could induce eight men into staying to act as our gaolers.

None of our original escorts had been chosen for guard duty; presumably they were considered to have done duties enough. The eight left to watch us were headed by Ulseg's other particular crony — I never learned his name — and included the three men who had carried our packs. These four seemed to be considered relatively trustworthy by Ulseg, if any trust could be reposed in so villainous a crew. Indeed, I am sure his trust in them was minimal. That we had been allowed to continue wearing our jupons was largely, I think, because Ulseg suspected that our pockets would be rifled otherwise.

We had indeed been tied up very firmly. We had each been made to sit down upon a crudely-constructed, but very heavy, wooden bench of small width. Our wrists had been crossed and placed behind us and our feet pulled backward under the narrow seats, to be tied to our wrists. Further ropes had been wrapped about our chests, stomachs and thighs, attaching our bodies firmly to the seats.

Fortunately we had not been gagged. Indeed, the guards had brought us a share of the food and given us a few swallows of beer from a very battered pewter beaker. They seemed to regard us with no particular animosity and even rather to admire Robin after his exploit, the recollection of which occasioned recurrent jocularity. However, they had not freed our hands while feeding us and had left no implements in the room that we might use to free ourselves.

Or so they thought; but, of course, they had not removed my boots. Moreover, the fashion in which they had tied me, highly effective though it would have been under other circumstances, was almost ideally suited to enable me to reach either of the knives concealed in my boot-shanks. (I blessed the inspiration that had caused me to persuade the Bristol cobbler to make those concealed sheaths!) I was reasonably confident that I could free my two friends and myself; but what then? Since our own weapons had been piled, along with our packs, in the outer room under the guards' eyes and since those guards were themselves heavily armed, how might we pass them?

Even supposing that we did, could we find our way back through Kradsunar's warren of narrow streets to the gate, without going

48

through the square? I had no concept of the town plan or the nature of the fortifications; the keep might be near to or far from the gate, the walls easily traversable or impassable. Moreover, if we did find the gate and fought our way out past its guards, how could we evade the inevitable pursuit in such barren terrain?

Avran had fallen into a deep slumber. Because of his cramped position, perhaps, he was snoring quite loudly. It was unlikely that our guards were listening but, if they were, the noise of his snoring would drown my words, providing I spoke softly. Hastily I outlined the problems to Robin.

His eyes took fire, and he sat up straighter, when I told him of my knives. Although he listened patiently when I expressed my various anxieties, he seemed not to share my disquiet.

'Free us, lad; that's the first and greatest step. We'll fret about the other matters when the time comes. And, you know, if those villains outside keep at their drinking, they may not present so great a problem after all. Even if we're armed only with knives, we might yet be able to surprise 'em!'

The freeing proved more difficult than I had anticipated. If I strained backward, I could just about reach down with my right hand to my left boot. However, with only my two middle fingers to use, at first I could not tug the knife free from its sheath. Eventually, after much arching and relaxing of my foot, I managed to push the knife upward a little with my heel; but then, as the knife was freed, I came perilously close to dropping it. When I had succeeded in grasping the knife firmly, its blade proved too awkwardly angled to reach any of the ropes. I had to use my other hand to push it into a position that would allow me to saw at the rope linking wrist to ankle.

Matters moved more swiftly thereafter. The knife was extremely sharp and the rope, though fairly thick, of poor quality. When it was sheared through, I was able easily to reverse the blade and cut through the rope linking my left wrist to my right ankle. It was a relief to have my feet free and I paused to stretch them awhile. Then, turning the knife about and holding its hilt between my two hands, I cut away at the rope linking my wrists. Ah! the joy, when I felt that rope part!

After that, the ropes about my body were untied swiftly enough.

I stumbled on rising to my feet, recovered and then stretched luxuriously, before hastening over to free a delighted Robin.

Avran was still snoringly asleep; it was only when his ankles were unfastened that he was aroused. I covered his mouth hastily with my hand to stifle any awakening cry, but none came; indeed, he seemed still sleep-dazed. Not until all ropes were off him and he also had risen and stretched did he make his one quiet comment: 'Simon my friend, you're quite a useful man to have around one in a tight place!'

'Well, happen so,' I muttered in response, 'but we're not out of the tight place yet. There are the guards outside to be dealt with, first off.'

'Yet they're strangely silent, aren't they?' Robin was listening with head cocked to one side, reminding me for the first time of the little English redbreast whose name was echoed by his own. 'Harken for a while!'

It was quite true. Earlier in the evening, as the beer began to circulate outside, we had heard coarse voices from time to time, upraised in ribald comment or in bawdy song. Now, though we were listening carefully, we could catch no sound at all. Indeed, it occurred to me that I had heard no noises for some considerable time. Surely it was not possible that all eight ruffians had sunk so swiftly into a drunken stupor?

However, when I had given knives to Robin and Avran and we opened the heavy wooden door — it moved so reluctantly, and groaned so loudly on its unoiled hinges, that a surprise attack would have been impossible — the scene meeting our eyes suggested exactly that.

The outer chamber was much more brightly lit, by two torches placed into wall-brackets. To our left the stone staircase ascended into darkness, while on the farther side of the chamber was the door through which we had entered. (I had thought it small, but saw now that it was merely a wicket in one of two much more massive doors whose rusty hinges and cover of cobwebs proclaimed that they had not been opened in many years.) Between the doorway and us were chairs arranged in a horseshoe, with a trestle table between on which were platters bearing the remains of the guards' ample repast, a small sprung keg of ale and six pewter tankards. A seventh tankard had dropped onto the floor and emptied its contents there, while the eighth was dribbling ale onto the lap of the man holding it. He had slumped backward in his chair, as had four of his fellow guards. Two others had collapsed forward onto the table, their heads cradled in their arms. The eighth, Ulseg's crony, had risen and then fallen forward onto the stone floor; it was his tankard that had spilled.

I wondered briefly whether they might be, not drunk, but dead. However, this was not so. The sitting men, at least, were merely deeply asleep, their chests heaving rhythmically and their jaws hanging open. The three others proved, when we examined them, to be sleeping also.

'That must have been strong ale!' Avran sounded awed.

'No, it was not just the ale,' Robin replied puzzledly. 'Look around you; there is little ale spilled, little disturbance. These men have just fallen quietly into slumber, though this one' — he prodded their sleeping leader with a gentle toe – 'fought against it. It is as if they were all put under some spell.'

'Wizard's work, indeed!' Avran was even more awed. 'And fortunate for us. Might Vedlen Obiran have a hand in this? Is his arm so long?'

Robin hesitated, then shook his head. 'I do not believe this is the work of Vedlen. Well, we must not waste time in idle speculation. Put on your sword-belts — quickly, now! Then we'll tie up these sleeping beauties and pop them into that inner room.'

Yet to truss up eight men does take time; to carry them, heavy and inert, from one room to another is quite a task also. Since we were the younger men, Avran and I undertook both jobs, while Robin stood on watch.

As we left the inner room, Avran paused to blow out the candle and then, shutting the door, whispered: 'Sleep sweet, my darlings!'

So well had he mimicked a considerate mother that I found myself chuckling and Robin laughed also. Then we put on our still-unrifled packs. Avran and I attached the quivers of arrows to our belts and picked up the bow-staves, preparatory to departure.

At that very moment we heard a small sound. Someone was cautiously turning the handle of the outer door, for the latch was stirring reluctantly in its bed and beginning to lift.

Since Robin and I chanced to be further from the door than he, Avran gestured at us to hide in the shadow by the staircase. For his

51

own part, he set down his bowstave carefully and moved soft-footed to stand against the wall just behind the door.

Slowly it opened, a widening rectangle of darkness. Then we saw a hooded head peering within at the seemingly empty chamber. There was a pause of hesitation, then someone stepped within — a slight figure, wrapped in a long and very ragged cloak and with a dagger held in one hand, its blade directed upward.

At that moment, Avran pounced. With his right hand he seized the wrist wielding the knife, while the crook of his left arm went about the neck of the hooded figure.

The dagger dropped with a clatter onto the stones and, in a trice, Avran had both arms of that person pinioned. Indeed, there had been no real struggle; Avran's attack seemed to have been too much of a shock, and his strength to have proven too great, for his victim even to try to fight him.

Then the hood was tossed back and I understood why. Gazing at us, breathlessly perhaps but quite calmly, was a girl — the girl who had dropped the jug, the girl whom Robin's swiftness had saved from a second assault.

I was entirely astonished by this development and Avran quite discountenanced; he let go of the girl as quickly as if she had become suddenly red-hot. As for Robin, he merely nodded to himself, as one for whom a mystery has been solved.

It was the girl who spoke first. 'Thank you,' she said. Presumably this was addressed to Avran, though she did not spare him any glance; her eyes were on Robin. 'Well, gentlemen, I had thought to rescue you; but it seems my efforts were not needed.'

She was speaking in Reschorese, of course. Her voice was crisp and clear. It was not especially feminine; more like that of a boy, or of a girl who has grown up among boys and has adopted their intonations. She had an accent unfamiliar to me, but not strong enough to present any problems in comprehension. Her hair was fair, curly and trimmed fairly short, her face a young one, yet there were lines of experience graven upon it — more lines than so young a face should have borne. I could not see the colour of her eyes.

'On the contrary, we are deeply indebted to you,' responded Robin. 'Whilst it was my friend here' — he gestured at me — 'who freed

52

us from our ropes, we could not have dealt easily with our guards. I take it that it was you who, er, lulled them into slumber?'

She nodded. (It is simplest to describe the act thus, though in fact the Reschorese signify agreement by moving their heads from side to side with chins dipped.) 'I owed you a debt,' she said, 'and I am anxious to leave this dreadful place. You are the first man I have seen in many months who has seemed worthy of trust. Will you take me with you?'

'Of course, with great pleasure! Indeed, we'll be glad of your guidance. We had been wondering how to escape from this city and traverse the country beyond; perhaps you might advise us?'

'As to the city, I know it well. As to the country beyond . . . Where are you headed?'

'Northward, to Reschora.'

She pondered. 'That might prove awkward . . . Well, we must leave Kradsunar first, wherever we are heading. What did you do with the guards?'

'We bound them and put them in the inner room.'

'Excellent! Then let us be leaving. Most of Darnay's men are deeply gone in drink by now and the rest are far from sober. We must travel as far as we can before they recover their wits.'

Without more ado she bent to pick up the dagger and, straightening, thrust it into her belt. Then she shook the hood forward over her face and turned toward the door. Cautiously she opened the wicket and looked outside. The alley was still a pit of darkness and, apart from a distant echo of revelry, the only sound was the chirping of some cricket-like insect from a recess of a wall.

'Follow me closely, now.' She spoke quietly over her shoulder. 'The way is devious and we must be swift!'

Indeed, the route by which she took us was so circuitous as to bewilder me. Soon I lost my sense of direction wholly, if ever I had it. Mostly we hastened down dark, dirt-strewn passages, only dimly lit by the stars overhead: since April was at its end, there was no moon. Where the passages were arched over, even this poor light was denied to us. Moreover, on three occasions we were led in through the doorway of a ruined building and out through a gap in its farther wall.

The girl went fast, with never a pause for any further word or for the catching of breath. Robin was always close at her heels, but Avran and I were hard put to it to keep up with them and came near to losing them on occasion.

At last the girl halted and spoke again to Robin; not yet had she either addressed a direct word to Avran and me or seemed even to look at us.

'We have still to traverse the wall. An old storm-drain passes beneath it, just a few poles from here. Darnay's men know of the drain, but it is hard to find and they do not trouble to post a guard over it — no, not even on an ordinary night, let alone on one of feasting. Usually the drain is reasonably dry but, after the rain, I am afraid that passing through it will not be very pleasant.'

I could not see her face, but I could detect a certain amusement in her voice.

'Pleasant or not, we shall go that way, if you recommend it.' Robin's tone was quite positive.

'I do, for there is none other that is safe. Yet the way is dark and far from easy, for the drains divide beneath the wall. I shall go first, of course, and you must follow me. I suggest that your men keep contact with you by means of those bow-staves. If two of you each hold an end of a stave, the middle man holding both other ends, you should not go adrift. Understood? Very well, then.'

For a moment I glimpsed her slender shape in the star-glow. Then she was gone into shadow, with Robin again at her heels. A dozen careful, swift steps followed before she called back: 'I have found the place. Link up, now!'

It chanced that I was last. Hastily Avran thrust forward his stave, Robin grasping it under his left arm. Then I thrust forward mine, to be clasped by Avran's left hand and under the crook of that arm.

'Good. Once we are within the drain, there is little need for speed and much for care. The slope is steep at first and the way slippery. Very well; follow me once more — and watch your footing!'

Steep indeed it was at first, a sharp downward plunge into the darkness, with the wet stones under one's feet sometimes loose and always too sharply pitched for a secure foothold. Though the girl seemed entirely sure-footed, we others descended into the drain in a sort of stumbling run. Twice I came close to cascading forward upon Avran. How he managed to maintain balance, while clutching those two ends of bowstaves, is beyond my understanding.

When the slope eased, the danger of a fall lessened. However, our passage became even less pleasant, for we were by then in entire blackness and splashing ankle-deep through nauseously odorous water. Moreover, the upper curve of the drain was so low as to force us to bend almost double.

A steady drip, drip of water fell on our lowered heads and bent backs, causing me to wish I had donned my cloak: alas, it was rolled up in my pack! Nor was there any pause during which I might fetch it out. Instead, we lurched onward steadily, occasional draughts and trickling sounds indicating that we were passing the mouths of other drains.

How the girl found her way so confidently and swiftly, I could not imagine. The drain seemed surprisingly long; surely we must be beyond the wall by now? The water swirling about our ankles was becoming deeper, though somewhat less foul.

Abruptly Avran stumbled and lost hold of my bowstave. Without his support, I fell forward into that water with a loud splash.

Avran was on his feet before me. Unwisely, however, he stretched up, hitting his head against the drain arch and gasping in pain.

Warned by this, I rose only into a half-crouch. I could not see Avran but, raising my dripping bowstave, I was able to push it forward so that he could again clasp it. Then, without commenting on the mishap or even cursing it, we resumed our lurching onward steps.

At last I noted a lightening of the blackness ahead of us and knew we must be approaching the further end of the drain. I was truly grateful, for my back was aching from being bent so low for so long.

Just then the girl called back: 'Keep to the right side and watch your step again. There's a deep mire to the left; don't fall into it!'

Somehow we contrived not to do so. The water could not have long submerged the mud at right, for its surface remained firm enough, if slippery. Robin, whom I could see ahead of me now, was supporting himself with one hand on the drain's side. I emulated him and managed well enough, but Avran had to grunt, slip and slither along unhappily without that support.

At length I saw Robin straighten and realized that the two sides

55

of the drain were swinging away from us; we were at its end and emerging into a gorge little broader than the drain had been.

The girl stopped and said: 'You can unlink now, gentlemen, but you'll need to do a little climbing instead. The path is steep, but it is not difficult. Follow me carefully and you'll encounter no further problems.'

Steep it was and, despite her words, difficult enough for three travellers with packs on their backs and with sheathed swords swinging from their belts to catch awkwardly in the rocks. The bowstaves helped, however, for Avran and I could use them like staffs in mounting the slope. As we climbed, the sky was lightening overhead and the stars fading with the coming of day. However, we were still in deep shadow and must feel our way, for we could not see it.

One last upward step, then we emerged from the gorge and into the light of the dawn. Though only pale, it seemed bright enough to us, after the complete darkness of the drain and the gloom of the gorge — bright and very welcome. Against the distant horizon below which the orb of the sun was yet concealed, I could see the jagged outline of distant mountains — the Rockaine Hills, perhaps, or the Stoney Mountains?

South of us they were; why, then, we must be on the east side of Kradsunar, between that gloomy city and the Rimbedreth! I looked over to my right. Yes, there was the city, not so very far away from us. Behind and beyond it was a dark mass of other mountains — the Northern Mountains of Rockall, at last!

They were yet far away and I was very tired. Nevertheless, after our escapes from river storms and evil men, my heart was high. Soon, I was sure, we would be among those mountains.

Chapter Seven

ESSA

All of us stood for a while, gazing toward the rising sun and enjoying the slight breeze, so refreshing after the foul odours of the drain and the sweaty ascent. Then I became aware how wet I was and, while shivering, saw that Avran was shivering also. He was quite as sodden as I and very much muddier — or so I thought, until I looked down at my own boots, hosen and sleeves.

The girl saw my glances and laughed, then said to Robin: 'Why, sir, your men look as bedraggled as two kittens thrown into a duck-pond!'

Though he smiled in response, our friend was more sympathetic. 'Well, my lady, that was not the cleanliest of paths to follow! More-over, I must correct you. These are not my men; rather, they are companions with whom I have been privileged to travel. May I present them to you? This gentleman at right is Avran Estantesec, Prince of Sandastre, a realm far to the south beyond the great forests.'

Avran bowed.

'Indeed?' She sounded startled, even disconcerted. 'Then he has travelled far.'

'And our other companion even farther. This is Simon Branth-waite,' — he managed the name well — 'called Simon Vasianavar here in Rockall; but he came originally from England.'

I did my best to emulate Avran's bow, but was conscious that I performed the act much less gracefully.

'For my own part I am Sir Robert Randwulf, originally from Odunseth but now without a country. All three of us hold ourselves to be deeply in your debt.' His bow was even more courtly than Avran's. 'Would you honour us by divulging your own name?'

'Oh, I'm Essa. I am no-one special; I have no honorific titles.' Her disclaimer suggested embarrassment. 'I appreciate your kind words, Sir Robert, but let us cease all this talk of indebtedness. I have not forgotten your courtesy to me when you thought me merely a servant of your enemies, nor shall I forget it. However, we must not stay bandying words here. In this open land, we're as conspicuous as a fly on the pate of a monk.'

Robin laughed. 'A good image, my lady: and, indeed, you're quite right. I take it that we're on the south side of Kradsunar and that those are the Elnekar Vekher, the Trident Mountains, beyond?'

'Southeast, to be precise. The gate of Kradsunar is on its northeast side.'

'Ah yes. I have not visited Kradsunar before, but I've seen something of this country; I crossed it once, many years ago. Stony ground here, of course; and, if I remember correctly, there are grasslands on the eastern flank of the mountains. It affords small prospect indeed of cover, where fugitives such as we might hide.'

'True enough; so we must cross it quickly. There is a place of concealment just beyond the city, however — a place where Darnay pastures his mounts — or rather, the mounts of the travellers upon whom he and his band have preyed.' Her voice was bitter.

'Then the beasts will have no strong ties to their present masters! Might we hope to, er, reappropriate those mounts for our own use?'

'That, I believe, should be our aim.' Essa sounded faintly amused, like a tutor whose pupil has triumphantly extracted an obvious truth from a text. 'The beasts are guarded, of course, but at this hour, their guards should be drowsy — easy to bemuse, perhaps. Darnay's men, as you've noticed, are *not* of the highest type. However, we should act speedily. Come, now.'

Off she set again. This time we walked with her, Robin beside her and Avran and I close behind. I was glad to be moving, for I had become extremely cold; indeed, for the second time that night, I was wishing I had put on my cloak.

As before, Essa set a fast pace but, since our strides were longer than hers, it was not hard for us to keep up with her on this open terrain. One had to watch one's footing, however. Not only were there lines of slate sticking up through the grass and broken into many loose blocks and splinters, but also one must watch for the vegetation — barrel-like plants growing just high enough to trip the unwary, trailing creepers that would clutch bramble-like at one's heels, and clustering masses of spiky leaves, sometimes so sharply pointed as to pierce the upper of an unwary boot. Nor were the plants easy to see, when the oblique light of the still-hidden sun threw such long shadows. Moreover, I was extremely tired; to watch my footfalls and to keep moving was about all I could manage.

Once or twice I glanced over to my right, at the city from which we had escaped; our course was taking us obliquely in toward its walls. However, there were no lights to be seen, no signs of life. All cities seem asleep in the earliest hours of morning, but Kradsunar seemed dead and forsaken: had I not known otherwise, I should have been sure it was deserted. As things were, I wondered uneasily if unseen guards might be watching us. I would have been happier if we had been heading in any other direction.

Avran, after his brief sleep in the guardhouse, was in brighter spirits than I. He was humming cheerfully to himself and striding out like a yeoman off to a fair. Robin, in contrast, seemed quite tired. I recall him asking only a single question.

'The leader of those ruffians — you call him just "Darnay", yet his men styled him "Lord Darnay". Is he not a lord, then?'

Essa laughed abruptly. 'What, he a lord? Nay, he's just a common cut-purse from the alleys of Vachnagar, chased away from his home-land and roosting here in the wilderness. They styled their last leader "Lord" Akhaseng. When Darnay slew Akhaseng — an even blacker villain than he, I might remark — why, he became "Lord" Darnay in his turn.'

She fell silent and Robin said no more.

As we walked, the rising sun began pouring its molten metal upon the southern horizon and the glow grew steadily. Soon we were almost under the shadows of Kradsunar's walls. I saw now that they had been constructed of blocks of some massive stone, like Pennine limestone but much darker in hue. They had been built well, for it was evident that they had withstood long years of neglect. I wondered why so strong a city should have fallen into decay. Had there been less need for silence, I might have asked Essa; but to speak when so close to the walls would have been folly. Why, indeed, were we approaching the city so nearly? Was it simply to make our route shorter?

In the lee of Kradsunar's walls on this western side, there was a thicket of bushes. Any conscientious castellan would have rooted them out, I was sure, for they grew right up to the base of the walls and might have screened an approaching enemy. However, Darnay's men — I had jettisoned the 'Lord' from my thoughts of him — were not likely to take such care.

As we approached this thicket, Essa addressed us quietly: 'When you reach the bushes, drop to your hands and knees, then go forward silently and carefully. In a moment, you will see why.'

Belatedly it occurred to me that Essa spoke not at all like a serving-wench. Though she had neither the accent nor the verbal mannerisms of a gentlewoman — or, at least, of such gentlewomen as I had encountered — she spoke with authority, as if accustomed to giving instructions and being obeyed, not just by other women but even by men. Yet she was not old; whatever could be her background?

Well, there was no time to puzzle it out, for we were almost among the bushes. Obediently I dropped into a crouch, then crawled forward, striving to keep my hands and knees clear of the thorns. Swiftly and lithely Essa crawled ahead, with Robin following her closely. Then she stopped and, with her hand, restrained him from further forward movement. They were between two bushes that had the slightly dusty look of evergreens; intergrown branches bearing slender, grooved leaves screened the view ahead.

With great care, Essa parted two branches and said to Robin: 'Look, now!'

As he did so, I saw his start of surprise. Then he moved back, giving place to Avran. He in turn gazed outward between the branches for a while, then motioned me forward.

Yes, the sight was indeed surprising. Before me, the ground fell steeply away into a broad hollow, about a furlong in diameter and densely grown with trees. Among those trees, some thirty beasts were browsing. Most were rafneyen, familiar creatures to me by now with their dapple-brown hides, their single, blunt nasal horn and their pair of five-tined, forwardly curving brow-horns. The very sight of them made me wish I were astride Galahad and, with Avran mounted on Lancelot, riding again through the great forests.

60

However, there were a number of other creatures also; quite different beasts, solider, shorter-legged and less graceful. These were not hasedain nor yet sevdreyen, but animals quite new to me. Their hides were dull grey in hue, with irregular lateral streaks of white and brown that made them hard to see clearly in this early-morning light. Their heads were carried lower than that of a rafenu and bore, not two horns like a deer or a hasedu, not three like a rafenu or four like a sevdru, but — my goodness! — *six* horns! The two foremost were set on the tips of their muzzles; these horns were short, but as sharp as a boar's tusks. The middle pair were of moderate length and set just behind their eyes, like gigantic outswept eyebrows. The third pair, at the backs of their heads behind their cocked ears, were the longest, branching in Y-fashion with one tine directed forward, the other upward. Well, I had grown accustomed to riding three- and four-horned beasts; but *six* horns . . .

I looked again about the hollow and saw that it had been a quarry, no doubt the quarry from which the stones used to build the city had been extracted long ago. Some trimmed blocks had been left in a stack on the farther side and there was a great rubble-heap of broken stones at the centre. On top of that heap grew a single tree, of no great height. In its shade were lounging eight guards. All of them were wrapped in heavy cloaks; four were armed with long-bows and the others with big spears much like boar-spears, for they had cross-pieces at mid-length.

As I watched, one guard rose and stretched. Something hanging about his neck shone briefly and brassily, causing me to glance at him again. I perceived then that it was a curving trumpet, a clarion, upon which, no doubt, an alarm would be sounded at need.

Essa was becoming impatient; her sharp elbow dug into my shoulder. Reluctantly I moved back. As I did so, she lowered the branch gently into place, then turned to us.

'Have you seen enough, then? The guards, the rafneyen and the veludain?'

'So that is what those creatures are!' Avran was interested. 'I have never seen them before.'

'Have you not? Well, those are what we should strive to obtain, if we can.' Robin was speaking now. 'A veludu is not so fast-running as a rafenu on open ground like these plains, but veludain are much swifter on rugged slopes and steep hillsides — as sure-footed as the goats of your English mountains, Simon.'

'Yet we have to cross grasslands,' Avran was doubtful. 'On flat lands, as you say, a rafenu is faster.'

'You speak as though you had a free choice!' Essa sounded scornful. 'You do not. The rafneyen have all been here a long time and will have become accustomed to their new masters, thieves though they be. Only two days ago, though, six veludain were brought in, among the loot from a raid on a Raffettean farm. We have a chance of obtaining four of them, if we are cunning.'

'But why might we not simply slay the guards and choose the mounts we want, driving away the other beasts?' Clearly Avran was impatient for action. 'We have our long-bows and we are in deep cover. They are well within bowshot, you know. I am a fair archer and Simon is a superb one.'

'Did you not see the clarion? Could you guarantee to kill all eight guards, before an alarm was sounded? And would you truly wish to slay eight men needlessly?'

Essa's face was still shadowed by her hood, hiding her expression; but she sounded so disgusted that Avran looked abashed.

Robin spoke again, quite quietly. 'I take it that you have a better plan, my lady?'

She sniffed. 'Well, it may seem a little devious to our friend the Prince here, who seems all for warfare and bloodshed. But, yes, I think my plan will work, provided our other friend here is capable of a little play-acting.'

With a toss of her head, she flung back the hood and gazed at me, calmly, questioningly. I saw now that her eyes were blue, the blue of the sky on a sunny winter's day when there is snow on the ground; not an azure blue, but lighter, clearer, more jewel-like. Her face had been grave but, as she looked at me enquiringly, there was the flicker of a smile about her lips.

I hesitated. 'Well, I am somewhat weary . . . Yet, yes, I'm prepared to try whatever you suggest.'

'Good. It has to be you, Master Simon, I'm afraid. You must personate a stripling from Kradsunar, bearing a message from Darnay. I cannot go, for Darnay would never employ a girl as messenger — nor, indeed, willingly permit any woman to pass outside the city walls. Sir Robert here is too old, too trim and too clean; and, while Prince Avran is quite dirty enough' — her lips twitched again, and Avran glowered — 'he is too large to wear my cloak, nor does he seem, er, weary and harried enough.'

She scrutinized me again, then went on: 'Your boots and hosen are sufficiently muddy, Master Simon, that their quality is not obvious. Your tiredness is an asset, for of course you have been carousing all night and have run from the gates, bearing Darnay's message. As for your other clothes, why, if you wrap yourself in my cloak, they'll not be noticed. Here now, I'll give it to you.'

She slipped off the cloak. Under it she was wearing a long surcoat that had lost much of its blue colour with age and many washings, and beneath that an undertunic that had once been white but was now much discoloured. Both garments were somewhat too small for her, slim though she was and not tall; I guessed that she had outgrown them but had been unable to replace them. I noticed for the first time that her feet were bare; her toes were scarred and her nails much scratched, probably during the ascent from the gorge.

She saw me looking at her feet, blushed and tucked them out of view. However, she did not protest when, anticipating Avran, I fetched out my cloak and draped it about her shoulders.

It seemed that Essa had recognized the head guard, the man bearing the clarion, and knew his name. That was one part of the hasty instructions I was given before I was sent on my way. Her last words were: 'Remember that these are not clever men. You can surely fool them, Master Simon, if you use your wits!'

Wrapped in Essa's cloak and thus adjured, I made my careful way back out of the thicket, straightened thankfully and then walked out from the walls. I followed the thicket's fringe until I reached the track that led down into the quarry. Long ago it had been a waggon-road, for the grooves of the wheels were still to be seen, though now half-obscured by the slow creep of the stony soil and the growth of barbed-leaved plants. Many shallower marks of the cloven hooves of rafneyen, and somewhat different impressions presumably left by those of veludain, were of much more recent date. I gazed at these interestedly. Then, remembering my role, I began to run in a tired jog down into the quarry.

As I was already well aware, the domesticated animals of Rockall —

and some wild ones also — have perceptions outside the reach of a horse or even a dog. Yet, though several beasts raised their heads to look at me and I could sense the awareness of the others, I knew also that I was not considered a menace; I looked too much like one of Darnay's men.

Well, if I could fool the beasts, surely I might also fool their guards? I hoped so, for I had left my long-bow, my sword and my belt of throwing-knives behind. My only weapon was Essa's long knife, thrust into the belt of her cloak — the weapon she considered appropriate for a young ragamuffin in Darnay's rag-tag following.

As I ran toward the guards, I was aware that they were watching my approach. Though most of them were still sprawled on comfortably flat stone slabs under the tree, the man with the clarion had again risen to his feet. He was wrapped in robes of hasedu-hide, a massive creature with a bunchy black beard streaked with grey, black hair matted with dirt, and a red face marred by scars and pockmarks. His eyes peered out from under tufty brows, as bleak and mistrustful as those of a he-goat. Indeed, there was something animal-like about all of the guards; not so much goat-like, more akin to mongrel hounds grouped about their pack-leader.

I climbed up the rock-mound as if altogether weary and then stood eyeing the red-faced man awhile, panting and with chest heaving, as if I'd run a long way.

He eyed me, not suspiciously but as if anticipating tiresome news, then spoke contemptuously. 'Did ye drink so much last night that you can't run and can't speak? Lucky you were! As for us, we've had to stay out in the cold and watch these accursed beasts! Blast you, what's the message, then?'

'Lord Darnay . . . he has an order for Messer Ashenart.' I panted the words, rather than spoke them. 'Are you . . . are you he?'

He spat disgustedly. 'Who else would be here? What do you think I am, then — some sort of lizard among the stones? You're a fool, boy!'

He made as if to strike me and I cowered back, crooking my left arm before my face like any frightened street urchin. The other guards chuckled at this.

'The message, damn you!'

64

'Lord Darnay — he says you're to send him four of the veludain that were got two days ago. I'm to take them to him.'

'You, take them to him! Can you even ride? I'll be bound *you're* not to have one of them — a raw stripling like you! Look at him — not even a proper beard, yet!'

He seized my nose and pulled it, then thrust me away so that I fell backward among the stones. The other men were guffawing now.

Rubbing my nose, I got to my feet in a timorous, sidewise fashion — the fashion in which the street urchin I was personating would have risen. I spoke in an appropriately defiant squeak: 'Am I to tell Lord Darnay, then, that you won't send him the beasts?'

'Nay, you can take them. If our beloved leader instructs, we must obey.' This caused the other listening guards again to chuckle coarsely. 'Who are they destined for, d'you know?' He was eyeing me with a sort of resentful curiosity.

'I don't know, but I can make a hazard. Hand me a drink, and I'll tell ye.' There was a half-full flask on the ground beside him, which I eyed thirstily.

'Very well,' he grunted. 'Give him a drink; only a small swig, mind!'

The man sitting next to Drak Ashenart — for that, according to Essa, was the guard's name — seized the flask and, rising reluctantly, offered it to me. It contained a coarse, acid-tasting wine of a sort unknown to me. Scarce had I begun to drink, however, before the flask was snatched away.

'Well, then, what's your guess?' Ashenart was impatient.

I wiped my lips with the back of my hand, then replied: 'For Messer Ulseg and his cronies, I think. They made a rich capture, yesterday on the river, or so folks say; and they're to be rewarded.'

His face darkened. 'That accursed Ulseg again! Aiming to be leader, *he* is: Lord Darnay should take care! Ach... Well, show him the beasts, Dan Wyert; and if he can't ride, then tie him on!'

Once more the other guards laughed, rather obsequiously I thought; evidently they were afraid of Ashenart.

An elderly, scrubby-looking man rose reluctantly. Beckoning to me, he led me down the farther side of the stone pile. As we walked, he eyed me curiously and said: 'I can't put a mind to seein' you before, young man. Who be ye?'

65

The question was disconcerting, but I answered boldly: 'For that matter, I can't bring to mind that I've seen *you* before, grandpa. And I'd never forget your lovely whiskers!'

This cheeky response provoked a resentful mutter, but prevented further questions. Instead he led me over to the farther side of the quarry where, among a group of dark-leaved bushes, six veludain were browsing. They seemed more nervous than the other beasts, for they raised their heads and turned about at our approach.

The old man squatted down on his heels and gestured at them: 'Take your pick! They're a poor bunch, so they'll suit that Ulseg and his hangers-on well enough.'

Indeed, all of the veludain had a scruffy, neglected look, as if their previous owners had not been kind. The foremost lowered his head warningly: those six horns were indeed a formidable battery! Yet this did not deter me, nor did the fact that I had never before tried to mount a veludu.

I have striven earlier to describe how one makes mental contact with a creature of Rockall and, no doubt, failed; to explain it to one who has not the ability is as hard as trying to make a stone-deaf man appreciate sounds. All I can say is that I reached out to the creature with my thoughts, not striving to give it orders but merely offering my friendship; that the creature at first shied away mentally from my approach, then hesitantly reached out in return; and that, quite suddenly, it raised its head and began stepping toward me, as cautiously and daintily as a court lady crossing a muddy lane. Then I was stroking a soft muzzle, caressing the creature's head between those out-arching horns and scratching its brow. In another minute, I was sitting contentedly on its back and surveying the other five veludain.

The old man grunted in surprise and rose stiffly to his feet. 'Well, ye can handle beasts, right enough. Ye'll not need me.'

He sounded quite disappointed. In a moment he had turned his back on me and shuffled away to rejoin the other guards on the mound.

I am not sure whether it was by my own thoughts, or through those of the veludu on whose back I was riding, that I called three more veludain to follow us — the three that looked in best condition. I could sense the disappointment of the two not called and could even share in it a little; how strange this business of mental linkage is! I knew already that my mount, a stag, was called Proudhorn — in Reschorese, *Ikhilturin*. I had become aware also that he was the leader of the six, that two of the others following us were females and one a male, even though at that time I could not have discerned the difference. In fact, both sexes of veludain look much alike, though the nasal horns of the does are somewhat shorter.

For the moment, I was happy to be riding out of the quarry. The guards watched me pass with apparent impassivity; there were no farewell shouts and even Drak Ashenart seemed to have sunk back into somnolence.

Up the track we went, Proudhorn and I in the lead, the other beasts following, out of the deep shade of the trees and into the bright sunlight. It was good to be riding again; tired though I was, my heart was as light as the morning breeze. All was going well again. No more being a cramped passenger in a river-tossed boat; no more tedious walking across stony plains. Now, truly, we were on our way!

Chapter Eight

PURSUIT

However, as hour succeeded hour and we rode steadily west-ward, my high spirits began to sink. Essa and my two friends had met me at the first point beyond the old quarry where the trees gave an adequate screen from any watchers on the walls. Through Proudhorn, I had sensed their waiting presence before I saw them and had given a calming message to the veludain.

Essa had chosen first, selecting and making friends with the smaller of the two does. She had pinned up the skirts of her tunics and was riding a-straddle. She was not very confident at first — I guessed rightly that it was long since she had last ridden — but, after an hour or so, she became much more at ease, quite evidently enjoying the experience and the bright sunshine.

To my surprise, Robin had chosen to ride the other doe, leaving the second stag for Avran. (It is, perhaps, wrong to speak of velu-dain — or of rafneyen, for that matter — as 'stags' and 'does,' when both sexes have horns retained year-long, not shed like the antlers of a deer; but the Rockalese words have no more exact English equivalents.) Avran's mount was called Highback (in Reschorese, *Esdehan*): he was the biggest and strongest of the veludain but, I thought, less quick-witted than Proudhorn. The two does, Essa's and Robin's mounts, were named in Reschorese *Rengahé* and *Seddesim*; but I will call them Stripenose and Browntail.

The four of us were riding in a spread-out line, quite far apart. This was Robin's idea. He thought that any pursuers, seeing us only from a distance, might not perceive that we were a group travelling together, the group they were seeking, but might mistake our mounts for wild animals and ignore us.

True enough, there were other swift-footed creatures roaming these grasslands — for the stony country had been already left behind. These were of a sort I had not seen and whose name, since I was not close to Robin or Essa, I had not yet learned. Slim, long-necked beasts they were, with short, knobbly horns; their graceful fleetness was quite different from the slow jog of a veludu. Only the most impercipient pursuer could mistake the one beast for the other; I had little faith in Robin's stratagem.

The motion of a veludu, as felt by a rider used to horses, is quite strange, being more uncomfortably jolting and, on flat land, much less speedy. A trotting horse, or a rafenu going at moderate pace, covers almost three leagues in an hour, but a veludu can scarcely manage two. If Darnay and his men had discovered our departure early in the morning, found our tracks and chosen to pursue us on rafneyen, they would be gaining on us quite rapidly.

That thought was depressing enough. A more immediate problem was that I was so dreadfully tired, a condition made worse by my body's unfamiliarity with the motion of my mount. I found myself swaying in my saddle and twice came near to slumping forward upon Proudhorn's sharp brow-horns — not, of course, that he would have permitted them to injure me, when he was so sensitive to my thoughts and movements and so easily able to duck his head forward.

Avran perceived my condition and called out to Robin: 'Simon is almost asleep. Can we not have a brief rest, and some food perhaps?'

Robin hesitated before responding reluctantly: 'If we must stop, then we must; yet I wish we were closer to the hills.'

Browntail's jog-trot dropped to a walk, then she halted. Our veludain converged upon her and stopped also. After we had all dismounted, the veludain spread about us in a watchful half-ring. Ever and again they would drop their muzzles to graze, but only to raise them while the fresh spring grasses — green grasses here, as in England — were being munched. So veludain, like hasedain but unlike sevdreyen or rafneyen, could graze as well as browse . . .

To our surprise and pleasure, Robin produced from his pack two broken loaves of reasonably fresh bread and some hunks of meat, wrapped up carefully in a piece of torn cloth. Providently he had taken these from the table in Kradsunar keep, while Avran and I were busy tying up the slumbering guards and hauling them into the inner chamber.

70

Not only that, but Robin had filled his travelling-flask with some of the boatmen's beer on a previous day and, as it chanced, had not drunk from it subsequently. When he first offered the flask round, Essa expressed concern until reassured that it had *not* been taken from the drugged keg in the Kradsunar keep!

Altogether, it was a much better meal than I had hoped for. It was delightful also to sit at ease with friends in the sunlight. After my securing of the veludain, even Essa was smiling upon me, though she talked mostly with Robin. She continued to pay small attention to Avran.

Of herself she would not speak, but she did tell us a little about Kradsunar. Its builders had been venturesome folk from the mountain kingdom of Raffette, who had desired lands richer and broader than their own narrow valleys and steep hillsides. The name Kradsunar, she told us, signified in the Raffettean dialect 'bright hope'. Indeed, the settlers had prospered for a while — how long a while, she did not know: for a century or so, she thought. Then, alas, the hope had foundered.

At first, wheat and oats had been grown and hasedain kept in the open lands about the city. However, the ground had become progressively drier as the Etolen Dunes spread westward, while the level of water in the wells had dropped steadily. The growing of crops had become impossible and the finding of pasture for beasts ever more difficult. Eventually its people had forsaken Kradsunar and retreated, going either northward back to their former homeland or southwestward to establish new farms in Lukeyne. The brave colony became just another part of the Lordless Lands, the lands the Templars had spurned.

Kradsunar had long stood empty, its buildings steadily crumbling. Eventually, almost exactly seven years ago, the self-styled 'Lord' Akhaseng and his cutthroat gang had taken up abode there. After that, Kradsunar had become a base for their predatory attacks, northward and westward against the farms of Reschora and Raffette or southward into the Templars' territories, Lukeyne or Devoria. The caravans of Mentonese merchants, travelling east to their trading base at Trayad-in-Riotte, had also been a favourite prey until, for self-protection, they were made so large and manned so stoutly as to deter the robbers. Captured veludain were taken to Dakhanar and sold to Kelcestrian merchants deliberately uninquisitive concerning their origin. The rafneyen were mostly kept for use in the swift raids in which Akhaseng had delighted.

Twice within the time that Essa had lived there, Kradsunar had been visited by parties of Reschorese soldiers seeking vengeance on the marauding gang. However, Akhaseng and his men had concealed themselves so effectively among the crumbling alleys that the soldiers had gone away, satisfied that the city was still deserted.

As Essa talked, I was wondering whether it might have been raiders from Kradsunar who had sacked Vedlen Obiran's home. Later I learned that Robin had wondered this also. He had asked Essa; but, among the wearisome boasting of Akhaseng's ruffians, she had heard no echoes of any such raid, so far into the mountains and so many years ago. She did recount how Akhaseng had been slain while drunk by Darnay, but found no cause for regret in that memory. Indeed, whenever she spoke of Akhaseng, her voice was so very bitter that I was sure he must have done her some grievous wrong.

While she and Robin were still conversing, I slipped quietly into a deep sleep. I believe they permitted me to slumber for about an hour, but it seemed to me that I had no sooner closed my eyes than Avran was shaking me into wakefulness.

'Rouse yourself, Simon my friend,' he was saying. 'The veludain are uneasy; we believe that we are being pursued!'

At these ominous words, I became fully awake. I stretched, then leapt to my feet to find Proudhorn beside me, Avran mounting Highback and Essa and Robin already mounted.

Robin was gazing back across the grasslands. He spoke anxiously. 'Yes, there are men on rafneyen away to the east of us; Darnay's men, for sure. We are not far from the mountains now, but I cannot say whether we will reach them in time. Make haste, Simon; we must be away!'

Once again the four of us spread out, though there was now little hope that this would bemuse our pursuers. I had thought the jog-trot pace of a veludu uncomfortable enough. Their gallop, if that term can properly be applied to a gait little faster than a horse's trot, was much more so. Indeed, in the first few yards I came close to falling from Proudhorn's back, so unexpected and so jolting was his motion. I sensed his apologetic surprise and after that, with some help from him, managed better.

The noonday heat, in combination with the effects of yesterday's rain, served to blanket the mountains in haze. It was hard to tell how close they were or to estimate whether we might hope to reach them before our pursuers caught us up.

How many of Darnay's ruffians could be riding after us, I wondered? If all the rafneyen of Kradsunar had been pastured in the old quarry, as I suspected, we could not have more than twenty pursuers, perhaps not even so many as that. But twenty against three — Essa could not be counted, for she was effectively weaponless — was heavy odds.

The ride seemed an unduly long one. Moreover, it was depressing to know that we were being steadily overhauled; gamely though our veludain were striving, they were indeed outpaced by the rafneyen of our pursuers. All too soon we were within the view of Darnay's men — I suspected, correctly, that the fat giant himself had remained behind in Kradsunar — and could hear their exultant shouts.

I noticed that the country was changing; an increasing scatter of taller plants and low bushes were growing among the grass. Surely we could not be far, now, from the mountain-foot? But would we reach it? Our veludain had their heads down and were going their hardest, but Darnay's men had so much caught up on us that we were within distant bowshot. I crouched lower upon Proudhorn, my arms about his neck. This was simply to aid him, however. Though some of those men, as I knew, wielded long-bows, it is so hard to shoot from the back of a running animal that few archers even attempt it. For the moment, we were safe from arrows.

At last the haze thinned and the mountains — or, rather, their outer foothills — rose before us, as sharply from the grassland as did the southern face of the Stoney Mountains from the forests, though these were darker hills and more densely vegetated. One level of my mind registered these observations quite calmly; at other levels, though, I was close to panicking. Our pursuers were now only a few poles behind us and still gaining on us steadily.

A coarse voice — surely Ulseg's? — called out to us: 'Hold back, now! Time to end this race! Ye've had a good run, but you're caught. Surrender, and we may spare you. Resist, and ye'll surely be slain!'

Could that be true, I wondered dully? Had my bright morning optimism been groundless? Would all our efforts at escape prove vain, after all? And what would be Essa's fate, if we were captured — Essa, who had risked so much for us? (Since she had wrapped herself in her cloak, its hood forward over her head, and was crouching low on Stripenose's back, I doubted whether they had yet recognized her.) No, we could not surrender, whatever might befall us.

Fortunately, the very sight of the hills ahead seemed to have given our veludain a second wind. When they felt the land beginning to rise under their hooves, their pace seemed to accelerate; or was it that the speed of the pursuing rafneyen was slackening? Soon we were climbing a steepening slope, with a rocky knoll just above us and a higher ridge beyond.

Was that Robin calling to me? Yes, indeed. 'Simon, when we reach the crest, you and Essa must ride ahead and you must string your bow. Avran and I will try to hold back these ruffians, but we'll need the aid of your arrows!'

When the knoll was attained — it was a narrow place, only a few yards across, of bare rock perilously seamed with deep cracks — they turned their mounts about. After unslinging their packs from their backs, they drew out their swords.

Essa and I rode upward to the ridge. When we reached it Proudhorn stopped, obedient to my thought. I dropped to the ground, shouting to Essa to ride onward and find safety. However, she ignored me and dismounted also. The two veludain scampered down into the hollow behind the ridge, out of our view.

By that time I had extracted my bowstave from my pack, from which it had been protruding like a flagpole; also I had got out my bowstring from its pocket. Swiftly I bent the bow and strung it. I knelt so that the slope would shield me a little, unhitched the quiver from my belt and set it before me, then put my first arrow to string and looked back down the hill.

With the advantage of their veludain's pace on the slope, Robin and Simon had gained some ground from their pursuers. Nevertheless they were ringed already by six mounted men, while others were pouring up the slope toward them.

One, however, had dismounted at the hillfoot and had strung his own bow. He must be my first target, before he could loose arrow

74

at my friends. Quickly I aimed and shot. To my relief, the arrow was true; he staggered and fell.

As I reached for another arrow, it was thrust into my hands: Essa was crouching beside me, eager to give aid.

Robin and Avran were already engaged, the clash of swords ringing out in the clear air. However, a rafenu-rider in a faded scarlet surcoat had edged unnoticed behind Avran. He had one of the long spears in hand and was about to thrust it murderously into my friend's back.

My arrow was quicker. The spear fell from his grasp and he dropped from his mount, his body rolling limply away downslope. As this happened, a brass object was caught by a plant stem and lodged shining there — a clarion. So the dead man must be Drak Ashenart!

Already I had seized another arrow from Essa, set it to string and loosed it into the mass of rafenu-riders. One of the ruffians cried out, clutching his arrow-pierced shoulder. His rafenu collided with another. Beasts and men fell in a tangle downslope, bringing down a third rafenu and its rider as they tumbled.

A fourth rafenu was racing away riderless; the thief who had ridden it must have fallen victim either to Avran or to Robin. Their swords were indeed weaving a quicksilver pattern that had driven back most of Darnay's villains, no less than twelve of whom were ringing them in an unenthusiastic circle.

However, a massive man in a mailcoat was riding upward toward them, on an equally massive rafenu; Ulseg himself! Beside him was another mail-clad figure, that one of his cronies whom, yesterday evening, Robin had tumbled in the puddle. Yelling with fury, he hurled himself upon Robin.

Meanwhile, Ulseg was assaulting Avran. The robber was wielding a massive, two-handed sword, so much longer than Avran's own that my friend's weapon seemed little more than a toothpick. As Ulseg's rafenu leapt upward toward Avran, the great sword wheeled down upon him in a bright arc, like some terrible cleaver.

It met only empty air. At Avran's thought, Highback had jumped sideways. Then, while Ulseg was still out of balance from the mightiness of his stroke, the veludu and Avran launched themselves forward.

So forceful was Avran's thrust that his sword pierced right through the rusty chain mail. Ulseg gave a groaning sigh, clutched at his chest and toppled sideways onto the rocks of the knoll.

Meantime, Robin was engaged with Ulseg's crony, an able swordsman. However, I could not watch their duel; I was too busy with my bow, loosing arrow after arrow at the ring of men about the skirts of the knoll. A rafenu staggered and fell, rather to my sorrow, for I hated to slay such beautiful animals; its rider rolled away downslope willy-nilly, losing his spear in the process. Another man received an arrow in the shoulder, a third in the thigh: both of them turned their rafneyen about and fled.

Indeed, with the fall of Ulseg, much of the heart seemed to have gone out of our attackers. I heard a groan from them as Robin dispatched Ulseg's crony, the very fury of whose assault seemed to have betrayed him. Then all of Darnay's ruffians were in full flight — or so, at least, I thought.

With a sigh of relief, I set down my bow and stood up — most unwisely. One of our assailants had stopped at the bottom of the slope, to loose a single, vengeful arrow before fleeing. That arrow took me in the left shoulder and flung me about, causing me to fall heavily onto the stones of the ridge.

My head hit a rock. As my senses whirled, I saw the horror on Essa's face, but it turned swiftly into a white blur and faded into the blackness of unconsciousness.

Chapter Nine

An Unexpected Encounter

I was aware of a steady throbbing in my head, regular and yet unpleasant, like some convulsive heart-beat; then of another, more continuous ache in my shoulder. There was a brightness, too; a brightness above me, perceptible even through my closed eyelids. To avoid it I turned my head, provoking so violent a throb that I groaned.

I felt a dampness about my forehead; someone was wiping it gently with a cool, wet cloth. The sensation was pleasant, soothing. I enjoyed it quite passively for a while, then began to wonder who was tending me so gently. I opened my eyes, to find that I was looking up straight into the blue eyes of Essa.

I was lying on a spread cloak; she was kneeling beside me with the bright sunshine of late afternoon behind her. There was a pervasive smell; what was it? I sniffed, then realized that the cloth must have been dipped in ale, presumably from Robin's flask, for we had not emptied it during our repast.

Essa was continuing to bathe my temples and to gaze down on me calmly; yet she was aware I was awake, for she was smiling.

Without moving my head, I breathed deeply and stretched, only to wish immediately, at the fierce pain from my shoulder, that I hadn't. I tried to smile in response, then said: 'Thank you . . . Thank you, that feels pleasant. You must not make me drunk, though, with all that beer!'

At this Essa chuckled. I had not seen her laugh before and was surprised how youthful it made her seem, driving from her face those lines traced by premature hardship. She sat back on her heels and said approvingly: 'You're a high-mettled one, Simon Vasianavar!'

'Yes, he can be valiant, our friend here.' I had not noticed Robin until he spoke. He was standing just beyond Essa, his arm about the neck of his veludu Browntail.

Tilting my head cautiously in order to provoke no more sudden pains, I saw that we were on the southern, sunny side of the ridge, with three of the veludain close by. I sensed the grave concern of Proudhorn even before I saw him. As our minds made contact, he trotted forward eagerly and pressed a soft, snuffling muzzle against my cheek. Carefully I caressed his head and scratched his ears, unconcerned that those sharp horns of his were so close to my face, for I knew he would never injure me.

Essa rose to her feet in a single, graceful motion. Saying decisively, 'I think Simon should sit up,' she fetched over a pack to prop my back.

My elevation into this new posture caused me to blench with pain and close my eyes, but soon I felt better and could open them again. I realized by then that the arrow had been withdrawn from my left shoulder and the wound bandaged very competently.

'Thank you again,' I said a little gaspingly. 'Someone here is a skilled leech. Was it Avran who tended my wound?' I was remembering what we had both learned while travelling with the wizard.

It was Robin who replied: 'Avran helped, but mostly it was Essa. This young lady seems to have the skills, both of a physician and of an apothecary.'

'Aye, she does indeed. Is she not the daughter of Lerenet Falquen? A great man he was, and a good.'

That voice was one that I had expected never again to hear! It so startled me that I glanced abruptly sideways, wincing at the throbbing pain this induced. Yes indeed; there, perched on a rock, was the scrawny, elderly man whom Drak Ashenart had sent with me to find the veludain! His right leg must have been broken, for it was thrust out before him and bound by broad strips of cloth to a rather clumsy splint made, I guessed, from a spear-shaft.

At my evident surprise, he grinned. 'Didn't think you'd meet *me* again, did ye, young man? "Grandpa", forsooth! I made sure I'd never seen *you* in Kradsunar, and I was right, wasn't I? But you fooled that Drak Ashenart proper, you did! And he lying dead now, with your arrow through him. Serve him right — a bullying brute he was, to be sure.'

'Yes, you were right,' I agreed soberly. I was searching my mind for his name... Ah! I had it: Dan Wyert! 'But who is Lerenet Falquen?'

'Why, he was physician, chirurgeon, apothecary, all rolled into one. Many's the man whose life he's saved, aye, and woman too, in the years we were at Kradsunar and in the wandering years before. I remember him cutting out an arrow from my arm, neat and tidy as you please; and he drunk at the time, at that. A fine man. I grieved greatly when he died.'

'When he was slain, you mean. Slain by "Lord" Akhaseng, in one of his mindless furies.' Essa's voice was bleak. She was sitting up tensely now, her hands clutched together; the lines were back in her face.

'Aye, lass; I should not have mentioned it.' The old man's voice was strangely gentle. 'But your father taught ye well, and you've saved many a life since.'

'Lives mostly not worth saving,' Essa responded bitterly. 'Men who had been wounded while raiding and pillaging, and who would then go out to raid and pillage again.'

'Aye, well, just so.' The old man sounded abashed. 'Still, they did appreciate it.'

'They let me alone for a while. But that would not have lasted much longer, as you well know, now that I am grown into a woman. I am very much beholden to you, Sir Robert, for bringing me away from that place.'

The bitterness had gone from Essa's voice; it had become somewhat tremulous. Aware that I was looking at her again, she gave me another quick smile, then glanced away; but I had seen the tears in her eyes.

To spare her by changing the subject, and also because the question was coming to concern me, I asked: 'Where is Avran? Is all well with him?'

'He's fit enough,' Robin replied. 'He survived our little skirmish quite unscathed. He's ridden away to seek aid for you — gone to find a Reschorese settlement. The men of Reschora are mostly good folk, you'll discover.'

'Why, I am not so very grievously wounded. Could I not ride there

79

myself?' The ache in my head was fading somewhat and I was beginning to feel more confident.

'No, Simon, you could not.' Robin was quite definite. 'Essa did well for you. She found some plant with healing virtues and wrung juices from its stem to treat your arrow-wound, after washing it with the ale: yet that wound is deep. Moreover, you have lain long insensible — for two hours and more. You may think you can ride and indeed, perhaps you *might* ride, for a while; but it would wreak ill upon your wound — and do no good to your head, either.'

Remembering the bouncy jogtrot of a veludu, I realized that he was right. Indeed, I winced at the very thought of riding. Apologetically I resumed my caressing of Proudhorn. 'So Darnay's men have fled?'

'Aye, though they left seven dead behind them, including our old friend Ulseg. His slaying of the man Vatsarg brought swift retribution, did it not? Such murderous actions are an affront to God.' Robin's voice held deep disgust.

'What, was Vatsarg slain?' The quick question came from Essa. 'He was not a good man, but I thought him less evil than Ulseg.'

In the briefest of fashions, Robin recounted the episode we had witnessed. Essa sighed and said: 'That was an action all too typical of Kradsunar, I am afraid.'

'So it was!' Dan Wyert was speaking again, a quivering indignation in his tone. 'Look at what happened to me! There was I, lying at the bottom of the slope with me leg broken after falling down the hill; and what do they do? Do they give me a hand up onto a rafenu? No, not they! "Don't bother with Dan," they said. "He's too old to be worth saving. We'll give his rafenu to someone more useful." Those were their very words; and off they go, taking the riderless beasts with 'em.'

'Not many of them,' put in Robin. 'Two rafneyen were killed and three fled away southward; no doubt they'll join the wild herds. Darnay's men can only have taken three.'

'Aye, maybe; but I could have been riding one of those three.'

'Would you really wish to go back to Kradsunar? Don't you realize that the city is finished as a hideout? Very soon now, the Reschorese will know where your "Lord" Darnay' — there was profound contempt in Robin's voice — 'has been lairing up: nor will they be long in fetching him out, you may be sure. And, if you'd gone back there, would anyone have troubled to bind up that broken leg of yours and set it in splints? Not they! They'd be too busy preparing for battle — or, more likely, running away.'

The cold logic of Robin's words was not lost on the old man. 'Well, perhaps so; and I'm greatly beholden to ye, Mistress Essa, for your kindness. But . . . but what will the Reschorese do to me, when they know I'm one of Darnay's men?' There was a note of desperation in his voice now. 'Likely enough they'll kill me, or at best they'll prison me up somewhere and leave me to rot. I'm done for, whichever way things turn out.'

Robin's voice was bleak. 'Well, do you not deserve it? For how many men's deaths have you been responsible?'

'None at all! None at all, except in battle; and that's been fair enough!' Dan Wyert's protestations sounded almost frantic.

'Battle?' Robin was contemptuous. 'D'you call it "battle", those raids on innocent farmers and peaceful traders?'

'Nay, but I didn't — mostly I didn't go on the raids, and when I did it was to look after the beasts. I've not slain any man, not since I was fighting for the Duke of Tarnevost against Hezalor and Bayansavar, years ago!'

'Is that true?' The question was addressed to Essa, not to Dan.

'I think so,' Essa spoke as if pensively. 'Usually they did leave Dan in charge of the beasts; he has a way with rafneyen. Dan was never considered a fighter.'

'Do you reckon him worth saving, then?' Evidently Robin was relenting a little.

'I'm not sure.' She sounded doubtful, but she had given me a quick wink, so that I knew she was play-acting. 'Is it worth the trouble, when he's been a robber for so long? Do you suppose he's yet capable of being honest, of living a decent life? He's rather old now to be a brigand, I'll admit; but, as they say, a badger does not lose his stripes, however venerable he grows.'

I smiled to myself at hearing this unexpected mention of the animal that was the emblem of the Branthwaites; and, indeed, the saying was new to me. But the unfortunate Dan Wyert was quite terrified.

'Nay, Mistress Essa, to be sure I'll be honest; I swear I'll be honest — and I'll keep my word, you'll see! Only save me from those Reschorese, and I'll be your servant for the rest of my days.'

I think he wanted to throw himself on his knees before Essa, for he strove to rise to his feet; but the stout, unyielding splint prevented this.

'Well, Sir Robert, shall we stake a hazard on him? Shall we give his good intentions a try?' Essa still sounded doubtful, but I was sure she had long since decided to seek mercy for Dan.

'If you so wish, my lady.' Robin spoke reluctantly, as one persuaded against his own better judgement.

'Thank ye, Sir Robert; thank ye, Mistress Essa.' Poor Dan sounded quite tearful. 'Ye'll not regret it; I'll see ye'll not regret it.'

'Very well. Then we'll say that you aided our escape from Kradsunar; that should satisfy the Reschorese and incline them to mercy. Agreed, Essa? Simon? Good; but we must warn Avran, so that he does not betray you inadvertently.'

That proved to be easily managed. When, only a few minutes later, Avran came riding along the hill-crest towards us, he was alone. As he dismounted from Highback, he said breathlessly: 'I've found help for us. There is a fortified farm on a hilltop, only a league away. The women received me kindly, but the men were away tending their beasts and had to be fetched. One man has gone to alert the Reschorese soldiers against Darnay and his reivers, but three others are following behind with a litter for Simon. How is he?'

Since I had been propped up facing southward away from the ridge, I had only heard, not seen, Avran's approach. When I called out, 'Well enough, Avran my friend,' he rushed to me and knelt to inspect me anxiously. A shining object was hanging about his neck from a string — a familiar object.

'Why, you're looking better,' he said relievedly. 'I'm so glad.' Then he saw my gaze fixed on the clarion, flushed and offered it to me. 'This should be yours, not mine. It was your arrow that slew Drak Ashenart.'

'Keep it, Avran my friend,' I laughed. 'You're the one that likes to blow on things. If I am to make music, I prefer a plucked instrument. Keep it by all means.'

'So Avran likes to blow his own horn?' Essa sounded coolly amused. 'That does not surprise me.'

Again Avran flushed, but this time with vexation. However, he pretended to ignore her comment.

After Avran had been told by Robin about Dan Wyert's altered status — this provoking a further flurry of thanks from the old man — we talked, while waiting for the relief party, about the skirmish and our escape. Dan, his spirits quite restored, chuckled when he heard how Essa had drugged our guards' ale. Darnay, we learned, had assumed that they'd drunk too much and had been so furiously angry that they were still locked up in the keep, with other guards posted over them. The tale of our escape through the drain came as less of a surprise to Dan, for he had guessed that had been the way Essa would choose. Of my concealed knives, he was not told.

The arrival of the three Reschorese farmers put an end to our conversation. Tall, wiry folk they were, unlike the wizard's men in build but like them in having deep brown eyes and dark hair. Their hair, however, was long and tied back behind their necks by narrow leather thongs. They were clad in jupons and hosen of a sober green, while each man had a sword swinging in a leather scabbard from his left hip and a short axe suspended in a loop at his right. Two of them were riding veludain much like ours, though in better condition; the third straddled the right-hand member of a pair of hasedain with a wickerwork litter slung between them.

The men gave us warm greetings; they were evidently delighted that Darnay's lair had been located at last. I was lifted into the litter (a briefly painful business), swathed in blankets and strapped in place, while Dan Wyert was lifted up to ride before Avran on High-back. Then the hasedain were turned about and, with Proudhorn trotting rather anxiously beside me, we set off up the ridge. As we turned, I caught a last glimpse of the Stoney Mountains far to the south, dark against the setting sun. Thereafter our faces were directed toward the north.

As Avran had told us, the distance to the farm was not great. However, it was mostly uphill — up along the ridge, then by a steep saddle to a higher ridge; along that for some way, then across a deep gully — a scrambling descent and ascent that, bounced about as I was in my litter, I found acutely uncomfortable. Hasedain were feeding in the gully, under the watchful eyes of herdboys who called out cheerful greetings.

Not far beyond, high on the top of a third ridge, stood the home of our escorts. Such buildings are called predin in Reschora, not so very different a word from the Sandastrian padin; and, indeed, the fortified farms of northern Rockall are not so very different from those of Sandastre. However, a Sandastrian padarn is always circular in plan. In contrast, every northern predan is built to some geometric shape, though that shape varies from region to region. The predin of Reschora are always pentagonal.

This particular predan was surrounded by a broad, deep ditch set with sharpened stakes, as closely spaced as the spines of a hedgehog. The ditch was crossed by a narrow drawbridge — a bridge that could be withdrawn at need, not upward, but inward into a slot beneath the predan's single massive, copper-sheathed door. All about the predan were steep, grassy slopes, barren of bushes or any other vegetation that might shield attackers from view; its outer face was, of course, stern and windowless. At its centre, however, there was a garden arranged about a pool whose tranquil waters reflected the bright colours of blossoming bushes and early-summer flowers.

From my first glimpse of that garden, I might have known that I would like the Reschorese people very much, even had I not already enjoyed the cheerful companionship of the wizard's men. As it was, I was expecting friendship and found it in abundance.

Not that I saw much of my hosts that night. A quiet room on the shadowed side of the predan was found for me and I was put efficiently to bed. A bowl of soup, hunks of fresh, grainy bread and some dried plums were brought, along with a stone beaker of hasedu-milk for beverage. Then, after Avran had checked the bandaging of my shoulder and rebandaged my head — he seemed temporarily to have usurped Essa in the task of tending me — I subsided gratefully into a deep, profoundly desirable sleep.

Chapter Ten

THE TIME OF DARKNESS

We spent three days in that hilltop predan, days of sunshine and welcome relaxation. On the first I slept long, to waken in mid-afternoon. It was not a particularly pleasant awakening. My body felt stiff and bruised, as much from veludu-riding as from my wounds. My mouth had the bitter taste and my mind the sluggishness that are so often a product of over-long sleep, even though that sleep be needed and beneficial.

Avran had been sitting on a three-legged stool by my bed and playing his pommer very quietly while he watched over me. Seeing that I was awake, he fetched me a drink of some aromatic herbal brew which cleared away both conditions. Then he assisted me to my feet and led me out into the garden.

There I sat on a wooden bench, my back supported by cushions placed against the trunk of a small tree, while my hosts were brought to greet and inspect me. The predan was inhabited by five families, all with the surname Denrateng; the oldest couple were grandparents to the youngest, but quite as busy as they in the doings of the farm. One of the wives was plump and blonde, the daughter of an English-descended family living in Lukeyne and called Mary. As to the names of the other Denratengs, I was never very clear; they were all so much alike, brown-haired and brown-eyed, lean and smiling. Well, distinguishing them does not matter, for we owed an equal debt to them all for their kindness.

This extended to a care for our clothes. The travel-stained garments of Robin, Avran and me were whisked away, to be returned two days later, meticulously laundered. In the meantime, we were lent green jupons and hosen like those of our hosts.

It was a particular pleasure to see Essa attired, not in the ragged garments she had so long outgrown, but in a long-sleeved, moss-green undergown and a sleeveless surcoat of tan colour, with soft boots of the same hue. I had not realized how small she was, slighter even than I. With her fair hair brushed back and shining and with a smile almost always on her face, she looked like some benign sprite of the countryside, come to work good for rustic folk who had remembered her with food and other tribute.

Smiles there were for our hosts and hostesses, for Sir Robert — Essa would never call him 'Robin' — and for me, but never for Avran. Though perfectly polite when she did address him, Essa continued, insofar as she might, to avoid doing so. Nor did her glances at my friend hold any kindness. I observed this hostility without comprehending it.

The transformation of Dan Wyert was even more marked. Not only had he been found fresh and better clothes, but also his skin seemed to have been scrubbed to new, pink freshness. His hair and beard had been washed and trimmed, in more careful a fashion than can have happened for many years. His broken leg had been bound to a lighter splint and he had been equipped with a pair of crutches on which he hopped round merrily.

Merrily, indeed, was the word; Dan had altogether shed his burden of fears and tensions and seemed as happy as a child at a fair. This was especially so when 'Mistress Essa' was by or when Dan was playing with the plump baby who was the only child present in the predan. All the other children — a half-dozen of them, we gathered — were gone away to Hasaring for the schooling that is as universal in Reschora as in Sandastre.

By the third day the throb in my shoulder had quite subsided, leaving a stiffness that was only replaced by pain when I made too unwisely sudden a move. Yet my head ... my head seemed to be aching worse than it had been on that first day. Something, as I was beginning to realize, was very wrong with me. My friends, I knew, were becoming anxious; Essa had twice insisted on rebandaging my head and had dosed me several times with a concoction of herbs, but to no effect.

On that evening I was sitting under the tree by the pool, watching the cloud reflections in its waters, when suddenly they blurred into a spreading whiteness. Then the waters seemed to rise up and engulf me and, at that, my senses swam away from me.

Evidently I had swooned. When I came to myself, I was wrapped in blankets and back in my darkened room. Essa must have been close by, for I heard her saying sorrowfully to someone: 'My skills are limited; Simon's condition is out of their reach.' Then I faded back into unconsciousness or sleep.

Of the next few days, I can recall only brief episodes — being wrapped in blankets and placed again into the wickerwork litter; seeing Robin riding solemn-faced beside me on his veludu Browntail; a steep descent into a valley, with rain falling gently and Essa again wrapped in her cloak; a splashy crossing of a shallow, stony river; two — or was it three? — nights in other predin, where unfamiliar faces gazed at me with sympathetic inquisitiveness; and a ride under dripping, lichen-grown trees, with attent hasedain all about us.

After that everything passed into a long haze of vagueness, through which reality and dreams moved in a confused procession that, ever and anon, turned into a strange, frightening dance. Yes, I recall being made to drink curious, unpleasant-tasting potions; but were there not also splendid feasts, with rich, unfamiliar viands and potent wines? Yes, there were the grave faces of Essa and of Avran gazing down at me; but did I not see also the wistful smile of my beloved Ilven? Surely I did; surely I groped for her, to be desolated when my arms could not enclose her. Yes, I remember the calm concern in Robin's voice and the worried dismay in Dan Wyert's; but did I not hear also the fond gruffness of my father, the jesting affection of my brother, even the sweet, almost-forgotten tones of my mother who had died before ever I came to know her?

And there were many other faces and voices; of bearded, furrow-browed elders and curious children, of bright-cheeked maidens and sulkily watchful youths. There were matrons giving that special smile, and speaking in that specially warm voice, reserved for the very sick. The faces would be still, the voices comprehensible; then they would move and rise, into a whirl, into a shout or a scream, until I seemed to be plunging into dark waters that were sucking me down, down to oblivion.

One unfamiliar countenance there was that I saw again and again — a face frowning in concentration, surrounded by a hood of purple. It was adorned by eyebrows as bristling as the brow-horns of a veludu and by a beard jutting as sharply forward as the prow of a ship. I came to know the voice associated with that face — a sort of exasperated growl, like that of a baited bear unable quite to reach the terriers tormenting it.

Eventually there came a day when, looking up at that face, I saw a beamed roof above it that did not move, a torch in a bracket that did not whirl; when my hot hands felt the coarseness of blankets beyond the soft sheets swathed about me; when I gasped, coughed, and knew clearly that I was awake, that these things were real.

'I believe we've brought him back.' The growl, for once, signified gratification. 'Essa, the cloth, please.'

Again my brow was being gently moistened and, this time, without any smell of ale. Yes, there was Essa, gazing at me over the man's shoulder, though it was he, not she, who was tending me; Essa looking very weary, but also very relieved.

On that occasion I said nothing; indeed I was not able, yet, to speak. After a very short while, I slipped away into sleep; but it was now a sleep with benign dreams, of tranquil meadows and grazing sheep, of blue skies and drifting, still bluer butterflies among blossoming celandines . . .

Next day — or was it some later day? Time had little meaning — I was awake for longer. I recall Avran's smile and Dan Wyert's delighted grin, but I did not speak to them, and I am unsure if they spoke to me, before I returned to my bright dream-meadow.

Then there were other days when I was propped up on pillows while I drank hasedu-milk from beakers held to my lips, swallowed spoonfuls of soup, or crunched crisp breads; and a shakily splendid one when I was raised up onto my feet, to totter a few steps round the room before returning thankfully to my bed.

There was a gazing into a polished-metal mirror, an unkind mirror that revealed a haggard face, little like my memory of Simon Branthwaite — a depressing sight until I saw the fringe of dark hair on cheeks and chin and realized, with sudden immense gratification, that my beard was sprouting at last! Eventually — after how many days? — I walked out of that dark chamber, one arm about Avran's shoulder; walked through an archway; and walked into a garden, as bright and colourful as in the best of my dreams.

By then, of course, I had learned where I was and whose garden this was. We were staying in the castle of Arravron, high on the ridge that forms the central prong of the Trident Mountains. That particular ridge, as I was to discover later, was formed of a curious red stone, almost the colour of blood, but mottled in places by lighter patches of brown, cream-colour or even white. However, the stone to build the castle had been brought from elsewhere and was quite different: and this, for the moment, enclosed my field of vision. It was a sombre enough material, a black stone of fine, close grain, that could be — and indeed, had been — highly polished.

The keep crowned the round knoll that capped the ridge. It was low and circular, with four subsidiary towers forming corners north, east, south and west. Falling below this knoll, like an apron below the pot-belly of a bibulous innkeeper, was the bailey, with the gatehouse lowermost and northernmost, two other towers and a high, machico-lated wall between. Black keep, black walls; it might have seemed a sinister place save for the garden that occupied the keep, with its many trees and blossoming bushes. Their colour and greenery were reflected in the polished surfaces of the walls, so that one quite forgot their own sombre hue.

As to whose garden it was, why, I had been brought for physicianly treatment to this place because it was the home of Dekhemet Arrav. He was the most skilled of the chirurgeons and the most formidable of the necromancers of the Trident Mountains — and thus, in the eyes of the Reschorese at least, the master wizard of all Rockall. I was by no means the only person whom he was treating: there were other men and women sitting on benches or lying on couches in that garden, each recovering from some formidable injury or ailment that lesser physicians could not treat. It was Dekhemet Arrav whose strange countenance had haunted my dreams; it was he whose sensi-tive touch had located the displacement of bone in my skull that had resulted from my heavy fall, and whose skilled manipulation had set it right; it was he whose salves and potions had brought healing to the wound and driven away the fever that had pulsed through my veins.

This had not been achieved quickly, but during a long battle for my life that had endured over many weeks. When I was first taken out into the garden, I asked Avran what day it was. When he replied

'Rimbalet talil' (July 15th), I could not at first believe him. But it was true. For almost a month and a half, with the flowers of summer blooming and fading outside, I had lain in a dark dream-world, while Dekhemet Arrav strove to bring me back from the boundaries of death and my friends came close to despairing of his success in those strivings.

Throughout all those weeks, someone had always been watching by my bed; Avran, Robin or Essa during the days (and, as he came to be trusted more, Dan Wyert also), one or other of the Reschorese women who assisted the wizard during the nights. Dekhemet Arrav had seen me at least once every day, each of his visits giving me some renewal of tranquillity — or so I was told, though I could not remember.

Well, now I was on the mend; but, for a long while, I felt as weak as a gutted herring. I was content to sit among the flowering bushes, listening to the piping of the birds and the throbbing hum of the bees, watching the meandering flight of the butterflies and the unsteady aerial tumblings of the ever-drunken-seeming beetles.

Better still was it when Avran brought his pommer and played to me the tunes of Sandastre and the less familiar ones of the Aramassa boatmen and the Reschorese farmers, or when Robin sang to me the court songs of Herador and Merania — songs always of lovemaking, hunting or war. It was pleasant also to listen to the conversations of my friends and of Dekhemet Arrav's other patients and still pleas-anter when, as the days went by, I was able to join fully in those talks, and even to sing.

During that time, I learned what had transpired at Kradsunar. Within hours of Avran's arriving at the Denrateng predan, a company of Reschorese soldiers had ridden out to that city. They found the rafneyen and veludain gone from the old quarry and the gates of Kradsunar closed and guarded.

The Reschorese were neither so strong nor so foolhardy as to assault so stout a fortification; they had merely encircled the city with a thin line of guards, awaiting reinforcements.

Four nights later, during the deepest darkness before dawn, the gates were quietly opened. A dozen of the robbers — all those who could find mounts — rode forth, not to attack the Reschorese but to try to evade them. However, they were detected and pursued.

There was a brisk and bloody battle in the early light of dawn, out on the open stony plain, between vengeful Reschorese and frantic brigands. In that battle, seven Reschorese soldiers had died; but all the robbers had been slain or taken.

Next morning, the remaining brigands awakened to find themselves deserted by most of their leaders. There was a panic and some of the men sallied forth on foot.

Though the majority of the Reschorese soldiers had gone in pursuit of the mounted robbers, a few remained on watch and there was a second skirmish. As it chanced, the long-awaited Reschorese reinforcements arrived while that fight was in progress. Their arrival caused the surviving robbers — several had already been slain — to throw down their arms and surrender.

'Lord' Darnay was not among those slain or captured. Somehow, while that second skirmish was in progress, he had contrived to escape from Kradsunar, perhaps through that same drain by which we had escaped. If a search had been begun quickly, he must surely have been found and taken; but, by the time the Reschorese realized he had eluded them, it was too late.

The people remaining in the city — mostly old men, women and children — saw no further hope and capitulated also, opening Kradsunar's gates to the Reschorese. Those folk had been treated gently enough. They were allowed the choice of going back to the lands from which they had come or of continuing to live in Kradsunar, as servants for the Reschorese garrison that thenceforward would be stationed there. Some left but most, rather surprisingly, chose to stay, perhaps because they were too fearful of retribution to dare to return to their homelands.

As for the robbers captured in battle, they were taken to Pretalaas for trial. It was unlikely that they would be executed, but unquestionably they faced imprisonment for their black crimes.

It was satisfying to know that the evil stain had been scoured from Kradsunar; but I doubted whether, in so arid a situation, it could ever again become the vital city it must once have been.

Though my own horizons were still confined by the high walls of the castle bailey, I learned in addition something of this Kingdom of Reschora to which we had travelled so perilously. It is not a rich realm, for the greater part of Reschora is mountainous, furnishing only scanty pasture for veludain; and indeed, its highest lands are so barren as to be of small value even for hunting. Only on the southern flanks of the hills and on sheltered valley slopes can hasedain be grazed, and even then they have to be driven down into the valley bottoms during the winter, feeding on the stubble of crops till snow comes and then on hay and grain till spring.

Moreover, even the growing of crops and keeping of beasts on those valley floors is a hazardous occupation. All the principal rivers of Reschora — the Shaludaith, the Hevedash, the Mentone, the Avronash and the Shadarth — flow through steep-sided, flat-bottomed valleys. After rain in the mountains, all are as prone as the Rimbedreth to go suddenly on the rampage. At such times, the farms and fields within reach of their waters may be devastated, crops and beasts being swept away down river and the unfortunate farmers having to rely on help from their neighbours till a more benign season comes.

Most Reschorese live well above those perilous valleys, usually in isolated predin perched on some crag or ridge that affords defensive advantages. Sometimes the predin may be clustered, forming a hamlet or small village; but, in this whole wide realm, there are only five small towns. Pretalaas, where the king holds court, is set on a hilltop high above the valley of the Shaludaith, while Shesvendray, an earlier capital, stands equally high above that of the Hevedash. The other three towns are built on flood-spared ridges beside the broad waters of the Mentone — Hasaring, just beyond the Trident Mountains; Delmansgay, where the swift waters of the Hevedash join that mightier stream: and Ingelot, closest of all Reschorese towns to that realm's northern boundary.

None of the towns boasts any special product, any particular craft or skill comparable to that of each Sandastrian — or, for that matter, of many English — towns. They serve merely as markets and as strong-points in times of war; for indeed, only a few centuries back, the region that is now Reschora had been the scene of bitter conflict, still not forgotten.

It was through the people of the Trident Mountains that Reschora had come to be unified under one king — though, oddly, not a king from that region — and it was from the Trident Mountains that

Reschora gained its special qualities, its particular renown among these northern realms.

As Felun Daretseng had told me many weeks before and as my friends were learning in their wanderings abroad, this was a very special region. No riches of silver or gold, or even of copper or tin, have been found there; instead, its strange earths, and the equally strange plants that grow in them, are of value because they can be used in the making of medicaments and in furnishing materials for magic.

Most of the folk of the Trident Mountains are simple farmers like the other Reschorese; yet it seems that at least one son or daughter of each predan is born endowed with special skills, of prognostication, precognition, sorcery, leechcraft or chirurgy. Such children are identified early, during their schooling in Hasaring. They are then sent to serve an apprenticeship in the home of some luminary of the particular art to which they show an inclination. Sometimes they remain with that person life-long, as disciples or adjuvants. Sometimes they go back to their home predan, practising locally the arts they have learned. Most often, however, they sally forth into the wider world beyond Reschora's borders, returning to their homeland only after many years — or never.

There are many such wanderers, in the great forests and in the southern realms of these northern Mountains. A few choose to be servants to particular rulers in this wide region, sometimes indeed attaining a mastery over those rulers; they become rich and powerful, either doing good or spreading terror according to their personal character and that of their masters. The majority, however, pass their lives in selfless service to the ordinary people of those lands. Vedlen Obiran, the wizard in whose train we had so recently adventured, was one of these; his name was honoured in Reschora.

Indirectly, both groups have given to their homeland a curious, special protection, for they have caused Reschora to be viewed with respect, awe or even fear by outsiders. Though sometimes harassed by robbers — ever a hazard in so thinly populated a land — Reschora has not been invaded for very many years. Nevertheless, because of those robbers and because greedy Kelcestre is so near a neighbour, the King of Reschora maintains a standing army. It is an army staffed from the other parts of his realm, for the people of the Trident

Mountains are not inclined to war. They feel themselves to be creators and sustainers, not destroyers.

Dekhemet Arrav had been Vedlen Obiran's mentor, long ago. He must have seen more than eighty summers, yet he was as strong and vital as a thirty-year-old and formidably knowledgeable. Moreover, he was possessed of a profound curiosity, undimmed by the passage of years — a curiosity that would cause him to investigate the profundities of alchemy or watch the mating flight of ants with equal avidity. He cross-questioned Avran so prolongedly about the geography, the peoples and the laws of southern Rockall as to leave my friend exhausted. Robin, for his part, had been astonished by Dekhemet's knowledge of England, France, Lower and Higher Germany and the Levant; he had gladly supplemented that knowledge. In evenings when Dekhemet was not tending some sick or injured person, he and Robin would play chess. Though as skilled a warrior on the board as in the field, Robin was almost always vanquished in those mock-wars.

As my recovery progressed, it came to be my turn to be interrogated concerning England, its wars, its customs and its courtesies, and even to recount to Dekhemet the small tales of Hallamshire. Never, however, did Dekhemet permit his questioning to tire me.

During the long lassitude of those summer days, Robin and Avran spent much time with me, assisting me when I embarked upon the exercises that Dekhemet Arrav had designed to strengthen my body anew. For their own exercisings with sword and long-bow, however, they had to ride out beyond the walls of Arravron Castle; such military pursuits were forbidden within its quiet walls.

After a while they rode farther, to see more of the Trident Mountains, and entertained me with strange tales on return. The ridges forming the outer prongs of the trident were made, they discovered, of rocks quite as black as the castle walls; indeed, they visited the quarry from which its stones had come. However, those black rocks were smeared and seamed by crystals and ochres of much stranger colours — pinks and saffrons, azure-blues, sulphur-yellows and unnatural greens. My friends spoke also of plants with weirdly colourful flowers and with leaves of curious shape, like spreading hands or closed fists, arranged in complex spirals or serried spikes; and they told me of brightly-coloured, flickering-tongued lizards and sluggish, horn-headed snakes, creatures which the Reschorese treated with respect and whose slaying was not permitted.

This sounded to be a bizarre place, indeed. As my body slowly mended and my mind shook off its prolonged torpor, I became increasingly eager to venture forth and see such strange sights. I asked many questions about the lands beyond Reschora, learning much about Raffette, Kelcestre and the realms further west. Of the realms to the north, however, the Reschorese seemed never willing to speak; and no-one had heard of Lyonesse.

Of Dan Wyert and Essa we saw little — Essa, because she was absorbed in the healing work of Arravron Castle, assisting and learning; Dan Wyert because, mindful of his vow, he was staying faithfully by Essa's side and lending his aid to her whenever he might. This appeared to suit him immensely; though Dan had not lost his rather mischievous sense of humour, he seemed to be attaining a new tranquillity. I wondered whether, when we left, the two of them would choose to travel with us or whether they would prefer to remain in Dekhemet's service.

And so the summer days went by, July turning into August, August into September. The blossoms on the bushes in the castle bailey were replaced by pendant clusters of berries or by oddly-shaped, hard-shelled fruits; the flowers faded and turned into seeds that were blown away by the wind.

Robin was enjoying this long, quiet period, but Avran was becoming increasingly bored and restless, going off on rides that were ever longer and finding ever less to say about them when he came back. My own energy was returning; I found myself envying the men and women who, having arrived injured or sick after I did, were leaving with health renewed long before I might.

I practised my Reschorese in conversations with those people and I learned some of their songs. These told of the life of the land, the hazards of the seasons and the pleasures and pains of love; never did they treat with war or evildoing, as do so many of our English ballads. Robin procured for me a timbelan, a strange stringed instrument with a bell-shaped, open-ended body made of dark, dense wood and with strings on both the upper and lower sides of the neck. Its tone is curiously mellow and resonant, but it is hard to play and, despite my skill on citole and psaltery, I found more frustration than pleasure in striving to make music on that instrument. Still, my attempts helped to occupy the long hours.

At last came an evening when Dekhemet Arrav, having examined me very thoroughly, looked at me from under those disconcertingly horn-like eyebrows and said: 'There is no occasion for you to remain here longer. Your body has mended itself; you require no more of my care.'

I strove to express my profound gratitude to him, but he brushed my words aside, with a response I found very strange: 'It was not only my pleasure to renew your health, but also my duty. Prince Avran and you have many tasks to perform, Simon Vasianavar — tasks that may alter the whole history of our island of Rockall. It is time for you to go forth.'

At my astonished expression, his face broadened into a smile, the point of his beard bobbing like a ship's prow in rough water. 'You do not understand? Neither do I. It is enough that I know.'

He seized my hands in the Rockalese grip of friendship, smiled at me again, then turned and left me in my bewilderment.

Chapter Eleven

IN THE CASTLE OF INGELOT

'Well, my friends, you would be wise to decide soon concerning your course. If you delay your setting forth, even by a little, you are at risk of being trapped in the high mountains by winter; and our winters can be savage. Yet still I trust that you will not elect to go northward.'

The speaker was Toril Evateng, zahar of Evatel, Reschora's northernmost province. Upon hearing his name, I surmised that he might be a distant cousin of Narel Evateng, who had been our companion in the wizard's train; and, when I asked him, this proved so. Indeed they were not unalike, being both lean and having the tanned and deeply lined countenances that result from prolonged exposure to bitter weather. However, Toril was somewhat less tall and considerably older. His hair, worn quite long and fastened back in a ring-comb of shining copper, was of the same silver grey as his neatly trimmed beard, while his eyes had faded to an indeterminate hue. Nevertheless there was still, in his gaze, such an all-comprehending percipience and authority that one gained no illusion of feebleness. Quite the contrary; this was a man who had spent a lifetime in tackling difficult problems without being ever daunted or dilatory in decision-making.

We were sitting in a chamber high in the keep of Ingelot Castle. The sunshine of late afternoon, streaming in through the three arrowslit windows that looked southward, made long paths of brightness across the otherwise shadowed room. If one gazed out westward, one looked down upon the waters of the Mentone, too broad to be bridged even so far from the sea as this and traversed only by an eight-oar ferry. Beyond were fields of stubble — the crop had been good this year — and, beyond again, the steep lower slopes of the Ferekar Dralehenar, the Highshadow Mountains.

If instead one looked eastward, one's immediate view was of a tract of commonland on which grew tall herbs and many bushes. An English castellan would have winced at such a prospect, preferring the easier visibility — and greater safety from fire — of close-scythed lawns about his keep. However, the plants were needed; they would serve as fodder when the town's veludain were brought there, to be safe from the blizzards of early winter and out of the reach of the Mentone's hungry waters at spring melt. Surrounding this common on its three other sides were close-spaced lines of houses, the farthermost built against the high, crenellated castle walls. Walls and houses alike had been constructed of a grey limestone, much like our good Pennine stone. Indeed, Ingelot might have passed for a small town in northern England, had not the mountains in whose shade it nestled been so much taller than any in my homeland. On this eastern side they were named the Ferekar Uvahanir, the Windrench Mountains; and windy indeed they must be in winter.

We had taken two days to prepare for departure from Arravron and three whole weeks to make our way to Ingelot. To my own great surprise and, I think, to Robin's also, Essa had elected to travel with us. She had so chosen without any least hesitation, so far as we could perceive. For Robin and me she had proved an agreeable companion, eagerly interested in every new plant that was seen and every new animal that was glimpsed, eager also to hear Robin's tales of his wanderings and to learn something from me of England.

Yet she manifested no comparable interest in the Rockalese realms south of the great forests — why, I could not understand. Moreover, she continued to maintain a barrier, spiritual if not actual, between herself and Avran. This distressed my friend greatly. It had caused him privately to implore me to explain what he had done to make Essa dislike him so; but I could not tell him. Friendly though she was to me, she kept her own councils. We had learned a little about Essa while I had lain wounded after the skirmish with Darnay's robbers but, since that time, nothing more.

Since Essa had decided to accompany us, naturally Dan Wyert had come along also. His broken leg had long since mended, leaving him without even a limp. A doe veludu called *Remdegel*, 'Longshank',

98

had been procured for Dan to ride. She was an ungainly-looking creature with curiously high hindquarters, but Dan liked her well enough. He had firmly taken upon himself the task of tending to and grooming all the veludain: he had proved very skilled at this, treating each with particular kindness. Consequently, all of them liked him — even Proudhorn, though he was a single-hearted creature and I had that heart.

I smiled to myself when I recalled how rapturously Proudhorn had greeted me, on my first emergence from Arravron's walls. Why, he was as exuberant as a hound whose master had been long away! He had curvetted about me, leaping into the air and tossing his horns, then nuzzling me with strange little snorts of pleasure. For my own part, I had shared his delight. When I said my prayers in the castle chapel — for in Christian northern Rockall, as in England, each castle has its chapel — Proudhorn had figured high among the many blessings for which I had given thanks.

After almost three months of rest, good fodder and careful grooming in the pastures about Arravron, all four veludain were in excellent fettle. They were a far cry indeed from the miserable-looking creatures we had stolen from Kradsunar. Nor had our ride northward done anything to worsen their condition. We had travelled only small distances at first, for Robin and Avran were anxious not to tire me unduly. Three full days had been taken over the short distance to Hasaring and two nights had been spent in that town. (Ostensibly this had been done so that we might meet and present gifts to the Denrateng children, whose parents had been so kind to us. Actually, though, I am sure the stay was designed to permit me further rest and recuperation.) Then we had ridden northward in benign weather, following the western bank of the Mentone. For three nights we had enjoyed the hospitality of the castellan of Delmansgay and his plump, cheerful lady and, on the other nights, humbler but no less pleasant entertainment in a series of hilltop predin.

Dekhemet Arrav had courteously furnished us with a scroll letter of introduction, not to any specific person but to whatever Reschorese folk we chanced to meet; his name was known to all his compatriots and almost all could read. However, though we had dutifully displayed this scroll to potential hosts at first, we had not needed it. Everywhere that we went in Reschora, we were made welcome.

Though far from rich in material possessions and having an arduous enough existence, the Reschorese are a most gracious and generous people. Never do they allow their hardships to subdue their spirits; instead, they are loud with the joy of life. So happy are their homes that each meal, however simple, seemed as delightful as a feast and each evening was one of music-making and the telling of tales. Any attempts that we made, on leaving, to pay for our beds and our food were refused with peremptory embarrassment; we were informed reprovingly that our company, our songs and our stories constituted payment enough.

On one such occasion, I became aware that Dan Wyert was weeping. He told me that, after so many years in Akhaseng's and Darnay's robber bands, he had forgotten how people could be so kind.

However, none of our hosts had furnished any help in planning our journey. The fact that the name 'Lyonesse' awoke no echoes in their minds occasioned no surprise; after all, neither Vedlen Obiran nor Dekhemet Arrav, mighty though their knowledge was, had ever heard of it. What continued to astonish me was how little the Reschorese seemed to know of the lands north of Reschora and Raffette, and how unwilling they were to speak about those lands. Though their information was meagre enough about the Mentonese lands to the west — the Mentonese, despite being such vigorous traders, do not permit strangers to cross their borders — they talked or speculated readily enough about Mentone. Of countries to the south and east, they knew a great deal and spoke freely. However, when we asked questions about the realms beyond Reschora's northern frontier, it was as if a shutter closed across their minds, allowing no light of information to pass.

Even Toril Evateng, lord though he was under the King of this northernmost region of Reschora, had refused to speak of those lands. Instead, when we had first talked to him about our quest, he had striven hard to persuade us against proceeding with it. Why waste time in seeking for a land that, he was sure, did not exist? Avran and I had travelled far and had survived many dangers; would it not be better for us, now that the summer had ended, to turn our faces south toward our own land? If we returned there, we would surely be honoured, for were we not the greatest travellers Rockall had ever known? Why not return home and share with the other peoples of southern Rockall the rich stores of knowledge we had gained? Why face further, wholly unnecessary hazards by pursuing a quest that was bound to fail?

However, I had fought my battle of conscience against inclination during that long night in Dellorain. I would not turn back now, even if I were compelled to go on alone.

Avran and Robin were quite as determined as I to continue the search, but for different reasons. They were not, like me, seeking to fulfil a burdensome duty that had torn them away from all they loved most; theirs was the desire that actuates the wanderer, the desire to see new lands. Consequently, this argument of Toril's was rejected swiftly enough by all three of us.

His second line of attack was much harder to combat. It was launched as we watched the interplay of sun and shadow in the upper chamber. Dan Wyert was not with us; probably he was chaffering with the old matrons in the castle's great hall or down in the kitchens wheedling sweetmeats, of which he had an inordinate fondness, from the cooks.

The sentence with which I began this chapter marked the renewal of Toril's onslaught. It began with a skilled sapping of our earlier defences.

Very well, then, we intended to pursue the quest to its end; Toril expressed admiration for our determination. Moreover, at this point he admitted that, yes, there might be lands unknown to him beyond the mountains. Unknown to the Reschorese, certainly; but surely they could not be unknown to the merchants of Warringtown, whose caravels traded along the whole northeast coast of Rockall. It would be stupid of us to head northward into the most dangerous region of the mountains, especially when winter was imminent. Why did we not travel instead to Warringtown? There we must surely find *someone* who knew the whereabouts of Lyonesse, if it existed. Mayhap we might even find a ship that would take us there!

Perceiving from our uneasy glances at each other that this was a possibility we had not considered, Toril Evateng developed his idea. We could turn back down the valley of the Mentone, he suggested, and follow the skirts of the mountains to Kaldensett in Raffette. Then we might traverse Kelcestre, Lantharm and Quenslang to Warringtown. Yes, indeed Kelcestre might prove a perilous realm,

101

but we were skilled with weapons and not rich enough to invite robbery. As for Lantharm and Quenslang, they were tranquil lands, where we would be made welcome; indeed, Lantharm was now ruled by the King of Herador with such benign justice that its people, although they were Reschorese, were perfectly contented to be under his sway. Going that way, we would be safe from winter storms, guaranteed of finding adequate provender for our beasts and able, by hunting, to eat adequately ourselves without being required to purchase food.

Well, then, if we thought that route would be too long and time-wasting, there was another and shorter, if rather more arduous, way that we might consider. Why should we not cross the Ferekar Uvah-anir, the Windrench Mountains, into northern Raffette and thence into Adira? We might manage that easily before the winter storms set in. Adira's capital, Garrandevor, was a most beautiful city and its ruler wise and benign: we could be sure of a welcome for the winter. Next spring it would prove a simple enough journey for us, onward through Chaskrand and the smaller realms of Quetalas and Tanswing to Warringtown. Why must we throw our lives away by insisting upon going northward?

We had all, I believe, become not only puzzled but deeply alarmed by the reluctance of these good people even to speak of the lands north of Reschora and Raffette, let alone to contemplate our journeying there. Thus Robin and I — and, perhaps, Essa also — could understand Avran's feelings when, under this further prodding from Toril Evateng, he blew up.

'What is the matter with you Reschorese? Always you advise us "Go south; go east; do not go north." Yet you will not say *why* we should not go north! Are the mountains there so much higher, so much steeper? Are the wild beasts so much fiercer? Is the weather so much more terrible? In God's name, cease treating us like ignorant children and tell us what you know!'

Toril was clearly both taken aback and angered by this outburst. Fortunately, Robin spoke to him more pacifically: 'You must forgive our friend's brusqueness, but it would truly be helpful if you did speak out. Though we have made so many friends here in Reschora, not one of them has been willing to speak freely to us. Why, we have not even learned the very names of the lands north of here! Mayhap,

102

as you imply, there are excellent reasons why we should turn aside, excellent reasons why we should seek another path. Can you not tell us those reasons?'

While Robin was speaking, the wrath had faded from Toril's countenance, to be replaced by an unwonted expression of doubt. He caressed his beard with his right hand for a while, then seemed to make up his mind. As I have remarked earlier, he was not one to lose time by hesitation.

'Very well, then, I will respond as you ask; though it is not a subject that gives pleasure to we of Reschora. Yet I can speak of those northern lands only from hearsay, for I have never travelled beyond the bounds of this Kingdom. Indeed, none of our people have ventured northward, during many generations. Why should that be, you will ask? Well, yes, there are good reasons. Yet how must I begin? Perhaps by saying first that, though the mountains themselves are indeed high and harsh and though there are indeed wild beasts enough among them, you are brave men and can face such hazards. It is not of the peaks, the moors and the beasts, nor even of the bitter winds and early snows that you must beware; it is of the people of those mountains.'

He hesitated and fell momentarily silent, but Robin prompted him: 'Tell us about those people, please. Tell us why they are to be feared.'

Toril Evateng leaned back and considered us, as if again assessing how to proceed. Robin and I were intent, Avran a little shame-faced as if repenting his explosion, and Essa curled up on her seat in the shadows, with feet tucked up under skirt, cool and withdrawn. There was a table at the centre of the chamber, constructed from a strange grey wood which, when polished, gleamed almost like silver. Toril's gaze dropped and he began tapping the table with his right fingers, in the abstracted fashion of one collecting his thoughts. Then he spoke again.

'If you wish to comprehend fully, then you must be patient, for I must cast memory far back. I must speak of a time of shame and bitter hardship for we of Reschora, a time now forgotten by most living folk. Know, then, that in the beginning, after Adam's seed had first spread across the earth, six different races lived in these mountains; or rather, two races, each divided into three great tribes. People

103

of the Veledreven race have fair skin and very dark hair; Simon here would look like one of them, if his eyes were green or pale blue instead of being brown. Oddly, though, some few of the Veledrevens are entirely white — white-haired, with palely pink eyes and skins so easily burned by the sun that they must robe and hood themselves closely when out of doors. All black or all white, that is the colour of the Veledrevens and that is their nature, or so men say. The other race, the Oburnassians, are such folk as we, brown-haired and most often brown-eyed. You are of our kind, Sir Robert, even though your forefathers came from across the sea.'

Robin and I glanced at each other rather furtively, each considering the other as exemplar of characteristics of a race of which we had never heard hitherto. Avran was smiling, knowing how little he accorded with either type; and there seemed an element of amusement even in Essa's cool consideration of us. However, the zahar was continuing his discourse.

'The three tribes of Veledrevens all dwelt on the northeastern flanks of these northern ranges. The Seleddens lived northernmost, on a great, rich lowland west of the black mountains. South and east of them, on the eastern side of those mountains and on a plain beyond, lived the Gadarrans. The third tribe, the Beladnens, dwelt south of both the other tribes, between the Chaluwand River and the Warringflow. In the past, as now, they were the only Veledreven tribe that showed friendship to we Oburnassians.

'Of the three tribes of Oburnassians, two were very numerous and the third quite small. The smallest tribe — they were called Sachak-kans in those ancient times — lived on the southeastern flanks of the mountains and in the grasslands beyond, between the Warring-flow and what men nowadays style the Green River, though it had an earlier name that even I now forget. The whole central and western region of the mountains was occupied by the two greater tribes. We, the Reschorese, lived in the south centre and southwest. To the north of us dwelt the greatest tribe of all, the Safaddnese.'

The zahar paused and drew in a deep breath, then let it out slowly, shaking his head very gently from side to side. He seemed both sad and wistful.

'That was a good time, if we are to believe the old stories. The summers were more benign then, and the winters infinitely less bleak. The rivers flowed more peaceably, flooding rarely if at all. The valley bottoms were green with fruiting trees and their sides bedecked by berry-laden bushes. Even on the high tops the grass grew lush and tall, so that one might pasture hasedain there — yes, hasedain, not just veludain — for eight moons in each twelvemonth. The fish in the rivers were bigger and fatter and the hunting was much, much better. Indeed all things, *all* things, were better. I do not say that the men of the six tribes never met in battle — can men ever live long at peace? — but conflicts were few. With such abundance, there was no hardship and little occasion for envy or jealousy. Ah! if only that happy time had never ended.' Toril sighed.

'Yet your people are among the most contented — and, I may say, among the most hospitable to strangers such as we — of any I have met; and in my travels, I have encountered many peoples.'

Robin's words brought a smile to Toril Evateng's lips. 'It pleases me that you should say so. Yes, it is true, we have recovered something of our former happiness, now that we live in freedom again. Well, let me tell you in brief the story of the long, black years.

'Trouble came upon us from the south. At that time, you must understand, forests grew right up to the southern slopes of the mountains in the west and in the east, while even the Etolen Dunes were then rich grasslands. Well, out of the forests there came a great army — or rather, two great armies in concerted onslaught. Swarthy, squat men they were, sheathed in mail of bronze and bearing shields, swords and spears of bronze or iron, whereas my forefathers of that time used only spears and axes of stone.

'Why those armies came to attack them, our forefathers never understood clearly. The southerners could hope for little plunder from we simple folk of the mountains. Indeed, after they had conquered us, they demanded little tribute and drove away only a few men and women to serve as slaves. Was it that their gods demanded a tribute of blood spilled in war? Was it that their rulers sought to hold the whole world in dominion or thralldom? Who can say? It happened long ago and they are long gone.

'Whatever the gale of desire that caused their coming, those two great armies swept up into the mountains like a storm-driven tide. The southern tribes broke under their impact; the Sachakkans, the Beladnens and yes, we Reschorese were swiftly overwhelmed.'

105

'Did those soldiers wear the device of the rising sun?' Avran was sitting forward eagerly in his chair. His words awoke in me the recollection of the grey riders, a memory that came like a breath of chill fog into that warm room.

'So men say.' Toril seemed startled. 'You are from the south; is that the emblem of your own people?'

'No indeed! That was the emblem of the Empire of old, the evil Empire whose armies conquered our realms of the southern hills in years before memory. Why, they held my forefathers in thralldom for more than a millenium! Yet we did not know that their foul grasp extended so far.'

Toril Evateng was deeply interested. 'You call it just "the Empire" and give it no other name? For their part, my people called the invaders just "the Southerners". For long years my ancestors looked southward only in hatred and fear.'

'Yet your ancestors were fortunate in that so little was taken from them.' Avran's voice was sombre. 'My own people paid heavy tribute, in goods, in toil, and in furnishing victims for sacrifice to their accursed gods.'

The zahar gazed at him in startlement. 'Did they indeed? Yet I can scarcely consider that we of the northern mountains were fortunate, in view of what was to follow. As I told you, the three southern tribes — the Beladnens, the Sachakkans and we Reschorese — were speedily conquered. However, the Gadarrans and Seleddens were not similarly taken by surprise. They fought back for a while; but then, to my ancestors' complete astonishment and their own lasting dishonour, they treated with the enemy while still undefeated. They made obeisance to the southern gods and became the creatures, the puppets, of the Southerners, serving as brutal intermediaries between their new masters and their cousins of the mountains.'

Even the memory of that betrayal disgusted the zahar. As he paused we made sounds expressive of understanding and sympathy; but he seemed scarcely even aware of that response.

'What caused them thus to sell their souls?' he asked rhetorically. 'We can only guess; we cannot know. Nearly two millenia have passed by since that shameful episode and, in so many years, much has been forgotten. Yet I think it was because of their priests. I believe the tribes were persuaded into abandoning their own, gentle gods and

106

worshipping the new, fiercer gods of the Southerners — gods whose power seemed so much greater, for had they not given metal weapons to their worshippers, weapons with much keener edges than any axe of stone?'

'But what of the Safaddnese? You have not mentioned them.' Avran's interest was now so deeply aroused that he had quite forgotten his embarrassment. He was sitting on the very edge of his chair, with arms akimbo and hands braced on his knees. As for Essa, she was gazing at him in a curiously troubled fashion, for which I could imagine no good cause.

'Ah! the Safaddnese! They went on fighting. They were driven back into the high mountains, yes, but they were never vanquished. From that terrible time of defeat, betrayal and enslavement, they alone emerged with honour untarnished. At first they beat off the Southerners with their simple stone weapons, but then they began to garner swords and spears of metal from their dead foes and used those newer weapons also. They learned never to meet the Southerners in open battle, but only in ambush. They proved adept at rolling rocks and causing stone-slides, so that the Southerners became afraid to venture up out of the valleys. Even in those valleys, the Southerners were not safe. The Safaddnese slew them from cover during the day — not in major attacks, but one or two at a time — and so harassed them at night that their fears prevented them from sleeping.

'After ten years, the Southerners and their allies gave up the struggle. They abandoned any thought of further conquest and, instead, erected a ring of fortifications to hem in the Safaddnese from south and east. Many of my ancestors found death as they strove to erect those fortifications under the merciless whips of the Seleddens and Gadarrans. Yet, if the Southerners had not defeated the Safaddnese, they had at least contained them; and the rest of the mountains were theirs.'

Robin was listening with an interest quite as deep as Avran's. 'I have heard a part of this story before, but never told so clearly or so fully.'

'The story is quite new to me,' said Avran. 'How long did these Southerners maintain their dominion, here in the north?'

'Not for many years; not nearly so long as their grasp upon your forefathers' lands, Prince Avran. Perhaps for two generations or three; not more. Then came a rumour, none knew from where, that the heartland of the Southerners had been destroyed; that the very ocean had risen against them in wrath at the insatiability of their appetite for evil. Whether it was true or not, I cannot say; but certainly these tidings caused the Southerners to lose faith in their gods and themselves. Their strong discipline softened like an icicle melting in spring sunshine and their power flowed away from them.'

The zahar smiled, the bitter smile of one who remembers a just vengeance. 'And so the Safaddnese came down out of the high peaks, slaying and burning, throwing down the enclosing walls that the Southerners had erected and tumbling their temples into ruin. Those few Southerners who were not slain fled back into the forests where, I understand, there lurked other men seeking vengeance upon the invaders. I question whether any can have found their way back to their homeland. Mayhap, indeed, as our legends tell, that homeland had been drowned by the sea.'

'It is true; the ocean did overwhelm that ancient, evil Empire.' Avran was speaking very earnestly. 'Only a few small islands were left. My forefathers witnessed that happening and, from it, gained their own freedom.'

The zahar sighed. 'Alas! if only freedom had been gained here in the north also — but no, it was not. After the Southerners had gone, my forefathers found they had merely exchanged one harsh master for another even more harsh.'

'However did that happen?' Avran was puzzled. 'Did those other two peoples — those Seleddens and Gadarrans — did they drive back the Safaddnese and hold your people in thralldom?'

'No indeed. Those two peoples were regarded with particular hatred by we other mountain tribes. They had ranged widely and gained high authority in the service of the Southerners but, when their masters fell, their own power was lost also. Maybe a few contrived to flee back to their homes, but most were slain.'

Toril Evateng paused again. When next he spoke, it was in a tone of surprised reflection. 'And, you know, it was as if the ocean was seeking vengeance on them also — or so it is asserted, in another legend told to me by my grandsire. Until now, I had almost forgotten it. You are interested, Avran? Then I will recount that legend.

'It is told that the King of the Seleddens — some name him Meliad or Melian, some call him Rivalin — was a cruel man, implacably harsh to his own subjects and treating captive enemies with particular brutality. Yet it is said that his son was more noble. The prince strove to persuade his father to forgo these cruelties, but in vain.

'There came one particular year when Melian proclaimed a great celebration of conquest, at which the King of the Gadarrans would be principal guest. To entertain him, a thousand Safaddnese were to be tortured to death. The son strove one last time to persuade his father into clemency, but failed utterly. In deep disgust, he bade farewell to his father's city and rode up into the mountains.

'As he reached ·the summit of a pass, he looked back. He saw an astonishing sight — a towering wave of the ocean thundering across the plain behind him, to break upon the evil city and destroy it utterly. The swash of that tremendous wave spread about the whole broad valley, lapping up to the very ridge from which the young prince was looking; nor did it ever ebb. People say that the place from which he watched came thereafter to be called "Hrensedlin" or, in our language, "the margin of vengeance".

'Not all the Gadarrans and Seleddens were drowned, of course, but their rich lowlands had vanished forever beneath the sea. Henceforward they would live only in the mountains that, formerly, had served merely as a spine to much broader lands. The survivors forsook the worship of the Southerners' gods and returned to the worship of their own ancient gods. As for the prince, it is said that he went off to venture in far lands. Indeed, some say that he became a knight of Christ.'

It was my turn to be sitting eagerly forward in my chair now. 'The prince — his name? Do your legends tell you his name?'

Toril was startled at the fervency of my question. 'His name? Let me think, now. Taran, was it? Or Tradam? No — I have it: Tristan.'

'Tristan!' At last I understood why Sir Arthur Thurlstone, when he voyaged with Sir John Warren and the other adventurers to settle a new land, had not thought it to be the 'Avallon' to which the mortally ill king, his namesake, had been taken. Instead he must have realized that he had discovered the homeland of another of the greatest heroes of chivalric romance. 'Tristan of Lyonesse!'

109

Thus by chance, after so many months, we had discovered the clue we had been seeking so long. At last, at long last, we knew where we were heading. Vedlen Obiran had guessed rightly. To the northward there did indeed lie the land we were seeking — the land of Lyonesse. Yet, paradoxically, we had learned this from a man who, of all the Reschorese we met, had tried hardest to turn our feet in other directions!

Chapter Twelve

TORIL EVATENG ENDS HIS TALE

'Tristan of Lyonesse! Of course!' Robin was marvelling at this sudden revelation. 'Tristan who came from the lost land, the land overwhelmed by the waves! When in the forests so many months agone, Simon, you asked me about Lyonesse, you brought his story back into my mind: yet I did not forge any link with this other tale I knew, of the drowning of the lands of the Seleddens and Gadarrans. Well, well! And indeed, it was always said that Tristan travelled to Cornwall from the west. So it was from Rockall that he came!'

Avran was beaming. 'This is great news! I am delighted. After so many months and so many leagues travelled with nary a word of Lyonesse, I must confess I was becoming sceptical. I was beginning to question whether we would ever find the land you sought, Simon. How good to know that our adventuring has not been in vain!'

Essa did not speak, but she was sitting forward in her chair and smiling at me — the smile of a mother whose child has received some well-merited, but quite unexpected, reward. As for Toril Evateng, he was not only taken aback but also deeply intrigued. He insisted that we narrate to him the epic of Tristan's later life. Since Robin professed to remembering only scraps of the tale, it was I that had to oblige.

It was my father who had told me of Tristan, sitting in the firelight in our hall at Holdworth on winter's evenings many years before. As I recounted the story, I was seeing again his face, benign but slightly abstracted, and hearing again his rich, firm tones. The memory made me long to see him once more, to hear his voice once more. Over the long leagues, my desire to please him by finding him, to show that still I shared the special love that had bound together my brother

111

Richard, my father and me, had dwindled into the doggedness with which a good staghound keeps his nose to an old and fading trail. These unexpected tidings gave new life to my old enthusiasm for finding Lyonesse.

So now it was my turn to recount a tale from the past. I told how Tristan had sailed from his home on a ship of the Northmen, to land in Cornwall with only a bow and a harp as his possessions. I told of Tristan's perilous adventures in that land and in Ireland; of his meeting with the beauteous Iseult and his speaking of her to his friend, King Mark; of how, after Mark and Iseult had become betrothed, Tristan had been bewitched into love with that fair maiden; of the further adventures that befell Tristan when, fleeing from a hopeless love, he took ship to Brittany; and of his eventual reunion with Iseult, a reunion that happened only in death. You will all have heard the story many times; I do not need to retell it in detail.

Toril listened intently, Avran and (to my surprise) Essa eagerly, while Robin sat back relaxedly, as one hearing a story so familiar that he need not pay it close attention. When I was done, Toril spoke reflectively.

'I am indebted to you, Simon. We knew from our own legends, of course, that Tristan had spoken up against his father's ill-doing. It is good to hear how, during his life, he conquered so many other evils and how, in the end, he died resisting temptation. Though he is little remembered nowadays in Rockall, truly Tristan deserves to rank among our greatest heroes. I trust that his spirit and Iseult's, though sundered on this earth, were united in the life hereafter.'

He paused, then continued with a smile: 'While you were speaking, Simon, the names of Meliad's kingdom and city came back to my memory. The realm was called Seleddnar, "land of the Seleddens"; but the city — why, it was called Laionesel! Easy to see how that name became transmuted into the nobler form "Lyonesse"! I trust that the fortunes of your settlers from England will not prove to be as Meliad's, but as Tristan's; that their realm may be, not one of wickedness and cruelty, but of kindness and of faith.'

'Amen to that,' said Robin briskly. 'Well, my lord, will you not complete your own story for us? We have learned much concerning the history of these mountains, and we are grateful indeed for that

112

knowledge. Yet we have still no clear picture of the dangers we must face, if we elect to guide our veludain northward.'

'Very well,' Toril responded. 'First, though, let us have some light, and perhaps some wine. This chamber is becoming dark and we require some lubrication for tongues, if we are to delve once more into our remembrances of past times.'

Slipping out a dagger from its sheath, he rapped loudly on the table with its knobbed hilt. Very soon a beaming manservant appeared, bringing a taper to light the torches in the wall-brackets. Within a few further minutes, we were each holding a beaker of a slightly tart wine, made from some berries of the highland moors and very refreshing.

Toril took a long draught, then resumed his story. 'As I have said, after the rule of the Southerners had been broken and long ere the richest lands of the Seleddens and Gadarrans were taken by the sea, the Safaddnese came down from the mountains to destroy what remained of the power of the invaders. Sadly, though my forefathers welcomed them as liberators, the Safaddnese behaved like conquerors. Yes, they threw down the enclosing walls and the temples erected by the Southerners, but they did not destroy their castles and strong-points — no, indeed! Instead, the Safaddnese lords moved into those castles and sent their soldiers to man those strong-points. Suddenly and belatedly, my ancestors became aware that a new empire had been established in these mountains — a Safaddnese empire. You say, Avran, that your land of Sandastre was under the domination of the Southerners for almost a millenium. Let me tell you that the Safaddnese empire endured here for much longer — for almost fifteen centuries!'

There were gasps of dismayed astonishment from Avran and me, but Robin and Essa registered no particular emotion. That was something they knew already.

'Yes, for a thousand years and half a thousand years again their empire persisted — a time during which my forefathers knew much toil and sweat but no joy, no liberty. The rule of the Safaddnese was strong and bitter. One-fourth of all crops a man produced, one in four of the beasts that he reared and tended, could be kept as food for his family and himself; three-fourths went as tribute to the Safaddnese.'

Reading our appalled reaction to this from our expressions, Toril smiled grimly. 'Indeed, it was a burdensome rule. Yet that man might compound for a part of that tribute. He might choose from two alternatives; either to furnish his own labour in building new fortifications for his oppressors, or to give a son or a daughter into their service.'

'A terrible choice indeed,' Robin murmured.

'Yet, Sir Robert, the Safaddnese kept strictly to their own rules.' The zahar spoke judicially, as if striving to be fair. 'Children were taken at seven years, never earlier, never later. A first-born child was never accepted, since such children are often the ones most prized and loved by their parents; and never would the Safaddnese take more than a single child out of four.'

'What was the fate of those children?' Avran asked. 'Were they treated well, or ill?'

'Not well, but not so ill either. The child taken would be brought up in service in some Safaddnese castle or town. If he or she attained an age of thirty-five years and was trusted, he and his family or she and her family — yes, they were allowed to marry other servants — would be placed as steward for the Safaddnese in some village or district. It was a privileged post, but one never allocated in the region from which that man or woman had come as child. Always they were sent far away from their home region, to serve as agents of the Safaddnese among some tribe with which they had no ties.'

'What a lonely life that must have been,' I commented sympathetically.

'Indeed so. My forefathers called such folk the *tazlantenar*, "the rootless ones". They were no longer a part of any tribe — any who did strive to return to their homelands were slain — and yet they were not Safaddnese. Moreover, the Safaddnese were rigorous in keeping themselves separate, apart. They would not intermarry with other peoples, no, not even with their servants. If a servant-woman bore a child to a Safaddnese man, it was always out of wedlock. The child became a servant also; and mother and child were sent away immediately to some other town or castle, so that the father might not cherish and favour his natural son or daughter. If a Safaddnese woman were unwise enough to bear a child to a servant, the child would be exposed on a mountaintop and the servant executed.'

114

'A harsh law,' Essa commented softly.

'Yes; but then, the Safaddnese were always stern, not only to others but also to themselves. They were very rigid in behaviour outside their castles, whatever might happen inside. Though Safaddnese warriors travelled throughout these mountains, there were no rapes, no by-blows left behind that might grow up with claims to be Safaddnese. Nor was any robbery or pillaging permitted. When demanding their tribute, they would never accept more than three-quarters, nor would they accept less. Yes, the Safaddnese might give back a little food or a few beasts in hard years; yet that heavy tribute was always taken.'

'Why did not your people rebel against so harsh a rule?' Avran was asking.

'Because they could not. In every region of the mountains, there was a strong-point and a garrison, almost always on a mountain-top. Castles such as this, set on a natural ridge or an artificial motte in a lowland — such castles were built after the Safaddnese were gone. The Safaddnese believed that their strength came from the mountains. They preferred their homes to be in high places and built their temples in still higher places, for they worshipped gods of the mountains, cold gods of stone. They sought to make themselves as hard as stone also, to toughen their bodies by arduous exercise and stern living, to expel from their lives any gentle emotions. Yes, they were harsh rulers, but they were not cruel — or not. at least, in the years when their power was unquestioned. Cruelty, like kindness, was a weakness, and they strove to eliminate all weaknesses.

'And, you know, it was as if the very climate changed to accord with their harshness. The winters became ever bleaker, the summers ever shorter. The great forests drew their skirts away from the mountains; the lesser woods in the valleys dwindled and altered strangely; and the mountains themselves became ever more barren. On the high moors where once hasedain had grazed, even veludain had difficulty in finding fodder. In the valleys, fruiting trees became fewer, berry bushes less prolific and crops harder to grow. Moreover the rivers, rising in spate, began to devastate our poor plantations and fields, in surges of anger that none could predict.'

'Surely that must have caused the Safaddnese to move down into the valleys, then?' Robin was asking. 'Was that what undermined their rule?'

'No, the Safaddnese never did forsake their homes among the higher peaks; mayhap they live there yet. However, as the centuries passed, they dwindled. The sons of tazlantenar came to be recruited as soldiers, then as officers, until many garrisons consisted wholly of tazlantenar under a single Safaddnese commander. Their grip on the mountains slowly slackened. And, while the Safaddnese themselves remained merely harsh and stern, the tazlantenar became cruel, so that my forefathers' hatred of their rule grew even greater.

'Moreover, other happenings militated against them. While the Safaddnese were still strong, a great fleet of ships brought the Mentonese from some far-distant land. They established colonies in the southwesternmost mountains, where the rocks are white and honeycombed with caves. Men say, indeed, that the Mentonese capital, Angmering, lies beneath the ground, though I find that hard to believe!'

'I have heard that also,' Avran commented. 'Yet I cannot say whether it is true. Though we Sandastrians trade with the Mentonese, as do neighbouring realms, we are never permitted to travel to Angmering.'

'Well, it is a matter of small importance. Of greater importance was the fact that, though the Safaddnese sought to drive away those unwelcome newcomers, they failed wholly. Indeed, after many bloody battles, the Safaddnese were forced to treat with the Mentonese — an unprecedented happening. The Mentonese were permitted to trade southward along the coast or eastward into the forests — in those days, there were still people dwelling in the forests — but not northward beyond their own coasts and never into the mountains. Even nowadays, the Mentonese continue to adhere to that treaty. To this very day, they will not send traders into our mountains, though their caravans often cross the grasslands on the mountain skirts. Mayhap, even now, they fear a renewal of war with the Safaddnese. I do not know; the Mentonese keep their own council.'

Toril's voice had become dry from over-use. He took a swig from his goblet and continued: 'Then came the Northmen. When? Oh, almost seven centuries ago, I believe; though, if Tristan did indeed sail with them to Cornwall, their ships must have been travelling

116

even earlier to Rockall. They raided along the coasts, again and again meeting the Safaddnese in battle, sometimes gaining a victory and spoils, sometimes being driven bloodily away. That happened in England also, you say, Simon? And did the Northmen decide, in the end, to settle your land? Ah, indeed! Here, that happened some three hundred years agone; but only in the northwest, where long wet fingers reach from the sea into the lands, providing quiet harbouring for their great ships. Yet the Northmen were contained; they could not outmatch the Mentonese in sea fights, nor could they outfight the Safaddnese on land. Their realm of Norroway survives still, but they have never spread far into the mountains.'

This impressed me greatly. 'They conquered most of England,' I commented ruefully. 'In our churches, men still pray to be spared the fury of the Northmen!'

'Yes, the Safaddnese fought them off, yet the attack was to cost them dearly. While they were engaged with the Mentonese, the northern Sachakkans had risen in revolt against the cruelty of the tazlantenar. The revolt succeeded for a while, but then the tribesmen were defeated and destroyed — destroyed so utterly and mercilessly that, men tell me, the hills west of the Chaluwand remain unpeopled to this day. Yet that terrible retribution did not have the effect that the Safaddnese anticipated. The tribes of the east were not cowed; instead, they were outraged. Their anger was so extreme that it overwhelmed their fears. The surviving Sachakkans rose in the south and the Seleddens and Gadarrans in the north, so that the whole eastern seaboard was aflame with rebellion.

'By that time the Safaddnese were engaged in the west, in their battles with the Northmen. Consequently, the armies sent eastward were weak and made up almost wholly of tazlantenar. Those armies were obliterated by the furious, vengeful tribesmen. Now, if the Safaddnese had marched east, as they had done before . . . But they did not. Afterwards it was easy enough for the Beladnens, a peaceable people and never strong in arms, to drive out their rulers also. And thus the eastern mountains were lost to the Safaddnese.'

'So *that* was how your people gained your freedom.' Avran believed he had perceived the resolution of this history.

Toril Evateng sighed. 'Not so, I fear. When we Reschorese sought, in our turn, to throw off the bonds of their dominion, the Safaddnese themselves came south upon us. I shall not recount to you the whole tale of the bitter fighting that ensued, for it is much too long and soon we must be descending to the hall for our banquet. Let me say simply that, for a century and a half, there was rising upon rising, battle upon battle. After each rising had been suppressed, there were executions and other punishments. Yet, whether because we were closer kin to them or because they dared not obliterate their only remaining source of servants, the Safaddnese never sought to destroy us, as they had destroyed the northern Sachakkans.

'As the years went by, Lantharm and Chaskrand freed themselves, with the aid of the Sachakkans; and then Adira. Next, a betrayal of their masters by some tazlantenar gave a shaky foundation to Kelcestre. That was — oh, three centuries back, maybe.'

Toril paused, gazing into his goblet; against the light from the window, the wine glowed warmly. He drank, then resumed his recounting.

'At about that time, the Christian message was first brought to us over the seas. The Beladnens accepted the Word gladly, for its tidings of peace accorded with their own inclinations. Nor were we Reschorese tardy in accepting the Divine message, ill though it accorded with the beliefs and desires of our Safaddnese masters. Yes, we had our martyrs — many of them.'

Robin made the sign of the Cross and Avran and I did likewise. Toril watched us sympathetically, then continued.

'Not all the mountain peoples responded thus, however. The Sachakkans divided sharply and fought bitterly, father against son and brother against brother, at first with words and later with sword in hand. Most accepted the good message in the end, setting up the Christian realms of Tanswing and Quetalas. The remainder retreated northward to continue their pagan practices under the shield of Seledden protection; they formed new realms in the mountains and on the sea-coast about the old city of Kledstrad. As for the Seleddens and Gadarrans, they cling to their old gods to this very day; though now, I hear, they are united into a single realm which they style Pavonara, "land of the drawn sword".'

Toril paused again to empty his goblet. After wiping his lips with a napkin, he went on: 'Regrettably, the bitter internal warring among the Sachakkans deprived we Reschorese of their support. Yet at the

118

same time the Word of our Saviour was strengthening us, for it made us understand how evil were the gods and the practices of our long-time rulers.

'As the Safaddnese fought ever more desperately and were ever more often defeated, their own religion, which had been merely stern and austere, crumbled into evil. Plunder and rape, hitherto shudderingly eschewed, became a common aftermath of any Safaddnese victory. Their poor Reschorese captives — men and women alike — died lingeringly in frantic offerings to gods that had never hitherto demanded sacrifice. That was a dire time indeed.

'Then came two culminating battles. One was fought not far north of Ingelot, on the east bank of the Mentone; the other over the mountains, in the vale of the Rimbedreth. In both combats, very many lives were forfeited, but from both my forefathers emerged narrowly triumphant. At long last, the Safaddnese were forced to treat with us. They relinquished their claim upon our realms, provided that we in turn undertook not to march further northwards into the lands that had been Safaddnese from the beginning. Boundaries were drawn, to separate our territories for all time. We swore never to cross those boundaries and the Safaddnese swore a matching oath.'

He paused, then eyed us in turn directly before speaking again. 'And you know, my friends, those undertakings have been kept to the letter. In two centuries, no-one, *no-one* has crossed those boundaries.'

We were all astounded at this: even Essa started up in her chair with surprise. It was Avran who voiced our thoughts: 'But surely, you must at least trade with the Safaddnese? There must be some exchanging of goods and news, some bartering, along your frontiers?'

'There is not. Let me assure you, Prince Avran and friends, that the oath taken by my forefathers has not been broken in any particular. During more than two hundred years, we of Reschora and our neighbours of Raffette have had no communication whatsoever with the Safaddnese. Thus I can tell you nothing very precise, nothing very useful about the dangers you may face, for my information about them is gained only from grandfathers' tales.'

Toril was gazing across the table now, not at Avran or me but past us, out through the window, to a horizon rimmed with the last orange light of an already-vanished sun. Yet it seemed to me that he was

119

scanning instead the parchments of his memory. When he spoke again it was in an intermittent flow of words, with many stops and starts, as one recollection prompted another.

'The Safaddnese — they never had a single king, you know. They were ruled by a general council of priests and of lords, from which a war-leader would be chosen at need. He would serve only until the time of need ended or until some failure caused him to be replaced and executed. For those stern people, failure was the greatest of weaknesses and quite beyond condoning.

'Strange people they were, those Safaddnese. All that was important to them came in nines. They had nine gods, each one hostile and merciless, not to be loved but to be appeased. There were nine regions, called *letzestrei*, "ninth-realms". Each letzestre was organized into nine districts. There were nine classes on their social ladder, with the letzahar and his family at top and the tazlantenar and servants occupying the two bottom rungs. There were nine levels of priesthood also, I believe, and nine ranks in their armies. Their predanar, their homes, were always nonagons, nine-sided in plan, while their greatest castles boasted nine towers. The hymns sung in their temples had always nine verses. Even their very laws were codified into groups of nine.

'Let me think now, what were those letzestrei, those nine realms? I am not sure I can recall all the names ... Ah yes, there was Aracundra in the west, hugging the skirts of the greatest of all our peaks, Fereyek Gradakhar, "Mount of Storms". On that mountain, they believed, their greatest god had his palace and entertained the other eight gods; thus Aracundra was their holiest land. Paladra surrounds the shores of a great, black lake, the Asunal Dralehin, "Lake Highshadow". It is more or less northwest of here and it is especially to be avoided, for men say that its people are given to practices of uttermost devilry. Exactly north of Reschora there lie two smaller letzestrei, Darega and Omega. Close though they are, I must confess to having no clear knowledge of them. Though our tales tell of witch-winds and menacing trees, I place no credence in such tales. North of Raffette and Adira lies Desume; its warriors had an especial reputation for ferocity. Beyond Omega and Desume lies Ayan, another land about which I have heard little that is worthy of belief. The other three Safaddnese realms lie along the north

120

coast. Strange names they have: from west to east, Vasanderim, Avakalim, Brelinderim.

'Nine realms, then — and each of them, I doubt not, having its own particular variety of evil. No, I can tell you nothing certain about them, as they are now. However, each was peopled in the past, and must still be peopled, by fierce warriors serving harsh gods that require to be appeased by bloody sacrifices. Take my advice, I beg of you, my friends: turn back or turn aside.'

Toril stopped speaking and toyed a while with his goblet. When he spoke again, his voice was at first gentle.

'However, you must please understand that, if you do elect to travel onward, I shall not strive to hinder you. Your peoples have spoken no oaths to the Safaddnese and are not bound by the oaths sworn by my forefathers.'

He paused, then added grimly: 'Yet, if you do go further into the mountains, I judge that you will never emerge alive from them. Moreover, since you will be entering the very heartland of the nine black gods, I fear also for your immortal souls. If you must pursue your quest for Lyonesse, go there by some other way, my friends. Do not continue on northward, I implore you!'

Chapter Thirteen

A PEACEMAKING AND A LEAVETAKING

After delivering his solemn warning, Toril Evateng would say no more. He rose, to lead us out of the chamber and down the winding stone stairs to the hall, where all was ready for the banquet. In the generous Reschorese fashion, we were lavishly entertained with food, wine and music; there was a timbelanist, I remember, whose playing put my poor efforts to shame. However, it seemed to me that there was an unwonted brittleness to the gaiety. Was it because, in this northernmost Reschorese town, there was still an awareness of the Safaddnese shadow brooding over the mountains, just beyond a frontier that was only a few hours' ride away? Or was it that Toril's words had brought that shadow into my own mind?

My comrades seemed likewise somewhat withdrawn and reflective — all, that is, save Dan Wyert who had not been a part of our discussions. He was full enough of good cheer, and, soon, of good food also. Unfortunately Dan had chosen to sit at a lower table, so we gained little benefit from his high spirits. As for Toril, he knew well that he had given us much on which to ponder. He did not urge us into conversation, nor did he allow others at our table to do so. Instead, he permitted us to tread the paths of our own thoughts.

Next morning, Robin met us at breakfast with the exhortation: 'Today we must decide which route we are to follow, Lady Essa and gentlemen. The day promises sunshine. In this friendly castle, we cannot in courtesy isolate ourselves; to do so would be to risk giving offence. I propose, instead, that we find our veludain and ride up onto the slopes of the Windrench Mountains. That will give us a wider view and the opportunity for unhindered discussion. What do you say?'

All of us assented. For me, at least, the idea had a particular attraction. I had slept poorly and, in my brief sleep, been visited by nightmares: I felt that the fresh winds of the mountains might drive the cloud of foreboding from my mind.

Our veludain, who had been feeding in the riverside meadows, were summoned to meet us at the western gate of Ingelot. After our pleasant and leisurely walk through the little town, we found them waiting, greeted and caressed them, and mounted.

We had all chosen bright raiment that day, perhaps to keep up our own spirits. Avran and I were both wearing our Doriolupata cloaks, freshly laundered and mended and with yellow sides turned outermost; Robin was wearing a pourpoint jacket, cap and hose of maroon velvet that he had purchased in Hasaring; and Dan Wyert was smart in chestnut-brown jupon and hose, with highly decorated boots of hasedu-leather of which he seemed particularly proud.

As for Essa, she was clad in a short dress of azure blue, with full sleeves, tight bodice and skirts short enough to permit her to ride a-straddle. (Indeed, most women in Rockall rode in that fashion; it was so rare to see one riding side-saddle that I had almost forgotten how the Rockalese style had once startled me.) Since our escape from Kradsunar, Essa had allowed her fair hair to grow longer, so that its curls now played about her shoulders, while the blue of her eyes quite matched that of her dress. On this bright morning, I was conscious of how pretty she looked; more than pretty, even beautiful. Fortunately, my love for Ilven was too firm for that consciousness to be distracting.

The ride was at first easy, for the rock mound on which Ingelot had been built declined at only a low angle toward the valley's flank. However, that eastern flank rose up very steeply indeed. The bridle path up the mountainside had all the twistiness of smoke eddying upward on a gusty day.

Briefly I longed to be riding a sevdru again — my beloved White-brow or the noble Yerezinth, now lost, alas! to the Montariotans — and racing confidently up this slope, instead of ascending it so laboriously and slowly. Then I felt ashamed of myself, for disloyalty to poor Proudhorn who was bearing me upward so patiently. At the very thought, I sensed his affection and relief; for, of course, he had been aware of my earlier brief discontent with him. To share thoughts with one's mount can cause difficulties at times!

Below us, the town seemed to shift away and dwindle. From this height, one did not perceive the size of the castle of Ingelot, nor even glimpse the houses huddled within its curtain walls. It looked, indeed, just like one of those toy castles with which young squires are instructed in the arts of fortification and defence. (Motte, bailey and moat; keep, curtain wall and flanking towers; castellation, machicolation and revetment; bastion, rampart and barbican — how those terms had been drummed into me!) I was sure I had never before climbed so high. Was it the height that was causing me to feel so breathless, even though it was Proudhorn who was exerting all the effort in climbing? He, in contrast, did not seem at all discomposed.

We ascended an especially steep place, then at last the slope eased. Strangely, a massive boulder was perched just at the point where the slope changed; a boulder so huge that we were all five able to dismount and climb onto its flat top, then sit there in comfort. Nor did it shift under our weight, even though poised on a precarious-seeming pedestal of rock.

The hour was approaching noon and the Mentone valley becoming occluded by autumnal haze. The veludain moved away upslope to browse on low bushes that grew here and there among the rocks. We were hungry also and were pleased when Dan Wyert produced our food from his pack. There were flat cakes, freshly baked and made sweet by dried berries much like bilberries; slices of cold cooked meat; some hard-stoned fruits that would have seemed like English plums, had they not been scarlet in colour (Robin called them *tetsenar*); and two generous flasks of Reschorese wine.

While we ate and drank, we talked, though only about minor matters, not about the major question that was exercising our minds. Essa, however, sat silent and seemed to be cogitating. When we had finished, she took a deep breath and turned determinedly toward Avran. Her cheeks were flushed and her expression unexpectedly tense. She spoke with the care of one who has rehearsed her words beforehand.

'Prince Avran, it is proper that I should express to you an apology. For too long, I have been bearing you a grudge that you have not

125

merited. You must understand that much of the history that the zahar Toril related to us was known to me already — indeed, had been familiar to me from childhood. My father told me often about the armies from the south, those Southerners who brought war into these mountains and changed them forever. He made me believe that anyone coming from the south must be an enemy; and you came from the south.'

She paused for a moment, then went on doggedly: 'Since you were a prince, I believed you must be some distant scion of that ancient, evil empire. Yes, I knew it had lost much of its power, but I believed it might have persisted in diminished form and might be eager to rise again. Moreover, at first you seemed to me far too eager to fight and to kill, even when there was little need for fighting and none at all for killing. Though, as the weeks went by, I found that was not your mood, I continued to distrust you. I wondered, even, whether you might be using Simon's quest merely as a screen — whether you might be spying out these mountains in readiness for some new invasion.'

Essa stopped a second time, visibly hesitated, then said embarrassedly: 'Yes, I realize that must sound stupid to you, and indeed I *was* stupid. I should have known that, with two such good friends as Simon and Sir Robert, you could not be any harbinger of evil. I recognize now how very unjust I have been to you — that your ancestors, like mine, were sufferers under that Empire of long ago and never willingly a part of it. I understand also that I've been attributing to you emotions that were never your own. I have been foolish and unkind. I am sorry; can you forgive me?'

For the very first time, she smiled at Avran — a tremulous, uncertain sort of smile — and held out her clasped hands to him, in the Rockalese gesture of friendship.

Avran, who was evidently both astonished and deeply moved, took Essa's hands within his own. For a long moment they sustained that grasp, Avran gazing raptly into her eyes. Then Essa drew her hands away and the clasp was broken; yet her smile had taken on a greater warmth.

'Henceforth we may count ourselves friends, then?' she enquired gently.

'Yes indeed!' Avran sounded fervent. 'Of course — of course I

126

will forgive you. After all, there is nothing to forgive. Already I was in your debt, and now . . . '

His voice trailed away, yet he was beaming in such fashion as I had rarely seen, well though I knew him.

'Good; then let us begin our discussion.' Robin spoke briskly; he seemed somewhat embarrassed. 'I am delighted to witness this, er, ending of the strain between the two of you; but really we must proceed to consider other matters. We are all agreed, I think, that we must continue our quest for Lyonesse, especially now that the prospects of discovering it seem so much more encouraging. Has anyone explained that to you, Dan? Ah, Essa has; good! Well then, the question is; shall we head on northward, as we had always intended, or shall we take Toril Evateng's advice? Shall we return back southward to the mountain skirts and then go east to Warringtown, or shall we cross the mountain ridges to Adira? That might indeed be a sound choice. In Garrendevor, they might well know the whereabouts of Lyonesse. If they do not, then we might go on to Warringtown after all! What say you, Simon?'

I had hoped not to be asked to speak first but, now that the ball had been tossed so firmly into my lap, I could not evade responding. Moreover, I had made up my mind already.

'As to turning back southward, I see no purpose in that. If Vedlen Obiran or Dekhemet Arrav had believed we would find an answer in Warringtown, they would have guided our steps eastward, not northward. You must remember also that Vedlen said: "Go to Reschora — go north from Reschora." He did not say: "Go to Adira".'

'That is true,' Robin admitted. 'Yet Vedlen did not know where Lyonesse was to be found. How *could* he direct our path exactly?'

His riposte took me aback. It was Avran who responded, with another question: 'Adira is the northernmost of the Oburnassian realms, is it not? The one farthest into the mountains?'

'Yes, that is correct.'

'And has Vedlen Obiran ever visited it?'

'I think so. Indeed, I'm certain he did, in the months after his wife and child were murdered — or, as he believes, abducted. He was very restless then and he roamed very widely.'

127

'And are the frontiers of Adira just as firmly closed on the northern side as those of Reschora and Raffette?'

'I'm not sure. I have not heard that the Adirans made any such pact with the Safaddnese, but . . . No, I'm not sure.'

'The Safaddnese realm north of Adira is Desume. There is no intercourse whatever between Adira and Desume.'

This flat pronouncement came, unexpectedly, from Essa. She spoke with such serene assurance that none of us questioned it; nor, until much later, did it occur to any of us to wonder how she knew this. As for Avran, it enabled him to press home his argument.

'If that is the case, then there can be no purpose in our heading east to Adira, can there? We would learn nothing more by doing so, and we would waste several months — the whole winter, in fact.'

'You are perfectly right, Avran,' Robin admitted — rather ruefully, I thought. 'Then we ignore Toril's warnings and travel northward?'

I had made my decision about this. 'I shall go on northward,' I said firmly, 'and I believe that Avran will go with me. Indeed, Dekhemet Arrav informed me that Avran and I are bound together, not merely by friendship but also by destiny.'

I paused to look round at my friends. Essa and Avran seemed tranquil enough, but Robin's brow was furrowed and Dan appeared definitely unhappy. It was in a gentler tone that I continued.

'Yet I see no reason why you should feel compelled to travel with us, Robin: and certainly I cannot see any need for you, Essa, or you, Dan, to face further perils without good cause. This land of Reschora seems a very happy one; can you not remain here? Or, if you three have a continuing desire to see new lands, why do you not head east to Garrandevor, the city of whose beauty the zahar Toril speaks so highly? You have faced risks enough in my company: why not instead find ease and peace?'

Surprisingly, it was Essa who responded first. 'I shall go with you, Simon. I wish to see more of these mountains.' She paused, then went on: 'You see, I am not at all afraid of the Safaddnese.'

So strange a note was there in her voice that all of us looked at Essa sharply; but she spoke no more.

After a further pause, Dan Wyert spoke quietly: 'If my mistress Essa goes northward, then I shall go northward also.' He did not sound enthusiastic.

Robin sighed. 'Well, it seems that our decision has been taken. I shall accompany you, of course; but I am far from certain that we are being wise. I pray that God will guard and guide our steps!'

When, on return to Ingelot, we told Toril Evateng of our decision, he sighed and looked distressed but did not try to argue us out of it. Instead, most generously, he undertook to ensure that we were properly prepared for the journey — and for winter in the mountains.

Furriers and tailors were called in, to fit us with pourpoint jackets, gloves and trews made from the fur of some creatures called amerals. Their pelts are essentially white, though with a scattering of black spots that reminded me of the heraldic rendition of 'ermine'. The ermine itself, or stoat as we call it when in its fox-brown summer coat, has black only at the tip of its tail; amerals, in contrast (or so we were told) bear the black spots all the year round, though their summer coats are grey. Otherwise they sound much like stoats, though inhabiting high moors and mountain ridges, not woodlands. Certainly their fur is decorative and makes clothing so warm that, when trying it on, we found ourselves perspiring.

Essa's garb was much like ours, though her jacket was cut to a fuller length. Also like us, she was furnished with light boots lined inside with hasedu-skin, to wear over her own boots. These overboots were fastened by so complicated a system of loops that I needed to be taught the skill, as did Robin and Avran. In contrast, to our surprise and that of the Ingelot bootmaker, Essa fastened hers correctly at first try, without instruction.

In addition, we were each furnished with sleeping-sacks lined with the long hair of rock-conies and given leggings, similarly lined, to slip over and fasten about the cannons and pasterns of our veludain before riding through snow. For the moment, all these items were placed into packs, to be carried by two additional veludain that had been found for us.

We stocked up also with food that might be eaten when hunting failed. All the remaining space in our saddle-packs and those of the two pack-veludain was filled by wrapped stacks of cadarand cakes, packets of dried sindleberries and slices of smoked, spiced meats of several different kinds. The cadarand cakes are of flour made from an acorn-like nut, mixed with honey and fats and covered with a

129

crust of dried rose-hip-like berries. We were to find that, if kept properly wrapped, they stay moist and flavourful for an extraordinarily long time.

Each of us was furnished also with a large flask of beer and a smaller one of efredat, a brandy-like spirit distilled from ground-up cadarand nuts, sindleberries and an aromatic herb that grows on the Mentone's banks. Efredat is clear brown in colour, like peaty water, and has a strange smoky flavour that I did not much like at first sampling. Nor did I ever drink enough to acquire any taste for it, as one does for so many flavours initially considered unpleasant.

Only with extreme difficulty could we persuade Toril to let us pay for our winter clothing and bedding and for the additional veludain and their gear. We were allowed to do so because we were giving the Heradorian gold and silver coins to men from the town, not to his servants or himself. For the food and drink, he would accept nothing. Indeed, I am sure Toril would have preferred to give us everything, so generous was he.

Our equipping took six further days. It was only at the end of the first week of the month that the Sandastrians call Besbalet, the Reschorese Bekkalet and we English October, that we were able to set out northward.

The zahar Toril must, I think, have issued firm orders to his people, to prevent any new warnings from being voiced to us after our return from the perched rock. However, we had been addressed in the intervening days with that uneasy warmth reserved for soldiers about to fight a hopeless battle. When our new friends bade us farewell, it was all too evident that they expected never to see us again — that they believed we were riding, valiantly but foolishly, to our doom.

Possibly Essa was entirely cheerful — I could not tell, for she was adept at concealing her emotions — but certainly we four males left friendly Ingelot with regret and misgiving. My own sense of responsibility pressed heavily upon me in that hour. Though Avran had rallied so strongly to my support, I knew that the decision to go on north had been primarily mine. In that hour of leave-taking, it seemed to me all too probable that Toril's gloomy predictions would be proven right.

Chapter Fourteen

THE GOLDEN BIRD

When I was growing up in Hallamshire, October had been the month I liked best of all. At other seasons, greens or browns were predominant — placid colours, among which the saffron of the stones and muds of the little iron-rich streams or the russet of the coats of the squirrels and foxes seemed to glow like brave flames. In October, the whole landscape seemed to be striving to match their bright tints. The bracken of the moorland slopes took on its own saffron hue and the leaves of the woodland trees were transformed into copper or gold. Those colours had been my favourites, even before I had set eyes on Avran Estantesec's saffron cloak and fallen so deeply in love with his auburn-haired sister.

There were other good reasons. October tended to be a month of sunshine and, in my rainy homeland, that was a rarity and a blessing. The harvest was over and the fruits and crops gathered in; one could run or ride unreprimanded across fields and through orchards. Moreover, apart from tending their beasts, one's elders had few tasks to perform. They were willing to talk to or play with lonely children like me, to sing songs to us or tell us stories. Yes, it had been a happy season.

The month of Bekkalet in northern Rockall had many of the same qualities. We had decided to ride along the Mentone's banks as far as we could, partly because it gave us a line to follow, partly because the Safaddnese, we had been told, lived on the high tops and might not be encountered by the waterside. The meadow grasses remained green, though they had been cropped to shortness by the veludain; but the taller weeds, the low bushes and the few trees growing in sufficiently sheltered spots above flood level had all taken on autumnal fire, their leaves flame-yellow, reddish brown or russet. The grey hides of the grazing veludain looked not so very different from those of Peakland sheep and the whistles and calls of their herds were much like those of English shepherds. Only the high lines of the mountains to west and east — the Ferekar Dralehenar and the Ferekar Uvahanir — proclaimed clearly that this was not England.

To make matters better during our first few days after setting forth from Ingelot, the sun shone brightly upon us and the sky was of a bright blue, with only a few floating pennants of cloud.

Moreover, we were not yet at the northern border of Reschora. There was a much-used road following the river's left bank, so that we were repeatedly cheered by encounters with other travellers, intent upon their own business and unaware of ours. Two more nights were spent enjoying generous hospitality in hilltop predin whose owners assumed, without enquiry, that we must be going no farther than the northern marges of their land. Nor, now, need we invite curiosity and arouse dismay by enquiring about Lyonesse and the lands to the north.

However, we noticed differences from southern Reschora. These predin were more carefully positioned in secure places and more elaborately embattled, while the travellers we met were more heavily armed. Even after two centuries, the people living here knew themselves to be frontiersmen and potentially at peril. The pressure of apprehension of the Safaddnese might have dwindled to a featherweight, yet it was still felt.

It was early afternoon on the third day since leaving Ingelot that we crossed Reschora's northern frontier. There was no mistaking it. Hitherto, the road along which we had ridden had paralleled the river edge pretty closely, though keeping about five poles away to avoid marshy patches. North of Ingelot, it had ceased to be paved. Even so, tributary streams were still crossed by stepping-stones, suitably positioned for veludain hooves, or sometimes by clapper bridges. At the frontier, however, the road swung sharply eastward and steeply uphill, becoming a flight of shallow rock-cut steps that ascended the mountainside until it passed out of view.

There was a drystone wall blocking our path, without stile or gate: not a defensive structure, this, but more like the limestone or gritstone walls with which Pennine farmers mark the limits of their lands. A large board had been erected at the point where the road

132

turned away from the river. Though ancient and affected by the weather of countless seasons, it stood sturdily yet; the painted words on it had been touched up freshly. They read bleakly '*Daliipel Rescheren. Lakhash rukhen*' — 'Boundary of Reschora. No crossing.'

We stopped our veludain and looked at one another uncertainly. Robin took a deep breath, then expelled it slowly. 'No crossing', he repeated. 'And yet, cross we must.'

He dismounted and, walking up to the wall, peered over; it rose no higher than his chest.

'There is no road beyond,' he announced. 'The weeds are growing quite tall; no beasts can have been grazed there for many years. There is a narrow track, though; an animal track of some sort. The wall is in good repair and seems to become higher to our right; there are no gaps in it. We might easily climb it, but our veludain cannot. Let us instead ride down to the river and see whether we can pass the wall's end.'

He remounted Browntail and led us down, parallel to the wall, to the water's edge. The river was low and, as we splashed past the wall's outer stones — it ended in very massive blocks, solid and heavy enough to withstand most spring floods — we found that the water was no more than pastern-deep.

As Robin had observed, while there were pastures for veludain south of the frontier, north of it there was merely a wilderness of unkempt land. We were now in the Safaddnese letzestre of Darega. Omega, that other letzestre whose name echoed so ominously the last letter of the Greek alphabet, lay on the further, right bank of the still-broad Mentone.

If the people of Darega needed to be advised against crossing the frontier, it was not evident. There was no warning placard on this northern side; nor was there any least indication that anyone had ventured close to the boundary during recent decades. The dense growth of tall weeds and bushes against the wall made it evident that all recent repairs had been done from the southern, Reschorese side.

We found the track quickly enough, but it proved frustratingly difficult to follow. It wove so elaborately among weeds and under bushes that it must have been made by animals no taller than hares. Perhaps the trackmakers were aquatic creatures; certainly, at one point, we disturbed without sighting some animal that fled squealing

133

away, to plunge splashily into the river. Though we crossed several broader paths, they were of no use to us, for they were directed toward the river and made by creatures coming down from the hill-slopes to drink.

Eventually, after seventy minutes or so of laboriously following that tiresome path, Avran became exasperated. 'This is ridiculous,' he said. 'It has taken us more than an hour to travel a league. We can't waste our time and energy like this; we must find a better way.'

Without more ado, he set Highback plunging obliquely across the overgrown meads toward the mountain-skirts. After a glance at each other, the rest of us followed.

Suddenly Avran checked Highback and dismounted, stooping to draw something out from among the deep growth of plants. As we came up to him, he lifted it high to show to us — a worn and weathered human skull, its crown cleft through, presumably by an axe-stroke. Then Avran bent again and, when he straightened, he held in his other hand a deeply corroded spear.

'We have chanced upon a battlefield,' he said. 'Look about you; there are many bones and the remains of quite a few weapons, all among these bushes. See there, the skeleton of some beast — a veludu, I think. And there, a rusting helmet. And over there; was that not a sword, before the long seasons ate it away? That must have been a mighty combat, when so many warriors and beasts were slain.'

Obediently we gazed about us. The ground here was gravelly, with a poor soil, even so close to the river, and the cover of plants not particularly dense. Among them were an abundance of yellowed bones, many tumbled and rusted helmets and, surprisingly, many decayed swords, spears and axes. Evidently so great a number of warriors had died here that the survivors had not even striven to recover their armour and weapons. A rusty-brown spider's-web was all that remained of a chain-mail tunic, whilst an ancient breast-plate was so deeply corroded that Proudhorn set a hoof right through it.

'Perhaps this was where that last, bitter battle was fought between the Reschorese rebels and their former Safaddnese masters,' I speculated. 'Did not the zahar Toril say it took place somewhere north of Ingelot?'

'Yes, that's so,' Avran responded. 'I believe you must be right.'

Essa had dismounted from Stripenose and was gazing quietly about her. Suddenly she gave a little cry and, dropping to her knees, delved among the plant roots. As she rose, she was blowing the dust from something held in her cupped left hand. Her face was flushed with pleasure.

'See here,' she said. 'Is this not beautiful?'

Lifting it carefully with her right fingers and then gripping it between both hands, she held up for our inspection a loose-linked chain that, though much discoloured, must surely be of silver. From this there hung a pendant in the shape of a bird in the position which heralds call 'displayed, wings inverted' — a bird looking to the right, with spread wings whose tips drooped downward.

Yet this was not one of the usual heraldic birds — not an erne, not a falcon, not even a peacock or a pelican. Rather it resembled a crane, for its bill was spear-like; but its neck was too short, and its tail too long, for any crane. It had been fashioned in gold, with two tiny blue gems for eyes. Even after so many years of exposure to wind and rain, the gold and jewels still glittered brightly in the sunshine.

Seeing our interest and puzzlement, Essa smiled. 'It is a taron,' she said, 'a bird that haunts the northern coasts of Rockall and plunges boldly even into the stormiest waters in quest for fish. Or so I have been told; I have never seen one, nor even seen the sea. This must have been worn by some great person among the Safaddnese, for the rulers of one of the letzestrei — Avakalim or Brelinderim, I am not sure which — used the taron as their exclusive emblem. I am sure *this* was not left deliberately on the battlefield.'

'How do you know these things?' Avran demanded surprisedly. 'Toril Evateng told us little about the letzestrei; how did you learn what their emblems were?'

'Oh, my father taught me much,' she answered dismissively.

Taking back the pendant into her left hand and producing a small cloth from her sleeve, Essa breathed on and polished the chain until it gleamed. Then, satisfied, she placed the loop of the chain over her head and, shaking back her hair, settled it until the golden bird shone at the centre of the halter-neck of her brown surcoat. Thus adorned, Essa smiled at us, clearly inviting our admiration. Indeed, the pendant gave a touch of royalty to her humble garb.

135

'Is that wise?' Avran asked doubtfully. 'That bird — it is an emblem of a people who fell into evil. It may prove an ill omen . . . Yet it looks well on you, I must confess.'

'It looks well,' she responded lightly. 'Let that be reason enough for my wearing it. Shall we proceed on our way, gentlemen?'

Without further ado she remounted Stripenose who, at her thought, began ambling slowly away from us, along the line that Avran had chosen. Avran started after her immediately, as did Dan Wyert. But Robin, who had hitherto said nothing, lingered and spoke quietly, I think more to himself than to me.

'Lady Essa keeps her own counsel. That she is more than a mere wench from a camp of robbers has long been evident; and indeed, she has confessed to being the daughter of a physician and chirurgeon, though of her mother, and indeed of her parents' origins, she has told us nothing at all. I respect her profoundly, but I speculate much about her.'

In another moment, at his master's desire, Browntail began following the other veludain. As Proudhorn and I did likewise, I had something new to ponder about. Well, at least it served to expel the cloud of apprehension from my mind for a while.

As we rode, I think we were all watching out for other valuable or interesting trouvailles among the relics of the battle — relics no longer grim, for the passage of the years and the overgrowth of flowers and weeds had reduced their poignancy. However, we found nothing more. Indeed, within a few hundred yards the gravels were left behind. The ground became marshy, with a tussocky growth of wetland grasses and reeds that obscured from our view any other remnants of that combat. Essa and Avran, who were riding alongside one another now and conversing cheerfully, swung their mounts more steeply upslope to avoid the mud.

The wet ground did not extend far; it ended against a narrow, high ridge traversing the meads and climbing up the valley side. On surmounting this ridge, our three friends paused to allow us to catch up. Avran had dismounted and was gazing about him doubtfully.

'I might be wrong, but — is this not the remains of a great wall? The stones are almost overgrown, but they seem very square. Surely they must have been mason's work?'

Robin dismounted also and, brushing away the grasses that had overgrown one of the stones, prised it from its place and lifted it up for our inspection. Avran was quite right; indeed, it had been shaped so crudely and hastily that the chisel-marks were clearly evident.

'This must have been a mighty wall, to have so broad a foundation,' Robin said thoughtfully. 'Yet the river muds have banked up high against it. The wall must be very ancient. I believe it must have been one of those built by the Southerners to enclose the Safaddnese, and tumbled by the Safaddnese when the ancient Empire was overthrown.'

'Likely enough,' commented Avran. 'In my own land, many structures that were constructed in the time of the Empire stand yet. Whatever their wrongdoings, its people were mighty builders. Maybe this will help us. If there is any road on this side of the valley, it must cross or cut through the wall.'

With Highback following him, Avran strode off briskly up the ridge. Robin remounted and the four of us followed after. By then we were at a considerable distance from the river, the eastern flank of the valley rising steeply before us.

Just before the change of slope, the ridge broadened, then narrowed quite sharply. Avran had stopped and was again looking about him.

'There was a fortification here, I think; see, there are the remains of other walls on this south side. And look there, high on the ridge; was that not once a tower?'

As the ancient wall climbed the valley side, it was less overgrown and its nature more obvious. If one's eye followed it upward, one perceived a sort of stone plinth on the skyline that might have served as base for some defensive work. To identify it as a tower was perhaps presuming too much, yet surely some building had stood there, long ago.

'Mayhap so,' said Robin a little impatiently. 'Yet we are seeking a road; and I think I have discerned one, or what remains of one. See — just where the ridge narrows, at the slope foot — that gouge in the grass? Obviously the road has been long abandoned, yet it may furnish us with a line to ride along, even now. I wonder why it is no more used? Do the Safaddnese stay only on the high tops in these days, shunning the valleys completely? Have you any ideas, Lady Essa? Did your father tell you anything about this region?'

137

'Nothing of value,' she answered, in the brusquely dismissive tones of one desiring no involvement in a discussion. Robin, thus rebuffed, fell silent.

Indeed, the road had been so long out of use that its course was not easy to follow. North of the old wall, it swung away from the slope foot and back toward the river, just far enough to carry it out of the reach of falling rocks. Nevertheless, the road stayed so close to the slope foot that it would have been hard to watch from above. Perhaps it had been constructed by Southerners fearful of a rock-rolling assault from the heights, perhaps at some later time; who could say? Yet it did provide an easier route for us than we had found among the overgrown meads.

We rode until the sun's last rays were gilding the Mentone's waters far to the south. Eventually, as we were crossing the riverside gully, where the swollen streams of winter had washed the stones of the road away, Robin halted.

'There is clean water here,' he said. 'We are sheltered and those bushes, down toward the river, will provide good fodder for our beasts. We have ridden throughout a long day and have not yet chanced into hazard. If we rest now, we can set forth early in the morning.'

So, for the first time, we sampled the provisions that Toril Evateng had so lavishly furnished. We found them good. Dan Wyert insisted on serving us and on laying out for us the light blankets in which we would sleep. We had each brought with us a flask of the Rescho-rese beer; one would be opened each day till all five were exhausted. Essa's was drunk first, to lighten her load. This beer was made, like efredat, from cadarand nuts and was even less flavourful. Yet some-how, in the open air, it tasted better than it had done in the hall of Ingelot.

Dan had been quiet all day: since crossing the frontier, he had been very nervous. Over the meal, however, he seemed eager to talk, the words pouring out of him faster than the beer from its flask.

I had guessed from his name that Dan's forefathers had travelled to Rockall from England. He confirmed this, but was vague as to which region they had come from. He knew only that it was some-where in the south and that they had fled after some calamitous defeat of their lord in the Wars of the Roses.

Dan had been born in Thraincross, not at that time the royal capital of Herador, though it became so later. His father was a soldier of fortune, his mother a sempstress. There had been five other children. After their father had gone away to fight in some war from which he had never returned, the Wyert family had lived in such dire poverty that the children were always hungry. Dan had begun pilfering food from market stalls and sharing his loot with his brothers and sisters. He had managed this so skilfully that his misdoings passed long unperceived.

Eventually, however, a neighbour had seen him stealing a loaf and had told his mother. She had been bitterly angry. Telling Dan that she wanted no thief in the family, she had expelled him from their home. He had been only ten years old at the time. Even after so many years, that memory distressed him.

After that, Dan's life had been more hazardous but, on the whole, merrier. He had worked as rafenu-boy with a group of travelling merchants, then as mercenary soldier in the little wars of the eastern plains. Some of his stories proved extremely entertaining. Indeed, his lively account of an incident in Camabray, when a drunken officer had collided with a cheesemonger's cart and caused the round cheeses to bounce and roll all over the market-place, was so amusing that it set us all laughing heartily.

The evening was well advanced by then and the gully in deep shadow. We had lit no fire and could see only each other's shapes as we sat among the rocks. Particularly disconcerting was it, therefore, when our laughter was responded to by some creature high above us on the mountainside.

The sound was most unpleasant, higher-pitched than our own laughter and having a frightening, maniacal quality. It so echoed among the crags that we seemed to hear a responsive chorus of grim amusement. Peal upon peal there came, ending in a scream that reverberated hideously among the rocks.

As the last sound died away, Avran spoke sturdily: 'Some sort of bird, I expect. No cause for being afraid, Lady Essa.'

'That was not a bird,' she answered soberly. 'That was the voice of an animal — a tasdavarl. They prowl at night and feed on carrion; I have heard and seen them often about Kradsunar — too often . . .

They are cowardly creatures and will not attack us, with the veludain on guard; yet I do not like them. I think I shall seek my blankets.'

Indeed, that weird laughter had taken the heart out of all of us. Trusting to the watchfulness of our beasts, we all followed Essa's example.

How well the others slept, I do not know. One of them was snoring, but I am not sure whom. For my part I lay long awake, wondering why this land was so empty, wondering about Essa, wondering what would befall us. Not until after midnight did sleep claim me; and even then, those horrible, mocking laughs seemed to ring through my dreams.

Chapter Fifteen

INTO THE WIND-FOREST

It was around noontide next day when we saw the first of the strange trees. The morning had brought more sunshine and a further following of the long-abandoned road beside the Mentone bank. During our ride, we had discovered no other ruins and, indeed, had found no clear indication that this country was still inhabited.

Once we came upon a dozen veludain drinking at the water's edge; but the initial curiosity that caused them to approach our own beasts, and the precipitate manner in which they fled on perceiving us riders, made it evident that those veludain were wild. A larger herd, on the further bank of the Mentone, watched our passing tranquilly from that safe distance. Whether they were domesticated we could not tell, but we saw no herdsmen. Avran thought he had spotted a tumbled tower, far away on the flank of the Highshadow Mountains. However, Robin considered it merely a crag of bare rock protruding through the grassy slope, and we others were not sure. A few birds passing overhead, a few small animals chittering and diving for cover, and a few late flowers to engage the eager attention of Essa were the only other small incidents of that morning.

The ride had been an easy one and ought to have been relaxed and enjoyable; yet, somehow, it was not. Since crossing the frontier from Reschora, we had all known ourselves to be in peril. Moreover, even though Essa had explained it, the mad laughter of the tasdavarl had graven a new pattern of uneasiness into our minds.

Only Essa seemed relaxed that morning. The rest of us were as tense as the strings of a tuned cittern — and as likely to vibrate at any touch. Though we rode closely together, our conversation came only in gusts, dying away quickly into a watchful silence.

One reason for this was that, among the open meads of the valley bottom, we knew ourselves to be so very conspicuous. Yesterday, the valley sides had been convex and the road, hugging the shelter of the slope-foot, must have been virtually invisible from above. Today the slopes had become much more irregular. In places they were still steep, but they were seamed by the hollows and marged by the mounds of centuries of landslides. There were many stream valleys, most of them dry and all of them steep and narrow, and there were many boulders. Some of these had rolled down to, or even across, the road; others were still perched on the valley sides. In such a jumble of ridges, declivities and rocks, anyone seeking to spy from concealment might do so with the greatest ease. In contrast, riders such as we, down below and in motion, would be spotted from a league away.

The rocks themselves were decidedly odd. Brass-coloured they were, and made up of some substance that formed thin, tortuously folded layers. I thought at first that they were formed of some metal ore; not gold, though, for they were not yellow enough. When we halted while Essa examined some flower, I picked up a loose piece and tested it with my fingers, only to find that it flaked easily into thin shards. Not metal, then; but, when I asked my companions what else it might be, none of them knew.

During this stop, one of us had looked upward and noticed that first tree, growing out from behind a boulder halfway up the valley side. Next we saw a thicket of such trees, in the shelter of a landslip hollow high above us. As we rode on northward, we began to see more and more of them, until there was a continuous frith along the lower slopes and spreading downward ever closer to the road.

The valley of the upper Mentone had not hitherto proved rich in trees. Apart from those planted about and within the little Reschorese towns, for shelter, as orchards, or to furnish fodder for hasedain and sevdreyen, we had seen very few. All of those few had been growing close to the river in some sheltered place. Small trees they had been, with brown bark and oval, serrated leaves much like those of an English alder, but of less height and with longer branches. Nothing very odd about them!

These trees, however, were utterly different from any I had seen. From a distance, they looked rather like short-stemmed toadstools,

142

for they had very round trunks and flat, broad tops that appeared scaly. The colour of the foliage seemed at first glance to be pale green. However, as we saw them more closely, we saw that it was of quite a deep green, but lavishly flecked with light brown and yellow.

When we saw a tree at close quarters, it proved even stranger than we had anticipated. All of us stopped upon impulse to examine it. The trunk was thick and the bark very smooth, smoother even than that of a beech and of a much darker hue. The branches did not grow out from the trunk at random, as in most trees. Instead, they radiated outward only at three distinct levels. Moreover, they were so arranged that each branch of the lowest group was placed exactly between two branches in the level above and exactly beneath a branch of the third, topmost level.

The lowest circle of branches was about ten feet above the ground; the second about a yard higher up, the topmost another yard higher. There were not many branches at any level; I counted them and found there were exactly nine. Nine branches . . . I recalled uneasily that nine was the sacred number of the Safaddnese. Could these, then, be sacred trees? I hoped not; I had had quite enough of sacred trees!

As for the branches themselves, and the leaves — well, they were even odder. The branches were quite long — disproportionately long, I felt. Each one divided into three and each of those three subsidiary branches separated into three branchlets — nine branchlets, another repetition of that sinister number! The branches were very thick and even the branchlets were quite stout, right up to their tips. There were no twigs and the leaves were without stalks, hanging down directly from the branches and branchlets in an alternating double row.

And such leaves! Very large they were, the size of the pennons one sees at a tournament and showing about the same variation in shape. The majority were long and tapering, like a heraldic standard; a few were swallow-tailed; and a number were short and almost square. Their colour varied also. The square leaves were almost always dark green, the green of an oak-leaf; but the long leaves were sometimes pale green at the base, shading to a darker green, and sometimes dark green at the base, changing to brown or even to yellow. The swallow-tailed leaves always had yellow or brown tips.

143

It was the leaves that gave the trees their scaly appearance, when seen from a distance; and only from a distance did they seem of uniform colour. As for fruit or seeds, I did not see any, on this tree or on any of the other trees we saw later.

My companions examined the tree with equal wonderment. It was Dan Wyert who was first to comment: 'Weird sort of vegetable, isn't it? Yet I won't say that I like it. Seems almost evil, doesn't it, masters?'

'In all the lands that I've travelled, I've never seen such a tree,' Robin marvelled. 'Have you heard of these trees, Essa? Can you give them a name?'

Essa hesitated. 'I'm not sure . . . No, I don't believe so. My father spoke of "wind-forests", but I do not remember him naming the trees that grow in them.'

'As to the wind-forest — why, mayhap it lies ahead.' Robin was pointing. 'Do you not see how, up the valley, the woodland is coming right down to the river? Well, that will hide us from prying eyes, but I'm not sure I fancy entering such a forest . . . It is time that we ate, anyway. Why should we not eat here?'

So we did. Though we were well into October, the sun was hot in the valley and the tree, odd though it might be, at least furnished some shade. Avran chose to set his back against its trunk. However, when he leaned restfully against it, the trunk moved a little, thick though it was, and the leaves rustled overhead as if disturbed by a light wind gust.

Surprisedly my friend rose and, bracing himself, pushed hard against the trunk. It bent backward and there was a distinct fluttering of the leaves, as pennons flutter when shaken. When Avran relaxed his pressure, the trunk returned to position.

'Curious!' said my friend. 'I would not have thought so thick a trunk could be so flexible. I should imagine the branches might make excellent bows.'

'Oh, come now, Avran!' I scoffed. 'You'll never make a bowyer. You might use the branchlets for a children's bow, perhaps, or to make a small bow for bird-hunting — but never a long-bow! It would bend much too readily; your arrows would travel no distance at all! And consider the thickness; would you truly be able to hold so stout a bow as those branches would make?'

In the ensuing argument about bowmanship and the properties of

144

woods, our meal was consumed and our unease about the tree forgotten. However, that unease returned when, an hour or so later, we rode into the forest.

At first the trees were spaced apart, with patches of grasses and taller plants between them, and the line of the road was easy to follow: but then the trees closed together. Not that their branches ever overlapped or entangled, as do those of trees in any ordinary forest. Instead, each tree seemed so spaced that the tips of its branchlets just avoided touching those of the next.

In between the canopies of neighbouring trees, enough sunlight penetrated to allow a narrow line of grasses and plants to grow (though mostly these looked rather pale and sickly). In the larger space between the circular canopies of each three or four adjacent taller trees, one or more saplings might be growing, their serried branches dividing only once and directed upward, as if praying for more light and space. The regular arrangement of the trees suggested an orchard, not a forest — that these trees had not grown naturally, but had been planted.

Under the trees there was deep shade and a coolness at first welcome, but soon rather chilling. No lesser plants grew beneath the circle of branches, but there was an accumulation of dead leaves. As we rode along, striving with increasing difficulty to follow the line of the road, I noticed that these dead leaves, though much curled, were always chevron-shaped or triangular. Whenever Proudhorn trod on one, there was a puff, as if of dust.

Why, these trees must shed in autumn, not their whole leaves, but their leaf-tips or corners! Pale green when young, the leaves must darken with age, as did other leaves, and eventually turn to brown or yellow. As for the seeds, why, they must form in those leaf-tips, just before they were shed!

I caught up with Avran and Essa — they were, as usual nowadays, riding together — and explained to them my deduction. Essa was interested and told me she was sure I must be right. Avran was entirely unresponsive; he seemed even to resent my joining them, for he scowled and said nothing. I wondered at this and presumed he must be particularly disliking the forest.

Robin and Dan were further ahead, while the two pack-veludain were lagging behind. Suddenly I was aware that all the veludain were listening intently. Yes, there was a crashing sound in the forest some way ahead of us, as if some great creature was forcing its way through the trees. If so, it was not coming towards us, for the sound faded away into silence.

Silence. Yes, that was the trouble with this forest — or one of the troubles; it was too silent. There was little wind that day but, out in the open heathland, there had been at least a few wafts of air beside the river and, always, the sound of the waters flowing. Here there were no such zephyrs and, even though the Mentone must be close by, we could no longer hear the river.

Moreover, quite soon we had to admit that we had lost the road entirely; it had been disused too long, too long overgrown by the forest. For an hour more we wove our irregular way northward, guided largely by the slope of the land. Then Avran, ever impatient, said: 'We're wasting time again! Let's ride down to the river edge and get out from among these accursed trees!'

The idea seemed good but, unfortunately, it could not be carried out. As we rode toward the Mentone, we found ourselves entering a maze of fallen and rotted trunks — trees killed, no doubt, by past floods — upon which tall, strangely coloured fungi flourished and through which both trees and saplings grew uninhibitedly upward. It was a struggle for our veludain to find any way through this tangle. Many times, we riders had to duck our heads as our beasts leapt over the fallen trees or brushed against decaying branches. When at last we had ferretted our way through, it was only to discover that the river was edged by marshes. So we had to turn back.

Nor was our second attempt to find a route any more successful. This time we sought a way along the valley side, above the forest. However, the trees grew very high on the slopes and, beyond the tree-line, the rocks were too steep to be ascended even by a veludu. Moreover, remembering the altitudinal preferences of the Safaddnese, we were not eager to adventure up into the mountains, even had that been possible. Consequently, we turned back downhill.

During our descent Robin's veludu, Browntail, slipped on a loose stone and cannoned against a tree-trunk. Immediately some large bird that had been roosting in the branches exploded into flight, its screams of alarm echoing through the trees.

By then we were becoming accustomed to the silence; consequently, we were all greatly startled. Indeed, the two pack-veludain bucketed past us downslope in a panic. Fortunately, when we reached the slope-foot, we found them waiting for us, safe and sound in a sunny place where a stream cascaded down from the heights.

Robin stopped also. 'Browntail has suffered a shaking and we've both had enough of travelling for today,' he announced rather brusquely; he had not enjoyed our riverward and upslope adventurings. 'The light is beginning to go and, in this forest, we may not easily chance on another stream. I believe we should pass our night here. Agreed?'

All of us were hot and perspiring by then — save perhaps Essa, who seemed always cool. The prospect of a refreshing wash in the stream waters was so attractive that we concurred readily with Robin's proposal. Soon Dan Wyert was unloading the pack-veludain, while we others unsaddled our beasts and spread our blankets.

Fodder for the veludain proved something of a problem. Like sevdreyen and rafneyen, veludain will not eat fallen leaves. Eventually Avran found a young tree whose lowest branches were just within his reach. Its leaves proved surprisingly tough; they could not be pulled off easily and had to be torn off by main force. Yet, most tiresomely, our beasts refused to eat even these green leaves. Instead they fed inadequately from what meagre grasses they could find around the stream, for they seemed reluctant to venture away from us into the forest.

As for us, we ate well enough; but it was an uneasy evening. While the last light was fading, we heard again the sound of some great creature crashing about among the trees, not very far from us. However, it did not approach nearer and none of us felt tempted to investigate.

Just after that noise had died away and darkness had fallen, there came the sound of a great flock of birds passing overhead, down from the mountains into the forest. They called cacophonously to each other in flight, after the fashion of rooks but in even harsher voices. On settling into the trees, they fell silent.

That night we found little to say to one another and sought our blankets early. As we were doing so, suddenly we heard again the high-pitched, insane-sounding laughter of a prowling tasdavarl. This

147

time, however, the beast was not responding to our laughter and, most certainly, its own voice evoked in us no amusement.

As I strove to find sleep, I was grateful for the cheerful tinkling of the little stream. I believe it soothed me, for I slept placidly and dreamlessly till morning.

Perhaps because the east side of the valley remained late in shadow, all of us slept longer than we had planned. We awoke to find the veludain uneasy and, when we were breakfasted and mounted, reluctant to move out from the stream valley into the forest.

Yet it was a bright morning and, by the time we rode forth, there were dusty shafts of sunshine striking down between the deep shade of the trees. Ahead of us, indeed, there seemed to be some sort of glade or clearing into which the sun was shining brightly. Almost automatically, we headed in that direction.

When we reached the place, we were all disconcerted. This was not a clearing. Instead, it was an area where some great creature, or creatures, had been feeding. Branches had been pulled down and stripped of their leaves; branchlets had been torn off. In the soft, smooth bark there were many deep scratch marks. Beneath the trees, the humus had been disturbed. In the patches of bare earth, there were the impressions of great, clawed feet.

Chapter Sixteen

THE CREATURES IN THE GLADE

'What can have been feeding here?' I asked, awed. 'Some mighty monster, surely. Might it have been a dragon?'

'I have never understood that dragons ate leaves,' Robin responded pensively. 'Mind you, I've never encountered any dragons, save in the art of heralds! And as for that, I cannot recall having been ever told what dragons *do* feed on! In all the stories one hears, they spend much of their time curled up with the loot of gold and jewels they've collected; and they cannot eat such indigestible items. Moreover, even when a dragon does manage to kill the odd knight, it might toast him with its hot breath but it does not usually devour him.'

'A dragon was slain quite close to my home in Hallamshire,' I remembered. 'At a place called Wantley near Rotherham, by Sir More of More-Hall. They say it ate trees; but they say also that it ate houses and churches, which sound to me even more indigestible.'

Avran laughed. 'Well, maybe you have dragons in Hallamshire, but I've never heard tell of any in Rockall — save, as Robin says, in the art of heralds. Moreover, as you mentioned, Robin, dragons are supposed to have fiery breath. These branches may be bent and broken, but none of them is charred. I cannot believe it was a dragon, I'm afraid, Simon.'

'Yet wyverns and griffins, they don't have fiery breath,' I argued. 'What else could have clawed feet, and yet be so huge? Some gigantic bird? What do you think, Lady Essa? Have you heard reports of any such creatures, here in these mountains?'

She was smiling at me. 'Not I. All the tales of dragon-slaying I have heard were set in some distant place — your own England, or the land of the Paynims, or the marches of the Holy Land itself.

149

Never in Rockall. Neither have I heard, Simon, that we have griffins or wyverns in these mountains, nor yet any gigantic birds. Yet mayhap I can guess what beasts were here . . . Mayhap . . . ' Her voice trailed away into silence.

'Tell us what you guess,' pleaded Avran. 'Some very perilous creature?'

'Any creature so large is likely to prove perilous,' she responded logically. 'But no, I shall not tell you my thought, for I am far from sure.'

Since we had found already how fruitless such endeavours were, none of us strove to persuade Essa to speak. Instead, we set off again. The tracks of the creatures, if there had been more than one — I could not be sure — led away westward toward the river. For our part, we headed on northward.

Keeping close to the slope-foot and with the sun behind us, we encountered no problems in finding our way. Moreover, with the undergrowth so extremely sparse and these strange trees shedding only a part of their leaves, the riding was easy enough; there was only an occasional fallen tree or root-hole to be avoided.

Why, then, was that ride so trying to one's nerves and temper? Partly, I think, because of our endless weaving around tree-trunks; partly because, when one was on veludu-back, the lowest leaves hung only just above one's head, seeming to press down upon one like an unduly low green ceiling; and partly because of the sheer monotony of the trees themselves.

I had loved to ride through English woodlands in sunshine, because of the countless small surprises presented by each new view. There are so many kinds of trees, all growing in close proximity. There is such a variety of ground cover; one might see the tall grace of foxgloves, the broad-spreading docks and spiky plantains, the fierce furriness of stinging-nettles, the bogus ferocity of dead-nettles and, in sunny spots, the curly-topped sprouts of bracken. There are squirrels chattering rebukes from the branches overhead, jays flying off with disapproving cackles, and the rippling songs or strident alarm-notes of a multitude of smaller birds.

In this forest, all those things were lacking. Yesterday it had reminded me of an orchard. However, even though all might have been planted at the same time, each plum or apple tree takes on its own character as the years pass — a different twist to its branches, a different gnarling of its trunk, a different manner in which its twigs and leaves have grown. Not only were these trees all of the same type but also, with the exception of the few saplings, they seemed all of about the same size. Their branches all divided in the same fashion and spread out to the same degree; and, though the leaves did vary, it was in a limited variety, endlessly repeated.

Perhaps, in the summer, there might have been insect noises — the militant hum of gnats, the fierce buzz of wasps or the drowsier drone of bees, the ticking of beetles or the shrill stridulations of grasshoppers — but the season was too late for such sounds and there seemed to be no birds or small animals. Instead, all was as quiet as in an empty church on a sunny day. There was only the rustle of veludu hooves among the few fallen leaves, a susurration no louder than one's steps cause among the rushes strewn on a church floor.

This quietness was so oppressive as to forbid speech. Dan Wyert was as dolefully silent as a mute at a funeral; Robin seemed impenetrably wrapped in the cloak of his own thoughts; and even Avran, riding again beside Essa, was finding nothing to say to her. We were all waiting for the sound that must surely come, to shatter this stifling silence and plunge us into new perils.

When that sound did come, it was not directly ahead of us, but some way over to our left, toward the river. So curious a noise was it that I find it hard to describe — somewhere between a scrape, a crunch and a rasp; rather as if someone were tearing a thin sheet of wood with huge metal pincers. The noise ceased for a while, then resumed. There was a creaking of branches also. As we rode onward, we heard a third sound — a steady soughing, like a strong wind blowing through a hole in a shutter.

We halted our veludain and looked at one another enquiringly. 'It is off our path, whatever it be,' Robin said quietly. 'We can pass on by.'

'Not I!' announced Essa. 'I propose to discover what the creature is.' She slid adroitly down from her saddle and stood beside Stripe-nose, listening intently.

'If you're going to look, then so shall I.' Avran dismounted rather

151

less adroitly from Highback, then ruffled his veludu's ears before going to stand by Essa.

'And I.' My curiosity was too urgent, after so much speculation about the great, clawed beasts, to permit me to remain behind.

Robin sighed. 'I believe we may be placing our lives foolishly at hazard — but so be it!' He dismounted also, then asked: 'Dan, would you stay with the veludain? Keep alert; we may need to flee from here at speed.'

I smiled to myself. Even if he disapproved of it, Robin would not miss the chance of an adventure! However, when he urged Avran and me to string our bows and take with us our quivers, we both recognized his wisdom and did as he bade.

Essa waited impatiently while we armed ourselves, then set off swiftly through the trees. I was at her heels, while Avran and Robin followed more slowly; they knew themselves to be less skilled than me at tracking and stalking. However, I believe they were as surprised as was I at Essa's confidence and evident pathfinding skill. Yet, if one avoided the drifts of dead leaves and took care, in choosing one's line, to use the tree-trunks as shield from the view of the creature ahead, it was not hard to move quietly and speedily through this forest.

I held my long-bow almost horizontally in my left hand as I went along, in the fashion of an English poacher. Though excited, I was also profoundly apprehensive and several times caressed my sword-hilt with my other hand. Would it be a dragon or wyvern, an oliphant or a griffin that we would see? Could we indeed hope to view it, without being discovered ourselves? And, if it did see and attack us, would we be able to slay it before it slew us? Recalling stories of the ferocity of such creatures, I felt disposed to turn back. Yet how could I, with Essa ranging ahead of me so fearlessly?

Suddenly she stopped and, gesturing to me to do likewise, dropped onto hands and knees. She wormed cautiously forward till she was able to look out from the shelter of a tree-trunk. It would not form enough cover for two, but there was that rarity, a fallen tree, just a little to her left. I made my careful way to this and, hands on its trunk, gazed into the glade ahead.

No, this also was not a natural glade; instead, like the other, it was a place where beasts had been feeding. Had been feeding?

Rather, were still feeding! Huge though they were, I did not see them at first, so dark were their hides and so deep the shade under the trees.

No, these were not of the dragon tribe, nor were they oliphants. They were beasts of a sort I had never seen depicted by heralds or heard described by story-tellers, beasts so queer that, as I looked at them, I felt the small hairs at the nape of my neck rising.

At first glance, they seemed like huge horses. At second look, however, they were something much stranger — nightmares, maybe? Their heads were long, small-eyed, small-eared and really very horse-like, while their bodies were almost equally horse-like, with a mane at the neck and a plumed tail.

Yet there was something altogether wrong about their proportions. Their front limbs were much longer than their hind limbs, so that their bodies sloped backward in a wholly unnatural fashion — or so it seemed to me. The front limbs, though so long, had more or less the shape and proportions of those of a horse; the short hind limbs, however, were much thicker and more solid. And, whilst a horse's limbs end decently in hooves, each foot of these bizarre creatures sprouted three massive, divergent claws.

At first, I noticed only three of the creatures. Two, by their size, were adults; the third was smaller and young. (I cannot, even now, bring myself to call it a foal!) As I watched, one of the adults reared up on its pillar-like hind limbs and, pulling a branch downward, began to feed. As its front teeth clipped off the thick, pennon-like leaves and its back teeth masticated them before swallowing, I heard again that strange sound we had first noticed — the wood-tearing sound.

Then I heard also that windy soughing, though not from one of the three beasts at which I was gazing: it came from higher. Looking upward, I perceived a fourth beast of the same kind, another young one, lying upon a stout tree-branch rather closer to us. Its head was thrown back and its mouth widely open as it wailed. I saw flattened front teeth, sloping forward and chisel-edged, that would act like clippers when brought together; and I began to understand how those tough leaves might be sheared through. Its back teeth I could not see properly, but they appeared more massive than those of any horse.

153

By then, Robin and Avran had joined me in the shelter of the fallen tree. Robin was well placed to obtain as good a view as mine, but Avran was not: he was positioned behind the tree's crown and his view was blocked by broken, decaying branches. In order to see better, he pulled himself upward, using the base of a thick branch as support. Well and good; but then he placed a knee on the trunk to lever himself higher.

That proved a mistake. We had all thought the trunk to be solidly resting on the forest floor, but it was not. As Avran moved and the balance of his weight altered, suddenly it shifted.

Robin and I fell flat as our support moved away; but Avran was caught off balance and thrown forward. He tumbled down in a heap, to be pinioned beneath the rolling trunk in full view of the huge horse-like creatures.

For a moment they remained frozen in startlement. Then the creature that had been feeding dropped onto all fours, making as it did so a loud, unpleasant noise, like a mighty, roaring yawn. Thereupon it and its equally massive mate advanced upon my helpless friend.

When they reached him, the first beast reared up above him. Again it gave that strange roaring yawn, towering over him and looking down on him with eyes bleakly red, like some mad stallion. The huge claws on its front feet were opening and closing convulsively.

Neither Robin nor I were able immediately to aid Avran. When he fell, Robin's cloak had become impaled upon a broken branch; he was struggling to free himself. My long-bow had become trapped beneath the trunk. After a vain attempt to free it, I reached instead for my sword. Though, being no St George, I had little faith in my ability to defend my friend, I was determined at least to strive to do so.

However, it was Essa who saved the situation — and in an extraordinary fashion. Leaping suddenly out from behind her treetrunk, she ran toward the great beasts, her hands clutching her cloak and flapping it about her head. As she ran, she screamed at them: 'Run away, you silly creatures!'

To my blank astonishment, they *did* run away! The beast that had been rearing up over Avran half-turned and flopped down onto all fours. Then, with hooting whinnies of fear, it and its mate lumbered off in panic flight. The younger beast that had been on the ground was already running away, lurching and snorting in fear.

Seeing itself apparently deserted, the fourth creature leapt down from its branch. It crashed through the leaves and, landing heavily, fled noisily after the others. There was a prolonged thudding of heavy feet, eventually dying away into silence.

Essa had halted and was laughing more heartily than I had ever seen her. Robin and I straightened, eyed one another rather shamefacedly, then began laughing also. Even Avran, though still trapped beneath the tree, was chuckling. That sudden transition of the beasts from menacing nightmares to panic-stricken buffoons was surely a reason both for amusement and joy in deliverance.

Indeed, we had fared better than we deserved. The tree-trunk was soon rolled back; its surprising lightness accounted for the ease with which it had moved. Avran was found to have suffered nothing worse than scrapes on hands and knees. Neither of our long-bows was damaged and, though Robin's cloak had been torn by the jagged branch, the tear was easily repaired later by needle and thread.

When Avran had risen from the ground, he hugged Essa delightedly and asked her: 'That was splendid! But however came you to suppose that such huge creatures might be so readily scared away?'

She was still quivering with amusement. 'Was it not hilarious?' she gasped. 'Such vast creatures, and yet so very cowardly! When I saw the claw-marks, I guessed right. My father had told me about *udreyen*: he had said that, though huge, they were timorous — that it was not hard to frighten them. And how — how very right he was!'

She dissolved again into laughter, in which we all joined.

The arrival of a worried Dan Wyert, riding Longshank and with the other veludain following behind, and the uncomprehending astonishment with which he contemplated our merriment, set us all laughing afresh. It was, indeed, some time before we were even able to explain to Dan what had transpired. Though he smiled politely, it was clear that he could not comprehend why we were so much amused. But then, he had not witnessed that sudden transformation!

Since this was a sunnier place than most in the forest, we ate our midday repast there. While we were eating, Essa recounted what little she knew concerning the udru and its ways. It was an animal

155

living only in the wind-forests and, she thought, the only creature able to devour and digest the leaves of the wind-trees. It lived alone or in family groups, never in herds. Though so large, it was truly dangerous only at mating season, in the spring; at all other times, it preferred to flee rather than to fight. Its meat was not good to eat and it was not hunted. Its only natural enemies were a large cat-like animal with immense, sickle-like canine teeth, called a *branath*, and some creatures called *xakathei*, which came down from the mountains in packs to invade the forests in the winter.

Thus ended my hopes of viewing a monster of the dragon kind; and, though I was destined to encounter many other strange beasts, I have never yet seen even a griffin or a wyvern. Avran and Essa were right; though such creatures may, for all I know, be encountered widely in this world, they are not to be found in Rockall.

Chapter Seventeen

The Wail of the Wind

'Simon, Simon, wake up! Something strange has transpired — something very strange! This forest — I believe it is bewitched!'

Though Avran was shaking me, it was not so much that action as the alarm in his voice that jerked me into wakefulness. When I opened my eyes and looked about me, I realized what he meant and felt equally disquieted.

We had ridden long yesterday, until the evening was well advanced. Though we had traversed two dry stream gullies, we had discovered no running water; and, in the end, we had settled down for the night in an arbitrarily chosen place, beneath the green canopy of a large wind-tree. We had felt no least breath of air that evening and the forest had been oppressively quiet. Before going to sleep, I had heard no sounds of birds or beasts; even my companions had been lying still and silent.

Now, all was different. It was as if we had been plunged suddenly from summer into winter. A bitter wind was blowing from the north. The branches overhead were moving apart and together, forward and backward, like seaweed fronds in a rising tide. But their leaves — *where were their leaves?* The green canopy was gone; I was looking up through a shifting framework of bare branches into a bleakly grey sky.

Why, if the leaves had fallen, I ought to have been covered by them — blanketed with leaves, like the lost children in the story who fell asleep in the wood! But I was not. As Avran straightened, I sat up hastily and looked around. Apart from a few brown, decayed relics of earlier years, there was nothing; not a single freshly fallen leaf was to be seen.

I turned a scared face to Avran. 'The trees . . . Their leaves . . . Whatever can have happened?'

His face was grim. 'Ask me not, friend — I don't know. I have no answer, nor has Robin.'

'And Essa? She seems to know most about these mountains.' Then I saw she was standing a little behind my friend, her cloak wrapped about her.

'I do not comprehend this either, Simon. When I was young, my interest was in beasts. My father told me many stories about the udreyen and other creatures, but he spoke little about trees. I do not think this is witchcraft, but I cannot explain it. And listen to the wind; is not its sound strange?'

Indeed it was. I had heard winds a-plenty, moaning among Hallam-shire crags or howling across Yorkshire moorlands, whistling between tightly-packed houses in towns or sighing about castle turrets, but I had heard nothing like this wind. Nor did its note resemble the noise with which the wizard had stricken fear into the hearts of Casimir's men. How, then, shall I describe the sound? Like the throbbing screech of a barn-owl, maybe, heard not close by but at some dis-tance; and never relapsing into silence, but only rising and falling, rising and falling. It was a most uneasy modulation, to which the rustles and creaks of the branches furnished an unpleasing counter-point.

I was rolling up my blankets — on that journey, with its perceived dangers, we took off only our cloaks before seeking slumber — when Robin joined us.

'I don't like this wind, friends. As for the veludain, they are hating it. Dan Wyert is striving to pacify them, but they are very restless. We must eat swiftly and be on our way, to see whether we can discover some way of escape from the trap of this forest.'

None of us had much heart for breakfast. Moreover, when our packs were loaded, we realized we could not hope to ride. The lowest boughs had been only just over our heads when we were on veludu-back, even yesterday when the air was so still. Today the motion of the branches was so great that, if we had mounted, we would have been swept swiftly from our saddles.

Well, we had at least one advantage. Had we been riding horses, we would have been obliged to hold on to their reins and lead, or

158

even tug, them along. There was no need for that with veludain; they would follow us upon mental instruction, however unwillingly.

I had considered the two previous days of riding through the forest unenjoyable, hating the silence and the sense of being shut in; but soon I was looking back upon those days almost with regret. This was much worse, this trudging beneath a low ceiling of tossing, writhing branches, with head and shoulders swathed in one's cloak, more for protection than for warmth. The veludain, as they followed us, held their heads low so that their horns might not be caught in the swirl of the boughs; they were indeed most unhappy. And always, above the hissing and groaning of the trees, there was that whining, throbbing whistle, becoming louder, more continuous and harder to endure as the wind strengthened to a half-gale.

Robin led the way and at his heels was Browntail, that brown tail twitching uneasily. Avran was walking with Essa; he seemed disposed to put his arm protectively about her, but she would not allow that. Highback and Stripenose followed them side by side. Dan Wyert and I likewise kept pace together; Dan seemed to be suffering especially from the wind, for he was shivering inside his cloak and not at all inclined to talk. Longshank and the two pack-veludain came next, while Proudhorn had dropped to the rear. That was the position of danger — as, somehow, I knew — in a travelling herd of wild veludain and the one always taken up by its leader. Yet, though my veludu was at his most watchful, I sensed in him no specific apprehension, just the general unhappiness that was oppressing us all.

And so the march went on, hour upon hour. I had wondered if the leaves lost from the trees might have been somehow blown into hollows, but I saw no such accumulations. In any case, the idea was ridiculous; how could green, fresh leaves have been blown away, when so many old, dry leaves were still lying undisturbed on the forest floor? I had wondered also whether some leaves might remain on the branches — just a few, on some trees. No, all were gone. The mystery of this, and the steadily waxing howl of that dreadful wind, did nothing to allay my apprehension.

Nor could we see any way of escaping from the forest. It was harder than ever to follow any line through the trees. The Mentone valley ran north-north-east, but the wind was coming exactly from

159

the north, so that its buffets hit us obliquely. This affected our sense of direction; again and again we strayed past the break of slope onto ground slanting sharply enough to be awkward to traverse. On each such occasion, when we looked upward through the dancing mesh-work of branches, the valley sides proved much too steep to be ascended. Indeed, they were topped by cliffs so nearly vertical as to be entirely daunting.

No, we could not escape that way. Perhaps there might have been open meadowland beside the Mentone's waters but, after our earlier experience, we were not confident enough to chance any second foray in that direction either.

Robin had spoken of the forest as a trap; increasingly it was seeming so. One had the sense that one was trudging, trudging vainly; that one was making no progress, expending effort to no purpose. When I considered the matter dispassionately, I knew that the trees we were passing must be different from those we had passed earlier, from those beneath which we had been encamped. Yet they did not look different — and, in that wind, it was hard to be dispassionate about any matter.

Every so often we passed a sapling, its obliquely-directed branches seeming to leap back and forth, back and forth like a sword-dancer's feet at a fair, or a fallen tree shifting to and fro in the gusts, like a weed in flowing water. Such sights were welcome, for they formed reference points to be reached, passed and left behind. Temporarily, one had a sense of progress. Otherwise, nothing changed.

Nothing, that is, save the sound of the wind. The whining whistle to which I had awakened had altered into a cacophony of separate noises, each having its own pattern and pitch. It was as if there were some demonic consort of shawms and curtals in the sky, striving to produce, not harmony, but the most extreme dissonance. To continue forward was ever more of an effort. The urge to turn and flee, in blind quest for shelter and quiet, was becoming almost insupportable.

Dan Wyert turned a desperate countenance to me: he was very pale and looked his full age. 'Must we go on, Master Simon? That noise — it's getting worse and worse, the further we progress.'

'I don't like it either, Dan: but where would we turn back to? We have passed no refuge. Mayhap, if we go on, we'll find a way out of this forest.'

He grunted depressedly. 'Wind-forest, Mistress Essa called it. I wondered why, at the time. Well, now I know. Windy indeed it is — a witches' wind, a Devil's wind!'

I strove to be cheerful. 'You know, Dan, I'm beginning to comprehend why the Safaddnese prefer the mountain-tops. At least, they avoid these trees!'

He did not respond to my feeble attempt at levity. 'Avoid them? Are you sure they didn't *plant* them, to snare strangers like us? And Master Simon, did you ever traverse a forest without finding some sign that there'd been fires? Mayhap not everywhere nor recent, but in a few areas at least and from a few years back — where lightning had struck? Yes, just so. Well then, have you noticed any signs of burning in *this* forest?'

Now that the point was put to me, I realized Dan was right; and how odd it was! 'No, Dan, I haven't.'

'An unnatural place, it is. Proper unnatural.'

He relapsed into silence; but indeed I am not sure I would have heard him, had he continued to speak. The wind was turning into a full gale, the ululation of spectral instruments becoming ever more discordant, ever more disconcerting. I found myself plugging my ears with my knuckles, in vain attempt to keep out that sound.

Looking ahead, I saw that Essa had swathed her head in a shawl fetched out from the pack-saddle, while Avran was closing his ears with clasped arms. Robin had already passed from view.

Progressively I became conscious that the ground underfoot was sloping upward; some spur from the mountains must be reaching down into the valley. Well, maybe it would furnish us with a route out of the forest. But the noise — why, it was becoming almost unendurable! Dan Wyert was staggering along in a half-crouch, with elbows forward and hands covering ears; and, as for the veludain, I could feel their deep alarm. Yet, faithful creatures, they did not turn tail even now.

Belatedly I realized something else, something more surprising. Why, we were again on a road. Could it be the same road, rediscovered after many leagues?

As we mounted the rise, I saw boulders protruding up through the forest loam in places; and then low crags, like irregular, overgrown shelves. Once again the rocks were strange-looking; in these

161

northern mountains, there was never a decent gritstone, limestone or shale to be seen. These rocks were red — an unpleasing red, the colour of drying blood — but containing convoluted layers of a dark, storm-sky blue. Some sort of granite, I presumed; a peculiar, sinister sort, fitted to this peculiar, sinister place.

Though wind-trees had rooted among those rocks, the road itself was now quite free of them. Was this just chance, or was it being maintained? Had any saplings or seedlings been removed by some human or unhuman hand?

The terrible pressure of sound — that blast of a grotesque aerial orchestra — into which we were ascending inhibited clear thought. Nevertheless, I contrived to look about me with reasonable care. However, apart from the new tracks of my companions, I saw never a sign of recent human or animal presence.

Then Dan Wyert grasped my sleeve urgently and pointed ahead. At first glance, I thought I saw cliffs barring our path; but then I realized that, in the grey light, the lack of shadows had misled me. I was looking at a great stairway cut into the rock. The steps were broad and low, well suited to veludain. And above — could that be some great wall, with only a narrow passageway through it? Was this some castle that we were approaching?

If so, then it was a veritable castle of the winds. Their caterwauling, with ear-drilling harmonies and growling dissonances, had reached a volume that was truly appalling. We seemed, as we climbed, to be pushing forward into a yielding barrier of noise, to be inclosed and battered mercilessly by sheer, intolerable din.

Perhaps I would have turned tail, left to myself; and I know that Dan Wyert and the veludain were climbing the stairs wholly against their will. To this day, I do not know why the beasts did not flee. Their trust in us must have been great indeed.

As for me, it was only my awareness that my companions were ahead that persuaded me on upward. Avran and Essa, with their veludain, were a dozen steps higher than me — a long way, it seemed, in that terrible cacophony. As for Robin — why, he and Browntail were already almost at the top!

A brief gleam of brightness against the dark rock told me that Robin had drawn his sword. Why was that? It was so hard to respond to any sight, to be even interested, so great was the pressure of sound

162

upon one's brain. Robin — his sword — did he perceive some danger? Dully I gazed upward, though I did not cease mechanically mounting the steps.

That wall ahead of us; its outline against the sky was odd — like the upper half of an octagon, almost, but with an extra elevation in the middle, just above the passageway. Moreover, it was perforated by many other holes — arrow-slits, maybe, for use by defending archers or spearmen? But if so, why were they so variable in size and outline? And did I see carvings on the wall — reliefs of strange animals and birds, words formed in that curious, angular Northern Rockalese alphabet?

Oh, if only that noise would cease! Under its unrelenting pressure, I could scarcely think. Even my eyes seemed not to be working as they should.

The light was brighter now, for we were above the tops of the trees, with bare rock on either side of the steps. In that archway, that central opening against the northern sky — surely I perceived a human figure? Was the guardian of this wall some mighty warrior? Or was he an enchanter, ready to destroy utterly we presumptuous adventurers, whom even his weapon of sound had not driven back? Certainly he was huge, a giant!

Yet, up ahead of us, Robin was advancing upon him without hesitation. Why, he had lowered his sword! Had enchantment so worked upon him that he could not even fight?

Those terrifying gale-caterwaulings were becoming still louder; I would have thought it impossible, but it was happening. If my friend was in peril, I must aid him; I must mount the stairs faster, I must pull out my own sword! Yet each step, each pressing forward into that wall of noise, was such an effort . . .

Avran and Essa were still ahead, still climbing upward together. Why was Avran not drawing *his* weapon? Why was Essa not moving back, to allow him freedom to fight? Were they also succumbing to enchantment?

Another upward step and yet another. Then, as I looked ahead, I realized why Robin had lowered his sword, why my other companions were not readying for combat. Yes, the guardian of that tunnel was gigantic indeed; but he was not human — he was carven, a statue!

My three friends had gone forward and were gathered about him.

163

Three more upward steps remained to be climbed; two; one — and I was myself walking along the flat passage that led through the rock wall.

As I did so the frightful, multi-throated wailing of the gale diminished sharply in volume. Four more forward paces, deeper into the shelter of the tunnel, and all that was left of that appalling cacophony was a deep-throated roaring, sufficiently low-pitched as to be perfectly bearable.

Thankfully I removed my knuckles from my ears. That was better, though my poor ears were still ringing and throbbing. I wrinkled up my face and swallowed effortlessly, then advanced to join my companions. Each of them was relaxing now, though the effects of prolonged strain were evident on all three faces.

'See the king of the wind-castle, Simon!' Avran said. He was trying to smile; yet there were fresh lines of tension on his forehead and cheeks. He slapped the left leg of the statue casually as he spoke.

Quite evidently, Essa did not approve of this levity. 'He is a god, not a king. This is the image of Daltharimbar, one of the nine gods of the Safaddnese — the god of the winds and the skies. He is the special deity of the people of Darega. Treat him with respect, I urge you.'

Avran was evidently startled; as, for that matter, was I. 'How did you know his name, Lady Essa?'

'I did not know it; I read it.' She was impatient. 'Do you not see the words carven on this wind-wall? They are writ in large enough letters! *Ksatashazen Daltharimbarem, vlatel Daregaengim, vlatel letzestrerim; zhatash Daregaengim, zhatash letzestrerim.*'

She intoned the words sonorously, almost reverently. Despite the steady roar of the gale, despite the throbbing of my own maltreated eardrums, I could detect that special note in her voice.

'I think I understand, though the language is not Reschorese,' Robin was speaking. "Praise to Daltharimbar; he who is the charge of the men of Darega, of the seventh letzestre; he who rules the men of Darega, the seventh letzestre." Have I it right?'

'Near enough.' Essa sounded almost indifferent; she seemed in an odd mood.

'Yet how did you know he is god of the winds, for these northerners

164

who do not accept the tidings of the true God? Did the inscription tell you that also?'

She laughed shortly. 'Why, are not the winds singing to him? Is this not a wind-temple, made to enable them to sing to him? When the wind blows, every opening in this rock wall chants in its own voice, all in honour of Daltharimbar!'

Avran winced. 'Yes, I heard their songs of praise; my whole head is still ringing with them. I cannot say, though, that I enjoyed it.'

She laughed again, almost derisively. 'Who are you, a mere man, to expect to enjoy hymns sung to a god of the mountains? You are in his realm now, at his mercy and that of his people. Take care, man of the south! Take great care!'

At this, my friend's face took on a stubborn look. 'I am a follower of Christ, not of any pagan diety — any mere god of stone. Daltharimbar is not alive; he is merely a carving. Why need I have any fear of him?'

Essa looked at him strangely. 'Perhaps you see only a carving. Yet, if your God enters into bread and wine in your communions, as your priests aver, cannot a god of the mountains enter, at will, into a statue of his own self? Gaze now upon Daltharimbar! Is he not mighty?'

Certainly the statue was impressive, a massive figure in kingly garb, with elaborately decorated tunic and baldric. Though its feet rested on the flatness of the passage through the rock, at the level of our own feet, the figure was so huge that even Avran could scarce have reached up to its sword-belt. For indeed, it sported a carven scabbard, from which the hilt of a mighty sword protruded. On its other flank was carven a device like a catapult, while upon its chest there hung a pipe of many reeds. Was that pipe supposed, when blown, to produce the winds? Was the catapult-like weapon conceived as propelling lightning bolts?

Then I looked further upward and was shocked. I have said 'it', 'its' — and rightly so. Daltharimbar had nothing of the look of a man; rather, he was a demon! He was prick-eared and horned at the brow like a bull. His head and cheeks, where hair and beard should have been, were covered instead by scales. And his hands — why, they were scaled also and ninc-fingered, each finger ending in a curving claw.

165

Essa was laughing yet again, as if delighted. She seemed almost fey, her eyes bright, her cheeks flushed. 'Is he not handsome and splendid?'

'No, he is not.' Avran was angry. 'He is bestial and hideous. He deserves to be cast down and this wailing wall of his to be destroyed.'

Essa's face changed in a moment from that weird hilarity to something close to black fury. I think Avran might have received the bitterest of responses. However, at that moment, there came a distraction.

We had all forgotten Dan Wyert. Now, at last, he had attained the top of the steps. He had been no longer walking up them, but crawling. As he reached the passage, he fell forward onto his face.

None of us had witnessed his arrival or his fall; we were not looking that way and the continuing grumble of the wind masked the small sound. Instead, we were alerted by Longshank. The veludu had followed his master into the tunnel and now stood over him, nuzzling him. It was Longshank's alarm and dismay that we sensed and, sensing it, turned about.

As we gazed and hesitated, the other three veludain came up into the tunnel and ranged themselves about the fallen body of our companion.

Chapter Eighteen

BACK TO THE WIND-FOREST

In a moment, Essa's mood altered from extreme wrath to profound contrition. She ran to her fallen servant, turned him over gently and knelt beside him, placing her ear against his chest.

As we joined the veludain in a circle about them, Essa straightened. 'His heart beats but faintly. Pass me a flask of efredat — quickly, please! Thank you, Simon. Now you must aid me by moving him further into the passage, away from the wind-noises. Good; that should serve. Sir Robert, would you dampen a cloth and hand it to me, please?'

Robin's beer-flask had been long since emptied and refilled with stream-water. While he obliged, Essa parted Dan's lips with her fingers and dribbled some of the efredat into his mouth. His face twitched and he swallowed. Setting aside the efredat flask, Essa took the moistened cloth and laid it across Dan's forehead. Then she began rhythmically to massage the back of his head and his neck with her strong fingers.

'Give Dan another taste of the efredat,' she ordered me.

As, leaning over her, I did so, Dan swallowed again, shuddered and opened his eyes.

'Strong stuff, that, Master Simon,' he gasped. 'Still, 'tis warming.' Then, becoming aware of Essa's ministrations, he shifted uneasily and tried to sit up. 'No cause for that, Mistress Essa. I'll be right enough in just a minute.'

'Lie still and be easy, Dan. Yes, you'll recover soon enough; but you must stay still and relax awhile.'

She continued her massaging; and, indeed, it was making the old man seem better, moment by moment. His cheeks had been as white as a linen napkin, but already they were regaining a little colour.

'That wind,' he murmured. 'It came nigh to finishing me. And those steps.'

I felt wretched. 'It was my fault, Dan. I should have stayed by you, not left you behind. I was not thinking straight.'

Essa glanced at me and smiled. 'Do not feel any guilt, Simon. Not one of us was thinking straight. When Daltharimbar's pipes are sounding loud, they can drive a man — or a woman — to distraction. I above all should have remembered Dan, but I did not. Yet he was courageous and climbed the steps, even without our aid. He will survive the ordeal well enough — will you not, Dan?'

'Aye, to be sure I will. But is this not a draughty drain of a place? Might we not go through to the other side? And I mislike the appearance of yond stone warrior; cannot we pass by him?'

'That is Daltharimbar and this is his hall,' she answered solemnly. 'Yet I believe we should indeed move on, to discover what lies beyond his temple. Sir Robert and Simon, can you aid Dan in rising and help him to walk?'

We managed this well enough. With Essa staying solicitously beside us and Avran, ignored and very much out of countenance, stalking behind, we set off northward through the tunnel. The veludain, following in the rear, were now in much better spirits and carried their heads high again.

The passage was level and evidently carefully engineered, with walls exactly vertical and ceiling forming a smooth curve high overhead. When we passed the statue of the god, Dan seemed about to make some remark but, catching Robin's eye, said nothing. Nor did any of us speak: and, as for Avran, he kept his eyes averted. Essa, however, bobbed her head, as if making a discreet obeisance.

Up to that point, the walls had been unadorned. Beyond it, however, they were graven with the images of men walking toward the god in solemn procession. Some appeared to be priests; they were tall, long-haired and long-robed, their heads lowered and their hands held together before them, with fingers directed downward, in what was doubtless some gesture of religious symbolism. Others were certainly warriors; they were equally tall, with heads held high and right hands on sword-hilts. Yet others were shorter and broader; they appeared to be serving-men, for their garments were coarsely cut and they were carrying bundles. The faces were not standardized;

each seemed to depict some particular human model. All were shown in groups of nine — three priests, three warriors, three servants. Angular Reschorese-style characters had been graven in the walls beneath the figures, but I did not attempt to read what was written. As for Essa, she seemed to be concentrating all her attention on Dan Wyert.

The noise of the wind diminished further as we progressed. Soon the grumbling mutter was replaced by a gusty soughing, no different from the normal sound of a gale in a narrow place. However, the wind was blowing as strongly as ever and felt now much colder.

Quite evidently, Dan was finding this hard to endure. His pace was slackening and, as I helped him along, I could feel his shivers. Indeed, we were all lowering our heads and hunching our shoulders as we went forward.

Abruptly, Essa halted us. 'Why are we enduring this chill?' she asked. 'Have we not good fur jackets in our packs? Dan needs his, and his gloves also; would you fetch them out for him, please, Simon? And I intend to put mine on. You gentlemen must suit yourselves.'

The suggestion was clearly so sensible that we all adopted it. Dan, though expostulating feebly concerning this new service to him, was stripped of his tan-coloured cloak and decorated boots and clad anew in the ameral jacket and gloves and the hasedu-skin-lined boots. Then we others sought our own packs and got out our own ameral jackets. However, we did not change boots and only Essa put on her gloves.

The benefit was immediate. Dan's shivering ceased and he gained more colour in his cheeks, while the rest of us felt much warmer. Though no words were spoken, I am sure that each of us was blessing the zahar Toril for his forethought.

The distance to the further end of the tunnel was not long, but it was far enough, since each step meant a fresh thrust forward against the force of the wind. I had thought Avran might lead the way, but he would not; he was still in too morose a mood. Instead, it was Essa who walked before us. I wondered if she would find another stairway on the northern side and, if so, how we might contrive to convey Dan down it.

In that mighty gale, the final few steps involved as much effort as if we had been wading chest-deep against the flow of a river. How-

169

ever, at last, we emerged from the tunnel, to look breathlessly out upon the landscape beyond.

It was at once a relief and a disappointment. There were no stairs to be faced, only a relatively gentle slope dipping away before us, covered with tufty grass that had been turned brown by autumn. Away over to our right was the broad Mentone. Some small distance northward, however, a spur of land separated two contributary streams; which of these was the Mentone proper, none of us knew. To west and northwest rose the mighty wall of the Ferekar Dralehenar, the Highshadow Mountains; on this grey day, they were shadowy indeed. Over to our right, the line of the Ferekar Uvahanir, the Windrench Mountains, continued unbroken. 'Windrench' seemed the proper name for them; had we not been drenched in wind all day? If this was indeed the realm of Daltharimbar, I liked it not at all.

As for signs of human habitation or cultivation, there were none. Instead, filling the whole valley on both banks and on the promontory between the converging rivers, there was a tossing, greyish-brown flood of leafless tree-tops — wind-trees once more.

Robin groaned. 'Must we again enter the wind-forest, then? I had hoped we had seen the last of it.'

'A vain hope, I fear, Sir Robert.' Essa sounded perfectly composed now. 'Yet I think we should move downslope ere we discuss our plans. The wind is positively funnelling into this entrance to the temple, doubtless in eagerness to meet its lord.'

At these words, Avran sighed exasperatedly. Fortunately, Essa ignored him and we others did not comment. Instead, we set off again downward.

With each step away from the tunnel mouth, progress became easier. However, we had almost reached the shore of that sea of trees before we felt able to stop and turn about, in a place where a great rock afforded some shelter from the gale. Thankfully Sir Robert and I lowered Dan into a place where he might sit in its lee; he had long since become a wearisome burden for us. Equally thankfully, Dan settled himself and almost immediately shut his eyes. Within minutes he was sleeping the deep slumber of utter exhaustion.

The ridge, with the wind-temple crowning it, could be seen once again before us, but now we were on its northern side and blessedly

170

spared the dreadful dissonances of that terrible wind-orchestra. The whole rock face was covered with elaborate carvings and inscriptions, with the phrase that Essa had quoted — yes, now that I had heard the words, I was just about able to read it — writ largest of all, in a curve above the tunnel entrance. Immediately over that inscription was an emblem of pan-pipes set upon an unsheathed sword, its blade directed obliquely upward; the badge of Darega, I presumed. From downslope and in this poor light, the many slots through the rock that generated the wind-noises could not be seen; even the passage we had traversed was not readily perceived.

The question was, could we ascend onto the mountain-tops from this ridge or must we again endure the monotony of the wind-forest? (We could not go·back; that, at least, was clear.) Surely there must be some path down from the mountains, by which Daltharimbar's worshippers might come from their high homes to offer him reverence? Yet the ridge on whose slope we were sitting did not extend upward very far and, to our left as we looked southward, the forbidding cliffs of the Ferekar Uvahanir showed no interruption.

While Robin and I were discussing this problem — Essa was sitting relaxedly with eyes closed, though evidently awake, and the veludain were feeding eagerly from the grass tufts — Avran rose impatiently to his feet.

'Stay you here, friends,' he said. 'I shall go to see.' Without waiting for any answer, he strode off uphill.

The afternoon had advanced two full hours before he returned. By then Robin, Essa and I had eaten and, after leaving Dan asleep for half that time and wakening him with difficulty, had induced him to eat also. Avran's report was brief.

'There was a stairway up the mountainside, but it has been destroyed by rock or snow slides — and not so very long ago, I would judge. It is unclimbable now, probably for men and certainly for veludain. There is no escape that way.'

Robin sighed. 'Then I fear we must indeed venture again among the wind-trees, though the prospect affords me no joy.'

We others acquiesced reluctantly in that decision. After Avran had eaten a hasty repast, we summoned our veludain. We mounted and continued down toward the forest, hastened by a spattering of raindrops that stung our cheeks as we rode.

171

Avran, still restless and ill at ease, took the lead and made it evident that he desired no company. Robin and I rode together behind him. Essa stayed alongside Dan, talking cheerfully to him to keep up his spirits, while the two pack-veludain came last.

I am sure that all of us, beasts and humans alike, re-entered the wind-forest with profound trepidation. We had to dismount before doing so, for the bare branches were still in turbulent motion in the strong tide of the gale. If there was any road, we saw no sign of it. Once again, therefore, we strove to keep to a line by following the break of slope at the mountain foot. However, this proved even less easy than before. There had been many rock-falls and landslides, recent or ancient, and we were again and again diverted toward the river.

There must have been many more udreyen on this northern side of the wind-temple. Often we noticed their great footprints in the forest humus; several times we crossed glades where they had fed; and on two occasions, groups of them were sufficiently close by for us to hear, even over the surfbreak-roar of the gale, the sounds of their crashing progress through the wind-trees. I speculated aloud why they should be more abundant here; and Robin glanced at me amusedly.

'I suspect, Simon, that they don't much enjoy those, er, wind-hymns we endured this morning. Winds from the north must be much commoner here than winds from the south, you know. Conceivably the udreyen are worshippers of Daltharimbar — Lady Essa might be able to instruct us on that point — but somehow I doubt it!'

If she overheard Robin's words, Essa made no response. Probably she did not, for she was a few paces behind us. For my part, I chuckled — for the very first time that day. Even though we were back in the forest, becoming ever wearier and still fighting the wind, the normalcy of its voice meant that we were all comparatively light-hearted — except Avran, that is.

Yet it was Avran who found for us our night's lodging — a semicircular wall of stones, so entirely overgrown by mosses and lichens that it seemed a place of welcome greenness amid the brown bleakness of leafless branches and bare trunks. What it had been, none of us could guess; not a fortification, for its walls were not massive and there were no earthworks about it.

In its shelter we ate our evening meal, organized for us by Essa, for she insisted that Dan should rest. Indeed, he settled so quickly into his sleeping-sack that it proved difficult even to awaken him for his meal. After eating and drinking only a little, he relapsed into slumber.

As darkness fell, the wind began at last to subside. We could hear distant sounds made by feeding udreyen, but they held no terrors for us now, especially when our line of veludain was guarding the open, southern flank of the ruin. (They were relatively contented, for they had fed well on weeds that had rooted within its walls.) Robin, Essa and I conversed a little but Avran, finding himself still ignored by Essa, was sulky and unresponsive. Then we rolled ourselves in our cloaks — the fur jackets had been returned to our packs — and sought slumber.

I think my companions found it more swiftly than did I, from the regularity of their breathing. Though for a while wakeful, I was in good spirits; the passing of the wind-temple seemed to have exorcised much of the evil from the forest.

Moreover, the motion of the branches had almost ceased as the wind dropped. Its failing breaths seemed to be producing a quiet, crackling sound, like the successive unrolling of many parchments in some great scriptorium. That sound was not alarming the veludain and did not alarm me. Instead, it soothed me to sleep and sent me back in dreams to the turret room in Sheffield Castle, where I had practised my letters under the stern eye of Lord Furnival's chaplain.

It was, I thought, his raised voice in reprimand that awakened me. But I was wrong; I had been roused by Avran's cry of astonishment.

'Robin, have you looked forth and seen the wind-trees? Why, they're in full leaf again!'

I threw aside my cloak and joined Robin and Avran at the gap between the ruin's walls, looking out into the forest. Yes, it was true. On that calm, bright morning, with the blue of the sky overhead masked only by a few unravelled streamers of cloud, there had been a mystic shift back to summer. Every tree branch was hung again with those thick, pennon-shaped leaves, of green sometimes shading to brown. The moss-grown ruin was no longer a haven of greenness

173

within a wilderness of bare boughs, but merely a more virent place in a general viridescence.

'I said it yesterday and I say it again today; this forest is enchanted.' Avran's tone was portentous. 'I wonder what new hazards we face today — what new tricks the gods of these mountains are going to play on us?'

'Yet I had understood that you did not believe in those gods, Prince Avran!' Essa had joined us, looking as fresh as a newly opened cornflower in her dress of blue — a dress she had not worn since leaving Ingelot. The golden taron shone upon her breast. 'If such gods do not exist, how might they work us evil?'

Under this teasing, Avran looked sour. 'Well, mayhap they do not. Nevertheless, there is wizardry or witchery in these trees. Look at them — bare as deep winter last night, yet in full foliage today. Is that not magic enough for you?'

'It is strange, certainly; but I do not consider it to be magic. Yet I confess I cannot explain it.'

Dan Wyert, having slept well and wakening to such bright weather, was in good spirits. He seemed to care not at all about the strangeness of the trees, now that the wind was gone; and certainly he had recovered very well from his collapse of yesterday. However, Essa watched him with a special solicitude, riding with him throughout that day.

She administered no further pin-pricks to Avran, but he remained in difficult spirits and disinclined for conversation. When we set forth — on veludu-back again — he took the lead firmly.

Unfortunately, Avran rode rather too fast and somewhat carelessly. At one time, indeed, he led us so far away from the mountain-foot that we plunged unaware into a glade in which three massive udreyen were feeding. Upon our coming, they turned toward us and two of them reared up on their hindquarters, their claws menacing us.

Highback stopped instantly, but did not strive to flee. As for Avran, he lifted the clarion that hung at his breast and blew a mighty blast. Instantly the udreyen turned about and lumbered off tumultuously.

Avran roared with laughter. Robin, however, was less amused.

'That was not wise, friend,' he rebuked. 'By sounding your horn, you have informed any listeners for leagues about that there are

174

travellers in the forest. Might you not have found some quieter means, as Essa did, for scaring them from our path?'

'Do you believe, then, that there are any ears in this forest to hear me, Robin?' Avran scoffed. 'I do not; at least, I believe we will be heard by no human ears. Have we not ridden for four whole days without seeing sign of any living man — or any woman or child, for that matter?' He looked challengingly at Essa. 'For my part, I believe that, if the Safaddnese lived ever in this land, they are long gone from it.'

She refrained from responding, but Robin said angrily: 'Though there may be no human listeners, you may be alerting to our presence other foes, quite as formidable or even more so. Have you forgotten already the enchantment that, according to your own expressed belief, lies on this forest? Do you consider yourself to be some valorous knight, challenging an ogre to come forth and do battle?'

Instantly, Avran became sober. 'You are right, Robin, and I am sorry. That was indeed foolish of me. I shall not sound the clarion again, unless our need becomes extreme.'

No immediate peril resulted from that horn-blowing; yet, from that moment onward, the weather began again to worsen. The cloud streamers spread and thickened, until they had driven the sun out of the southern sky. A breeze sprang up, a breeze from the north, causing the leaves to tremble. We had dismounted by then to eat our midday repast; this worsening of the weather caused us to finish hastily, don our cloaks and remount, with an aim to making as much progress as possible before the motion of the branches precluded riding.

The forest through which we were making our way was especially dense, with scarcely an interval between the branch-tips of any particular tree and those of the trees about it. As we rode and the sky became greyer, the green roof above our heads darkened and became more opaque.

Only for a while, however. As we continued onward and the wind strengthened, that roof of leaves seemed somehow to be becoming less dense, the glimpses of the sky more frequent. I heard also, amid the growing sound of the wind, that strange, creaky rustling that I had heard before going to sleep fifteen hours earlier. I gazed about me puzzledly — and suddenly I understood.

175

'Look, Robin, look — look overhead!' I cried. 'The leaves — they're curling up! And they're growing smaller — why, they're withdrawing inside the branches!'

Chapter Nineteen

A Bridge and a Tumble

So they were. When the wind began to strengthen, the leaves of the topmost tier must have been drawn within the branches from which they had hung. We had not seen this happen, but we had noticed how the green ceiling over our heads had seemed to lighten. Now, as we watched, leaf after leaf in the middle tier bent at its tip, flexed and then seemed to shorten as it curled back inside the branch. Occasionally a seed-burdened leaf-tip would break off and drift downward to the forest floor.

Before long, we perceived that the leaves of the lowest tier were likewise vanishing from view. After that, the forest looked exactly as bleak and wintry as it had done the morning before — when we had believed the change so wholly unnatural, so evidently a consequence of sorcery!

All too soon, the boughs were once more in vigorous motion in the steadily freshening wind. We had again to dismount and trudge along, our veludain following us with lowered horns.

When next we chanced upon a fallen tree, I paused to break off and examine one of the decaying branches. Why, no wonder the wood was so light! The branch was pierced with many spiral cavities, into each of which a leaf had once withdrawn. When I looked at the trunk, I found that it contained similar pits, extending deep into the wood and oozing a watery sap. On the outside, the openings were not at all conspicuous, looking simply like darker lines on the deep brown bark.

I displayed the broken-off branch to my companions. Robin, Essa and Dan Wyert were much interested; Dan in particular seemed quite relieved to know how the disappearance of the leaves was contrived.

Avran, in contrast, was merely glum. I could understand my friend's mood; he felt he had been foolish in believing the forest enchanted and it irritated him that Essa should have been proven right in questioning that belief. Nor did it help that she was taking as little heed of him as possible. For both of them, the episode in the wind-temple still rankled.

The rest of the day was a steady, tedious passage northward through the forest. The wind never attained the same buffeting strength as on the previous day, but very soon it was hurling raindrops into our faces. As the rain became heavier, the wind slackened and we were able to mount our veludain. Soon thereafter we were hearing again that strange parchment-crisp rustle, as leaves uncurled and emerged from the tree-boughs.

After the green roof had closed back over us, there followed a blessed period when it shielded us from the rain. Alas! that ended all too soon and conditions became worse than before. Not only was rain dripping down upon us from the boughs, but also those huge leaves held and concentrated the water so that it fell down, plop upon us, not in mere drips, but in gobletfuls.

The valley seemed to be narrowing about us as we rode along, for we heard more and more the noise of the turbulent, rain-fed river. On Robin's suggestion, we veered over toward its bank and, encountering neither any tangle of fallen and newly grown trees nor any marshland, reached the waterside without difficulty. Unfortunately, the bank was steep and the river rising in spate; if there had been a path along the river edge, it was submerged already. Moreover, there were now a whole series of brooks flowing vigorously down hitherto dry gulleys from the mountains into the river.

The first of these was discovered with pleasure; both the veludain and we drank eagerly and it was a relief to be able to fill up our flasks. However, the second and the many subsequent streams evoked less enthusiasm. Each was at its widest and deepest where it emptied into the river; each crossing posed a fresh problem. Again and again we were forced upstream, to seek narrow places that we and the veludain might leap or combinations of boulders that would permit a perilous traverse. After a couple of hours of this, we gave up our attempt to follow the riverside and returned instead to our earlier route along the mountain-foot.

178

In late afternoon we encountered a much larger stream, nearly as broad as the main river (was it still the Mentone?) and flowing to join that river from the east. So tumultuously turbulent were this stream's waters that we knew we could neither ford nor swim it. Reluctantly and dismally we rode eastward, seeking for a crossing-place and far from sure that there would be one to find.

Yet discover one we did, and at a distance of only three leagues — a high-arching bridge of stone, connecting a raised and overgrown causeway on the southern side with a ridge of land on the northern. The bridge was evidently very ancient and its eastern parapet had long since collapsed into the river, but it remained broad and other-wise still sturdy. Indeed, its stones had been so carefully and closely set that very few weeds had found root between them.

As we rode thankfully over that bridge, I looked about me for signs of human passage. I saw many claw marks of udreyen, causing me to wonder whether one of those clumsy beasts might have tum-bled the broken parapet; but of veludu hoofmarks or human foot-prints, I saw no sign. Had this land of Darega been wholly forsaken, or was it that the Safaddnese came no more into its valleys?

Avran who, despite his low spirits, was still insistently keeping the lead, paused to propose to us that we spend the night in the shelter of the ridge. However, Robin did not favour this, feeling we should move well away from that possible crossing-point of enemies, animal or human; and we others were too sodden to care much either way. So we rode onward, turning west to skirt that ridge and then heading northward again, for two more dreary hours.

Eventually we did halt, but in a very poor place — in a steep side-valley where a rock overhang and a leaning wind-tree, its roots almost washed out by the vigorous spate-waters of that valley's stream, combined to furnish some sort of shelter. Essa and Dan were allo-cated the only truly dry situations in which to spread their sleeping-sacks. The other three of us, with cloaks spread over our own sleeping sacks, huddled in what minimal shelter we could find and endured the continuing rain throughout a most uncomfortable night.

To start a day well-rested, dry and warm and to end it thoroughly soaked by a downpour is tiresome, but bearable. Far worse is it to begin the day wet, cold and unrested, with the prospect of a ride in continuing rain through a forest that is already thoroughly sodden. Such was our misfortune on that occasion.

Dan Wyert had slept poorly and was in little better state than we three. Though he strove bravely to light a fire beneath the rock overhang, the wet fuel and a perversely gusty draught frustrated him. As for Avran, Robin and me, no amount of foot-stamping and arm-beating could make us sufficiently warm to compensate for the damp-ness of our clothes. We ate a miserable breakfast and, on Robin's suggestion, put on our jackets of ameral fur beneath our wet cloaks before setting forth.

The warmth they furnished was welcome for a while. Exasperat-ingly soon, however, we became much too hot and sweaty. Before we had ridden a couple of leagues, Avran dismounted and bad-temperedly took off both his outer garments, stowing the fur jacket back into his pack and donning anew his wet cloak. I hesitated, then did likewise; and Robin followed our example. His brown woollen cloak from Flanders, lined with linen, had become even more water-soaked than had our double-sided cloaks from Doriolupata, woven as they were from vegetable fibre. (In this green land, we did not dare to turn them about and wear them yellow side outermost.) In consequence, Robin's usual ebullience was decidedly dampened. He had been riding with Dan Wyert, but they had spoken little to one another; and now Dan was busy with the pack-veludain, both of whose saddles required adjustment.

Only Essa was in good spirits, for she at least had slept well. She watched our proceedings with cool amusement, sitting relaxedly on Stripenose and looking, in her tan-coloured hood, cloak and boots, like some huntress newly ridden forth in benign weather. Quite disturbingly beautiful, she seemed to me.

Disturbing, certainly, to Avran. He was still enduring a conflict of emotions, as I knew well. An illogical annoyance at Essa's calm good humour and an exasperated disapproval of what he considered to be her heathen superstitions were warring with his consciousness of her attractions and his urgent desire to resume friendly relations with her.

For her part, Essa was making no attempt to bridge the gap between them. She continued to be formally polite to Avran whenever it became necessary to speak to him, whilst ensuring that such

180

occasions were few. At least she had refrained hitherto from teasing him, a fact for which I was grateful.

For my part, I had been much less disturbed than had Avran by Essa's apparent belief in the nine Safaddnese gods and their power. Was this because I was a less dutiful Christian than Avran? I did not think so. Was it because I was less concerned than he about her opinions? Perhaps so, but I did not believe that explained my attitude either. Rather, it was because her pronouncements in the wind-temple had furnished me with a new, important piece for the mosaic picture I was constructing of Essa — a picture that was still very incomplete.

Robin, I felt, shared my attitude. He had not been at all upset by her outburst — or, for that matter, by Avran's. Instead he was deeply interested, like a chess-player trying to read meaning into some novel gambit by his opponent.

When he remounted, Avran avoided looking at Essa and addressed himself to Robin. 'Will there soon be an end to this accursed wind-forest, think you, or does it stretch onward to eternity?'

Robin's response was equally morose. 'How can I tell? I know as much about these northern lands as you do; that is, nothing! And remember, I was not the one who chose this northward path; I spoke against it.'

This aroused my own ire. 'Yet you did choose to accompany us. You were under no compulsion to do so.'

Robin sighed. 'Aye, that is undeniable. It is true also that I have been too long a wanderer, guided only by my own whims. You must forgive me if, sometimes, I find it irksome to follow a furrow that another has ploughed.'

Avran uttered a short bark of laughter. 'A furrow, indeed! This valley is a mighty one, and a damnably tiresome and dismal one! Yet it is long since it has been ploughed — if ever it was. This is an unhuman land, suited only to udreyen — and maybe to wind-gods, if they chance to exist. It is no fit place for a man!'

Essa's voice was silky. 'Think you then, Prince Avran, that it is a fit place for a woman? And are you so readily dismayed, that one day of wind and two of rain can thus destroy your hardihood? Such a lack of fortitude is surprising in one who vaunts so much!'

181

Perceiving that Avran was beginning to swell with anger — he was ever touchy when his courage was impugned — I interposed hastily.

'I think that the tedium of riding this forest in such weather is disheartening us all, Lady Essa. It is as if we have all become shrunken to beetle size and are crawling endlessly among the damp reeds of some vast marsh. Yet we would be fools to turn back, after enduring so long. Perhaps we may soon reach the end of the forest; with the views so veiled by rain and mist, who can say? Might it not be better for us to ride onward, rather than to sit around here on our veludain, while our mounts and we merely become wetter and wetter?'

Essa laughed. 'You are right, Simon. For my part, I do prefer to ride onward!'

At her thought, Stripenose set off again at a much brisker pace than before, a pace approaching a canter — the fastest pace that could be managed with safety among so many trees. Robin and I glanced at one another, then fell in behind; and Avran followed at our veludain's heels rather shamefacedly. As for Dan Wyert, he remained firmly at the rear with the pack-veludain. Quite evidently he preferred their company to ours — even to that of his mistress — until that future time when the emotional storm-skies cleared.

This brisker pace did serve to cheer us, and indeed to warm us. Moreover, though the rain did not cease and the skies did not lighten, we began quite soon to notice changes. Belatedly I perceived that the trees about us were different from those we had been seeing for so long. Wind-trees they were still, but with a ridged, lighter-coloured bark, a lesser spread of branches and narrower leaves with jagged edges. Then I became aware that, though we were still following the break of slope at the mountain-foot, we were veering westward. The sound of the river was again growing louder; we must be approaching it more closely.

'Your prognosis was right,' Robin commented. 'I believe we are nearing the valley head and will soon see the end of this forest.'

'Oh, come now, Robin,' I said uncomfortably. 'It was scarcely a prognosis! I was simply striving to raise our spirits.'

He laughed. 'Do not be too honest, Simon! Often enough, one fails to receive earned praise for truly meritorious words and deeds: it does one no harm, now and then, to be given more praise than

182

one deserves! But hearken to the river; is it not noisy? I think we must be approaching some rapids.'

Essa was still some distance ahead of us, for Stripenose had maintained a steady pace and we had not striven to catch up with her. Almost as Robin spoke, her mount's pace slowed and she called back: 'Take care, friends! Just ahead, the ground falls away suddenly. The river is close below. I believe there has been a landslide. I am going to look.'

Stripenose stopped; Essa dismounted hastily and went forward on foot. As we came abreast of Stripenose and likewise dismounted, she called back to us again: 'Yes, a landslide — and very recent, I think. The trees that have gone down are still in green leaf.'

'Then take care!' Robin called back. 'The ground may be still unstable. Do not venture near the edge. Watch out, Essa! Ah . . . '

For his warning had not been heeded. Interested and incautious, Essa had gone to the very rim of that fresh landslide. As she did so, the ground beneath her feet crumbled. She cried out in alarm and threw herself backward — too late. She gave a wail of fear and, with arms flailing, slipped from our view.

Horrified, Robin and I ran forward and threw ourselves down on the ground, crawling carefully but rapidly till we could gaze over the edge. Though we had not noticed it, we must have been riding gently uphill for some hours. The river was now quite far below us. It was flowing swiftly indeed, a turmoil of brown waters and white spray among dark rocks.

The landslide must certainly have been recent, caused probably by the heavy rains and high waters of those two days. A great bite had been taken out of the bank, at the bottom of which was a tangle of fallen trees at the very edge of the water.

Into this tangle Essa had slipped. She had managed to halt her slide by seizing the outermost twigs of a fallen wind-tree and was lying far down on the slope, with her cloak spread out behind and over her. Already she was struggling to grope her way along the branch, toward the more promising haven of the tree crown. Seen thus from above, she looked valiant yet pathetic, like one of those ragged-winged butterflies one sees in gutters in late autumn, unable to fly yet still striving to do so.

As we watched, the tree shifted under her weight and slid, sending

183

a cascade of earth and stones down into the river. I feared for a moment that Essa was lost; but no, the tree stopped moving. Soon she had gained the insecure refuge she sought.

Avran had joined us now, his face white; and Dan Wyert was close behind him. It was Avran who spoke first: 'One of us must climb down to Essa, to try to rescue her. It is my task; I shall go.'

'That you will not, Prince Avran!' Dan spoke more vehemently than I had ever heard him. 'You're young and your life is valuable to many folk — your friends here and your family back in Sandastre. I'm old and of account to no-one. Let me go instead — though I can't say as I fancy my chances much!'

'Neither of you shall go,' Robin said firmly. 'Do not be so foolish! Instead, look properly at the slope below you. If either of you attempts it, beyond doubt you'll start another slide and merely send Mistress Essa into the river more quickly. But Simon and Avran, have you not ropes in your packs? I seem to recall your acquiring some, back in Arravron.'

Indeed we had but, in the shock of Essa's fall, neither of us had thought about them. Hastily we crawled back from the edge and fetched those ropes, returning to where Robin was watching.

'The tree has shifted again and slipped further down,' he told us. 'We cannot afford to lose time. How much rope have we?'

'Two lengths, each of around a dozen ells,' I answered. 'That should suffice, if we can knot the lengths together firmly enough.'

He smiled rather grimly. 'I can manage that: I have endured enough voyages to have mastered a few of the skills of mariners. Yet I do not see how we may convey the rope to Essa. The slope is not sufficiently vertical for us to be able to drop it to her. Nor dare we tie it to a stone. If we strove to roll anything down to her, we would surely cause a second landslip.'

Avran had been thinking furiously: 'But if the rope were attached to an arrow, what then? Simon, you're the archer, not I. Could you shoot a bolt into that tree trunk, think you?'

I looked down below me unhappily. 'There will be strange wind-currents above the water, I fear. Nor do I know how the weight of the rope will affect the arrow. Still, I suppose I must try . . . Very well, I'll fetch my bow.'

By the time I came back the ropes had been unrolled, two ends

184

knotted together, and the joined ropes neatly coiled. Robin exhibited his mariner's skills again when he attached the free end of one rope to the arrow.

'You'll need to allow me a long, loose length so that the arrow is not checked in flight,' I said consideringly. 'Will the coil run freely?'

'I think so,' Robin replied. 'I hope so.'

I took a deep breath, then expelled it slowly. 'I'll have to stand up, close to the edge, and lean forward. You must both hold my legs; and you, Dan, must be ready to free the rope if it shows sign of catching in the coil.'

Most hesitantly and fearfully I lifted my bow clear of the ground, straightened up from the knees and took the arrow. Setting it to bow I stood up, with Avran clutching my left leg and Robin my right. I swung the bow until its arc was transverse to my body and then, gripping arrow and bow with my left hand, tugged on the rope with my right to see how it was behaving. It was catching a little, but Dan flung the first three coils outward so that they trailed below us and the tension was eased. Taking another deep breath and trying not to think of that oversteepened, treacherous slope beneath me, I aimed and loosed.

I had not allowed sufficiently either for the rising air current or for the drag of the rope. The trajectory was too low and the arrow fell amply short. Worse, in trying vainly to reach out for it, Essa caused the fallen wind-tree to shift and slide once again. The waters were foaming perilously close beneath her now; it would take little to send tree and Essa down into them.

I settled back on my haunches, while Dan and Avran pulled up the rope and Robin deftly recoiled it. I could see lines of tension on Robin's face when he handed me back the arrow, yet he strove to speak reassuringly: 'That was a brave first try, Simon. Another such, and we'll save her yet.'

'Give me even more rope this time, please, Dan.'

Again I rose totteringly to my feet, loosed — and missed. The distance was right but the direction was not. The arrow plunged down among the tangle of fallen vegetation, amply to Essa's left. She was too wise by then — or too frightened — to try to reach it.

Nor was the rope easy to haul back: the arrow had caught among that tangle. When, after heaves that brought sweat to their brows

185

and sent new runnels of soil down the slope below them, Robin and Dan freed it, the rope came so suddenly loose that it almost upset their balance — and came up without the arrow, which must have broken under their tugging.

As Robin again re-coiled the rope, I commented: 'For the first time, I am glad these are not English arrows, nor yet Sandastrian ones. An arrow of ash or of ikhoras would not have broken so easily.'

Robin gave me a smile of approval: 'You do well to be so calm, Simon. Time to try again — and may the third loosing bring fortune!'

So, once more, I stood up perilously and, with the bow held before me, loosed. This time I shot higher than hitherto, directing my arrow into the rising current of air.

Ah! that was better. The arrow was veering, dropping toward Essa. Indeed, for one terrible moment, I thought it had been too accurate, that it would transfix her; but no, it plunged instead into the soft wood of the wind-tree trunk close by her shoulder. Under the impact the tree shifted and settled further, more stones and earth pouring from beneath it into the river.

'Excellent, Simon,' said Robin. 'Well shot, indeed! But we cannot pull up both Essa and the tree. Oh yes, of course, Essa has her dagger!'

Leaning over the edge, he called down. 'Essa, have you firm hold of the rope? Good; then fetch out your dagger — yes, your dagger! — and cut the rope free of the arrow. Excellent!'

We saw the flash of a blade as Essa obeyed; and both Robin and Dan felt the slight tug on the rope. Within seconds, Essa was beginning to climb frantically upward.

As she moved away from it, the wind-tree that had been her refuge rotated and slipped, causing a further cascade of soil and stones. This time, however, it did not find a new lodgement; instead, it plunged into the river. For a moment we could see its branches above the turmoil of the waters; then it was sucked down.

As for Essa, we brought her up the slope somehow. It was a scrambling ascent, the soil and stones ever and again slipping alarmingly from under her feet; but there was no second landslide. Avran, Dan and Robin hauled on the rope. For my part, I was trembling too much to help. Instead I flung myself flat, looking over the edge to watch Essa's progress and warn my friends if the slope showed sign of breaking away beneath them.

Most fortunately, it did not. After no more than five minutes of strenuous effort, Essa was brought up to the top. It was Robin who seized her hands and lifted her to safety. Her hair and garments were plastered with mud, her countenance tear-streaked and very pale. She looked Robin full in the face, seemed to begin to smile — and fainted into his arms.

I am sure Avran, at that moment, would have given much to change places with Robin!

Chapter Twenty

THE GOD IN THE PASSAGE

'Simon, I'm grateful — grateful for your skill as an archer. For a while, I . . . Well, I did not fancy a wetting in that river.'

Essa's recovery from her swoon had been reasonably quick. It had been aided by Dan Wyert's laving of her brow and cheeks with cold spring water from one of the flasks and by Robin's giving her a draught of efredat from another. However, she was still very pale and breathing gaspingly. Though her eyes had been open for some time, these were her first words.

'You must understand, Essa, that I had to do something quickly! Avran was determined to climb down to you, while Dan was just as determined to prevent him and go down himself. They were quite ready to fight for the privilege of rescuing you! If they'd tried, you'd have all gone into the river and I'd have had three friends the less! In seriousness, though, I wasn't thinking very clearly. It was Robin who remembered the ropes and tied them together so skilfully; and it was Avran who thought of attaching them to an arrow. And, remember, it was Avran, Dan and Robin who hauled you up, not I. You owe much to them and little enough to me.'

There was the flicker of a smile about her lips. 'I owe a great deal to you all,' she responded firmly. 'Yet I feel also as if I'd been rolling in a midden. Dan, would you please leave that water-flask by me? Then, if you would all kindly go away for a while . . . Might you not begin your midday repast? It must be long past noon.'

So we left her and walked back downhill to where the veludain were uneasily awaiting us. Stripenose, in particular, had been waiting tensely. Evidently she had been ordered to stay behind and had not felt able to disobey, even when she knew her mistress was in trouble.

189

As we approached, however, I suspect she received from Essa the summons to bring the pack. She bounded up past us, thrusting us aside with as little regard as if we had been merely bushes growing on the slope.

We had almost finished eating before Essa joined us, Stripenose following demurely behind. Essa appeared already very much better; there was colour in her cheeks again and all the clay had been removed from her garments and boots. Avran gazed at her amazedly and spoke hesitantly, yet fervently.

'Lady Essa, you appear miraculously recovered. I am delighted. You seem — well, altogether yourself again.'

'And who else would I be, indeed?' she answered sharply; but then relented. 'Yet it is thanks to you all that I am even still myself! I shall not forget that. Now, would you pass me one of those cadarand cakes, Dan?'

Nor did any of us refer again to the incident. However, when we rode onward, Robin and I were in the van and Avran riding beside Essa. They found little enough to say to one another but Avran, at least, seemed mightily pleased with that little.

Naturally enough, we had all lost our inclination for riding along the river-bank. Accordingly we headed back, to resume our old route along the foot of the cliffs that marged the valley. However, it was no longer possible to move far away from the river, for those cliffs were converging, as the sides of a spearhead converge upon its point. We had the impression that there might be a second, broader valley above ours, but the cliffs were too high, and the hanging rain clouds too obscuring, for us to be sure. The rain had slackened considerably, but it was still falling persistently and the air was clammily cold.

Though we were no longer in view of the river, its louder sound and changed note told us that its waters must be forcing their way through an ever narrower and deeper gorge. Moreover, as our valley narrowed, we found ourselves being directed steadily back toward the river's edge. Or not so steadily, maybe, for our course was by no means straight. There were still wind-trees to be circuited, but these had become few. However, there were many huge boulders littering the valley floor, and it was about these that our way wound.

A curious assemblage they were, those boulders. Since the cliffs were formed of that strange, brassy-coloured and sparkling stuff that we had noticed when entering the wind-forest, one might have expected the boulders to be of the same kind. Indeed, a few were — but only a few, those closest to the cliff-foot and most recently fallen. The rest were of many different sorts. Some were of a pink granite; some of purple slate like that about Cat Crags. Others were formed of multi-hued, tortuously-enfolded layers, like the rocks we had seen while approaching the wind-temple. Yet others were of a dark-coloured rock, studded with big green crystals that were lustrous even in the subdued light. Indeed, the colours of those boulders were so varied, and their distribution so random, that it was as if some giants had been playing jackstones with them and had abandoned their game in the middle.

Not only the roar of the waters, but also the strangeness of that place, caused us all to fall silent; yes, even Avran.

After a while, however, we discovered an easier line through this hemmed-in wilderness of boulders and trees; and there came the realization that we were again on a road. Though the largest boulders were circuited, smaller ones had been shifted aside, wind-trees removed and hollows levelled with smaller stones to form a surface upon which a cart might have been driven with ease.

As we rode along it, we saw that the road was leading us to the place where the cliffs from left and right came together; and, peering through the wet mist, we could perceive no gap. If the river penetrated those cliffs, then its gorge must become narrow indeed.

Inevitably also, as the valley sides converged, we were approaching the edge of that gorge ever more closely. I could sense that Proudhorn was not happy; or was it that he was perceiving and reflecting my mood? Certainly I was reluctant to tread again upon that perilous margin.

Nevertheless, as the road and our veludain swung left to pass a huge boulder of dark, crystal-glistening rock, we found ourselves once more on the very verge of the gorge. It was of solid rock here, fortunately, and the gorge so narrow that a reasonably agile sevdru might have leapt over with ease, though a veludu probably could not. The river was too far below, and in too deep shadow, to be seen, yet the roar of its waters was quite deafening.

Onward we went, our hands pressing our hoods against our ears

191

to keep out that tremendous din. The road was by now rising steadily, albeit not steeply.

We were not required to endure that noise long. When we neared the tip of the spear — the intersection of the cliffs — the sound of the waters diminished suddenly as rock closed right over the gorge. Words were carved into that rock, but the letters were too worn and moss-encrusted to be read.

As we rode onward, a throbbing of the ground below our veludain's hooves and a rumbling like the growling of a baited bear told us that the river must be still flowing deep beneath us. However, as the road climbed higher toward the valley head, the throbbing ceased and the sound diminished to a mere murmur.

Robin had already dropped his hands from his ears, as had I. Now, regardless of the still-persistent rain, he shrugged his hood back from his head and spoke.

'Well, Simon, that was not quite so desperate a din as when we climbed up to the wind-temple, but it was unpleasant enough. Think you that there is a way out of this valley or must we turn back, even now?'

'Indeed, we do seem to be heading straight for the cliffs; but can I not see some sort of opening — yes, there, between those two groves of wind-trees that are growing at the cliff-foot? Surely this road has been too well engineered to end in nothing at all! I suppose the opening might be only a cave, but I'll wager we'll find a stairway or passageway within, leading upwards. I propose that we investigate it, anyway.'

'Have a care then, Simon! And set arrow to your bow before you venture within. I distrust caves; who knows what fell beasts may lurk in them? If it be indeed a stairway, where will it lead, I wonder?'

We slowed so that our friends might catch us up, then approached the valley head in a watchful group. Soon the brassy cliffs were rearing high before us and we were riding between the wind-tree groves.

We observed with disquiet that those groves each consisted of nine trees set in a circle. A large boulder was situated at the centre of each grove; by chance or by design? We noted also that though the cliffs seemed to be crumbling, the road and the groves had been cleared of fallen stones.

192

The cave was directly before us, its opening a blacker arc within the deep shadow under the cliffs. Was it a natural cavern, I wondered, or might it have been made by mining, long ago?

'I like this not, Simon,' Robin said heavily. 'Certainly I am not willing to enter that dark portal without light. Let us seek branches that will burn, and make torches.'

Since wind-trees do not shed their branches and since the trees in the groves were all alive, three of us turned back down valley in quest for a dead tree. It was Dan Wyert who found one — a mere sapling with a single cycle of incompletely opened branches, uprooted and killed by a slide of rocks. Indeed, the trunk and centre of the crown were buried, but the branches protruded and were lopped off readily enough by Robin's and Dan's swords. We returned, bearing nine potential torches, to where Avran, Essa and the pack-veludain were sheltering under the cliff overhang before the cave mouth.

Robin decreed that, since we could not know how far into the cliff we might need to penetrate, we should utilize initially only three of the branches, keeping the others in reserve. Setting even those three alight proved far from easy, for their bark was sodden. However, eventually Dan coaxed the broken end of one into spluttering flame and used this to set fire to two others.

Avran and Robin each took one into his left hand; their unsheathed swords were grasped in their right hands. My hands were both engaged, for I had indeed set arrow to bow. Since Dan Wyert had been charged with the bundle of remaining branches, it was Essa who took the third torch. However, for the moment she and Dan remained behind with the veludain: it seemed that Essa's thirst for adventure had been quenched, at least for a while.

With some trepidation, therefore — at least on my part — Robin, Avran and I advanced into that dark mouth beneath the cliff. As we stepped inside and Robin raised his torch high, I gave a gasp of fear and, hastily raising my bow, drew back my arrow. Armed warriors were rushing upon us, shields before breasts and axes raised high to strike!

Then I sighed with relief and lowered my bow. These were merely warriors of stone, man-sized carvings cut so deeply into the rock that they seemed to stand out from it. It was only the swinging of the torch-flame that had lent them a semblance of motion.

193

As Avran raised his torch also, we were able to see them better. Each was depicted wearing light armour; mail-shirts curiously composed of overlapping metal lozenges, greaves ridged like a chesnut's bark, and helms topped with a mighty spike. Their shields had the shape of an inverted tear-drop, while their double-bladed axes were elaborately notched at the edges, like the shark's tooth that the Genoese traveller had shown me years ago. Never had I seen such armour, such shields or such axes, in reality or in picture.

'Safaddnese warriors, surely,' Robin commented softly. 'See, there are nine of them on each wall. But look beyond! For a second time today, Simon, your prediction has proven good. There is indeed a way out of the valley!'

As I gazed past the lines of warriors in the flickering torchlight, I saw what he had seen — a stairway leading upward into the rock. The stairs were shallow and broad; a veludu could mount them easily. Moreover, as I sniffed at the air, I realized not only that it was reasonably fresh, but also that there was movement in it; a slight wind was blowing from somewhere above us. The stairway could not be closed at its upper end, then, and I surmised optimistically that the ascent could not be unduly long. In that presumption, I was to be proved wrong.

By now, Essa had followed us within and was gazing about her interestedly. 'Do you see the emblems that they bear on shield and helm — the many-reeded pipe of Darega, that is also the divine symbol of Daltharimbar? I believe we are entering another of his temples.'

Robin shrugged. 'Well, pass through it we must. I do not desire to turn back into Daltharimbar's realm; I trust this stairway may lead us out of it. There is little wind today, mercifully. Perhaps Daltharimbar has gone away to some other land.'

I noticed that, in his words at least, Robin seemed to be conceding the existence of the god.

'Today is a day of Halrathhantor, god of the rain and of Ayan,' Essa answered seriously. 'Yet Daltharimbar never wholly leaves his land. Do you not feel his distant breath on your cheeks, and hear the murmur of it?'

Indeed, now that I was listening for it, I did notice a slight sound, the merest susurration, like the quiet breath of a tranquilly sleeping

194

animal. I glanced at Avran, to determine how he was receiving Essa's words. However, he had turned away, deliberately I am sure, and seemed to be trying to read an inscription carven into the wall below the stairway.

'Well, we should mount the stair before Daltharimbar returns wholly,' Robin stated firmly. 'Essa, will you summon Dan and the veludain?'

As we mounted the stairs, we passed many more carvings; not warriors merely, but groups of nine figures similar to those depicted in the other wind-temple — priests, warriors and servants, consistently in threes, but this time shown climbing upward and carven only into the left-hand wall. Always they were male, but as before they varied greatly in detail — in stature, style and length of hair, cut of beard and shape of eyes — as if real individuals had been depicted. Perhaps the angular letters inscribed beneath them told their names; perhaps they spelled out prayers or invocations. The characters were too strange for we men to read and Essa did not interpret them to us. Instead, she seemed wrapped within herself, as if deep in thought or prayer. I suspected the latter, but hoped I was wrong; these pagan gods disquieted me.

Indeed, apart from the uneasy murmur of the little wind and the small sounds made by our feet and the veludain's padded hooves, it was very silent within the cliff. The sound of the river had entirely died away.

The ascent was an arduous one, for the stairs led upward without break or turn. After a while, Avran's torch gave out, then Robin's; but Dan furnished fresh branches, which were easily kindled from the smouldering stumps. The torches emitted a slightly acrid odour, sufficiently like that of hot charcoal to carry my mind back to charcoal-burners' huts I had visited in Hallamshire woodlands, on sunny days in earlier years.

This pleasant memory so distracted me that only after prompting from Robin did I look about me for traces of earlier climbers of those stairs. Here and there I could see traces of boot- or sandal-prints. However, these were always covered by a film of newer dust, so that I was left unsure how long a time had passed since they were made. Though the steps were shallow enough to permit the ascent of veludain, the ceiling of the passage was too low to allow any riding up or down. Indeed, I saw no hoof-prints.

What I did see in the dust were prints of padded and nailed feet, like those of large dogs. These seemed much fresher than the human prints. This observation provoked in me renewed trepidations. I showed the footprints to Robin and Avran, who were likewise surprised and disquieted. Essa, who had fallen back to join Dan Wyert, did not hear our discussion.

We became very weary of that steady ascent, but ultimately it ended and we found ourselves entering upon a low, broad corridor. The flickering-out of Essa's torch gave reason for a pause. Dan sat down immediately to rest, his back against one wall; Avran thrust his sword back into its scabbard and, taking a branch from Dan, set it alight.

While he was doing this, Robin asked: 'Do the Safaddnese keep hounds, then, Essa? From the footmarks we've seen, it would seem so. Or might they be the tracks of wolves?'

'My father never mentioned that the Safaddnese kept hounds, or indeed any sort of dog. And "wolves"? What is a "wolve"? I have never heard that word.'

He chuckled and corrected her. 'A wolf, one would say. Well, it's a wild creature, much like a large, fierce dog. They hunt in packs. One may encounter them in France and Ireland — and in England also, Simon?'

'Not now. The last were killed — oh, before my grandfather's time.'

Essa shook her head. 'No, not of wolves either. I expect the footprints are those of xakathei. I mentioned them, do you remember? The creatures that hunt the udreyen in winter, or so my father said. Certainly they run in packs, but I do not believe they are much like dogs.'

'Do the Safaddnese keep xakathei as hunting animals?' I asked, rather apprehensively.

'I have not heard so,' she replied. She seemed uninterested in the discussion, for she had turned away and was examining the figures on the wall. Or rather, I should say, on the walls, for now there were figures at right as well as at left. Those at left continued to be shown going in the same direction as we; those at right, in the contrary direction. The right-hand figures had been incised less deeply and with less skill. Had they been carven more recently, I wondered?

But Robin was pressing Essa: 'How, then, my lady, do you account for the footprints in the dust?'

'I do not account for them.' She sounded impatient, as if Robin were a child tiresomely disturbing the serious thoughts of its parent. 'If its footmarks are here, then a xakath must have been here; surely that is evident?'

I was anxious to know something concerning the appearance of a xakath but, after Robin had suffered such a rebuff, I was deterred from asking. Since Essa's torch was burning well by then, Dan was assisted to his feet and we went on our way: none of us was anxious to risk running out of light before emerging from that place. Avran had unsheathed his sword again and, for my part, I was keeping my arrow at string.

As we walked along, I was disturbed to observe how much more frequent those blunt-clawed footprints were becoming. Why, there seemed at least one in each patch of dust!

'Robin,' I said hesitantly, 'the footprints — they're not all of one size and shape and they're often superposed. There has not been just one xakath here, but many xakathei — a whole pack of them.'

'That is ill news, Simon. One xakath, we might deal with readily enough; but a whole pack is a grim prospect! And I fear they cannot be very far from us. Do I not detect a beast-odour in the air about us?'

Yes, when I sniffed attentively, I could distinguish an unpleasant taint which the scent of the burning torches had masked. 'What must we do?' I asked nervously.

'Only press onward, keeping our weapons in hand,' Robin answered bleakly. 'As you know well, I was never of the opinion that we should even embark upon this journey. However, for better or worse, we are long past the point of turning back.'

He said nothing more, but his thought was clear — that I was the one who had chosen the route and had led us into all these perils. Yet, oddly enough, though I was apprehensive I was not deeply alarmed. Maybe the surmounting of so many dangers had given me a new valour, or maybe I was being imbued with confidence by

197

Proudhorn? Certainly the veludain seemed not to be apprehending any immediate danger.

Belatedly I became aware that ahead of us, penetrating vertically down into the deep gloom, there was a narrow beam of light. As we approached, the corridor widened into a circular space and the light into a bright column.

The illumination was coming from a shaft, driven upward through the rock. Beneath it, flanked by a high rim of dark stone, there was a broad, black pool, quite four poles in diameter and almost equally deep. At the centre of the pool was a plinth on which was carven the figure of a man scaled like a fish, with a trailing robe ending in the shape of a fish's flat tail. His spreading toes were webbed and there was webbing between fingers upraised in invocation or blessing. His head was thrown back, so that only his fishtail-forked beard could be seen. Indeed, it was not easy to see him properly, even from the rim of the pool, for he was surrounded by rain falling from above. Moreover, we were dazzled by the brightness into which we were gazing. Unless we plunged into the pool, we could not enter that column of light; we could only witness it from without.

'It is Halrathhantor,' Essa said soberly. 'See how he is bringing to himself the rain?'

She had walked away from Avran, to gaze into the pool. I do not think she heard him when he muttered: 'How absurd! That so-called god is not bringing the rain, it is the shaft in the rock that is conveying the rain to him!'

Robin spoke hastily, as if to prevent any louder repetition of that acid comment: 'Essa, does this mean we are in a rain-temple, not a wind-temple; a temple of Halrathhantor, not of Daltharimbar? Could it mean we are leaving Darega and entering Ayan?'

Since she turned around to reply, I could not see her expression, for she was merely a black shape against the light. Her voice, though, had a bantering sound.

'Why should it mean that? The Safaddnese gods are not at war; surely one is welcome in the temple of another? And as for our entering Ayan; that is possible, though I think Ayan lies yet some way to the north. Maybe the gods of these mountains will permit you to visit that land, Sir Robert; I know not. It is at their will, not at mine!'

At this, Avran spoke loudly and angrily: 'It is at the will of the One True God, not of any demons of the mountains!'

Certainly her voice was mocking now. 'Do you think it wise, prince of the south whose realm is so far away, thus to challenge the gods of a land that is not your own? For my part, I believe you are being very rash! Well, we shall see. Shall we go onward, then, gentlemen?'

She had set down her torch against the stone rim of the pool. When she picked it up, she turned again toward the figure of the god. Bowing her head and lifting the torch, she swung it in a curious sigmoid motion, chanting some phrase the while. As she lowered it, I saw that she was smiling, a strange inward smile.

Essa did not look again at Avran, nor did he seek her company as she went onward down the passage; for she was taking the lead now. As we and the beasts followed her, the column of light dwindled behind us till it faded completely from view.

Something new was troubling me. Since Avran was lagging behind, it was to Robin that I spoke. 'Up to the pool, I was sure we were travelling northward; but have we not turned? I would swear that we are now heading west, not north.'

He laughed grimly. 'You perceive correctly, yet you have not perceived all. You were too busy looking at the god in the rain, perhaps! At the pool, the corridor divided. One branch seemed to go eastward, but I felt no flow of air from or toward it and I believe it must be blocked. This corridor goes westward, but can you not feel the wind from it against your cheek? The strengthening breath of Daltharimbar, Essa will say. For my part, I believe this corridor leads to the surface — and at no great distance. Ah! See there, just ahead in the light of Essa's torch — more steps! Soon we'll be safely out of this dark place!'

His words were premature. Even as he spoke, I heard a sound ahead of and above us — a strange patter, as if many sandalled monks were running along a cloister. Then Essa turned about, her voice ringing out from the echoing space at the stair foot.

'I see eyes above me — many eyes! You have angered the gods indeed, Prince Avran! The xakathei are upon us!'

Chapter Twenty-one

THE COMBAT IN THE CORRIDOR

We were in an ill situation to defend ourselves. Had we been at the top, and not at the foot, of the stairway, matters would have been much better. As it was, the xakathei would be leaping down upon us, gaining an extra speed and momentum that would make their onslaught much harder to withstand.

Nor was there the chance for us to retreat far down the corridor; they were moving too fast for that. And so many of them! I could see already a close-packed mass of the creatures, coming down the stair in a rush like water flowing out of an overturned bucket.

Essa, torch still in hand, was running back to the shelter of our weapons. I wondered briefly whether the torches themselves could be used in our defence, but all three were burning low, even Essa's, the latest to be lit. How, then, to arrange that defence? Avran and Robin had courageously moved forward, their swords in hand; there was not time for Avran to get out his bow, unfortunately, and neither Essa nor even Dan Wyert was skilled in archery. Two swords would not protect us long from that cataract of attackers; nor had I enough arrows to slay many of them, even if each shot told.

While these alarmed thoughts were racing through my mind, the question of our defence was taken out of our hands. We had all forgotten the veludain and forgotten also that, over long years, veludain had developed their own defence against the onslaught of xakathei. Now they took control.

As the veludain surged forward, we were each warned in thought to step aside, then move back. In a trice, we were defended by an arc of beasts. Proudhorn, proud indeed now in anticipation of battle, was at the front of that arc, with the massive Highback at his left shoulder and one of the pack-veludain, a strong stag called

201

Twistbeam, at his right. The two riding-does, Stripenose and Brown-tail, stood close together at Twistbeam's right, while the other pack-animal, an older and larger doe called Feathertail, stood to the left of Highback, with Longshank between her and the wall. The seven animals blocked the corridor completely. Their serried mass of horns — remember, each had six, two at front of muzzle, two behind their eyes, and two branching horns at brow — must have been a formidable sight for the oncoming predators.

Quite evidently the xakathei found it so. The flood of animals checked, as the flow from a bucket will if its brim be suddenly tilted. I could not see the creatures clearly — the staircase was too dark for that — but I could hear a strange bombilation among the front rank of them, like a grunting snort many times repeated. Then, apparently through sheer pressure from behind, that dark, menacing tide began again to advance.

Hastily I lifted my bow, pulled back the string and loosed. A gurgling gasp suggested the arrow had struck home, but there was no other result. Quickly I plucked a second arrow from my quiver, set it to bow and loosed again. This time, one of the foremost xakathei snarled in pain and tumbled heels-over-head down the stairs to writhe at their foot, biting at the transfixing arrow, until death overcame it.

I am sure we each spared it at least a glance, for it was the first xakath we had seen clearly. A squat, broad beast it was, not very big, but like some diabolical fusion of cat and toad; short-legged and very broad-headed, with flaring nostrils and palely gleaming eyes set on the top, rather than at the sides, of that ugly head. Its fur was of a greyish tan streaked with darker lines, but there was a curious central ridge of bony plates down the middle of its back and along its long, twitching tail. Its enormous jaws, opening and shutting convulsively before they closed finally in death, showed multiple rows of pointed teeth. Such jaws would sever a limb at a single snap; I shuddered.

But it was time to loose another arrow. So I did, and another, and another. All took effect; the dreadful creatures were too tight-packed for any shot to miss. Yet the torrent of them was still flowing down the stairs and out into the corridor, the animals at front not at all eager to face those formidable horns but thrust forward by the pressure from behind. The injured and dying beasts were ignored —

pushed aside, stepped over or even stepped upon — as the great mass of xakathei advanced on us.

Then, suddenly, that terrible tide was being driven back! Proudhorn was leading a charge of the veludain, right into the oncoming pack. Their heads swept downward, then upward. I saw a xakath tossed high in the air, like a terrier tossed by a bull; and another; and another.

Forward the veludain went, cleaving deep into that phalanx of hideous creatures. Then the veludain withdrew a little, and charged again; twice, thrice, four times, till those evil beasts were driven back to the stairfoot and a score, at least, of dead or dying xakathei were being trampled beneath the veludain's hooves. Between arrow-shots — for I was still shooting steadily into the mass of xakathei above — I noticed Robin driving his sword into one wounded but dangerously-snapping beast, while Avran slew two others.

Whether our veludain could have charged onward up the stairs without coming to grief, I doubt. Fortunately, they did not need to do so. That pack of xakathei had suffered enough; moreover, it had lost its leaders.

The flow of beasts checked. There came another strange sound, like a gargling mew, which seemed to begin near the stairfoot and pass upward in a series of weird dissonances. Then the xakathei were in retreat, tumbling, slipping and thrusting as they fought to make their way back up the stairs. The danger was over.

Dropping my bow, I ran forward to throw my arms about Proudhorn's neck in frantic delight. Though I sensed his pleasure and pride, he did not turn about; rather did he raise his head higher, looking upward after his fleeing enemies. Nor did the other veludain break line till they were sure the last xakath — save for the many that had been slain — had gone from the stairway.

Only then did we realize that our valiant beasts had not come through the fray unscathed. Highback's shoulder had been torn by the claws of a xakath he had tossed, while Proudhorn's cheeks and muzzle and Browntail's flank showed slashmarks. However, their wounds were not severe. It was poor Stripenose who had come off worst. She had been most grievously bitten by a wounded xakath as she stepped over it. Indeed, her whole flank and belly were so torn

203

open that I marvelled how she had contrived to stand in line till the end. Now the peril was past, she collapsed.

Essa ran to her, knelt and sobbingly cradled the head of the veludu in her arms. I marked how, even in extremity, Stripenose was careful to tilt her head so that her horns might not hurt her mistress. Stroking Stripenose's muzzle and murmuring endearments to the dying doe, Essa appeared quite overwhelmed by distress. Yet, when Robin stood by sword in hand and looked at Essa interrogatively, she proved sufficiently in control of herself to nod briefly. A quick thrust put a merciful end to Stripenose's suffering.

I know that her death tore at the hearts of us all. Dan Wyert, fond as he was of all the veludain, was openly weeping. Essa laid her veludu's head gently on the ground and rose unsteadily to her feet, only to flare suddenly into anger at Avran.

'See what you have brought upon us, with your challenges to the high gods of these mountains! Only my supplications to Halrathhantor and to Daltharimbar have saved us — and at what cost!'

At this Avran, in turn, became angry. 'Say rather that our veludain have saved us! Moreover, notice that it is your Stripenose that died, not my Highback. How do you account for that?'

'Of course it was I who suffered the loss! Was it not proper that I be made to give the sacrifice, in order to save us all? How stupid you are!' Abruptly and astonishingly, Essa bowed her head and sobbed convulsively into her hands, as if her very heart was breaking.

While Avran stood by, quite discountenanced, Robin went to Essa and put his arm about her shoulders. After a while he said; 'You have blood on your surcoat and skirts, Lady Essa. If you desire to go back and wash in the pool, we will await you here.'

At this she tossed back her head and demanded indignantly: 'What, put blood into that pool — the pool of Halrathhantor? Certainly I shall not do that! It is sacred water, to be drunk sparingly perhaps, but not to be polluted. No, let us instead go out from here. The way is not far now; see, there is a gleam of light at the top of the stairs. Let us leave this place of death; I do not wish to stay here.'

She began weeping again, this time on Robin's shoulder while he endeavoured to comfort her. Then, again abruptly, she pulled away from him and ran off up the stairs.

Though Robin followed her immediately, his sword again in his hand, we others could not do so. Dan Wyert had already begun treating the wounds of the other veludain, using water from a flask and swabs and bandages from his bundle. I did my best to retrieve what arrows I could, for I had exhausted my quiver; however, two could not be withdrawn from the bodies of the beasts they had slain and several others had broken. Indeed, of twenty arrows, only twelve were now left to me. As for Avran, he transferred Essa's saddle to the back of Feathertail and divided Feathertail's load, adding half to Twistbeam's burden and finding space for the rest in the saddle-packs of the other veludain. Only when all those tasks had been performed could we follow Robin and Essa.

As we left that scene of carnage, I made a hasty count of the dead xakathei in corridor and on stairs. Fully thirty had been slain, yet we had not seemed to make any impression on that attacking mass. Why, there must have been hundreds of the creatures! Had they continued their onslaught, we would surely have been overwhelmed. We had indeed much to be grateful for. Stripenose's loss was grievous, but it was almost miraculous that the six other veludain and we five humans had survived. Perhaps, indeed, Essa's prayers *had* been answered . . .

We had lit two of the last three branches from Robin's and Avran's torches before they burned entirely out; but these soon ceased to be needed. The speck of light grew into a square and that square expanded steadily as we climbed up the stairs.

At their head was a short, wide space in the centre of which, on a high plinth, stood a mighty carven figure — a horned, prick-eared figure with sword, catapult, and pipes. Yes, it was a second image of the wind-god Daltharimbar but, this time, his back was to us, for he stood ready to defend his realm. Nor, mercifully, was the wind blowing much into this tunnel. I shuddered to think what we might have endured, had the wind been from the west and not from the northwest.

As I was eventually to learn, there were nine temples to Daltharimbar in Darega, one standing at each of the eight cardinal points of the Rockalese compass. From whatever direction the wind was blowing, Daltharimbar's pipes would be playing somewhere to his people. I did not envy them that music! The ninth and greatest temple, at the centre of his realm, was that into which we had strayed, to our pain. Now we were emerging from the western temple.

On this occasion, Avran uttered no word about the wind-god as we passed the great statue. Instead, he turned his head away.

When we were ascending the stairs, I had wondered if the upper corridor might be a den for the xakathei; but it was not. Though their footprints were everywhere in the dust — strangely doglike when seen separately, but quite different in track pattern, as I now perceived — there was little beast-odour here. Nor were there any of the other signs — shed hairs, chewed bones, or droppings — that characterize the habitations of predators. Instead, this upper temple was quite clean and its air altogether fresher than that of the lower corridor. Its walls were high and decorated from floor to roof with figures and inscriptions — inscriptions that we did not try to read.

Indeed we were in haste, for Essa and Robin were not within the temple. Only when we reached its further end and emerged through a high arch, to find another shallow stairway descending — though not for any great distance — before us, did we encounter one of our companions.

Robin was sitting on a step just below the top of the stairway, his unsheathed sword laid carefully within reach by his side. He had been gazing out into the still-falling rain. At our approach, he turned his head.

'Essa has gone forth; whether to clean herself of her veludu's blood with rainwater, or to offer further prayers to her mountain gods, or even to weep fresh tears for Stripenose, I cannot say. She called to me to await her here. Look about you, then, my friends. I fear it is a bleak prospect.'

So, indeed, was it. A broad slope of land fell away before us, veiled in wet mist and as strewn with great rocks as the valley had been. Mostly it was a barren prospect, in which only a few stunted bushes or tufts of spiky grass were struggling for life. Evidently we had seen the last of the wind-trees; I did not mourn that fact, but I found no encouragement in this view.

Avran tossed his torch out into the rain. It sputtered and flared alternately as it rolled down the steps and then, as it came to rest, burned brightly for a while. But soon the rain doused the flames and there was only a little plume of smoke fading upward into the mist.

Avran watched this sombrely, then sighed and sat down beside Robin. As for Dan Wyert, he stubbed the other torch carefully against a stone and, when it was quite out, stowed the unburnt remnant and the last wind-tree branch thriftily into his pack. Getting out his flask of efredat, he passed it around. I am sure we were all three glad to be warmed by that fiery liquid, though I came never to like its taste.

The six veludain ambled down the steps and out into the rain. Each beast stood for a while with head held high. I could sense that they were finding the rain refreshing; however, as the cloths he had used became sodden, I mourned a little for Dan's careful bandaging. Then the veludain spread out to obtain fodder from the sparse growth of plants. Clearly they apprehended no further danger.

Meantime, Dan Wyert had brought out his cloak of ameral fur, wrapped it about him and fallen almost instantly asleep. Remembering his earlier relapse into slumber and noticing the lines on his face, I realized how severely the strains of the last few days had told on poor Dan. I wondered how much more he would have to endure before we found Lyonesse — if ever we did attain that elusive land.

That thought brought another — that we needed to know our whereabouts and that I, at least, did not. I followed the veludain out into the rain, but my look-around told me little. Then I returned up the steps to sit beside my friends. Robin perceived my thoughts, or so it seemed from his comment.

'Yes, it is a question. Where, indeed, are we?'

'Far to the west of our planned route, that is certain,' I responded. 'It is hard to be sure in this mist and rain, but I think we must be on the western slope of the Highshadow Mountains.'

He sighed. 'Your conclusion matches my own. We are far off route. Yet I do not think we can turn back; I saw no other way out of that valley and I am certain that the eastward tunnel beyond the god's pool was blocked. Instead we must go northward and must try to find our way back over the mountains' crest. I fear it may prove no easy task.'

'Again, our thoughts march together. Yet, like you, I can conceive no better plan. This rain is bad enough; I trust it will not turn to snow. Our prospects are pretty disheartening, aren't they?'

Abruptly Avran laughed. 'Such gloom, my friends! One would not think you had both so recently escaped death. After we have survived so much, have you gained no faith in your fortunes? Surely we have cause to be, not doleful, but gay — not dejected, but exultant?'

At these words, we all three sat up straighter. 'You are right, Avran,' I admitted ruefully. 'We must be grateful to God that we are alive and well — and indeed, for my part, I *am* grateful. It's just that — well, I wish we were approaching the end of our journey. I long to know that Lyonesse is found, to see my father and brother again; but I long even more to be setting my face south toward Sandastre.'

'Will you do so, when the time comes?' Avran was trying to divert my thoughts and lighten my spirits. 'Might you not desire to stay with your father and brother in their northern home? Why would you choose to face so many more hazards, if there proves to be no good reason for doing so?'

'Of course I shall head south. Why, I long to see Sandarro again — and Ilven!' Then I realized he was teasing me and blushed rather sheepishly, before retaliating: 'But how about you, Avran my brother? Might you not find some reason to remain here in the north?'

It was his turn to blush, but he answered steadily: 'I see no cause to believe so — do you?'

'Peace, peace!' Robin broke in. 'Essa is returning; the veludain sense her coming. Ah! See, there she is, just beyond the stair-foot and walking fast. I wonder what is her mood now?'

She was looking fresh and vigorous again. All the stains of blood had been washed from her clothes and, indeed, she was very wet. However, she seemed unconcerned by that fact. Since she ran up the steps, it was evident also that she was in haste.

'Simon, could you come with me quickly? And Avran also, if he will bring his bow. We could all do with fresh meat; I believe I have found us some, if you can be swift and shoot well. We will not need the veludain; and, Sir Robert, would you remain with Dan, since he is sleeping?'

Robin agreed, though with little enthusiasm. As for Avran, he ran to Highback and fetched out bow and arrows. Then, as swiftly as we might, we followed Essa out into the rain.

After traversing about three furlongs of boulder-strewn slope, we found ourselves ascending a ridge that rose above the general level of the hillside. The last few yards were traversed cautiously, at Essa's urgent behest; she had kept the lead throughout. As we reached the ridge's crest, she gestured us to silence and pointed.

We found ourselves looking down into a hollow, beyond which a second, much higher ridge could be glimpsed dimly through the falling rain. In that hollow a half-score of dark-furred creatures, much like sheep but for their larger ears and longer tails, were grazing quietly, while a bigger creature of the same kind — the herd leader, I presumed — stood on watch upon a rock beyond.

We could not approach more closely, but the creatures were well within arrow-shot. Already Avran had strung his bow and I had restrung mine. We raised our weapons and, at my nod, loosed.

Both our arrows flew true. Two of the beasts fell, while the others raised their heads, snorted in fear and fled away into the mist.

Down we went into the hollow. However, when we reached the two slain beasts, we received something of a shock. It was Avran who noticed the oddity first.

'Lady Essa, these creatures — do you know what they are called? I have never seen such before.'

She was doubtful. 'They may be called "uvudain". My father mentioned beasts of some such kind, browsing on the highest hills where even veludain would not live. However, since he never limned one for me, I cannot be sure.'

'Did he say that the Safaddnese kept them?'

She was evidently surprised. 'No, I cannot recall him saying so. Why do you ask?'

'Because these creatures are wearing collars, look!'

Avran knelt and, with his fingers, probed beneath what I had thought to be a darker band about the neck of the dark-furred beast. Instead, it was indeed a leather collar, a thumb-span in width and marked with angular characters.

Essa knelt too and examined it concernedly. 'Yes, you are right. We have slain two beasts from someone's herd. I wonder who owned them, and where he dwells?'

Though the rain had scarcely slackened, the wind had been blowing ever more gustily and there had been some lightening of the southern horizon. As if in response to her question, there came a particularly strong gust and the mist thinned. We looked upward and shivered in the sudden draught; then we were still, transfixed by surprise.

Above us, revealed in their massiveness as the mist withdrew, loomed three stone towers. Not ruins, these, but stark strongholds in good order. However, if anyone lived within them, it was not obvious, for they stood dark against the brightening southern sky and there was no glimmer of light within.

Chapter Twenty-two

SNOW IN THE HIGHSHADOW MOUNTAINS

'And so Simon stayed to guard the beasts we'd shot, while Lady Essa and I tried to obtain a better look at those towers. But we could not approach them much closer. That further side of the valley is too steep; indeed, there are cliffs round three sides of the ridge upon which the towers stand. Then, when we went back uphill and climbed onto the ridge, we found it deeply breached and the gap filled by spiked stakes. There might well have been a drawbridge over the gap; but if one still exists, it has been raised. The mist was thickening again by then and it was not easy for us to see clearly.'

Avran was recounting our recent adventures to Dan Wyert and Robin. I had had a cold wait beside the dead uvudain, if that indeed is what the creatures were named, while Avran and Essa surveyed the towers. Even now that we were back within the shelter of the wind-temple's portico, I was still feeling chilled. Indeed, I was huddling as close as I could to the little fire that Dan, using as its first fuel the half-burned wind-tree branch, had lit for us.

With Avran's help, Dan had butchered an uvudu. Then he had made a spit by splitting the unburned wind-tree branch and sharpening one of the pieces. Now he was roasting a hunk of the meat. It smelled very good indeed and Essa was already using another piece of the wood as a second spit.

'So you could not tell whether the towers are still lived in?' Robin asked.

'Not for certain. The path leading along the ridge was well worn, certainly, but whether by beasts or men, I cannot say. As you know, I have not Simon's skill in reading tracks, but I saw none clear enough to tell me what or who was using the path. After all, we know already that there are other creatures about, don't we?'

'And we know that some, at least, of those creatures wear collars. Lady Essa, how do you read these letters?' Robin had one of the collars stretched between his hands.

Essa did not trouble to look at it. 'I have examined them already. Those are not letters, but symbols. Herdsmen's symbols, I presume. I guess that they identify the owner, but I cannot interpret them.'

'Still, if the beasts wear collars, some man must own them — or some woman.'

'Or one of those mountain gods, perhaps,' suggested Avran rather sourly. 'Or some other unhuman creature. Did you not say, Lady Essa, that you had never heard that the Safaddnese kept such beasts?'

'I am not equipped with an exhaustive knowledge concerning the customs of the Safaddnese,' she retorted annoyedly. 'Indeed, I recall only a few scraps of information from the tales recounted to me by my father. Please remember that.'

Before this exchange could turn into bickering, I spoke. 'There *have* been men about here, you know. In a patch of mud in the hollow, there were the marks of booted feet. Not made very recently, for the mud had dried and cracked before the last rains, but not made very long ago either.'

'So then, by lighting a fire in the entrance to this temple, we are inviting the attention of any vigilant Safaddnese warriors. And, more seriously perhaps, we are giving offence to those mountain gods of yours, Lady Essa!'

Avran was speaking provocatively again. He seemed to be positively inviting a conflict with Essa.

'Say rather, the attentions of Omegan warriors, for we must be in their land by now. And, as for the mountain gods, they are not mine; rather, we are their playthings.'

Essa paused, then went on less confidently: 'Yet I do not believe they would refuse us the shelter of this portico. We are not now within the realm of Daltharimbar. That commences where he stands, in the passage.'

'Who, then, is the god of Omega?'

'I do not know his name. My father never told it to me and I have not seen it inscribed on the walls of this temple. Yet I remember that he is the god of all living creatures — of tame and wild kine, of birds, insects and all small beasts that move upon or within this earth.'

'Then I know his name better than you,' Avran spoke triumphantly. 'The one true God, three in one and one in three. Does not our Bible say that he is the Alpha and the Omega?'

'Omega is the name of a land, not of a god!' Essa retorted derisively. 'And Alpha — what is Alpha? Another name of that threefold god of yours, who contrives also to be one? I have not heard that Alpha has any powers here, nor yet your Omega. Bear in mind, prince of the south, that you are far from your own realm!'

Then her mood changed again and she spoke earnestly. 'Once more I implore you: do not mock the gods of these mountains! If you persist, then you will bring yet more trouble upon us.'

Avran was not proof against this pleading. As Robin looked at him interrogatively, he responded in a tone that was a mixture of acquiescence and exasperation: 'Very well, then, I will say no more. But I shall keep silence for your sake, Lady Essa, and not out of respect for these Safaddnese gods. In them, I have no belief; nor shall I come to believe in them, whatever transpires. What do *you* think, Simon? And you, Robin?'

Robin spoke decisively. 'Whatever my own thoughts, I shall also respect your wishes, Lady Essa.'

I hastened to concur, using almost the same phrase. Yet, as I did so, I felt myself a traitor to my faith. I admired Avran's courage, even if I regretted what I considered to be his unwisdom. Were we not now outside Christendom, in heathen lands where the old, evil gods might yet retain their power?

For her part, Essa seemed satisfied. 'Thank you, gentlemen; your words give me ease. For my part, I shall continue to implore the nine gods of these mountains to be charitable to us. Sir Robert, this piece of meat seems quite adequately cooked; would you care to sample it?'

We ate well that night and, with the veludain in unceasing watch over us, slept well also. Before I fell asleep, I reflected that I could colour in more of my picture of Essa. It was, I supposed, unsurprising that she had grown up in that robber's camp without learning anything of Christianity. Belatedly I remembered that, when Robin,

Avran and I had gone to pray in the chapels of Arravron and Ingelot, Essa had never accompanied us. And if her father — what had Dan Wyert called him? Oh yes, Lerenet Falquen — had taught Essa nothing of our religion, why, I could understand that also! For surely her father must have been Safaddnese; that, at least, was becoming evident.

I think all of us slept long, but we awoke to so grey a day that it was hard to tell whether it be early or late. The wind had shifted to the westward and a moaning sound from the temple behind us intimated that Daltharimbar was once more crooning to his worshippers, if any yet lived. However, this was again a day of Halrathhantor, for the cloud had settled anew on the mountains and rain was falling lightly but persistently.

All in all, the prospects were so unpleasing that, when we saddled the veludain and set forth, we did so entirely without enthusiasm. Even Essa, mounted now on Feathertail, was reluctant to leave the protection of the temple portico.

It was hard to find a track along the mountain shoulder, in such conditions and among so many boulders. Once we came close to riding down another small herd of uvudain, but they fled from us so swiftly that we could not see whether they bore collars. A few birds, calling harshly among the rocks, were not even glimpsed.

We ate our midday repast in the partial shelter of a large boulder, a shelter that we forsook even more reluctantly than we had left the temple. By then, indeed, the rain was heavier and the mist thicker. Since we could see neither the valley below nor any peaks above, we were judging our route by the wind on our left cheeks and the slope of the ground.

Though the terrain seemed to become ever more barren and the weather ever colder, it was only when we found ourselves obliquely approaching the bare face of a crag that we realized how a shifting wind had betrayed us into heading upslope. Of course, we did intend eventually to cross back over the Highshadows; in such weather, however, we were not foolhardy enough to attempt such a feat.

By then it was late afternoon and we knew we had made little progress northward. Not that we much cared; by then our only desire was to escape from the rain and cold. Consequently, when in turning

214

downhill we happened upon a stone structure that promised some protection, we agreed immediately to stay there for the night.

What was that structure? I do not really know, but it struck me as much like a Pennine sheepfold — an uvudu-fold, maybe? There was a circle of high drystone walling, with an opening only on the upslope, eastern side. Inside the circle was a crude stone shelter of moderate size, roofed by slabs that showed signs of having been worked. Its single small doorway was also on the eastern side, protected from the wind.

That shelter was a little odorous within and none too clean, but at least it was dry. We were able to light no fire that night, for there was neither hearth nor chimney. Consequently we were early in seeking our blankets.

The veludain, though less fortunate than we, had at least the partial protection of the stone wall. I woke once in the early hours, sensing their unease; but, whatever the danger was, it passed and I fell again into deep sleep.

Next morning's weather was considerably worse. The wind was so much stronger that the rain was being driven almost horizontally. Avran, the first to venture forth, came back in with a glum face.

'A foul day indeed, friends. The wind comes from the north and, when we ride out, we shall have the rain in our faces. It is not a happy prospect, I fear.'

'Then must we go forth today?' I put the question tentatively. 'Yesterday, in somewhat better conditions, we made small enough progress. In today's weather, our progress could only be smaller yet. We have been enduring much strenuous adventure; do you not think that a day of rest might be good for us all?'

'You are correct, of course, Simon.' Robin spoke concernedly. 'Nevertheless, I have misgivings. We must pass beyond these mountains before winter settles in and makes any crossing impossible. Already Besbalet — what do you call it in English? Oh yes, October — is more than half gone and we have not yet even reached the highest peaks. Can we afford to linger for a day, even in such foul weather?'

He paused and studied each of us in turn. However, he must have perceived from our expressions that not one of us was anxious to brave the elements, for he went on: 'Well then, let us agree to spend the forenoon here. Yet if the weather proves any fairer after noon, we must venture forth and travel as far as we are able.'

So we breakfasted in leisurely fashion. Afterwards, Dan went out to see how the veludain were faring. When he came back, he told us that the wall was furnishing better shelter for them, with the rain so wind-driven, and that they were contented enough. We were aware of their contentment, of course, as indeed we were always aware of their mood. However, the comment served to set us talking about veludain, horses and other beasts. Indeed, though Dan was soon drowsing, we others passed the hours till midday wholly in talk.

Since by noon the rain had not abated, we spent the rest of the day equally relaxedly. Though we had no fire we were warm enough, wrapped in our cloaks and within the small space of the byre. Indeed, with this opportunity for idleness, we were quite as content as the veludain. Avran played on his pommer tunes that he had learned in Arravron; I brought out the timbelan from my pack and sang songs from Reschora and from my homeland; Robin told tales of his farings into distant lands and Dan, yarns from his days as a mercenary.

As for Essa, she would neither sing nor join in the storytelling; she merely listened. She seemed quite to enjoy the music and smiled sometimes at the stories, that rare smile which so lit up her face. However, at other times when I glanced at her, she looked so abstracted that I knew her thoughts had roamed far away from that stone byre. I wondered where they wandered, and in what company.

We sought our sleeping-sacks early, trusting that we would awaken to better conditions. We had no such fortune. Next day's weather was still worse, for the wind was just as strong and the rain had turned into sleet. To sally forth, with no certain prospect of finding shelter of any kind, would have been so manifestly foolish that we did not even consider doing so.

Yet that second day proved not nearly so pleasant as the first had been. The gloom of the byre and the closeness of our quarters were becoming irksome. Avran and I tried over some tunes on pommer and timbelan, but with little enthusiasm. Dan extracted a hunk of wood from his pack and whittled away at it persistently with his knife: though I could not determine what he was trying to shape, I did not even feel inclined to ask. Robin talked quietly with Essa, principally about his life in the courts of Herador and Merania; in this she

216

seemed quite interested, asking many questions. And so, somehow, the day passed. I am sure that, by evening, each of us was praying that better weather next day might free us from this confinement.

For a second time, our hopes proved vain. The wind did indeed drop overnight, enabling us to fall asleep in a mood of false optimism. Unfortunately, we woke to find it again whining about the stone byre and driving, not just sleet, but snow — a dry, gritty snow that stung one's face.

Toward noon, I sallied forth briefly for the private reasons that enforce such venturings. I found that snow had banked up against the back of the byre and against the wall behind which the veludain were sheltering, giving them an extra protection from the wind. They seemed not to be greatly desiring the fodder that, by now, they must be needing, for there was none within the pen. Instead, they had relapsed into that condition of semi-wakefulness by which sheep and cattle also endure such weather; none of them, not even Proudhorn, responded to my presence in any way. I returned to our shelter feeling rebuffed and altogether out of sorts.

Within the byre I found no contentment, for my friends were in no better mood. We had little inclination for music that day. I strummed my timbelan half-heartedly for a while, but soon put it away. Avran did not even fetch out his pommer and no-one wished to sing. Robin made a brave attempt at cheerful conversation but gained little response, even from Essa.

The only topic that interested us was the weather. Would the blizzard continue for many days or would it soon cease? Would there be only a thin cover of snow or would it pile up deeply? There were already drifts against boulders and walls, of course, but the mountainside might be otherwise swept clear by the wind.

Avran had seen snow only rarely and knew little about it; he asked many questions. The other three had experienced it often enough, but only in the lowlands. Thus I found myself, after my Pennine childhood, considered the expert on snow in the mountains. Yet, for my part, I had never been in mountains so high as these and doubted the value of my own pronouncements.

When we sought our blankets on that fourth night, I am sure our prayers for better weather were even more fervent than hitherto. For my part, I was beginning to fear that we were indeed suffering from the malignity of the mountain gods, Daltharimbar and Halrathhantor and those other seven deities of the Safaddnese whose very names I did not know. In my prayers, I implored my patron saint to befriend us. Was he not a zealot, a warrior, who should be able to vanquish these pagan gods? Well, perhaps; but he had lived far from this land of Rockall and I found myself doubtful of his influence here. In such questioning mood I fell asleep.

Maybe those doubts were unjustified; maybe St Simon had interceded for us, or maybe Essa's prayers to those mountain deities had persuaded them to relent for a while. Whatever the reason, we woke the next morning to stillness. The blizzard had ended and the wind was no longer blowing.

When I went outside delightedly, I discovered there was even sunshine! Of a pale and watery sort, maybe, and coming uncertainly from a sky in which there was still much grey cloud; but it was the first occasion on which we had seen the sun in many days. The snow was banked high against the back of the byre and had curled round its front in two horns; there was snow heaped against the eastern walls of the beast-pen; but elsewhere, the snow had indeed been swept away by the wind. The veludain were stretching, stamping and snorting, eager to be away.

After the hastiest of breakfasts, we repacked our blankets and the other possessions we had strewn about, then left byre and pen without regret. We had put on the overboots from Ingelot, but were warm enough not to need the rest of the winter gear.

As we were expecting, though snow was piled against each boulder and though patches of plants held it also, much of the mountainside was clear. We did not mount immediately, for we wished to allow the veludain to forage for fodder. It was amusing to see them sticking their noses into the snowbanks while they tugged at plant fronds and to hear their indignant little snorts as the snow chilled their muzzles.

Indeed, we were all in a cheerful mood, Avran and I quite exuberant. We made snowballs to sling at the boulders and at each other, Avran shouting gleefully when one hit me on the nose and fleeing in pretended terror when I pursued him with another. Soon Robin was joining in our game. Dan was laughing at us; his rest had certainly done him good. Even Essa was smiling on that bright morning.

218

After a while we ceased our games, mounted our now-adequately-fed beasts and set off resolutely. We perceived quickly enough that, in the rain and mist four days before, we had been misled by the slope of the ground and had strayed very far from our intended path. We were now on a rock-strewn upland, quite out of sight of any river valley. If Lyonesse were somewhere to the northwestward, as we presumed, then it was in that direction we must head. However, I found it hard to turn away from the sunshine and wished most heartily that I could direct my steps southward to my desire.

As if offended by our turning our backs upon it, the sun soon withdrew behind cloud. Soon also, a wind began to build up again. I say 'a wind', yet it was little more than a breeze and waxed, waned and changed direction so frequently as to seem like many little winds.

The upland we were traversing lacked dramatic topography, yet it was by no means flat. There were ridges that seemed at first to furnish a good line for us, but which then divided or faded away. There were many declivities, some so shallow as to be revealed to us only by the patch of snow they had entrapped, some deep enough to be spiked by marsh-grasses or even to contain an ice-encrusted pool that we must skirt.

In addition to the many solitary boulders, again and again we came upon mounds of stones. Sometimes these were broad and low, much like the boulder patches one finds below English gritstone edges. At other times, however, the piles were much higher and as steep-sided as walls. Perhaps, indeed, they *were* walls, or perhaps they were mounds raised over the graves of fallen Safaddnese chieftains. It was hard to see why anyone should choose to live in such a bleak land, yet we had been told that the Safaddnese loved these mountains.

When we needed to traverse one of the boulder ridges, our mounts moved even more slowly, fearful of entrapping a foot in some unseen, snow-filled cavity between the stones. The steepest ridges, like the pools, had to be skirted. We had hoped to travel rapidly in a consistent direction; instead, we were winding along like caterpillars in a pebble-heap.

That was bad enough. A worse problem was that, without either the sun or a steady wind to guide us and having no experience of such country, we were uncertain of our way. That we were by then much higher in the mountains was evident from the greater depth and greater extent of the snow. Avran, ever optimistic, thought we might be crossing the saddle of the Highshadows, but I doubted it. How could such broad uplands be called 'mountains'? Moorlands they were — or stone-lands, rather.

There were footprints in some of the snow-patches. Several times we noticed trails of uvudain (I was more sure of their track pattern than of their name), travelling singly or in small herds. Once we saw the trail of a pack of xakathei — nothing like so large a pack as had attacked us, but large enough for us to be relieved we were crossing, not following, its path. We observed no human tracks, however, nor any of veludain, loose or mounted. (Yes, I could tell the difference readily enough.) Indeed, we had quite decided that this bleak upland must be uninhabited when we were surprised to see ahead of us, at no great distance, a tower.

Since the tower seemed more or less in the direction we thought we should be heading, we made for it. This was rash, perhaps, since any people encountered were likely to be hostile; but, by then, our curiosity about these elusive Safaddnese had quite overcome our fear of them. Moreover, from the outset we had little expectation that the tower would prove to be lived in. As we drew closer, the lack of lights or of smoke, even on so dark and cold an afternoon, showed us pretty clearly that it was not.

The tower was circular in shape and quite tall, set high on an isolated rock pinnacle with cliffs on all sides. The only access was by a flight of steep steps, so narrow and exposed that no enemy could attain unscathed even to the mighty copper door that served as entry to the tower — a door overhung and protected by machicolations. When we reached the foot of the steps and peered upward, we could perceive a gap in the stone-work immediately above the door, through which stones might be dropped or boiling oils poured at need. It would indeed be a foolish captain who strove to take such a tower by storm.

'Whoever built this tower has not long abandoned it,' Robin said, almost to himself.

'Why do you say that?' I asked surprisedly. 'I see no tracks in the snow hereabouts. Indeed, I have seen nothing today to suggest any human presence.'

'Look at the door, man, look at the door! Copper it is, and highly polished. How long do you suppose such metal would survive, in such a damp, high place, without turning green with verdigris? A few short years, at most; and such a high polish would have dulled in a matter of months.'

Avran shivered. 'When we were in the wind-forests, I thought them bewitched. Maybe my reasoning then was not good, but now I think again of witchcraft. Where *are* the Safaddnese? They have wrought so much and yet they have left it all behind, to the winds and the wild beasts. They seem even to have forsaken their herds. It is not natural.'

He looked challengingly at Essa, but she made no answer. Instead, Robin asked: 'Well, since we have already ridden so far, shall we spend our night here? There is shelter of a sort in the lee of the steps.'

To our startlement, it was Dan who protested; perhaps Avran's words had alarmed him.

'No, my masters, we must not stay here. Maybe this place is bewitched, maybe it is not. Like enough, though, that some man or some creature be watching us from high in that tower! I could not sleep easy by it; we are not safe here. Let us go on our way, I beg you, my mistress, my masters! Let us find a resting place hidden from its view.'

'As to safety, nowhere in these mountains can we find that,' Robin stated flatly. 'For my part, I would feel as safe — or as unsafe — here as anywhere. Still, darkness is not yet upon us. We can ride on awhile, if you wish.'

'Then we should be on our way,' responded Avran; evidently his own apprehensions had been reinforced by Dan's words. Without more ado, he urged Highback into movement.

Dan gazed imploringly at Essa, evidently feeling he had spoken out of place. Then, since she showed sign neither of approving his plaint nor of reproving him, he rode off unhappily on Longshank after Avran. Robin glanced at me and shrugged his shoulders, then the other three of us followed. However, Dan kept at a discreet distance from his mistress during the rest of that day's ride.

Not until two further hours of wearisome winding among stone-piles and snowbanks had gone by did we pass finally from the view of that tower. When eventually the deepening darkness forced us to seek a resting-place for the night, the best shelter we could find was in the lee of a boulder mound.

Over a supper of cold uvudu-meat and chill draughts of water from our flasks, we discovered little about which to converse. Our optimism of the morning had quite dwindled away.

Nor did it cheer us when we heard, for the first time in many days, the high, insane-sounding laughter of a tasdavarl prowling somewhere nearby. Moreover, our guardian ring of veludain was decidedly nervous. Under such circumstances we dared not seek sleep. Only when, well after midnight, we sensed that they were relaxing did my comrades and I crawl into our sleeping-sacks.

We woke to a bleaker cold; yet the wind had dropped and there was no more snow. Instead, that dreary upland was enveloped in mist. It was not so dense a mist as Avran and I had endured in the Trantevrin Hills, so many months ago. Nevertheless, it was quite enough to finally overthrow our sense of the direction in which we should travel — a sense which, in my case, had been lost the after-noon before.

The task of finding the way was entirely ours; the veludain could not aid us. A veludu, though so much more at home in rocky terrain — our beasts were still in excellent condition — lacks the perception and special intelligence of a sevdru or a rafenu. Its rider cannot simply decide a direction, leaving his mount to find that direction. A veludu, like a horse, needs to be guided.

After our brief breakfast, we set out boldly enough. By riding in line, with the man in the middle — Robin during the forenoon, Avran afterward — calling out corrections whenever those before him went off direction, we hoped to maintain a consistent course.

Normally, in open country, this method works well. Here, however, it did not. There were too many boulders to be circuited; too many rock mounds to be avoided or traversed. At the end of a frustrating day, we were in terrain looking pretty much the same as when we started. Whether we were on line or not, I could not tell. All of us were in low spirits when we sought our sleeping-sacks. Fortunately, no tasdavarl was about and the veludain apprehended no danger. We fell swiftly into the sleep of exhaustion and slept long and calmly.

It was well that we slept, for the third day of that journey was a dreary repetition of the second. The mist was no thicker, but no less

222

dense either. Each rock mound and each deep snow patch presented fresh difficulties, but all have blurred into sameness in my memory, into a monotony of arduous endeavour.

At that day's end, when we had unrolled our sleeping-sacks in the poor shelter afforded by a single, massive boulder, Robin voiced openly the thought that was in all our minds.

'Lady Essa and gentlemen, I must say bluntly that I have no clear idea where we are. We have not encountered any high peaks and, for that reason, I believe we are now to the north of the Ferekar Dralehenar, the Highshadows. However, whether we are east of their line or whether we have strayed west of it, I cannot say.'

He looked around at us, expecting a comment or protest; but we were silent. Indeed Avran, who had served as our other principal guide, was nodding gently, his expression grim.

So Robin went on: 'Nor do I know what to suggest for the morrow. Unless there be more snow, I believe Simon might have skill enough to lead us back on our tracks, all the way to that second temple of Daltharimbar. I fear I can conceive of no other method by which we might be sure to reach any definite place. What think you? Should we turn back?'

None of us liked that idea, but we could produce no other that was better. If the sky had cleared, giving us a sight of the stars, we might have risked travelling by night, despite the hazards of rock and snow; but, since we had entered the wind-forest, every night had been cloudy. And on the morrow, what then? If we were vouchsafed a sight of the sun, route-finding would be easy enough. Even a wind blowing from a consistent direction would help. If there was no wind and if the mist persisted, none of us could conceive any means by which we might determine our way. It was a disheartening prospect.

When we had fallen into silence, there came the mocking laughter of a tasdavarl, somewhere among the rocks to my left. Then another joined in, from somewhere on my right; and another; and another, till we were ringed about by the sound of their hideous mirth.

The veludain were on their feet and tense. Hastily we armed ourselves. However, as we awaited the onslaught of the pack that must be circling us, we realized that Essa was still lying composedly in her sleeping sack.

'You have no need to be fearful, gentlemen,' she reproved us.

'Remember, a tasdavarl is a cowardly creature. They make noise enough, but they will never attack — not while our beasts keep their vigil. Leave your swords unsheathed, if you must; but relax and conserve your strength. Be assured, anyway, that the tasdavarlei will all be gone to their dens by midnight. It is always their way. They are hunters of the gloaming, not of the full night.'

We looked at one another; then Robin lowered his sword and sat down on his sleeping sack. As Avran, Dan and I followed suit, Robin responded surprisedly: 'We are grateful for your advice as always, Lady Essa; but why did you not tell us this two nights back, when we heard that other tasdavarl? The veludain were equally watchful then.'

'Yes, they were afraid, but not of the tasdavarl. A solitary tasdavarl would not dare to attack them, though a pack might if they relaxed their vigilance. No, on that night some other, more formidable creature was prowling nearby. What it was, we shall never know now; a branath, mayhap. I am only thankful it did not attack us.'

For my part, even after Essa's reassurance, I could not relax while the tasdavarls were rendering the night so hideous with their howls. Though, as she had predicted, the sound ceased long ere the new day began, I was not comforted. I felt that it was not the tasdavarls, but Daltharimbar, Halrathhantor and those other seven gods who were laughing at us. Had they not lured us deep into their realm, so that we might wander as helplessly as lost lambs till they chose to butcher us?

My prayers to God and St Simon, fervent though they were, brought me little consolation. Even in my sleep, I seemed to see grinning stone faces of beasts and of gods, and to hear those peals of mirthless, merciless laughter.

Chapter Twenty-three

THE CITY BY THE SHORE

'Simon, do I not hear water trickling, somewhere ahead? Can we be coming to the end of this dreary wasteland at last?'

Avran was in the lead and I just behind him. That morning, on setting out for a third time into the mist, we had agreed not to turn back but to continue, as best we might, in yesterday's direction. There had been a few changes — snow patches that were shallower and less extensive, a greater number of plants — that suggested we might be moving gently downhill; nothing conclusive. But this — why, it was the first time we had heard the sound of running water since entering the tunnel, eight long days earlier!

When the others caught us up, they agreed without hesitation that we should abandon our course and follow, instead, that of the stream. Certainly it must lead to lower ground, even perhaps to the sea itself! As we sought the stream, that thought gave us new vigour.

Its peat-brown waters were flowing out from a little bog, set in a hollow of the moor. The veludain drank eagerly and so did I, for I knew how sweet such waters could taste. After watching me hesitantly for a while, my friends drank also of the brown waters and each of us recharged our flasks. Then we rode alongside the stream as it wound its hesitant way across the boulder-strewn upland, wondering as we did so whether it was indeed flowing to the sea or whether it might merely empty into some larger morass.

Fortunately, it did not. Instead we began to be conscious, despite the mist, that we were riding down a shallow valley. This was not easy travelling, for the valley had trapped the snow and the veludain were often more than fetlock-deep. However, since at last we had a sense that we were making progress, our spirits remained high.

After a couple of hours' riding, the valley steepened and we saw

225

the loom of crags to left and right through the mist. We traversed what was surely a tumbled wall; we passed a heap of stones that seemed once to have been a byre; and we startled a herd of uvudain that scurried away among the rocks too swiftly for me to loose an arrow.

Beyond that jumble of stones the valley narrowed and deepened, the stream forcing a swifter and more clamorous passage among boulders and down little rapids and waterfalls. Since there were steep rock walls on either side of us, it was well that there was little snow. As it was, the rocky banks provided only a perilous footing, even for a veludu; had there been deeper snow or ice, the valley would have been impassable. Yet the precipitous descent afforded extra excitement; yes, we were leaving that desolate upland behind us!

The valley wound sinuously to the left. Then, quite abruptly, the wall of rock at right seemed to fall away. There came a wind, fumbling at the fringes of the mist until it was torn back past us; and suddenly we were looking out upon a wider view than had been vouchsafed to us in many days.

Below there stretched a long slope, scored deeply by our stream. Its waters were tumbling noisily down steeper rapids and greater waterfalls to plunge, far below us, into the quieter waters of a small river. The further slopes of that river's valley ascended before us into the mist. However, as we looked leftward — ah! as we looked leftward, we could see that river emptying into a much larger body of dark water, marged by silver-grey sands. That greater water stretched away into the haze of distance without giving any hint of a further shore. The sea! Surely it must be the sea, at last!

There was a babble of excitement. Each of us gazed at the others in wonder and joy. Then Robin pointed and cried: 'See, there is a road beside the river — yes, there, at the very foot of the slope. And do I not perceive a bridge away downstream, and another road beyond the bridge?'

'Yes, you see all those things, Robin,' responded Avran. 'But I can see something yet more remarkable! Follow with your eyes the curve of the shore to the westward. Do you see it also? — in the point of land reaching out into the water, in the farthest distance to which one's eyes can reach. Can I not see many buildings, and even lights? Is that not a city?'

226

All of us strained our eyes, gazing into the haze. I drew in my breath, then expelled it slowly. 'A city! Could it be the town of Sir Arthur Thurlstone and Sir John Warren? I have heard that it is on a bay. Lady Essa! Gentlemen! We may be looking down upon Lyonesse!'

Robin, Avran and Dan exclaimed in delight, but Essa was doubtful. 'I am not sure . . . Perhaps you are right, Simon; I trust so; but there may be other cities on the northern sea. Do not build your hopes too high.'

'Well, let us go to find out.' I was impatient, now that my particular Promised Land seemed so close. 'If this be not Lyonesse, then surely the people of the city will at least set us on our way.'

'Yes, let us seek the city,' Robin echoed. 'But let us also take care! The descent is a steep one. We must not urge our veludain along so fast that they lose their footing. Nor can we expect to reach the city today, with noon already past, the days so short and the way so long. We can scarcely hope to reach the bridge before evenfall, and there will be many more hours of riding ere we can attain the city's gates. Remember also, we do not know to what land we are coming. Caution is more important than haste!'

Then, perceiving that his admonitions had dampened our spirits somewhat, he laughed: 'Be of good heart and patience, my friends! Only a short time agone, we were wandering in the mist with no goal in prospect. Now, if it be God's will, we shall reach the city at a few hours past noon tomorrow — a good time for an arrival!'

The descent proved even more difficult than Robin had forseen. There were still patches of snow, crusted with ice, and more extensive stretches where snowmelt water had frozen again. At one point, Highback quite lost his footing and Avran came close to being thrown. However, urged to even greater caution by that near-mishap, we completed our descent without accident.

Before darkness, we had found ourselves a good refuge — a ring of strong stonework set on a rocky knoll, about a league short of the bridge. High on the wall was set an iron brazier and, beneath a protective stone slab, there was an ample store of logs and kindling. Clearly this brazier would serve as a beacon in time of danger. Equally clearly, since the watchtower was not manned, no danger could be apprehended by the people of the city, whoever they were.

We crossed the stone bridge in the early light of next morning; not a very bright light, for the day was heavily overcast, but with only a slight haze to remind us of the dismal mists of previous days. The bridge was fortified by twin towers at either end, between which were massive gates of burnished copper; but those gates had been fastened back and the fortifications, like the watchtower, were unmanned.

The roads to and beyond the bridge, and the bridge itself, all showed signs of use and there were tracks of veludain and uvudain in patches of roadside mud. However, the use did not seem to have been recent and the tracks were old — two months old or more, I estimated. Nor, for that matter, did we find any indication that the valley was occupied. We saw neither farm nor byre and, when we passed walls, they were either in need of repair or had already collapsed. There were coppices of trees, so neatly circumscribed that they seemed like planted groves, orchards even; but the trees were not of kinds known to us and very much in need of tending.

All in all, as we followed the road on that bright morning, there came to us that too-familiar sense of being in an empty land — a land that had once been peopled, but whose people had died out or gone away. Surely Lyonesse could not seem thus? I found my confidence waning fast. Eventually I voiced my thought to Robin.

'Not Lyonesse? Well, perhaps you're right, Simon. And look across the sands there' — for, by then, we had passed the river's mouth — 'the water is very quiet. Either the tide is out, or there is little tide and the water not deep. If this be the northern sea, as I supposed, we must have chanced upon a very sheltered bay. Not a likely landfall for your English knights, Simon!'

'Perhaps this is a sea under enchantment.' That was Avran speaking; we were riding along the road in a group. 'I am coming to believe these whole mountains are enchanted.'

'And yet, Prince Avran, you do not respect the power of our northern gods!' Essa was mocking him again. 'For my part, I am sure we are travelling to some Safaddnese city, not to one constructed by knights from afar. This road, for example; it is an old road, not one made or renewed recently.'

She was perfectly correct, of course; my spirits sank further. 'The

Safaddnese realms on the northern sea — what were their names, Lady Essa?' I asked. 'Vasanderim was one, was it not?'

'Yes; and Avakalim, and Brelinderim. Vasanderim is the western-most realm, close to the lands that the Norsemen hold; we cannot have travelled so far. This must, I think, be a city of Avakalim, the midmost realm.'

'The land of your golden bird — of the taron?'

'Perhaps. Strange, though, is it not, that we have seen no sea-birds?'

'Not so strange.' Avran was speaking again. 'Such birds gain their food from the tides; they do not congregate in sheltered bays.'

'Or mayhap the enchantment has driven them away?' Essa was teasing him again.

On that morning, however, Avran did not respond as she hoped. His only answer was: 'Mayhap.'

After that, we all relapsed into silence. However, my thoughts were busy. Where *was* Lyonesse, in relation to those two realms? To the east, I guessed. How great a journey did we face, then, before we could gain Sir Arthur Thurlstone's city? A long one, I feared. And how would the Safaddnese treat us? Would they aid us on that journey, or would they strive to prevent us from making it? Was there a chance of travelling by ship? If so, would Reschorese gold serve to buy our passages? Who would be the mariners — Safaddnese, or men from Warringtown perhaps? Not Mentonese, surely, for if Toril Evateng was to be credited, their vessels did not visit these northern shores.

Yet the question that most troubled my mind was — why were there no other travellers? Why, even so close to a city, was the land still so empty?

We took our midday repast on the shore. I was a little cheered by the sight of a crested, cormorant-like bird that swam and dived quite close to the sand's edge where we were sitting, quite unconcerned by humans or veludain. There were waves breaking on that shore, but only very gentle ones; this must indeed be a sheltered bay, to have so small a tide. I sniffed the air: it did not smell of salt, but perhaps that was not surprising, so close to a river mouth. For the same reason, it might not taste salty. Nor did it, when I cupped my hands and drank.

Far to our right was the line of stonework that was the city's wall, but it was in shadow and I could discern no details. Did I see smoke arising from fires within? I thought so, but I could not be sure. Beyond, everything faded into grey haze.

The city had been built upon the very tip of a promontory reaching out into the water, like the extended thumb of a right hand. In its last stretch before the city gate, the road climbed a little, and rocks, not sands, formed the shore. The city wall rose high before us — a wall without towers, built of massive blocks of purple stone. It was separated from the road by a deep, broad moat, that curved across the promontory, dark and evil-looking.

The moat was crossed only by a single, narrow stone bridge; this was shaped like a blunted spearhead, its base against the road, its tip touching the wall. At that point, there was a doorway into the wall, closed by two tall doors of burnished copper. As for the road, it curved back along the further side of the promontory, thereafter following the shore away into the distance.

When we came close to this bridge, we saw that its farthest portion, just before the door — the tip of the spear — was separate from the rest and that there was a cavity in the wall into which it could be withdrawn. The drawbridge was surfaced with copper, that favourite metal of the people of this land; but the copper was green, not burnished. We saw also that the walls were battlemented; however, no guards were visible upon those battlements. Was it the strange colour of the stone, was it the bleakness of the face it presented to the road, or was it sheer lifelessness that made this city seem so very forbidding?

We halted at the landward end of the bridge, then gazed at one another. 'An enchanted city in an enchanted land,' Avran observed softly.

Essa gave him a twisted smile. 'And what does a valiant knight do, when such a prospect confronts him?'

Avran looked at her, then suddenly he laughed gaily. 'Why, he rides up to the enchanted gate and he blows his horn!'

Promptly he rode forward across the bridge, the padded hooves of Highback silent on the stonework but clamorous on the copper. Then, pulling his clarion out from beneath his cloak and setting it to his lips, Avran blew a mighty blast: 'Tooroo, tooroo!'

The sound echoed against the walls, then dwindled away into silence.

A second time Avran blew: 'Tooroo, tooroo! Tooroo, tooroo!' Again, there was no response.

After hesitating a while longer, we others rode across the bridge to join Avran before the gate. He had proved his valour and was conscious of the fact; when he turned toward us, he was smiling.

'No-one appears to be at home,' he said simply. 'Yet I would swear I saw lights, yesterday from the mountainside; and Simon, did you not see smoke?'

'I thought that I did,' I answered doubtfully.

Unlike the drawbridge, the great copper doors had been polished — and recently, it seemed — for they gleamed dully red in the shadow of the wall. On each, there was a great knob in the ferocious form of an animal's head with staring eyes, gaping jaws and sharp fangs.

We gazed rather helplessly at the doors for a while; then Essa dismounted and said: 'I shall see whether these doors will open.'

Avran and I dismounted also and hastened forward to aid her. However, she waved us back. 'Mayhap I shall need your strength, gentlemen, but first let me try.'

Obediently we stood and waited, each of us sure that the doors would not budge. Yet they did. Using both hands, Essa grasped the beast's-head knob of the right-hand door by its ears — and turned it. As we watched, astonished, the door swung inward.

231

Chapter Twenty-four

THE EYE OF THE GOD

Essa was, I am sure, quite as surprised as we. She released her hold and, allowing the door to swing unchecked, gazed in through the shadowed doorway.

'There is a stone-walled tunnel,' she called rather breathlessly. 'The wall must be very thick. There are other doors at the tunnel's inner end, but they're standing open. I'm going inside.'

Without more ado, she walked briskly into the tunnel and vanished from our view. That act was rash, but Avran's was almost equally so. Plucking his sword from its scabbard, he ran after her.

I was more cautious — or more cowardly. I returned to Proud-horn's side, to extract from its loops my bow, string it, and attach the quiver to my belt. Then I stood for a moment, drawing in my breath, as I summoned up courage to enter the open door.

Robin had dismounted by then and drawn out his own sword. There was a grim smile upon his face. 'Like you, Simon, I fancy not the prospect. Yet, like you, I feel we must follow our impetuous friends into the city. I take comfort only in the fact that our veludain seem not to be afraid. Dan, will you stay here with them?'

'Nay, not I!' The old man was deeply alarmed. 'How would I fare, if you came not back? Rather I'll go with you, whatever may chance.'

'Very well, then, let us all enter the city, beasts and folk alike. However, I suggest that you and I should enter it on foot, Simon, so that you may keep your bow ready and I, my sword.'

As we went cautiously in, Robin paused to open the other door, to allow the veludain an easier passage; it swung inward as easily as the first. Dan, still mounted on Longshank, led the beasts in. He had drawn his own sword and was striving to look fierce and purpose-ful, though with small success.

Perhaps we should have closed the doors, but we did not. It seemed better, somehow, to leave our line of retreat open.

The tunnel was just about broad enough to accommodate a tumbril or small coach — a narrow enough entry to so large a city. It was arched over by tightly fitted stones, but there were shafts overhead down which unpleasant objects might be dropped, or dread liquids poured, upon any unfortunates trapped within. That day our passage was easy, since the inner doors stood open. Even so, I was glad to pass beyond the tunnel.

Within, there was a circular paved space like a sort of inner barbican, surrounded by a second defensive wall. This inner wall, however, was not starkly plain, like the outer. Instead it was elaborately carven with figures of mail-clad soldiers with weapons held at the ready. Their swords, axes and spears were all of unfamiliar form and yet surely Safaddnese; my last hope that this might be a city of Lyonesse was extinguished. Crystal had been set into the eyes of the guardian figures, causing those eyes to glisten coldly. The soldiers seemed to be watching and waiting, eager to advance in war upon us. I found them disquieting.

However, there was a second tunnel through this inner wall; not in line with the first, but somewhat to one side. Its doors also were open and through it we passed, more quickly since the inner wall was much less massive than the outer. I was not sorry to leave those carven warriors behind me, yet I did not like knowing there were three sets of doors and two tunnels to be traversed before we might make our exit.

Once inside, the three of us paused to gaze in disbelief. The veludain ranged about us, gazing also.

We had entered upon a wondrous place that seemed part city, part forest, part garden. There were houses, to be sure, in rows radiating inward from the walls of that great inner bailey, like spokes from the felloe of a cartwheel. Tall houses they were, with burnished copper doors and fine, high windows, glazed and leaded like those of a church. Between the rows of houses there were many trees, even taller than the houses and still in full green leaf — an astonishing sight for us, after so many days traversing those bare mountains.

A road led before us into a glade of trees that seemed to mark the centre of the city. We could not see beyond that glade, for its trees blocked any view of the more distant city wall. Beside the road and in banks before the houses, there grew many aromatic plants. Some were yet in flower and there were butterflies of strange shapes feeding upon, or flying about, them.

All was beautiful, yet so unexpected as to seem quite wrong, almost baneful. Though Avran was not beside me to prompt the thought, I found my lips were framing the word: 'Witchcraft!'

Before we had time to begin looking for them, Essa and Avran emerged from the door of one of the houses. Avran, I noticed, had sheathed his sword; but Essa looked puzzled, even frightened.

'This is a strange city indeed, gentlemen! Those houses — we have been inside three of them. Each is fully and richly furnished, with chests, benches, woven hangings — oh! and much else! I am sure they have been lived in recently. Indeed, it is as if their owners have only just left.'

Avran was looking even more troubled. 'There is even food. No, not on the tables — no signs of feasts newly abandoned. Yet there are dried herbs and hams hanging from the rafters; there are firkins of salted butter and kilderkins of beer — all the sorts of food that can be left in storage for a while. But the people — where have they gone? Why have they gone?'

'Or are they somewhere about us, watching us?' I was quite disconcerted by this news.

Robin shook his head slowly. 'If we were being watched, the veludain would know it. As you'll be aware, they are not altogether easy in mind — perhaps because *we* are uneasy — but they do not perceive any immediate danger. No, I am forced to believe that this city has been forsaken, abandoned.'

This puzzled me even more. 'If the people left deliberately, then why did they not take their food?'

It was Essa who responded, though she was not directly answering me. 'They have left no fresh or perishable food. They seem also to have taken their clothes, for I saw none. Nor did I notice any children's toys.'

'Maybe they have no children, the people of this city. Maybe they wear no clothes. Maybe this be a place of ghosts — of spirits.' Dan's nervousness was flaring up again.

Essa laughed. 'What — ghosts that eat ham and butter and drink beer? I have never heard of any such!'

We others laughed also, feeling a sudden, brief lightening of heart.

Dan seemed considerably cheered. 'Shall we let the veludain browse for a while, then?' he asked. 'There's fodder here, the like of which they've not enjoyed in many weeks.'

'By all means,' answered Robin. 'For my part, though, I'd like to explore further. Shall we walk along the road, to see what lies in the grove and beyond?'

Despite that moment of laughter, I remained apprehensive of this place. I was remembering the adventures of Arthur's knights — Sir Gawain, Sir Bedivere and the many other worthies of the Table Round who had chanced upon benign-seeming places and, upon entering them trustfully, had been caught up in webs of malign enchantment. Though I contrived to sound cheerful when I agreed to accompany my friends, I kept my bow at the ready and my arrows close by my hand.

Only Dan Wyert remained behind. 'Someone ought to stay with the beasts,' he said. 'Mayhap they don't need watching, but I mislike leaving them alone. I'll keep with them if you don't mind, mistress and masters.'

It was a strange afternoon, brighter than the morning had been and with a sort of luminescence, yet without sunshine. Moreover, there was an elusive haziness. The air seemed clear, yet one could not see very far — certainly not more than a furlong. There was no wind within these city walls and we could no longer hear the sounds of the shore. On the paved road, our soft boots made little noise and, when we spoke, our words seemed to be sucked away into silence.

After a while, indeed, we ceased to converse. Instead we walked slowly, looking intently about us. All four of us felt uneasy, especially when we passed in among the trees. Robin had not sheathed his sword and was now clasping it with blade foremost; Avran's hand was at the hilt of his.

Outermost there was a double ring of trees of no great height, too densely set to be counted. There the road narrowed to a path, though it remained paved. Then we entered a broad space in which herbs grew in such abundance that the air was redolent with their scent,

236

an unfamiliar odour and soothing to the senses. However, when Essa bent to break off a frond and sniff it, she made a face and cast it away.

Next we passed in through a single ring of taller trees, with dark, needle-like leaves; some sort of pine, I presumed. Between each two grey trunks was a block of stone exactly the oblong shape and size of the stone tombs one sees in English parish churches, yet without the carven figures usually placed upon such tombs. Into the surfaces of each, however, words had been inscribed in the strange Safaddnese lettering and weird symbols graven.

As I gazed at the one nearest to me, I saw there was a line deeply scored parallel to, and just below, the flat top. I shivered; perhaps these *were* tombs, then! However, I did not ask Essa about them, for I was not sure I wished to hear her reply.

Between that third ring of trees and the innermost, there were banks of flowers, waxy yellow in colour and strange in shape, their petals like five open fingers. Neither butterflies nor bees flew about those flowers, yet they smelled sweet enough. Or did they? As I sniffed, I was less sure that I liked their odour; nor did Essa stoop to pick one.

The path divided, to form a broad paved circle about the innermost ring of trees. These were the tallest of all, with delicate, feathery-fronded branches and leaves of the palest green, almost white. Though there was no wind, those pale leaves were fluttering in an unceasing, uneasy motion, as if something were breathing gaspingly upon them. I am fond of trees, but I did not like those trees.

I counted them. Nine trees; well, I had expected it.

In the exact middle of the glade was a huge black stone. At first I thought it formless and irregular, and so did my companions. Only when we had walked past it and chanced to look back did we perceive, with a start, its character.

The great stone had been carved and polished into a human shape — the semblance of a vast, cloaked figure, seated cross-legged and with hands clasped before him. We had approached him from the back, for he was facing toward the sea; the city wall was less high on that side, and the trees of the outer rings had a gap in them, giving him vision across the water. Yet he was not looking that way. Instead, his head was lowered and his eyes hidden.

As I looked more closely at the statue, I began to perceive that, after all, he was *not* altogether human in form. I noticed he had strange, misshapen ears, then that the fingers on those clasped hands were unduly long, their nails stretching past his wrists. Moreover, his knuckles were not merely swollen, but barbed. I was reminded of the figure of Daltharimbar in the tunnel. This must surely be another of those accursed Safaddnese gods!

Suddenly I was conscious that Essa, standing beside me, had stiffened, as if in shock. Then her breast heaved and she cried out, in a sort of desperate wail: 'Aiee, it is Mesnakech, god of magic and of evil! I had trusted never to set eyes upon his grim shape! Why, this must be his city, Sasliith! What an ill chance!'

As we gazed at her in startlement, she threw back her head and gave a sort of convulsive sob. Then, with both hands, she made an outward circular gesture, afterwards clasping them and bowing her head forward. Somehow I knew that these were motions to ward off evil.

Perhaps they comforted her, for she relaxed a little. Nevertheless, Essa's face, when turned to us, was so solemn that my heart seemed to congeal within me even before she spoke.

'Gentlemen, I must give you ill news. We were indeed lost; or perhaps our feet were being set upon a path we would not have chosen to tread. We have not traversed the mountains; we are not on the coast of the northern sea. Instead, we are by the shore of the Asunal Dralehin, the great water which in your tongue, Simon, men call Lake Highshadow.'

We exclaimed in horror and gazed at one another in bewildered dismay. Yet Essa was not done; she was already speaking again.

'Those are harsh tidings, but I must give you worse. As my father told me and as Toril Evateng told you, the letzestre of Paladra has an ill name — and with reason. In the wars that once tore these mountains, its people performed the darkest deeds. Their letzahar and his priests performed human sacrifices and many other acts of black cruelty. By that means, they sought to gain the complete mastery of their god; for the Safaddnese at once control, and are controlled by, their gods, just as the inscription in the wind-tunnel told you. Mesnakech, the god of the Paladrans, is the master of magic and the unseen; his searching mind reaches into the depths of the

238

earth and out beyond the stars. The Paladrans strove to harness, through Mesnakech, all those powers within and without this world that are least comprehended and most dreaded.'

'It seems, then, that Mesnakech is but another name for Mephistopheles or for Satan.'

Avran was speaking quietly and, if Essa heard him, I do not think she comprehended him. Instead, she went on speaking, with the determination of one who feels it necessary to tell a story in full, however little her listeners might like what they are going to hear.

'Had the Paladrans succeeded, perhaps the Safaddnese Empire would have endured till now — or perhaps those forces would have torn it, and these very mountains, asunder; I do not know. But the other Safaddnese rallied against them. They were shocked by the deeds of the Paladrans and by the intent of those deeds. The other Safaddnese gods moved against Mesnakech, at once to control and to aid him. And, with god striving against god and man against man, the Safaddnese lost their dominion over the other peoples of these mountains.'

This was a part of the story that Toril Evateng had not known; or, if he had known it, he had not told it. 'Was Mesnakech destroyed, then?' I asked. 'And his people?'

She laughed, a ripple of amusement as cool as the rattling of ice in a jar. 'Nay, Mesnakech was not destroyed. He cannot be destroyed, for is he not a god? Is he not sitting behind you, as you stand here? And do you not see about you a city, the city of his people? The Paladrans remain Safaddnese. The people of the other letzestrei might seek to divert them from evil courses, but they would never seek to destroy them. The nine gods and nine peoples are all part of one great pattern. That pattern cannot, must not be broken.'

Essa had been speaking on a rising note and ended in a strange, chanting cadence as one repeating a litany. She stopped abruptly, however; and when she spoke again, it was in a more normal tone.

'Yes, gentlemen, we are in Paladra — in Sasliith, the city of Mesnakech, and at the very heart of the sacred grove of Mesnakech, where his power is strongest. We are in great peril. If it be not too late, then we must flee from this city. Yet I fear it is already too late.'

At that very moment, her words received a terrifying endorsement. Sounding through the trees from our left there came the mighty

239

stroke of a great bell. Then came a second stroke; and, after that, stroke upon stroke, with the regularity of a great heartbeat.

We turned toward the sound, then gazed at one another in wild surmise. What could this sound mean, so loud and so sudden? For my part, I was sheerly terrified.

For some reason, Avran glanced back toward the statue. He froze, his expression aghast; then, with shaking hand, he pointed. We looked back apprehensively. Why, the statue *had raised its head*! Instead of looking down, it was staring at us, with flaring animal nostrils and blazing eyes!

At that our nerve broke entirely. Incontinently we fled, prince and maiden, warrior and English lad alike, out of the ring of trees, past the stone tombs and back along the path.

Nothing happened to stop us. When we regained the road, there was Dan Wyert, mounted on Longshank and waiting for us with the other veludain — an act of great courage, for he was shaking with fright. We hurled ourselves onto our mounts and rode frantically toward the city gate.

I think all of us expected to find the inner tunnel closed against us; yet its doors still stood wide. Through it we went and across the barbican — a frightening traverse, for the stone warriors, eyes shining redly, seemed to be reaching out at us with their weapons. Did I hear shouted threats and curses, or did I imagine them? I know not.

The doors to the outer tunnel were likewise standing open. Through it also we rode, in such pellmell haste that I did not concern myself with menaces from above. Nor was anything dropped upon us. Yet that tunnel seemed to resound with evil voices; or was some strange echo produced by our panic haste?

Out over the bridge we fled, the veludain's hooves drumming on its copper sheathing. The very road seemed a threat; we turned neither to right nor to left, but sped across it.

Only the high peaks seemed to offer any refuge from the terror behind us. Up a stony ridge we rode, the ridge that formed the spine of the promontory, urging our poor beasts to greater effort as the slope slowed them. We were all in frantic fear that, even now, some hand might be reaching out to grasp us. From ridge to mountain slope we passed, our pace slowing as the angle of the land steepened but our fear of some pursuit, physical or spectral, no whit diminishing.

Yet only the clangour of that great bell pursued us — a dwindling sound, as we rode onward and upward. When at last I glanced back, I saw that the shining copper doors had closed behind us.

Our panic flight ended in a common consent of exhaustion, just as darkness was beginning to fall. By then we were high on a saddle of the mountains, with the ridge by which we had ascended behind and below us. We could still hear the sound of the great bell: a stroke as regular as a pulse and, by now, sounding little louder. Sasliith itself was already hidden in the gathering gloom.

We dismounted and eyed one another in embarrassment, each now ashamed of the fears which, so recently, had been so overmastering. Typically, it was Robin Randwulf who spoke first. His voice sounded weary and gruff.

'Well, we escaped — or we were permitted to escape, I know not which.'

Avran sighed. 'Aye, we escaped; and I give thanks for that. Yet from what were we fleeing? Were there men in that city after all, or were there only evil spirits? I liked not that bell.'

'You fled from the presence of the god, in fear of his wrath, as men must.' Essa was quite sure. 'Were not his eyes upon us?'

Now that I was recovering my courage, I was beginning also to doubt. 'Yes, but *were* those eyes? Might they not have been crystals, or jewels perhaps, like those of the stone soldiers in the barbican walls? Maybe the light of the sun was catching them.'

Robin shook his head. 'No, Simon, that won't do. There was no sunlight; and the god, did he not raise his head to gaze at us? And the bell — how do you account for the bell? I saw no belfry and certainly I saw no bellringers. Moreover, the day was windless. You cannot explain it away, friend, strive though you might.'

I was prepared to be stubborn. 'Yet we have all travelled with Vedlen Obiran. We have seen deeds performed by him that would have seemed miracles, had we not known the truth of them.'

'The truth of them, Simon?' It was Avran who was responding. 'Did you fully comprehend how Vedlen achieved his feats? I know

241

that I did not; yet he was a worker of benign magic. This time, we have been close to great evil. Did you not sense it?'

I capitulated; indeed, I was too tired to argue further with my friends. 'Yes, I sensed a malevolence. And no, I cannot explain it. Whether it was the evil of man, spirit or god, I cannot say.'

'Nor I.' Avran shivered in the reminiscence of fear. 'All I know is that I have been very much afraid, more so than ever before. When I blew my horn before that gate, I was challenging forces greater than I knew.'

'As for me,' said Robin, 'when I left these mountains, I did so with gladness. Now I am glad again to be among them.'

Then he stiffened. 'Look there! No, not back toward the city — along the lake shore. Yes, there! Do I not see torches?'

Indeed he did. In this last, fading light of the day, the Asunal Dralehin shone dully, its face wrinkled with shadow. On its black margin, away to the northwest, we could see many pinpoints of bluish light.

'See, they are moving. They must be carried by riders — many riders.' Essa was speaking quietly. 'It must be the worshippers of Mesnakech — the people of Sasliith returning to their city.'

'They'll know that we've been there! They'll come after us!' Dan was in a renewed panic; his voice was shaking. 'See, there's lights in the city now!'

It was true. Those lights were brighter, but fewer; just nine of them, and red lights, not blue. I had not understood till then that the walls of Sasliith formed a nonagon, but now it was obvious, for there was a bright light at each angle. Mighty torches they must be, to seem so large when seen from so far and to cast so bright a glow on the purple walls. But who, or what, had lit them?

Yet Essa was speaking calmingly. 'No, Dan, I do not think they will pursue us. Mesnakech had us within his grasp, yet his hand did not close upon us. If their god did not strive to hold us, then the men of Sasliith will not seek to catch us. Mayhap we should set a watch tonight, but I believe we have little to fear. We have been in great peril, but we have been permitted to escape it — for a while, at least.'

She was right, for we had a night free from other alarms. I was the first on watch and, despite my weariness, did not find it hard to keep awake, for I remained profoundly uneasy in mind. I watched the torches moving steadily toward Sasliith — a great company, certainly, but of what nature I could not tell from so far. I trusted it was a company of people, yet feared it was one of evil spirits. That was irrational, perhaps; would spirits need to bear torches? Yet, it was hard to be rational at such an hour, and after such a day.

By the gate of the city, the lights divided. Some part of the company went within, so that the city came to be lit by blue lights as well as red. At that time, the great bell fell silent at last. As for the rest of the company, they continued along the lake shore and passed from my view.

These mountains had been empty; or so it had seemed. They would not be empty henceforward.

Chapter Twenty-five

SNOW AND SPECULATION

When Avran had taken over watch I had plunged, like a diver, deep into the river of sleep. Indeed, I dreamed that I was being carried helplessly along in a current toward a black lake. Though I knew there was a means for escaping from those swift waters, I was quite unable to recall it, strive though I might. When I was awakened, I gasped and panted like a drowning man pulled ashore just in time — and felt the same relief.

Dan Wyert was looking down at me anxiously. 'Be you all right, Master Simon? It was powerful hard to rouse ye!'

'Yes, I'm all right; thanks, Dan. But is not the hour very early? It is entirely dark still.'

'Not quite sun-up. Yet Sir Robert, he thinks we should be over the mountain-top before dawn — before any sharp-eyed Paladrans can spot us.'

Since we were so high and among so many rocks, it seemed to me unlikely that we could be seen. Surely an old campaigner like Robin Randwulf would know how well concealed we were from view? But then I thought to myself: perhaps those watchers from Sasliith have special powers — after all, they might not be human! I was shivering, and not entirely from the cold, as I slipped out from and rolled up my sleeping-sack.

Almost as soon as I had stowed it and mounted Proudhorn, we were on our way again. When I glanced apprehensively back toward Sasliith, I could not see it; the lights had been extinguished and the city was cloaked in shadow. Even that very hiddenness was disturbing. Despite my brave, doubting words of yestereve, I had not wholly recovered from my earlier terror. In that hasty departure, I sensed its echo among my companions.

However, with dawn and the realization that there was a ridge-crest of solid rock between Sasliith and us, my spirits began rising. The sky was cloudy, but the clouds were high. It would not be a bright day, but there was no threat of severe weather. I was becoming hungry and was glad when Robin called a breakfast halt.

When we had dismounted and were preparing to eat, Avran grumbled good-humouredly: 'Dried uvudu meat and cadarand cakes as usual, I suppose, and brown water from the stream. Solid, sustaining nourishment, of course; yet our sight of all that good food in the houses yesterday made me long for a change.'

'You should be grateful to be alive, my friend,' Robin rebuked him.

'So I am; but to be alive is to be hungry.'

Dan eyed them both with a strange, rather mischievous smile, then went over to unload some parcels from Twistbeam's pack. Returning, he asked: 'Might you prefer a little rafenu-ham or some veludu-cheese, then, Master Avran? And a sip of wine, maybe?'

Avran groaned. 'Don't tease me.'

Yet he was not being teased. Dan proceeded to lay before us what seemed, to our eyes, an unbelievable feast. There was indeed a ham, there was cheese and there were earthenware flasks of wine. Bread was lacking, but the cadarand cakes would substitute well for that. Our eyes lit up; but Essa was shocked.

'Dan Wyert, you stole this food and this wine from Sasliith!'

Since Dan was so sensitive to Essa's opinions, I expected him to quail before this accusation. However, he seemed not even slightly abashed.

'Well, Mistress Essa, an old soldier does scrounge food from wherever he finds it. Yet steal this I did not. In each of the houses I visited, I left behind a good Heradorian gold coin — ample payment, surely?'

Quite evidently Essa was taken aback by this response. However, in a moment her expression relaxed and she gave one of her rare laughs. When her face lit up, as it did then, I could quite understand why Avran found her so attractive.

'Aye, that would be ample payment. There is little gold among the Safaddnese, and that little they dedicate to their gods. Why, the Paladrans might well consider your coins to be gifts from Mesnakech himself! And maybe they were, Dan; maybe they were. I am glad that you left the gold.'

So was I. Indeed I wondered whether, if Dan had not, we would have been permitted to escape from Sasliith. As circumstances were, I was able to tuck into the food with great pleasure; and so did the others. When we rode onward, we felt that special contentment of body and mind which comes from having eaten unexpectedly well. It gave us heart for the further weary days among the mountains that seemed in prospect.

Since we had witnessed the onset of morning light from the southeast, it was easy for us to set a northeastward course. The land was rising steadily and there were peaks to our north, clad still in snow. These we were aiming to skirt rather than climb.

As the hours passed by the weather grew cooler, the wind becoming brisk and blowing steadily into our faces. On that day, having once donned those excellent ameral-fur jackets, we were not tempted to doff them. Indeed I wished I had put on the fur trews and boots also, for I was by no means warm. However, since the others — even Dan and Essa — had not done so, I could not; it would have made me too ashamed of my lack of hardihood. Consequently, I endured the chill and managed to keep smiling.

By late afternoon the mountain peaks rose before us. For a while we were able to find a route across the wind-stripped tongues of rock that thrust out southward from under their snow-caked faces. Soon, however, we found ourselves traversing a wilderness of snow through which many rocks protruded, like plums through the crust of a pudding. By then we were less sure of our direction, for the light had worsened. However, by generally keeping the wind in our faces, we assumed that we must still be heading northeastward.

I know now that our presumption was incorrect. Without our realizing it, the wind had swung more to the east. Consequently, instead of crossing the line of the mountains directly, we were doing so obliquely. That error was to bring about many chances and mischances.

However, we were confident that we were making good progress and, despite the cold, we were all in ebullient spirits. I was in the lead for once, singing some favourite English ballads to myself and watching for tracks in the snow. Avran was chatting briskly to Essa, who was responding much more freely than usual. At the rear, Robin and Dan were deep in reminiscences about their soldiering experiences. They took care to keep watch for signs of any pursuit but, in such a landscape, it was not easy to be sure concerning the nature of dark, distant objects.

However, we saw nothing that day to cause us disquiet. Our night, spent in a snow-free place behind a stone-ridge, was chilly but tranquil. Nor did the Safaddnese gods haunt my dreams.

During the early part of next morning, we completed our traverse of the snowfield and passed on to high moorland, with parched-looking grey-brown soils, tufty plants whose leaves were almost as grey as the soils, and rocks mottled with faded lichens. This change made us feel that the highest mountains were behind us; it renewed our false confidence in our route. Consequently our spirits remained high.

I think that, after our escape from Sasliith, we all believed the Safaddnese gods had relented; or maybe, that our strong Christian saints had placed over us the shield of their protection. Yet we knew now that there were men among these mountains, so we continued to keep a careful watch, throughout that day and, after a second uneventful night, during the next.

Insofar as we could, that is; for that third day was suited neither to watch-keeping nor to direction-finding. We had woken under a sky exactly of the hue of the lead they use in Derbyshire to sheathe the gutters of church roofs — and seeming about as heavy. There was little wind, and that wind came in irregular gusts, each time from some new direction. Quite soon a drizzle of rain began to fall, veiling the distances from our view.

I had kept on my ameral-fur jacket overnight and, on rising, had put my Doriolupatan cloak over it — green side out, though indeed yellow and green would be equally conspicuous in so sombre a landscape. Avran had dressed similarly, each of us finding the combination satisfactorily warm and waterproof. Robin and Dan were wearing their woollen cloaks over their fur jackets and looked rather too hot. However, apparently Essa found her hooded cloak a sufficient protection against the weather; before donning it, she had slipped off and put away her fur jacket. I was beginning to believe that, though a woman, she was the hardiest of us all.

With the rain the soils darkened, the plants appeared greener and the colours of the lichens brightened to chestnuts and golds. The very rocks, hitherto so dull-looking, were seen now to be blotched with red, green and even, in places, pale blue. Since we were riding along in our own little enclosed world, its limits defined by the opacity of the surrounding rain-clouds, one noticed and appreciated such details.

Yet it was hard to know what course we were following. Avran and Robin still seemed sure that we were riding northeastward; Dan Wyert was trustful and Essa seemed uncaring. For my part, however, I was beginning to wonder uneasily whether we might be again heading deeper into the mountains. My recollection of our haphazard wanderings among the Ferekar Dralehenar was all too vivid; I was no longer able entirely to trust my friends' direction-finding abilities. Yet, when we stopped for our brief midday repast, I did not disturb their high spirits by voicing my uncertainties.

Although the winds continued to be light and intermittent, the day was turning ever chillier. The rain had not ceased, but there was soon an intermingling of snowflakes — large, wet flakes that melted when they settled. Before we had ridden even another league after lunch, the raindrops were becoming fewer and the snowflakes more frequent. Moreover, they were melting much less swiftly. They were forming a dusting of white over the land surface, like the powdering of flour on a housewife's arms after breadmaking.

'I like this not at all,' remarked Robin. 'If this snowfall becomes heavier, we shall need to seek shelter. Yet there is little prospect of that, unless we find lower ground.'

Since we had bunched together, conversation was easy enough. It was Avran who responded: 'The only lower ground I know of is behind us — more than a day's ride back. Whatever else may chance, I do not fancy a return to Sasliith: do you?'

Since the answer was obvious, Robin ignored the question. 'I had expected that, by now, we would have traversed the highest land and would be descending toward the sea. What say you, Lady Essa? May we hope soon to find refuge in some valley?'

'As to that, Sir Robert, you can hazard a guess quite as well as I,' Essa answered coolly. 'These mountains lie outside my knowledge. I cannot even give them a name.'

'But can you tell us which letzestre we are in?' I asked.

'No, not even that. Yet I think we have left Paladra behind us.'

'I hope so,' commented Avran. 'I liked not that land.'

'But you are enjoying its ham and its cheese, are you not?' Essa was teasing him again, but much more gently now. Indeed, she was smiling at him.

Avran laughed. 'Yes indeed! I was thoroughly tired of dry meat and stale cakes. Yet I could wish we had prospect of some warm shelter, in which we might relax and properly enjoy that good food.'

However, as we rode onward, our circumstances merely worsened. Soon there were no more raindrops but only snowflakes, drifting or swirling about us as the wind-gusts weakened or strengthened, coating the earth and forming white caps on the rocks. The visibility decreased till we could maintain our direction only as we had done in the mist, by riding in a spaced-out line and calling corrections to one another when there were divergences from that line.

Nor did we find lower ground, though we rode till the day's end. The best shelter we could discover was the snow-drifted lee of a crescent-shaped rock mound. We dug out the snow and formed it into a wall on what we took to be the north side. Huddled into our sleeping-sacks between rocks and snow wall, we did not fare too ill.

The snow ceased and the wind dropped as night fell. Unfortunately, it began to snow again next morning. All day the snowflakes swirled about us in a shifting wind. Smaller flakes these were, that felt gritty when they blew against one's face. Since the snow was beginning to reach fetlock-depth, concealing the stones, we had to ride slowly and carefully to avoid falls. Yet sure-footed the veludain were, even in such conditions. Though there were a few stumbles on hidden stones, and consequent clutchings of horns by we their riders, there were no falls.

We had by then donned the full winter gear that Toril Evateng had provided — boots, leggings and all. Our black-flecked white furs would have looked agreeably expensive, and would have attracted much admiration, amid the bustle and colour of a royal court. Here, however, they made us so much a part of the snowy landscape that, if one were hindmost in line, it was hard to see one's leaders.

When it was my turn to serve as back-herd, I realized that I was not finding it easy even to see the veludain that were farthest ahead.

In sudden enlightenment, I looked more carefully at Proudhorn. Why, the hair of his hide was thickening and lengthening — and, yes, all the new hairs were white! Within another week, or perhaps in only a few days, those longer hairs would have overgrown the shorter grey ones and Proudhorn would be almost as white as the snow about us.

Throughout that day, we strove to maintain a steady direction. However, it was hard to tell whether we were succeeding, for the view seemed not to change. From morn until evening, all that we saw was the white blanket of snow, strewn with dark, snow-capped rocks that caused it to mirror, on a larger scale, the flecked pattern of our furs.

At that day's end we could find no shelter at all. So we made one for ourselves, shaping a wall of snow about us in the fashion in which English children build snow-castles. That gave us protection from the night winds and we had the Paladran ham, cheese and wine to cheer us.

As for the veludain, they seemed quite able to find food even in such conditions, digging into the snow with spreading fore-hooves — I had not realized how widely those hooves could spread — and feeding snortingly upon the plants thus exposed. Indeed, while browsing in this fashion, the veludain made almost as much noise as piglets in a sty. However, they had become quiet and watchful by the time of moonrise, as if there were some special danger to be feared.

Yes, the sky had cleared enough for us to see the moon — a slender rind only, for we were near the end of October now. Since we watched the moon's rising, we could identify a definite direction for the first time in three days. Moreover, though the whole sky did not clear, we were able to see also those stars that the Sandastrians called Ebuvrior, the Sky Saucepan, and that we Englishmen style Arthur's Wain in tribute to the king who will come again. Thus, without seeing it, we were able to locate the star called by the Sandastrians Lakhretmar, the Unmoving One, and by we English the Lodestar.[1]

Robin marked the northward direction by pressing with hands into

---

[1] Nowadays the Pole Star

251

the top of the snow wall to form a deep groove. As he sat back upon his sleeping-sack, he sighed and spoke to us in bitter self-contempt.

'Of little value am I as a pathfinder for you! I am reckoned a good guide through cultivated lands and forests; I have not been lost even among the mountains of Armenia and the deserts about Antioch; yet, in these stony moorlands, I have been twice at fault in a sennight! Yes, we have endured mist and snow, but even so we should not have gone so far astray. Maybe my powers are failing. Maybe it is time that I ended my wanderings; or maybe they'll be ended for me, somewhere among these bleak highlands.'

'Speak not thus, Robin.' Avran was distressed. 'You have striven well in difficult circumstances. I grew up among high hills, yet I have been equally at fault. These northern ranges are great and bewildering; you need not chastise yourself because we have lost our path among them.'

'Lost our path?' Essa was sitting in deep shadow, yet I could see the brightness in her eyes, as if some of the moonlight had found lodgement in them. 'Mayhap so; but are you sure a path is not being found for us? Not one of our choosing, maybe, but yet a path. Were we not conducted into Paladra, where we never desired to set foot? Were we not spared by Mesnakech to have our feet set, by him or by the other great gods of these mountains, upon this other path that it has never been our intent to tread? No, Sir Robert, I do not think we are lost. Rather, I think that we are being guided.'

Avran was sitting close by me. He had been made both weary and irritable by so arduous and frustrating a day. While Essa spoke, I could sense my friend's rising wrath. I was unsurprised, therefore, when he burst out at her.

'What nonsense! If we have been spared and if we are being guided, it is by the hand and mind of the One True God, not of any of your false mountain divinities.'

'Oh indeed!' observed Essa chillingly. 'And yet, Prince Avran, was I not with you, little more than three days ago, when you quailed before the very gaze of one of those "mountain divinities" whom you despise so much? Yes, you tootled bravely on that little horn of yours; but, when Mesnakech turned his eyes upon you, how very swiftly you fled!'

This rejoinder was devastating; it caused Avran to splutter like a hot coal that has been wetted. Before he found coherent words, Robin broke in. The threat of a quarrel must have jerked him out of his mood of self-castigation, for he spoke calmly and calmingly.

'Whether we be astray or whether we be following a path set for us, I cannot tell. I know only that, when morning comes, we may at least set off in the direction we desire — northward and, I trust, out of these mountains. After that — well, we must await what else chances, if chances these are! Let us sleep now, ere the stars fade.'

Little did we suppose what the next day would bring. If we had had foreknowledge, we might have slept scarcely at all; but, in our ignorance, we slept soundly.

Chapter Twenty-six

A FALCON IN THE SKY

That next morning I woke slowly and reluctantly, catching at the fringes of what I knew had been a wonderful dream. However, my dream shredded as I strove to seize it and was forever lost. The sky overhead was dark still, but there was a paleness in the southeast that betokened the sun's rising. There was a steady soughing also; a wind from the southward, a warm wind.

I had thought myself the first to awaken, for Avran was lying slack-jawed in sleep beside me, Robin was snoring jerkily and Essa, in the further shadow of the snow wall, lay still and silent. But Dan was up already and preparing our repast. Seeing that I was awake, he nodded to me cheerily.

'It fares to be a better day, Master Simon. We're done with snow for a while, I reckon.'

'Aye; and that's good.' However, I added cautiously: 'Yet if the day turn too warm, the riding may become difficult.'

'Happen so, Master Simon, happen so. Yet a little warmth — why, it'll nicely take the chill from my old bones.'

The others were soon roused. While we were breakfasting, we heard a high, throbbing whistle. Looking upward in surprise, we saw a bird circling overhead. By its manner of flight, it was a bird of prey and by its pointed wings and long tail, a falcon. Yet this was a much bigger bird than any falcon I had seen, bigger even than a gyrfalcon and much more brightly coloured — creamy white underneath and with upper parts of cerulean blue, much darker than the limpid morning sky.

Three times the falcon circled over our snow-shelter, though it whistled only once more. Then it was gone, flying purposefully away eastward.

This was the first other living thing we had seen in several days, and much the most beautiful in many weeks. All of us, I am sure, considered the bird to be an omen — perhaps a harbinger of evil but more likely an augury of good. For me, it caused a lift of the heart, for it brought the recollection of Sandastrian night-hawks and thus of Ilven. I think Avran also was reminded of his old, and my new, homeland, so far away to the south. Yet it was Essa who responded most positively. Indeed, she was beaming with delight.

'It is a gherek!' she cried. 'It is a sacred bird, the bird of Horulgavar, greatest of the gods — the bird of good fortune! My father described them to me, but I have never been so blessed as to see one. It has flown away eastwards and we, why we must follow!'

Remembering Avran's forceful protests whenever Essa made reference, even indirectly, to her mountain gods, I expected him to object to this idea. To my surprise, it was Robin who did so.

'No, Lady Essa,' he said heavily, 'we cannot do that. Already we are too far east and too deep into the mountains. We must strike northward now, hoping to leave these high lands before we are trapped by another and harsher blizzard. We cannot risk following any bird, however fortunate. I'm sorry.'

The pleasure faded from Essa's face, as swiftly as light is cut out when one drops a shutter. 'You are wrong, Sir Robert. Believe me, you are wrong. If we do not follow the gherek, we shall be spurning good fortune and inviting ill. Only grief will result, be sure of that!'

Robin's countenance had set into stubbornness, a stubbornness echoed in the stiffness of his tone. 'I believed we had agreed, yestere'en, that we would travel north today. That seemed to me then, and seems to me now, the only proper plan.'

'And yet, Sir Robert, have you not always been one to follow wherever fortune leads?' Essa's tone was pleading, almost desperate. 'So, at least, you have told us. Why, now, must you abandon that principle of a lifetime?'

'I would not be following fortune; I would be following only a bird.' Robin was uncompromising. 'However handsome that bird be, it can only be flying back to its roost. That roost must be in the mountains, not by the shore — not in Lyonesse, for sure. Why, when we are striving to find an English settlement, should we choose to follow a Safaddnese bird? That would seem to me quite beyond reason. What think you, gentlemen?'

His eye fell first on me, no doubt because this quest was mine. 'I don't know,' I stammered. 'Your observations make sense, Robin. And yet, your ideas have most often proved sound, Lady Essa. But I think — well, northward does seem the logical course. We have always been going north, or striving to do so. Yes, northward, I suppose.'

'And you, Prince Avran?'

He sighed and looked embarrassed. 'I too am one to follow fortune, all of you know that. Yet . . . Well, I have vowed to go wherever you go, Simon. If you elect to head northward, why then I must fare northward also. I am sorry, Lady Essa; most sincerely I am sorry.'

'Dan?'

Our companion wriggled uncomfortably. 'Nay, Sir Robert, 'tis not for me to say. I shall go wherever you choose — you and Mistress Essa.'

'Very well, then.' Essa's tone was bleak. 'Northward we go. Yet I fear we may all rue this choice.'

On that day it was an easy direction to find. The wind blew steadily from behind us as we rode, becoming ever warmer, so that our backs were soon quite hot. Having slept in her fur jacket, Essa had packed it away at rising; we others did so within an hour of setting forth.

As the snow began to melt, icicles grew to form glistening fringes beneath the snow-caps of the rocks. However, these also melted away as the sun became still warmer. Soon the hooves of our veludain were sinking quite deeply into the softening snow. Nevertheless, they were enjoying the sunshine, making that strange sniffling sound which, in a veludu, signifies happiness. Ever and anon, after giving us mental notice, they would bend their heads to crop off a frond of one of the plants that were emerging from the snow. Then, since those fronds were beaded with water-droplets, they would shake their muzzles, throwing out a spray that sparkled briefly before vanishing into the whiteness.

Once we crossed a broad line of many hoofprints, but by then the snow had melted so much as to enlarge them beyond the point at which they were at all informative. Probably they were tracks of veludain, but whether wild or ridden, even whether heading west or east, I could not determine. Nor was I much concerned. Though Essa's prediction had troubled me at first, the sunshine, the bright blue sky and the high spirits of Proudhorn had caused my spirits to rise also. Surely nothing ill could happen on so bright a day!

Yet there was too much snow to vanish in a single day's melting. The upland extended before us in a seeming endlessness of white, broken only by the varied colours of the emergent, lichen-mottled rocks and by the dripping grey-green fronds of the few tall plants. Hour upon hour went by without anything seeming to change — a steady jog through the increasingly sloppy snow, under the blue curve of a cloudless sky.

Noon was long past when we perceived, with pleasurable surprise, that we were riding down a gentle slope. To be sure, the land was rising again in the distance, but there must surely be a valley between, even if we could not yet see it. A valley; then a river, and perchance a route to the sea!

Infected by our rising excitement — though mayhap Essa was not excited, for she had withdrawn into herself and would not speak to us — our veludain increased their pace to something approaching a trot, regardless of conditions underhoof. Then they checked, for the slope was becoming dangerously steep.

We were approaching the verge of a great line of cliffs. They curved in from our right and extended away before us to a distance beyond our view. As we gazed northward, we saw that the height of those cliffs increased in that direction. We might follow their line, certainly, keeping well to the left on safe, flat ground. However, if we did so, there was no guarantee that we would find a way down into the valley that lay green below us.

When we looked to the right and southward, the prospect was more encouraging. The cliffs were somewhat less high and had been much bitten into by landslips. These had formed a series of broad steps that might, with a little scrambling and a certain amount of luck, be descended. It was hard to be sure, though, for the inner sides of those landslip terraces were hidden in deep blue shadow.

The sudden view instituted a flurry of comments, but then we all fell silent, wondering what we should do. Yet this was not a time for hesitation. The weather was showing sign of changing again; long fingers of white cloud were stretching from the south toward us. I felt uneasily that Halrathhantor, the Safaddnese god of the skies, was reaching out to clasp us again within one of his storms. Consequently I became impatient.

'Shall we start downward, friends? It would be well to make the descent before night closes about us.'

'Indeed we should, Simon.' Robin was nodding his head. 'And since it was I that determined our course today, it is for me to find us a path. Take heed how your beasts tread, Lady Essa and gentlemen! On such slopes, the snow may prove treacherous.'

At Robin's thought, Browntail set off along the cliff edge until, within only a few poles of our lookout, she found a way downward — steep enough, but quite possible for a spread-hoofed veludu. Avran went next, with Highback stepping mincingly, as if disdaining the wet snow. Essa was behind him, looking too small to be riding the big, bony doe Feathertail; and Dan was on her heels on the tough, if ungainly, Longshank. Our surviving pack-veludu, the massive Twistbeam, trod behind Longshank. Proudhorn and I brought up the rear, as indeed we had been doing for much of that afternoon.

The descent onto the highest landslip terrace was not at all arduous. After that, however, matters became more difficult. The next descent was a glissade, our veludain spreading out their forelimbs and sitting back on their haunches as they skidded downward. Twistbeam almost cannoned into Longshank, for Dan had unwisely paused to regain breath and self-assurance; but somehow a collision was avoided.

By that time we were in the cold blue shadow of the cliff, where the snow had piled up deeply and melted scarcely at all. When Robin rode onward to the further side of that second terrace, poor Browntail had to thrust her way through the snow, as effortfully as an inexpert swimmer breasting a strong current.

At length Robin dismounted. 'There appears to be a way down,' he called back. 'There's a line of snow down the cliff face, trapped in some sort of a crack. I believe it'll make a path for us. We'll need to watch our steps, though; we must not risk provoking any falls of rock or snow. You'd better all dismount and lead your beasts. And go slowly!'

I could not see Robin as, followed by his veludu, he embarked upon that third stage of our descent. However, I did see Avran dismount and set off after him. Avran seemed to have been gone a long time before Essa in turn dismounted and, with Feathertail on her heels, followed also.

By then Proudhorn and I were waiting in the snow slot behind Twistbeam. He seemed especially unenthusiastic; I sensed in him, and also in Proudhorn, some disquiet not caused wholly by the difficult descent. However, eventually Twistbeam, after turning his muzzle about uncertainly and tossing his horns, likewise began to descend.

When, having slipped down from Proudhorn's back, I ventured to the edge of the terrace and prospected our path, I found my own reasons for disquiet. Yes, there was indeed a snow-filled crack winding sinuously down, forming a white line against the dark rock; but it was very narrow, quite frighteningly narrow, and the drop beneath was of thirty ells at least. I was grateful that I had not been the first to venture down!

Far below me, I could see the rump of Browntail; Robin must be just ahead of her and within a few paces of the next terrace. My other companions and their veludain were well spaced out, as indeed they should be when there was such danger of accidents. To our left, not so very much further below, I could see many treetops and, among them, glimpse the foaming waters of a swift-flowing river. Why, we were quite halfway down the cliff already — excellent!

I unfastened the bowstave from my saddle to serve me as staff. Then, when Twistbeam was far enough ahead to be safe from any slips by Proudhorn or me, I set off downward.

It was not so hard a descent, after all. Earlier feet and hooves had packed the snow pretty firmly into the crack and, since it had never melted, that snow was not slippery. Moreover, my bowstave gave me confidence and I made sure to lean inward against the dark rock. Nevertheless I kept my eyes firmly on the path and avoided gazing left into those dizzifying depths.

Proudhorn was already following me down and finding secure hoof-hold. However, I sensed that his unease, instead of diminishing, was increasing. I could not understand this, but it aroused anew my own disquiet.

Yet all seemed well. That third terrace was the broadest so far and, as I now perceived, there was even a thicket of bushes growing upon it. Since their foliage was snow-encased, these bushes had been invisible from above, but now I was close enough to glimpse dark branches. Robin and Browntail had vanished from view into that thicket; Avran was just leaping down onto the terrace and Highback about to do so. Essa had been descending more slowly and she and Feathertail had made only half the traverse. Though Dan, the other beasts and I had still further to go before we attained the terrace, there seemed no particular cause for Proudhorn's unease.

And then it happened. There came a throaty roar that echoed against the cliffs, a startled, inarticulate cry from Robin and the chilling, gurgling shriek of a veludu in agony.

Avran drew his sword and flourished it to exercise his arm. Then, shouting: 'I'm coming!' he vanished from my view.

We others knew we should go to the aid of Robin and Avran, but that was not easy. The veludain were evincing none of the courage with which they had faced the xakathei. Whatever the animal was that had attacked Robin, it was quite terrifying them — I could sense their terror. Highback had leapt down onto the terrace, but he would advance no further. His horns were lowered, but he was swinging his head from side to side and seemed quite ready to flee. Essa was running — yes, running! — down that perilously narrow track, but Feathertail was stock-still, so completely blocking Dan's way that he could not follow his mistress. Though Dan shouted and even cursed, the veludu would not budge.

As for me, with two veludain blocking my path, I could not hope to reach the terrace in time to render assistance. Nor might I use my bow, even if any target came within view. Certainly the bowstave was in my hand and the string in my pouch, but the quiver of arrows was fastened to the saddle at Proudhorn's right side and, consequently, inextricably pressed against the rock face.

Forgetting that I had no need to use speech, I shouted at Proudhorn, demanding that he edge backward to some place where I might reach my arrows. For the first time, however, he would not obey me. Frantically I gazed about but, though my fear of heights was temporarily forgotten, I could see no way forward. The rock above was crumbling and ominously overhung by snow, while below me the cliff fell sheer.

By that time, Essa had leapt down onto the terrace and was pushing past Highback. She had drawn out her knife. Highback flourished his horns at her, as if in warning. However, though he permited her to pass him, he would not follow her.

When his mistress passed from view, Dan Wyert became quite frantic. If he could have thrust Feathertail from the path and into the depths below, I'm sure he would have done so. However, she was standing with hooves braced so solidly that he might neither shift nor pass her.

Suddenly Dan's feet slipped from under him and he came close to falling from the path. That quenched his ardour; having pulled himself to safety, he huddled terrified against the rock.

So there we were, Dan and I, each quite unable to aid our friends in what we knew must be their extreme danger. Instead we listened fearfully to the noises below; the growls, the cries and the sounds of movement. Then, abruptly, there came silence.

The veludain raised their muzzles skyward, not listening but, rather, employing that other strange sense which they and many other Rockalese beasts have, the special perception that so often warns them of danger.

After a few moments, Highback lowered his muzzle and began to move forward into the thicket. His steps were hesitant, however, and he stopped before passing out of view. Feathertail began again to advance down the crack. Dan, trembling now and stumbling so awkwardly that I feared he might fall, followed close behind. Long-shank and Twistbeam were soon also in motion; indeed, they were moving with a sort of half-fearful eagerness. And, of course, Proud-horn and I followed them down.

However, when the veludain reached the terrace, they all halted behind Highback. Were they unwilling to venture further because of continuing danger, I wondered? Yet Dan and I were permitted to pass among them without difficulty.

Between the thicket and the terrace edge there was an open space, in which the snow had been much trampled. It presented a scene I shall never forget.

Avran was standing stiffly. His right arm and shoulder were bloody, the sleeves of his fur jacket torn and his expression grim. At his feet there lay on its back a great beast, its chest transfixed by his sword. Its thick fur was creamy-white, irregularly streaked with grey-brown.

By the sharply pointed claws that it had flexed in death, it must have been some mighty relative of the cat, like the lion or the tyger. Yet such teeth it had! — two great sickles, curving down from its upper jaw and now pointing skyward.

Beyond was lying the veludu doe, Browntail. From her position, she might have been sleeping; but I knew she was dead. Beyond again, at the very edge of the terrace, Robin was lying in the snow, his sword fallen from his hand. As for Essa, she was kneeling beside him and weeping.

Chapter Twenty-seven

A Climb from Danger

Dan gave a wordless groan and stumbled over to Essa, dropping onto his knees beside her. 'Sir Robert,' he quavered. 'Is he — is he gone, then?'

She looked up at him bleakly. 'Nay, he lives. Yet he is sorely wounded — wounded beyond my skill of healing, I fear. Yet fetch the satchel from my saddle, Dan; I must do what I may for him.'

'Let me go instead,' I urged. 'Dan came close to falling; he was badly shaken, even before this.' And I ran back to where the veludain were waiting.

After I had handed the satchel to Essa, I asked Avran: 'Well, my friend, you seem to have slain the beast, but not without scathe. I've been useless enough so far; let me at least tend your wounds.'

'Yes, I slew it; but too late. Oh, very well, do what you wish.'

Avran's shoulder had been scratched severely enough, but the great gashes cut by the beast's claws into his arm were much more serious. Having washed off the most part of the blood, I placed handfuls of snow on those wounds to staunch its flow. When the bleeding appeared to have ceased, I fetched some bandages from Essa's satchel and, remembering the skills learned from the wizard's men, contrived to bind up the wounds neatly and firmly.

Avran suffered me to do this in silence. Indeed, it was evident that he was in considerable pain. His face looked grey and strained, now that the grimness had faded from it.

Only when the wounds had been wrapped did I ask him: 'What happened, friend? We could hear only the noises; we could not see.'

'I did not witness the beginning of it, but I assume that the beast — Essa calls it a branath — must have attacked Robin, or his mount, from the thicket. It used those great teeth like daggers, striking down with them from its open jaw. I think it must have leapt upon Browntail first, for she was already lying dead when I arrived and Robin striving to fight off the beast. It was leaping at him again and again, yet always avoiding his sword strokes. It moved astonishingly fast and, I believe, was trying to drive him over the cliff.'

'How strange!' I said. 'I would have thought it would have wanted — well, to slay and devour him.'

'Mayhap branaths prefer veludu flesh,' Avran answered wryly. 'Well, my arrival distracted it and, for a while, we two kept it at bay. But then Robin slipped in the snow and fell. Immediately the branath leapt upon him. I rushed forward but before I could reach Robin, it had driven those terrible teeth into him.'

'What an ill chance! But then, what happened?'

He gave me a twisted smile. 'I had a hot few minutes, I can tell you! That creature moved more swiftly than any human opponent I've ever encountered. Again and again I feared I was finished. But then Essa arrived. That distracted me, yet maybe it saved me. As I turned to shout a warning, the branath was upon me. Fortunately I was grasping my sword in both hands and, as I turned back, it leapt full onto my blade. It knocked me over and clawed at me, as you see; but — well, I'm alive and it's dead and all is over.'

His voice was trailing off as he spoke and he was looking quite ill. I spread my cloak for him, bidding him sit down upon it and relax. Then I went over to join Dan and Essa.

Between them, they had cleansed and strapped up Robin's wounds. They had wrapped his cloak about him and had somehow contrived to ease him into his sleeping-sack. He was breathing gaspingly and looked deathly pale.

'Dan tried to give him some efredat,' Essa said quietly. 'We parted his lips and dribbled it into his mouth, but he could not swallow.'

'Where was he wounded?'

'In his left shoulder — two deep wounds where those great teeth drove in. We have washed them and staunched the bleeding, but it was difficult. He is almost certain to lose his use of that arm, yet if he could only receive proper care, I think he might live. As it is — well, we are far from shelter.'

'You expected this, did you not, Essa? When we would not follow the gherek? I grieve that we did not take your advice.'

'I expected trouble, yes. Yet do not blame yourself, Simon.' Her tone was unexpectedly quiet and gentle. 'It was Sir Robert, not you, who was firmest that we should head northward.'

I sighed. 'Well, I had better see whether we can find an easy onward route. We cannot stay here, especially with Sir Robert in such case.'

Since my prospecting did not prove straightforward, a fair time elapsed before I returned. When I did so, I found Avran, Essa and Dan all seated on their cloaks beside the still-unconscious Robin. Dan had turned Avran's fur jacket inside out and was sewing up the rents with quick, neat motions of the needle. He had confessed to us — for it is not a proud admission, from a soldier — that he had once worked as a tailor, and quite evidently he retained his skills.

I watched him for a while before I noticed that Essa was cuddling something in her arms. At first, I took it to be a fragment of the fur of the slain branath. Then I noticed a sudden movement and found that two bright green eyes were looking at me.

'Whatever is that?' I cried.

'Why, only a kitten,' she responded rather hesitantly. 'A branath kitten. I wondered why the beast had attacked Robin — it was a female, you know — for branaths do not usually attack humans. Or so my father told me. I wondered also why our veludain would not come closer. They must have sensed that another branath was still alive. So I sought for the den and found this pretty little beast.'

'It is so tiny,' I marvelled. 'How can so small a creature grow so huge and formidable?'

'Yes, small indeed; it must have been a very late birth and quite out of season. Yet the kitten is past weaning, for it has eaten a piece of uvudu-meat.'

'I wanted to slay the creature,' interjected Avran. 'After all, its dam has caused us sad scathe. Yet Essa would not allow me to do so.'

'No indeed!' Essa was instantly defensive. 'Its mother attacked only because she thought her kitten was menaced. I grieve that Browntail was slain and Sir Robert injured, but this kitten is not to be blamed.'

Avran appeared quite willing to let the subject lapse; he was

267

evidently weary and, moreover, not desirous of offending Essa. 'Well, Simon, did you find us a good path?'

I shook my head, gazing at them bleakly. 'There is no onward way. On all sides, the slopes are too steep to be descended. Moreover, if we *did* get down, it would serve no purpose. The river flows right at the slope-foot — indeed, the slope is dangerously undercut in places — and it is flowing much too swiftly to be swum or waded, even without an injured companion. No, my friends; it pains me to tell you this, but we have reached only a dead end. We must return to the clifftop, if we can.'

All three were deeply dismayed. 'Say not so!' groaned Avran. 'That we have climbed down so far, and suffered such injury, all in vain?'

'I fear that is true. Moreover, the weather is worsening; we must not risk staying down here.'

Avran rose reluctantly and awkwardly to his feet. It was clear that his right arm was almost unuseable — though, I trusted, only for a while. 'Well, if return up the cliff we must, then return up the cliff we shall,' he said determinedly.

However, before we might even begin the attempt, we had much to do. At first all went well. I had expected that the veludain would shy away from the branath kitten, which Essa had determined should go with us. An attractive creature it was, with its mottled fur and bright eyes, and too small to be a menace; but still — it was a branath. However, when she brought it and showed it to them, they seemed to accept Essa's mental assurance that it was harmless. Indeed, they surged about us with a sort of embarrassed friendliness. They reminded me of children that had fled in fright, leaving another child to face a savage dog, and returned only after the dog had been vanquished.

Then there came the problem of redistributing our food and other possessions, since Twistbeam must bear Robin henceforward — at least, for such time as he needed a mount. That time, I feared, might not prove long. Then there was the problem of strapping Robin, still unconscious and wrapped in the bulky sleeping-sack, onto Twistbeam's back in a fashion that would be both secure and comfortable for mount and man.

Yet both tasks were achieved with relative ease. Our possessions had dwindled in bulk, now that we were wearing our winter gear and with the stock of food so much reduced. As for Twistbeam, I could sense that he was deeply gratified and satisfied at last to be bearing a human burden, not a mere collection of packs!

After that, however, matters took on a nightmare quality. The descent of that perilous path, down the irregular crack in the cliff-face, had seemed arduous enough. The ascent was to prove infinitely worse.

As we began it, rain commenced to fall and changed quickly to sleet. The snow surface was soon becoming sodden and slippery. Moreover, water began to drip down from the overhang above us, making a snow-slide all too probable. If that happened, the crumbling rock face might well also collapse, sweeping us down into the depths below. The hazards were indeed alarming.

I had ample time to consider them, for I was to be last in line. I had urged Dan Wyert to go first, for he was light and not over-burdened. However, he was suffering still from the reaction from his earlier near-fall and the mere idea terrified him.

Instead, Essa took the lead, the branath kitten cradled in the crook of her right arm while she steadied herself against the cliff with her left. Behind her stepped Feathertail. When they set off, the snow was still dry and firm. Though it became slippier before they reached the middle terrace, they did so without undue difficulty.

Dan followed close after. He had quite lost his nerve and climbed up the crack with eyes half-shut — or rather, crawled, for he made most of the ascent on all fours. Even so, he slipped several times and his gasping breaths became sobs of fear. I was relieved when Essa returned to assist him up the last stretch. Without her help, I am not sure Dan would ever have reached the top.

Yet perhaps he might, for Longshank was following close behind him and seemed as anxious as a mother with a stumbling child. Each time Dan slipped I saw Longshank brace himself, as if ready to lend assistance somehow. However, as I have said, Essa's help got Dan there without aid from Longshank.

Then it was the turn of Twistbeam and his burden, the grievously injured Robin. The veludu climbed slowly and with extreme care, stamping his hooves into the snow to gain better purchase. Even so, he slipped several times, causing me to fear that beast and man might tumble together into the void. Yet, somehow, he recovered his footing and climbed onward. I could see Essa watching anxiously from above and I saw her caressing Twistbeam's muzzle after he had completed the ascent safely.

Next it was Avran's turn. Fortunately, since it was his right arm and shoulder that had been injured, he was able to steady himself with his other arm as he climbed. Unlike Dan he walked up, seeking to place his feet into the hollows stamped by Twistbeam's hooves. However, several times one foot slipped and, once, both feet; Avran stumbled and could barely manage to drag himself upright again. Proud though he was, he did not disdain Essa's assistance on the last stretch and I was relieved to see him complete it.

When I had witnessed the extreme slowness with which Highback made the ascent — he was the biggest and, after Proudhorn, the strongest of the veludain — I knew I was in for trouble.

It was indeed a terrifying climb. The snow surface had become very wet by then. I realized immediately that I could not walk upright as Avran had done, but must instead ascend, like Dan, upon all fours. I kept my eyes firmly on my path, careful to ensure that my hands and feet would find the hollows. Though I did not dare even to glance into the vertiginous depths to my right, I was ever conscious of them.

All went well for a while, if such a phrase can be used for so effortful an ordeal. Then, suddenly, both my feet slipped. Since my hands found nothing to grip, I glissaded backward in panic fear that my last hour had come.

Fortunately, Proudhorn was following close behind me. Before I could slip far, he had lowered his head and was holding me against the slope with his six horns. His two nasal horns pressed firmly against the small of my back and his two brow horns against my mid-shoulders. His principal horns were set down on either side of my head, shielding my eyes — by chance or by design — from the vision of the abyss.

I lay there for a while, quite inert and with heart thudding in my chest. Then, somehow, I found purchase for my feet and, as Proudhorn relaxed his pressure, climbed on upward. When the ordeal was over and my veludu and I had safely gained the middle terrace, I pressed my cheek against Proudhorn's muzzle and tried to express to him my gratitude. Sensing his surge of affection, I knew that he understood.

However, our problems were far from being over. When we had descended, the veludain had glissaded cheerfully down the steep, short slope from the upper to the middle terrace. That slope now presented a second hazard for us.

How we surmounted it can be told shortly, though it was an arduous enough labour. Between us, Essa and I — she using her long knife and I, more awkwardly, my sword — cut a series of shallow, slippery steps up that slope. Then, having reached the top, I uncoiled the rope. Essa took it back down while I retained firm hold of one end. Hauling themselves with their left hands, Avran and Dan came up to join me.

Essa, who had stayed below, then tied the rope about Feathertail's brow horns. Though the smallest of the surviving veludain, she was big and heavy enough to make hauling her up a grim task, even for the three of us. When it was done, I ran down to give Essa the free end of the rope and then, with Feathertail serving as anchor at the top, hauled myself back up — a slippery but scarcely alarming second ascent. With Feathertail continuing to serve as anchor at the top and Dan, Avran and I hauling, the other veludain were brought up in turn. Essa came up last, coiling the rope as she climbed and not at all deterred by the frequency with which her feet slipped.

By that time the sleet had turned into snow. It would have been easy enough to ascend from that upper terrace to the cliff-top but, once there, we could not hope to find shelter. Between terrace and cliff there was at least protection from the wind.

Under Essa's instructions Dan and I dug into the snow until we found its drier, deeper levels. After shaping snow walls, we spread Robin's coat within. Still unconscious and sleeping-sack-enwrapped, he was lowered into the shelter we had made, Twistbeam settling down protectively on the open, valleyward side. We others dug similar but simpler trenches for ourselves, huddling into them and passing around food and drink, while our veludain stayed close by.

The snow slackened before midnight, but continued to fall gently. I had not expected to find sleep, but exhaustion overwhelmed my apprehension.

In the early hours, I was awakened by a violent trembling of the

271

ground and a roar which mounted and then died away. I sat up, shaking the snow from my face, and gazed wild-eyed into the blackness about me.

Before I could speak, Dan cried out in fear: 'What was that, masters? What wakened me?'

It was Avran who answered; he was sleeping farthest to my right. 'A snowslide and rock-fall, I think — and a big one.'

'Should we move — get away from here?'

'How can we, in such darkness? And where would we go?' Essa was speaking now, with some asperity. 'Turn over, Dan, and go back to sleep. We can do nothing now. In the morning, we shall see what has happened.'

We all fell silent and, for my part, I drifted back into sleep.

When, long after dawn, we did rise and look about us, the sight was disconcerting. Not only had there been a snow-slide, but also the whole rock face had collapsed. The crack up which we had ascended had gaped open, leaving beneath it a great scar of bare, dark rock.

As for that lower terrace upon which Robin and Avran had battled, it was gone. Looking down, we saw that the river was foaming as it sought a new channel about a great landslide. Somewhere beneath it poor Browntail, forgotten by us in our concern for Robin, had found a fitting burial.

Chapter Twenty-eight

A CHANGE OF DIRECTION

There is a certain shuddering satisfaction in knowing that, in part by hard effort and in larger part by good fortune, one has survived great perils. Moreover, the snow had ceased and the brightness of the morning sky seemed to promise a fair day. Had it not been for Robin's condition, we might all have been cheerful enough as we breakfasted. Instead, our mood was shadowed over by our awareness that, with each passing hour, there was less and less likelihood that our friend would ever regain consciousness. Consequently, it was a silent and introspective meal.

The greatest trouble, for me, was that we had no plan of action. Though Essa, Avran and I each had some skill in the art of healing, Robin's wounds presented problems beyond our abilities. Clearly we must find aid for him, but where was such aid to be found? Not behind us, that was certain. Only in Paladra had we seen recent evidence of humankind (perhaps; I was still not sure, in my heart, whether the inhabitants of Sasliith were truly human). Even had we dared to return there, it was too long and arduous a journey for one so gravely injured. We must go onward, then; onward toward Lyonesse, for want of any other destination; but in what direction did that elusive land lie? Indeed, was Lyonesse sufficiently close that, when we reached it, our friend might still be alive? That seemed depressingly improbable.

Moreover, though it had been I who had determined our destination, Robin had been effectively our leader. Since our dramatic first meeting with Sir Robert Randwulf back among the forests, Avran and I had come not only to regard him with deep affection but also to respect his experience and wisdom. As for Essa, not only did she consider herself profoundly indebted to him, but also she

273

evinced for him a similar affectionate respect. For neither Avran nor me did she have a comparable regard; neither of us could rely upon her support in any decision we might make.

That was my opinion as I drank the last of my ale that morning. Its correctness was to be made swiftly evident.

'Well, friends, we must decide what to do next. The only refuge we can seek in these bleak lands must be Lyonesse; I'm sure you'll all agree on that. As to our route, I presume we must aim to go northward, to seek the sea-coast.'

'That's well and good in theory, Simon,' protested Avran. 'Yet how *can* we head northward? Even before the landslide, you could find us no path down to the river. Moreover, I continue to mislike the look of those cliffs north of here. For my part, I think we should go *southward* and seek a path into the valley.'

'Yet that would do us no good, Avran,' I objected. 'As I told you yesterday, even if we did get down to the riverside we couldn't follow it. There is no passage. We need to ride along east of the river and trust that, further north, we may find a way down. If so, mayhap the valley will be broader and we'll be able to ride along the bank.'

'And how, my friend, do you propose to cross the river, to attain that eastern side?' Avran was becoming exasperated. 'We cannot fly, for we have no wings; and it is well beyond veludu-leap!'

I sighed. 'Yes, of course; how stupid of me! Very well, we'll head south till we find a place where we can traverse the river gorge. Then we'll turn northward.'

'That we will *not*, Simon!' Essa's eyes were blazing. 'Have you *no* thought for Sir Robert? What value is there in seeking for Lyonesse, a land that may be near but is more likely still to be far away? If we pursue such a will-o'-the-wisp, Sir Robert will certainly die.'

I was quite taken aback. 'Why then, what would you have us do, Lady Essa?'

'I would have us do what we should have done yestermorn; follow the gherek. That bird was giving us wise counsel of direction. Only because we ignored it did we encounter this — this disaster.'

'But the gherek has long since flown away!' Avran sounded bewildered.

'Prince Avran, are you really so stupid? You saw its direction of flight, did you not? What we must do is surely clear. We must ride back southward to our camp of yestermorn, then turn east.'

'But . . . Why, that will lose us a whole day of riding!'

'Have you, then, some desired objective, some other place of refuge, that you can attain more quickly? If so, pray tell me of it.'

Essa's scorn was stinging; Avran bit his lip and made no reply. Perceiving that she had vanquished him, Essa turned upon me. 'What say you, then, Simon? You are usually clearer-thinking than this valiant woodenhead here.'

The comment was manifestly unfair; had not Avran perceived the flaw in my own plan? Yet I did not waste time in rallying to my friend's defence, when the need for a decision was so urgent.

'Your idea is perhaps a good one, Lady Essa,' I answered hesitantly. 'If the gherek was indeed flying to some habitation of the Safaddnese . . . But was it? And, if so, how long was that flight? If we turn south, we shall spend almost a day in merely retracing our steps. How much farther shall we then need to ride? And Sir Robert — can he last so long?'

Her aggressiveness subsided and she looked merely anxious. 'I cannot predict that, Simon; I can only trust . . . As for the distance from our old camp to the gherek's destination, again I cannot say. Not far, I think. Not more than another day's ride.'

'And if the weather worsens?'

Essa shrugged helplessly. 'How can I answer? Once more I repeat; I cannot say, I can only trust.'

She lowered her head and I saw her lips moving. I suspected she was uttering some prayer to one of those mountain gods of hers. The suspicion did not comfort me, for I knew that mine was the burden of decision. Essa was for going back, then; and Dan Wyert would, I knew, side with her. Perhaps Avran and I might override their wishes. Yet if so, and if Robin died in consequence, they would certainly hold me responsible. Indeed, I would hold myself responsible.

I sighed. 'Very well, then. We shall head southward, seek our old camp and then follow the gherek. Yestermorn, as you know, Essa, I was hesitant but chose to vote with Sir Robert. Today I will place my whole trust in your judgement.'

She raised her head and looked me straight in the eye. Her own

275

eyes seemed to change in hue with her mood, from the soft blue of a spring sky to the bright gleam of sapphire. That day they seemed as pale and bleak as ice.

'Yes, that is your only proper course, Simon. Well then, we must set forth soon. There will be sunshine for a while but not, I think, for long. We have far to go and we cannot travel quickly.'

I was not sure whether her sudden, strong gaze had given me confidence; nor did I find her words entirely reassuring. However, my choice had been made and our route decided.

We had ridden north in good spirits, enjoying the warm wind at our backs. When we rode back southward, it was into a cooler wind whose fitful gusts accorded with our uncertain mood. My friend had not challenged my decision, nor even commented upon it; yet I was far from sure that he approved it. I think Avran accepted it only because he could not frame any adequate counter-argument.

Certainly Avran evinced no desire, that day, for Essa's company. Instead he rode beside me at the rear; but, even to me, he found little to say. Dan Wyert seemed unhappy also. He stayed close beside Twistbeam, ever watchful for changes in Robin's condition. However, our unfortunate friend showed no sign of recovering consciousness.

Only Essa seemed confident and reasonably happy — surprisingly so, indeed. It was as if she had discovered a solution to some longstanding problem and was lighthearted in consequence. Once more she rode in the van.

It was not hard for her to find the way; despite the melting of the snow, our tracks of yesterday were plain to view. It was too cold for there to be any further melting and, as Essa had predicted, the weather was indeed soon worsening. The wind shifted first to the southwest and then to the west, in which direction the skies were darkening ominously.

When Dan Wyert's anxiety about Robin's condition and dressings enforced a pause, we snatched a midday repast and fed some meat scraps to the branath kitten. I noticed that our veludain were biting off and gulping down the exposed plant fronds with unusual haste and determination, as if apprehensive that such food might soon become unattainable. This also seemed ominous to me.

I am sure that my companions likewise remarked the veludain's

276

behaviour and made deductions similar to mine. However, no-one offered any comment. Indeed, our meal was as silent as our ride had been. It was a relief when we headed on southward.

Within an hour we were riding beneath a surging mass of cloud and enduring an onslaught of hail. The hailstones were about the size of cherry-pits; they rattled against our saddles and stung our arms and cheeks, even through cloak and hood. Proudhorn and the other veludain tilted their heads leftward, but continued their steady ambling undeterred; and the hail soon ceased.

However, it was succeeded by an abrupt blast of rain, driven so hard by the wind that we were almost blown from our saddles. Dan Wyert, on the ungainly Longshank, came so close to colliding with Twistbeam that I feared for Twistbeam's burden. However, the effect was to shield Robin from that first violent blast.

Thereafter the wind dropped, nor did the rain long continue. Moreover, a brightness in the west gave us hope of a surcease from the weather's severity. Indeed, we were granted an interval of sunshine. However, the sky had a yellowish look that I misliked and there were more clouds massing to westward. That first storm had been brief, no more than a line-squall; but I feared it would prove merely a prelude to a much greater tempest. Already I was ruing our decision to head south.

My fears were justified. The developing storm-clouds had a statelier onset, for the wind had lost much of its strength; but they rolled upon us with an inexorability that was even more alarming. I reflected uneasily that this was the very last day of October and that, in these mountains, winter began early in November — or so the Reschorese had told us. Soon we were overarched with blackness; yet only after the last brightness had been blotted from the eastern sky did the first snowflakes begin to drift down.

We had been riding in silence for so long that I was quite surprised when Avran spoke.

'We should have followed the river,' he said. 'We might have been across it by now, and heading northward into finer weather. Little good can come of this — this rash venturing back into the grasp of those accursed Safaddnese deities.'

I found his words mildly amusing. 'Yet I thought you had no belief in those gods, Avran! Have you changed your opinions?'

He laughed bitterly. 'I do not believe them to be gods, be assured of that. Yet I am coming to consider they may be minions of the Devil. And this bleak land — why, it is surely a fitting habitation for demons!'

He paused, then continued more calmly: 'Let's suppose, Simon, that we do find a Safaddnese stronghold. What assurance of welcome have we? They have received no visitors from outside for centuries, we're told. Why should they greet us with rapture or treat us with kindness?'

'Why indeed?' I echoed. 'Yet, for my part, I think that our hope lies in Essa.' Though she was riding far ahead of us, we were not so distant from Dan; consequently I lowered my voice before continuing. 'She learned much about these mountains from that father of hers; so much, indeed, that I believe he must have been Safaddnese. Is that not your opinion also, my friend?'

'Yes, mayhap.' Avran was pensive and spoke equally quietly. 'Yet how might that help us? If her father was indeed Safaddnese, why did he depart from these mountains and join up with Darnay's ruffians? Was he some fighter on a losing side, fleeing defeat? Or was he a criminal escaping the consequences of his acts? In either case, would he or his kith be welcomed back?'

This reasoning disconcerted me; my own thinking had not progressed so far. 'But — well, after all there are nine Safaddnese realms . . . Mayhap he was not from this particular letzestre. Mayhap there are no evil memories of him — no memories at all.'

Avran found small comfort in this suggestion. 'Very well, then. Assume he is not known at all in this letzestre; that he fled south from, say, Desume and that his daughter has no kin hereabouts. How might that help us? Will it not mean simply that Essa, like us, is a stranger and therefore unwelcome?'

Snow was falling steadily by then, in big, white flakes that were the size of English halfpence and looked almost as solid. Depressed as much by this as by Avran's arguments, I found nothing to say; but Avran laughed suddenly.

'Well, after all these weeks in the wilderness, it would at least make a change to meet some other folk. Even if the encounter be hostile, I believe I might welcome it!'

The snow continued unrelentingly throughout the rest of that day.

278

When Essa began to find difficulty in distinguishing our northward tracks, she asked me to take the lead. Soon, however, they were buried too deeply to be perceived even by my eyes. In the whiteness of the blizzard, visibility had decreased to a few poles and the wind had by then so much dwindled that it gave us no help in direction-finding. So we tried again the method we had used in the mountain mist. I kept the lead, with the others well spaced out in line behind me, though Dan stayed beside Robin. Avran, from the rear, called to us corrections whenever he thought we were going off line.

For my part, I kept peering into the snowflake haze and hoping to see the rampart which had marked our camp. However, I was far from confident of doing so. It might have melted enough yesterday to collapse. If it still stood, we would only need to be a few paces off direction to miss it entirely, even in so featureless a landscape.

Nor could I estimate at all accurately when we might reach the camp. When we had ridden north, it had been at a faster pace than we could now manage. I guessed that we were likely to take an hour longer than yesterday to cover the same distance, but I dared not rely on my guess.

As we approached the time of vespers, I became more and more certain we had missed that small spot in the wasteland of white. Moreover, the snow was becoming heavier and the visibility ever worse.

At last I turned and shouted back to Essa, the next in line: 'What think you? Shall we stop for the night, while we have still time and energy enough to build some snow-walls? Surely we'll never discover our camp now!'

'No,' she called back briefly. 'Go on. We shall find it.'

'Very well.' I turned back and, thinking hard thoughts about the tiresome obstinacy of womankind, urged Proudhorn forward into the blizzard.

We had ridden another league, and my meditations on women were becoming ever more bitter, when Proudhorn suddenly swung westward, out of the line we had been following. There were dismayed calls from Avran, echoed by Dan — though not, I noticed, by Essa. However, Proudhorn ignored them and, by that strange mental interchange, stilled my own doubts. Then I noticed a slight darkening ahead, suggesting a declivity; and, in a moment, I realized that I could distinguish at last the snow walls we had built about our camp, two nights back.

How Proudhorn found the place I do not clearly understand, for veludain lack the direction-finding prowess of sevdreyen and rafne-yen. Yet, of course, they are much more used to high country and to snow; and I know that Proudhorn must have sensed the purpose of our ride. Well, however he might have done it, he had found the camp for us. That was all that mattered.

There was a period of gratified activity, during which we cleared some of the new-fallen snow from within the walls and built them up higher. Robin was lifted from Twistbeam's back, Essa and Dan settling him down in the most sheltered corner and striving to ensure he would be kept warm. Then we ate at leisure, though with little conversation, and afterwards sought our sleeping-sacks.

I did so in no mood of tranquillity, for I had found a new cause for unease. When we had cleared the fresh-fallen snow, it had seemed to me that the interior of our snow-ramparts was more trampled than I remembered, and by unfamiliar feet. With the light so poor and new snow accumulating so fast, I could not be sure: thus I did not mention my suspicion to my companions. Yet my impression that the camp had been visited by strangers — Safaddnese, presumably — came for a while between me and my sleep. However, there was nothing to be done; eventually I gave a mental shrug and subsided into slumber.

As happens so often, the snow ceased overnight. When I was young, my father used to tell me that this was because the Snowman had gone away to bed. If so, then the Snowman oftentimes reawakens with the dawn; and certainly, when we awoke, it was again snowing steadily.

Essa was more than ever concerned about Robin's condition. He had still shown no sign of recovering consciousness; moreover, he seemed to be breathing even more irregularly and weakly. Conse-quently she made us hasten our breakfasts and, as soon as possible, had us mounted and ready to depart.

Yet, paradoxically, Essa seemed still quite cheerful. I noticed with surprise that she was wearing the golden taron on the outside of her ameral jacket.

Since the groove that Robin had cut at the north point of the snow rampart was still visible, it was easy enough for us to start eastward. Without seeking permission or even commenting, Essa took the lead. Rather annoyedly I followed behind her, though at some distance since it was necessary to mark our line.

I was suffering from a deepening disquiet. Were we indeed heading for some Safaddnese stronghold? If so, what would be our reception? If not, then we must be heading still further into the mountains. It would have relieved my feelings to talk with Avran, but Dan was behind me with our injured friend and Avran away at the back of the line.

Dan Wyert was himself becoming a matter for concern. He was showing increasing signs of physical strain and appeared not to have recovered from the shocks suffered in the river gorge. Moreover, Dan seemed neither to have shared, nor even to have been encouraged by, Essa's new mood; rather, he appeared to distrust it. If Dan fell ill, our problems would indeed become formidable. But then, in such vile weather the survival, not merely of Robin but of all of us, was in highest degree unlikely.

By the morning's end, the snow was so deep that it was becoming hard to ride. After dismounting around noon to snatch a brief repast, we did not again mount. Nor did Essa take the lead when we set forth, for the breaking of the trail was becoming an arduous task. Normally Avran, the strongest of us, would have taken this over; but his injuries had drained away part of that strength and he had not yet recovered the use of his arm. Thus it was I who must lead once again.

In the morning I had resented Essa's usurpation of my role as leader; in the afternoon, I resumed that role reluctantly, for I doubted my own powers — and rightly. Within a league, I was becoming tired; within three leagues, I was wellnigh exhausted and stumbling along like a weary horse in soft sand. Each fresh step seemed a little harder than the last. Moreover, my eyes were blurring so badly that only the calls from behind — calls ever more frequent — kept me on line. Lift a foot; set it forward. Lift the other foot; set it forward. Repeat once, twice, endlessly, with limbs aching. It was long past time that I relinquished the lead, but the very concept of doing so was more than I could manage. Another step . . . Another step . . .

Was there no end to it — no end to this swirling snow, this terrible whiteness?

Only when the warrior in furs barred my way with his great axe did I become aware that he was there. Even then, I stumbled forward and almost fell against its edge. Moreover, the startled cries of my companions were needed to make me belatedly aware of the ring of other warriors about us.

However, by then I had recognized the warrior's weapon, from memories of the carvings in the tunnels. A double-bladed axe it was, with the edges of the blade elaborately notched; and his shield was oval, prolonged into a downward point . . . There could be no doubt. At long last, we had encountered the Safaddnese!

Glossary of Rockalese Words

All Rockalese words are defined when first used in this account. However, for the convenience of any reader who finds them hard to remember, they are brought together here for ready reference. Three Rockalese languages are represented — Sandastrian (Sand.), Reschorese (Resch.) and Safaddnese (Saf.): where words are common to two or more languages, this is indicated. In addition, at the request of an early reader, Sandastrian words for the days of the week, the months of the year and the principal numbers are given in full.

A **af,** *suff.* one (number); also used to identify the principal member or leader, in a group of humans or animals (Sand.)

aftal, *n.* one hundred (Sand.)

ameral (*pl.* **ameralen**), *n.* small, long-bodied and short-legged carnivore of the high moors and mountains of northern Rockall; pelt grey with black spots in summer, white with black spots (*cf.* ermine) in winter, when it is much sought for its fur (Resch.: Saf.)

askatal, *n.* one thousand (Sand.)

asunal (*pl.* **asunalar**), *n.* lake (Resch.: Saf.)

av, *pref.* one (number) (Sand.)

avar, *suff.* friend of, ally of (Sand.)

Avbalet, *n.* January (Sand.)

B **baz,** *adv.* here (Sand.: Resch.)

Beladnen, *n.* or *adj.* pertaining to, or a member of, the southernmost of the three principal **Veledreven** tribes: resident in the southeastern region of the northern mountains, between the Chaluwand and Warringflow (Perringvane) Rivers (Resch.: Sand.)

bes, *pref.* or *suff.* ten

Besbalet, *n.* October (Sand.)

branath (*pl.* **branathen**), *n.* sabre-toothed carnivore of the northern mountains; fur honey-brown, with darker brown streaks, in summer; creamy white, with grey-brown streaks, in winter; size and build like a tiger; solitary and ferocious (Resch.)

C **cadarand** (*pl.* **cadarandai**), *n.* small shrub growing in protected positions on the slopes of the northern mountains, producing acorn-like nuts which are distilled to produce **efredat** or ground to make flour. **Cadarand cakes** are made of this flour, with honey and fats, and crusted with the dried berries of the **pedelend** bush (Resch.)

D **daliipel** (*pl.* **daliipelei**), *n.* boundary, frontier (Resch.)

Daltharimbar, *n.* god of the winds in the Safaddnese nonarchy of deities: the particular god of Darega (Saf.)

dalu, *pron.* or *adj.* that (Resch.: Saf.)

danar, *v.* to be, exist (Resch.: Saf.)

datsemar, *v.* to travel a particular path or route (Resch.)

def, *suff.* two (Sand.)

degal, *adj.* or *suff.* long (Resch.)

dev, *pref.* two (Sand.)

deva, *n.* two (Sand.)

Devbalet, *n.* February (Sand.)

diev, *prep.* without (Resch.)

drale, dralé (*pl.* **draleyen**), *n.* shadow (Resch.: Saf.)

E **eburé** (*pl.* **ebureyen**), *n.* saucepan (Sand.)

Ebuvrior, *n.* 'sky saucepan' — the constellation of stars called, in England, Arthur's Wain or the Great Bear (Sand.)

efredat, *n.* brown spirit, much like brandy but with a smokey taste, distilled from **cadarand** nuts (Resch.: Saf.)

ehan, *adj.* high, elevated (Resch.)

esde (*pl.* **eseden**), *n.* back (of an animal) (Resch.)

esim, *adj.* brown (Resch.)

evyé, *adv.* or *conj.* why (Resch.: Saf.)

F **ferek** (*pl.* **ferekar**), *n.* hill, mountain (Resch.: Saf.)

fereyek (*pl.* **fereyekar**), *n.* an isolated, very high mountain (Resch.: Saf.)

G **Gadarran,** *n.* or *adj.* pertaining to, or a member of, the most central of the three principal **Veledreven** tribes; resident on the eastern flank of the northern mountains (Resch.: Saf.)

gahe (**gahé**), *adj.* streaked (Sand.: Resch.)

gelatar, *v.* to bring, fetch (Resch.)

gherek (*pl.* **gherekelei**), *n.* falcon of the northern mountains; size large; plumage cerulean blue above, creamy white beneath; wings acutely pointed, tail long. Considered to signify good fortune (Saf.)

glagrang (*pl.* **glagrangen**), *n.* carnivorous riverine turtle with carapace broader than long; head blunt, with flaring nostrils and pale eyes; and foreflippers larger than hind. Lives in the Great Marshes and the Aramassa and Mentone river systems. Old specimens grow to great size (Resch.)

gradakh (*pl.* **gradakhar**), *n.* a violent storm (Saf.)

H **Halrathhantor,** *n.* god of the rains and of terrestrial waters in the Safaddnese nonarchy of deities; the particular god of Ayan (Saf.)

hanar, *v.* to drench, saturate (Resch.: Saf.)

Horulgavar, *n.* leader of the gods and god of the Earth in the Safaddnese nonarchy of deities; the particular god of Aracundra (Saf.)

I **igha,** *conj.* and (*cf.* Sand. **iga**) (Resch.)

iildrih SEE **yildrih**

ikhil (*pl.* **ikhilien**), *n.* horn (Resch.)

il, *n.*, *pref.* or *suff.* five (Sand.)

284

Ilbalet, *n.* May (Sand.)

Indegis, *n.* Tuesday (Sand.)

K kadarand SEE cadarand

kel, *n.*, *pref.* or *suff.* six (Sand.)

Kelbalet, *n.* June (Sand.)

kheter, *adj.* several (i.e. more than two but fewer than many!) (Resch.)

krad (*pl.* kradar), *n.* hope (Resch.; but used in Raffette only)

L lakhash, *n.* or *adj.* not permitted; forbidden; proscribed (Resch.)

Lakhretmar, *n.*, the Lodestar or Pole Star (Sand.)

lama, lamé, *adj.*, *adv.* or *suff.* small, little (Resch.: Saf.)

lat, *n.*, *pref.* or *suff.* nine (Sand.)

Latbalet, *n.* September (Sand.)

let, *n.*, *pref.* or *suff.* nine: *cf.* Sand. lat (Resch.: Saf.)

letzahar (*pl.* letzaharei), *n.* the ruler of a letzestre (Saf.)

letzestre (*pl.* letzestrei), *n.* 'ninth-realm' — one of the nine divisions of Safaddné (Saf.)

M Mesnakech, *n.* god of enchantment, sorcery and evil in the Safaddnese nonarchy of deities; the particular god of Paladra (Saf.)

Murtegis, *n.* Monday (Sand.)

N nus, *n.*, *pref.* or *suff.* eight (Sand.)

Nusbalet, *n.* August (Sand.)

O Oburnassian, *adj.* or *n.* pertaining to, or a member of, the larger of the two major racial groups of the northern mountains, usually stocky, brachycephalic to mesocephalic, brown-haired and brown-eyed (Resch.: Saf.)

olk, *n.*, *pref.* or *suff.* twelve (Sand.)

Olkbalet, *n.* December (Sand.)

Ortegis, *n.* Friday (Sand.)

P pedelend (*pl.* pedelendai), *n.* small bush, related to the rose, growing on high slopes of the northern mountains; leaves greyish-green; hips dried and used for crusting cadarand cakes or utilized in winemaking (Resch.)

predan (*pl.* predin), *n.* fortified farm or dwelling of geometric plan (in Reschora, always pentagonal); *cf.* padarn of Sandastre (Resch.)

Q quet, *adj.* great, eminent, noteworthy (Resch.)

R rafenu (*pl.* rafneyen), *n.* antelope-like forest herbivore having one nasal and two brow horns; nasal horn directed forward, brow horns five-tined with three foremost tines curving and moderately long, two rear tines shorter and straight; pelage walnut-brown, flecked with creamy spots; used as a mount and capable of simple telepathic exchanges with its rider (Resch.)

Rastegis, *n.* Thursday (Sand.)

ren (*pl.* **renin**), *n.* nose of a man: muzzle of an animal (Resch.)

Rescheren SEE **Reschorese**

Reschorese, *adj.* or *n.* 1. pertaining to, or a member of, the large **Oburnassian** tribe occupying the central southern region of the northern mountains; 2. the language of that region; 3. pertaining to, or a citizen of, the Kingdom of Reschora (English variant of Resch. **Rescheren**)

rim, *n.*, *pref.* or *suff.* seven (Sand.; Resch.)

Rimbalet, *n.* July (Sand.)

rior, *n.* sky (always singular; never plural, as in English 'skies') (Sand.)

rukhar, *v.* to cross (Resch.)

S **Sachakkan,** *adj.* or *n.* pertaining to, or a member of, the smallest of the three **Oburnassian** tribes, occupying the extreme southeast region of the northern mountains and adjacent plains between the Warringflow (Perringvane) and Green Rivers (Resch.: Saf.)

Safaddnen, SEE **Safaddnese**

Safaddnese, *adj.* or *n.* 1. pertaining to, or a member of, the formerly large **Oburnassian** tribe occupying the northwestern, northern and north central region of the northern mountains; 2. the language of that region (English variant of Resch.; Saf. **Safaddnen**)

sedde (*pl.* **seddeden**), *n.* tail (Resch.)

Seledden, *adj.* or *n.* pertaining to, or a member of, the northernmost of the three **Veledreven** tribes, occupying the extreme northeast region of the northern mountains and the island of Aetselor (Resch.: Saf.)

sen, *n.*, *pref.* or *suff.* four (Sand.)

Senbalet, *n.* April (Sand.)

sevdru (*pl.* **sevdreyen**), *n.* antelope-like herbivore having two forwardly-directed nasal horns and two brow horns, branching twice symmetrically in Y-fashion so that each horn has four tines; pelage grey, with white underparts and central white line down neck and back; used as a mount and capable of simple telepathic exchanges with its rider (Sand.)

sunar, *adj.* bright, shining (Resch.; but used in Raffette only)

T **tal,** *n.*, *pref.* or *suff.* ten (Sand.)

Talbalet, *n.* October (Sand.)

Taltegis, *n.* Sunday (Sand.)

taron (*pl.* **taronen**), *n.* fish-eating sea-bird of Rockall's northern shores; plumage white, with flight feathers edged in yellow; body short and chunky; neck short; bill long; bill and feet greenish-black (Saf.)

tasdavarl (*pl.* **tasdavalnen**), *n.* nocturnal carnivore and scavenger of the northern mountains and adjacent grasslands; of fox-size but shorter legged; canine teeth strong and conical, first premolars modified into carnassials, other premolars and molars broad and strong, for bone-crushing; hide dull brown, blotched with black in summer, turning to light grey or white, with darker blotches in winter; eyes large, ears long and flat; cry a peal of maniacal laughter (Resch.: Saf.)

taza, (*pl.* **tazai**), *n.* root (Resch.: Saf.)

tazlantil (*pl.* **tazlantenar**), *n.* a 'rootless one'; a second-class citizen of Safaddné. May be 1. a man or woman taken in childhood by **Safaddnese** rulers, brought up by them and sent away to serve them in a place other than his or her own birthplace; 2. the child of two **tazlantenar**; 3. orig. the child of a **Safaddnese** father and **tazlantil** mother (later, the child of such a union was accepted as **Safaddnese**); 4. the orphan child of a **tazlantil** father and **Safaddnese** mother, its parents slain as punishment (Resch.: Saf.)

tetsen (*pl.* **tetsenar**), *n.* a deciduous shrub of sheltered valleys in the northern mountains, yielding a scarlet fruit, hard-stoned and plumlike (Resch.)

timbelan (*pl.* **timbelanin**), *n.* musical instrument having a bell-shaped, open-ended body made of dark, close-grained wood and a neck with strings on both its upper and lower sides (Resch.: Saf.)

turin, *adj.* proud (Resch.)

U **udru** (*pl.* **udreyen**), *n.* large, horse-like herbivore, with mane on neck and plumed tail; eyes small; fore-limbs longer than hind; feet each bearing three large, curving claws; chisel-like incisors and canines, front two premolars missing (leaving a gap), rear premolars and molars massive, grinding teeth. A browser on wind-trees, in part arboreal (Resch.: Saf.)

uvai (*pl.* **uvaien**), *n.* wind (Resch.)

uvudu (*pl.* **uvudain**), *n.* herbivore of northern mountains; very sheep-like, but hornless and having three hooves on each foot; fleece dark in colour; gregarious and sometimes domesticated; wool and skin used extensively for clothing (Resch.: Saf.)

V **vasian** (*pl.* **vasianar**), *n.* small, tarsier-like arboreal primate of southern Rockall, large-eyed and with grey pelage; capable of moderately extensive telepathic interchanges with its owner; very faithful (Sand.)

vek, *n.*, *pref.* or *suff.* three (Sand.)

Vekbalet, *n.*. March (Sand.)

vekhen (*pl.* **vekhnen**), *n.* trident (Resch.)

Veledreven, *adj.* or *n.* pertaining to, or a member of, the smaller of the two major racial groups of the northern mountains, inhabiting their eastern regions; usually rather tall, dolichocephalic to mesocephalic, fair-skinned and with green or pale blue eyes; albinos not infrequent (Resch.: Saf.)

Veltegis, *n.* Monday (Sand.)

veludu (*pl.* **veludain**), *n.* antelope-like herbivore of northern mountains, rather short-legged, having three pairs of horns — short, sharp nasal horns, brow-horns of moderate length and unbranched, and horns at back of head dividing symmetrically into two tines, one directed forward, one upward; pelage dull grey in summer, with irregular lateral streaks of white and brown, but turning wholly white in winter; used as a mount and capable of simple telepathic interchanges with its rider, but less intelligent and less speedy on flat ground than a **rafenu** or a **sevdru** (Resch.: Saf.)

viré, *pron.* you (*cf.* Sand. **vre**) (Resch.: Saf.)

vlatar, *v.* to be subject to, ruled by (Saf.)

Vortegis, *n.* Wednesday (Sand.)

X **xakath** (*pl.* **xakathei**), *n.* short-legged, very broad-headed carnivore of northern mountains; nostrils flaring; eyes on top of skull and large; central ridge of bony plates down back; hide greyish tan with dark longitudinal streaks in summer, turning white with grey streaks in winter; four rows of pointed teeth, the outer two in use, with lateral teeth replacement by whole row. Gregarious, congregating in large numbers in late autumn or early spring for southward or northward migration; but hunting packs usually do not exceed two score members in summer and are often smaller in mid to late winter (Resch.: Saf.)

Y **yildrih** (*pl.* **yildrihen**), *n.* broad, flat-bottomed boats propelled by two or more oarsmen; used by the boat people of the Mentone, Aramassa and Atelone river systems (Resch.)

Z **zahar** (*pl.* **zaharei**), *n.* lord (Resch.)
zhatar, *v.* to rule (Saf.)

COMPARISON OF THE SANDASTRIAN AND RESCHORESE ALPHABETS

The Sandastrian Alphabet

The Reschorese Alphabet